TWELVE FORTY LELAND STREET

Inspired from true events Four Generations of Decker's

Samanthy Jane

ISBN: 1539386686
ISBN 13: 9781539386681
Library of Congress Control Number: 2016916963
CreateSpace Independent Publishing Platform
North Charleston, South Carolina

Life is a series of choices.
With each choice comes opportunity and consequence,
What we do with that opportunity and consequence
will determine our lives.

To my two sons,
Chad and William,
the two loves of my life.

Special thanks to
Marvin Perry

CHAPTER ONE

Harry Decker
March 15, 2004
1240 Leland Street, Gladwin, Michigan
In-Home Hospice Care

Garnet, the somber one of my hospice nurses, injects sedation into the PICC line taped securely to my right arm. She is meticulous and efficient in her actions, yet I sense she no longer carries the love or desire she once had for her work. "Good night, Harry," she mutters, turning out the lights. "Sweet dreams." I smile at the thought of having a sweet dream, or even a different dream, but I only have one dream, always the same, never wavering, even in the smallest degree.

Lying inside the stilled darkness, consumed with sadness and longing, I whisper my nightly prayer. The grandfather clock strikes on the hour as the muffled sounds echo in my ears. "Seven, eight, nine," I mutter along to its chimes. "Ten." Closing my tired, sedated eyes, I allow my dream to begin...once again.

In the far corner of my bedroom, the silhouette of a young woman appears. Although her face is kept hidden within the shadows, her eyes seem to exude a quiet sadness as she stands silent in her corner cove. Every night, I beg to understand her nightly visits. Every night, I strain from the confines of my bed to recognize her face, but to no avail. She maintains a constant vigil from inside the shadows, as well as her silence, throughout the dream.

Off in the distance, late in the dream, there's a soft, irritating noise that cries out for me. "Talk to me," I plead to the lady, hearing its cry. "Please talk to me." The sound comes closer, demanding my attention. "Please." I struggle against its powerful call. "I beg of you! Step from the shadows! Show me your face!" The lady only recedes deeper into the shadows, while the noise screeches its victory.

"Good morning, Harry." Garnet turns off the alarm. "How are you feeling today? I see by your chart you turned eighty-four yesterday—happy belated birthday." I can feel my old tired eyes wrinkle as I smile in response. A single tear runs down my cheek as I realize once again my prayer was not answered.

"Why don't we try and eat a little breakfast this morning, Harry?" Garnet wipes the tear from my face, placing a bib over my chest. "It's your favorite, apple-cinnamon oatmeal." She brings the food to my mouth.

"*No*!" Shaking my head, I knock the oatmeal from the spoon onto my chest.

"Harry! You have to eat." Garnet scrapes up the oatmeal in displeasure. "Shall we try this again?" A halfhearted smile crosses her face.

"*No*!" I grumble defiantly, pressing my lips tightly, firmly together.

"All right, Harry." Garnet removes the soiled bib. "Have it your way." She leaves the room in defeat, with the uneaten bowl of oatmeal.

Slowly scanning the room that has now become my purgatory, my eyes come to rest on a photo of me as a young boxer. My stance is confident and determined. Chest bare and muscular. Fists are up and positioned. I'm ready to conquer. Ready to fight.

Lifting my hands, I struggle to make a fist in imitation, but my sore, arthritic hands refuse to close. "Where has all your strength and power gone?" I turn my crippled hands back and forth in confused amazement. "When did your betrayal start? Why have you chosen to abandon me?" I struggle once again, determined to make a fist, only to drop my hands in defeated exhaustion.

Looking to the heavens, consumed with frustration, I turn my thoughts to yesteryear. Closing my tired eyes, I inhale deeply; the smells of O'Hare's fill my nostrils, taking me back…"You're late, Southpaw," Pappy's gruff voice grumbles. "Grab a broom, boy. The gym's not going to clean itself." I smile nostalgically as I hear the young boy reply. "Yes, sir, Mr. Pappy, right away, sir." Returning to younger days, better days, I leave my meek, humble existence behind.

CHAPTER TWO

October 1932

I was twelve years old when I walked into O'Hare's gym and met Pappy O'Hare for the first time. The moment I opened the gym doors, the pungent odor of sweating men and the sounds of punches being thrown told me I was in the right place. A place where I could learn to fight.

"What are you doing in here, kid?" a voice grumbled from behind me. My eyes desperately tried to adjust from sunshine to the dim lighting of the gym. A stout, broad-shouldered man came into view.

"Uh…I'm looking for Pappy O'Hare, sir…the trainer?"

"Well, you've found him, kid. I'm Pappy." He stopped for only a moment to give me the once-over before continuing to sweep the floor. The legendary trainer was smaller than I thought he would be. His left ear was cauliflower, and his nose looked like it had taken too many punches, but he was still the most intimidating man I had ever met.

"Ah, Mr. Pappy...sir. I need to learn how to fight, and I hear you're the man to teach me."

"Well, you heard wrong, boy." He flashed a look of irritation. "I don't teach street fighting. I train boxers, and I sure don't teach kids."

"I'm not a kid!" My voice was defiant. "I'm twelve! Just a little small for my age, but I'll grow—you'll see. I'll be as big as I need to be, to become the best fighter, boxer, in this gym!"

"Is that right?" Pappy looked me straight in the eye. "There are two things you need to become a good boxer, kid: heart and strength. You might have the heart, but you got no muscle." He eyed my small, puny arms. "Come back when you're bigger, kid, and then we'll see what you've got. Now move along, boy; I'm busy here."

"But, Mr. Pappy? You don't understand. I can't wait till I'm bigger. There's this kid at my school. We call him Big John. He wants my lunch money. He wants my nickel, but I won't give it to him. Please, Mr. Pappy. I can't keep running. I won't keep running. I have to learn to fight, and you need to teach me...*now*!"

The old trainer gave me a slow, steady stare. I didn't know it then, but years later I would discover it's known as the boxer's stare. A stare given to size a man up, discover his worth. "I like your spunk, kid, so I'll tell you what." He rubbed his scruffy chin. "You come here every day after school, help me clean the gym, and I'll teach you how to box. At least good enough to keep your nickel."

"You mean it, Mr. Pappy?"

"Yeah, I mean it, kid, but the first time you're not here to clean"—he gave me the ole stare once again—"the deal's off."

"You don't have to worry about that, Mr. Pappy. I'll be here every day, right after school." I took the broom from the old trainer's hand.

"What are you doing, kid? I didn't expect you to start today."

"I clean the gym. You start my training. That's our deal, Mr. Pappy." I looked him square in the eye. A half smile crossed ole Pappy's face, his eyes flashing a look of respect.

"What's your name, kid?"

"Harry, Harry Decker," I stated proudly, standing tall.

"Well, put down the broom, Harry Decker, and come over here."

"Yes, sir, Mr. Pappy." I quickly set down the broom, realizing even then that you did what Pappy said, and you did it timely.

"Put up your fists, kid, and let me see your stance." Nervously I took a cockeyed stance in front of the legendary trainer, tucking my thumbs inside my fists.

"Boy!" Pappy shook his head, untucked my thumbs, and placed them firmly on the outside of my closed hands. "Thumbs always on the outside." Looking me square in the eye, he firmly held my small fist inside his strong hands. "Loosen up, boy." Swooping down, he shook my legs loose from the floor, adjusting my cockeyed legs into a boxer's stance. "Okay, kid." He took a stance in front of me. Hands up, palms out. "Let's see what you've got."

"What I've got, Mr. Pappy?" I looked at his giant hands in confusion.

"My palms, kid." He punched the insides of his hands hard. "Hit 'em!"

"Hit 'em, Mr. Pappy?" My eyes darted nervously around the gym.

"Let's go, boy…hit 'em!" Nervously, with hesitation, I threw my first punch. The moment it made contact with Pappy's palm, a strange sensation coursed through my body. A sensation of power, confidence, and strength. I threw a few more, thoroughly enjoying this newfound feeling.

"Enough." Pappy dropped his hands. "You're a southpaw, kid."

"A southpaw?"

"It means you're a left-handed boxer, kid." He took the broom from the floor and pushed it toward me. "Make sure you get the corners, boy."

"Yes, sir, Mr. Pappy." I brushed a cobweb from the corner. "Your gym will be spick-and-span when I'm done." I whistled a happy tune.

"Hey, kid!" Pappy called out from across the gym.

"Yes, sir, Mr. Pappy." I stood to attention.

"Drop the Mister, kid; the name's Pappy."

"Yes, sir, Pappy." Returning to my chores, I continued to whistle, feeling euphoric.

So that's the way it went. Every day after school, I cleaned O'Hare's gym. In exchange, Pappy trained my mind, as well as my body, to become a fighter. For weeks, I was able to avoid Big John as he took his bullying out on the other kids, but my luck was soon to run out. Shortly before Christmas break, my newly acquired fighting skills would be tested.

December 1932

"Students, button up your coats; it's cold out there," Miss Turner shouted over the recess bell.

Quickly, haphazardly, I buttoned only two buttons before running out the door. I was halfway to the playground when I stopped dead in my tracks, spotting Big John next to the monkey bars, abusing Ernie Mills. Our eyes met for only a second, but it was long enough.

"Hey, Decker!" Big John hollered, sending a shiver up my back. "Give me your nickel, and I'll let you live to see another day." Quickly I turned around and nervously headed back toward the school.

"Hey! Where you goin', Decker?" Big John's voice boomed from behind.

"Just leave me alone!" I muttered through clenched teeth, picking up the pace. I felt Big John hot on my tail.

"Hey, Decker! I'm talking to you." Big John pushed me hard from behind, causing me to stumble.

This is it, my mind warned as I caught my fall. I knew there was nowhere to go, nowhere to run—heart pounding, adrenaline pumping. Quickly and without thought, I spun around, delivering a solid left hook straight to Big John's nose, feeling it flatten beneath my fist. Big John fell to the ground, moaning in pain, blood gushing through his fingers.

"Decker just laid you out!" taunted Ollie Wells, a member of Big John's crew.

I looked at my fist in awe, amazed, before common sense told me to run. I ran all the way to O'Hare's, afraid that if I slowed down, Big John and his crew would be there to catch me. "Pappy!" I busted through the doors of O'Hare's. "I did it!"

"Did what, boy?" Pappy was preoccupied, adjusting a drooping speed bag.

"*It*!" was all I could say as I caught my breath.

"Calm down, boy, and tell me what *it* is you've done?"

"I hit Big John right in the nose." I swallowed hard, trying to calm myself. "He tried to take my nickel, Pappy, but I wouldn't let it happen. I decided right then and there I'd go down fighting before I would give it up." Smiling proudly, I displayed the nickel resting in the palm of my hand.

"Good for you, boy. Good for you. You were faced with a powerful opponent, and you conquered. With some hard work and training, you just might become a boxer yet."

"Do you think so, Pappy? I wanna be a boxer more than anything in the world."

"Well, if you really want to be a boxer, kid, the first thing we're gonna need to do is change your name."

"Change my name? What's wrong with my name?"

"Well, boy, a boxer's name is the first gesture of intimidation, and I just don't see Harry intimidating anyone."

"Okay, Pappy, we can change my name. What do you think my name should be?" Fascinated at the thought, I fidgeted in front of him.

"Well, let me think here for a minute, kid." He rubbed his cauliflower ear. "Let me see…Jimmy Whips? Nah. Tommy the Tank?" I nodded eagerly. "Nah, you're not nearly big enough to be called 'the Tank.'" I stood there for what seemed like forever before he finally mumbled, "The Southpaw Slugger."

He paused and continued, "You know, kid, I always said if I had a son, I would name him Jack Collins O'Hare. Never had any kids, Harry; never even got married. Yeah, Jack Collins." He nodded his head in approval. "Your name is going to be Jack Collins, 'the Southpaw Slugger."

"Jack Collins, 'the Southpaw Slugger,'" I proudly murmured, standing tall. "The best boxer in the world." My eyes were shining bright.

The Next Day

On the way to school the next morning, I was still feeling pretty proud of myself until Frankie Connors ran past me shouting, "You're a dead man walking, Decker." It was then that the reality of what I had done to Big John, and his nose, made me wonder if going to school was such a good idea. Contemplating the devastation that Big John and his crew were capable of, I slowed my pace.

Then I remembered the words written on Pappy's wall: "A man is either a coward or a fighter. Which one are you?" The thought of seeing Big John made me nervous, but the thought of not facing him made me a coward. I knew I had no choice but to go to school and face whatever was waiting for me there.

Taking a few deep breaths for courage, I resumed my pace and headed for school. The moment I stepped onto the grounds of

Buchanan Junior High, the sun disappeared behind a large black cloud. The loss of sunshine made the old school look as if it contained nothing but gloom and doom inside.

With every ounce of courage I could muster, I climbed the steps that could lead to my demise. Pulling open the heavy doors, I ducked my head inside, nervously looking up and down the halls for any signs of Big John or his crew. They were nowhere to be found. Breathing a sigh of relief, I hurried down the hall to my classroom and quickly took my seat. I opened my history book and pretended to read.

Within seconds, Ollie Wells was looming over me. He dropped a note atop my book before taking his own seat behind me. As I looked at the dreaded piece of paper, my mind and stomach began to churn. Keeping my head down I glanced up to my classmates. Their eyes were wide with fear and excitement. Apprehensively, I picked up the note. "You're a DEAD MAN, Decker" was all it said.

"Quiet down now, class." Miss Turner clapped her hands, bringing the class to order. "Take out your history books and finish reading chapter seven. Then do questions one through five on page forty-two."

Following Miss Turner's instructions, I turned to chapter seven, but I was having a hard time concentrating on my studies. All I could think about were the different ways I could die. My mind played out scene after scene of torture and death. I just hoped that when the time came, whatever punishment Big John chose to inflict would be quick and not too embarrassing. I was deep in my thoughts of impending death when the first-hour bell sounded, announcing the class's end.

"Close your books, class, and line up single file." Miss Turner took a stance at the door. Doing as instructed, I closed my book and took my place in line. Ollie Wells quickly stood behind me. I felt his hot breath on my neck as he mumbled intimidations in the name of Big John.

"Harry, could you please stay behind and clean erasers?" Miss Turner softly smiled.

"Sure, Miss Turner." Quickly stepping out of line, I breathed a sigh of relief.

"Straight to your next class now, children. No dawdling in the halls." Miss Turner looked directly at Ollie Wells.

Collecting the erasers, I began brushing them lightly over the squared wired box. I took my time, in hopes of assuring empty halls. I clapped the last eraser clean as I heard the bell announce the beginning of second hour. "All finished, Miss Turner." I brushed the chalk from my hands.

"Thank you, Harry, and here's a note for Mr. Hardy explaining your tardiness."

"Thank you, Miss Turner." Tucking my books under my arm, I walked the hall quickly to second hour.

"You're late, Harry." Mr. Hardy gave me a look of disappointment.

"Sorry, Mr. Hardy." I handed him Miss Turner's note, waiting for instruction.

"Take your seat, Harry." Mr. Hardy returned to the math problems written on the board. "Now, class, how would you begin to solve the first story problem? If it's two hundred miles to Albany, New York, and the train left the station at two p.m. traveling at a speed of forty miles per hour, making one stop that delayed the train by thirty minutes, what time would the train arrive in New York? Anyone?" He searched the sea of faces. "Ernie?" He pointed to the smartest kid in the school.

"The train would arrive at seven thirty, Mr. Hardy."

"Einstein Ernie...Einstein Ernie," a few of my classmates teased.

"Okay, class, that's enough," Mr. Hardy scolded. "You have until the end of class to finish the remaining problems. I suggest you get started."

"Pssst, Harry, is it true?" Ernie called out to me in a low voice. "Did you break Big John's nose yesterday?"

I shrugged my shoulders, unsure of exactly what I had done to Big John. My mind began to race, replacing problem five with a story problem of my own. *If a guy broke Big John's nose on Tuesday, how long would he have to live on Wednesday?* The answer...*Until Big John found him.* Shaking my head to clear my thoughts, I read problem five as it was written.

If you filled a gallon jug with water three times, how many quarts would you have? Answer...*There are four quarts in a gallon. So there would be twelve quarts.* Moving on to the next problem, I looked at the clock on the wall. Twenty minutes, plenty of time to finish.

"Okay, class, time's up." The bell announced the end of second hour. "Line up single file for dismissal, and leave the finished papers on my desk. For those of you who didn't finish, enjoy your homework. Mr. Decker, would you mind staying behind a moment?"

"Sure, Mr. Hardy." I dropped my paper in the finished pile and stepped aside, allowing my classmates to pass.

"Harry?" Mr. Hardy closed the door. "Sometimes taking a few lumps in life is absolutely necessary." He flipped Miss Turner's note between his fingers.

"I know Mr. Hardy." I gave a nervous smile. "Is that all, Mr. Hardy?"

"Yes, Harry, that's all." Taking the small pile of finished papers, he placed them securely inside his briefcase.

After contemplating Mr. Hardy's words, I decided not to wait for Big John to find me but to seek him out—after school, of course. Leaving Mr. Hardy's room, I felt good, relaxed, almost comfortable in my decision—until later that afternoon, when the reality of the confrontation presented itself.

As I closed my locker and headed toward the cafeteria, lunch box in hand, it happened. Big John was coming down the hall straight toward me. His nose was covered with a white bandage, both eyes badly bruised. My eyes darted nervously around the hall, and I knew there was no escape. Dread consumed me as I watched my classmates part like the Red Sea. The hall grew eerily quiet. Big John's steps grew louder and louder, echoing inside my ears. Swallowing hard, I dropped my lunch box, bracing myself for a fight—a possible beating if necessary.

Big John slowed for only a moment, but it was long enough for me to see the fear and embarrassment in his eyes before he turned away in shame, passing me by. I stood there for a moment, unsure of what had just happened. Glancing around the hall to my fellow classmates, I gave a sigh of relief. The boys, including members of Big John's crew, nodded their heads in respect. The girls just smiled, looking at me in a way they never had before. Quickly composing myself and picking up my lunch box, I straightened my shoulders, puffed out my chest, and confidently walked down the hall of Buchanan Junior High.

School was never the same for me after that, and Big John never tried to take my nickel again. From that day on, Harry Decker no longer existed. I became Jack Collins inside and out of O'Hare's gym. I took on the persona of the Southpaw Slugger. I lived and breathed the world of a boxer, honing my skills. I learned how to size up my opponents in the first few minutes of confrontation, quickly recognizing their strengths as well as their weaknesses. It was there in Pappy's gym I met Joe Riley. The guy who would become my cornerman and best friend. The gym became my second home, and I grew to love ole Pappy as I became one of the best boxers to ever come out of O'Hare's gym.

CHAPTER THREE

September 1941
Harry Decker, a.k.a. Jack Collins,
"The Southpaw Slugger"

It's seven in the morning. My alarm clock screeched that it was time to get up. Suddenly but not unexpectedly, my best friend, Joe, burst into my bedroom. "What do you call a guy that's in the best shape of his life, is quick on his feet, can jab, punch, and knock a guy out in the first round?"

"I don't know, Joe." I rolled over sluggishly. "A boxer?"

"*No*! We call him Jaaaack Collins." He emphasized his words like an MC. "The Southpaw Slugger. Now get up, and get showered." He pulled off my covers. "Pappy wants us at the gym, seven thirty sharp!"

I had met Joe Riley a few years back…via Pappy. At the time, I was being groomed to go pro, and Pappy felt it was time for an assistant/cornerman to help with my training. His job was to keep me focused on my training, and away from the women. Needless to say I wasn't happy, and I had no intentions of accepting the changes, but despite all my objections, one afternoon my future assistant trainer/cornerman entered the gym.

"Excuse me, aren't you Jack Collins, the Southpaw Slugger?"

"Yeah, and who might you be?" I gave a glance of disregard, knowing full well he was Pappy's new man.

"My name's Joe Riley. I have an appointment with Mr. O'Hare this afternoon...is he around?" He gave the gym a quick once-over.

"Yeah, Pappy's around, but there's no need for a meeting. I've got all the help I need, inside and out of the ring. So move along, Mr. Riley." I gave the heavy bag a solid left hook.

"I think you've got things a little wrong here, Mr. Collins." He refused to be intimidated. "First, let me say I've got nothing but respect for you as a boxer, and in time...I'll let you know what I think of you as a man. Second, I'm not here to interfere in your personal life. I'm here to help you become one of the best middleweight boxers in the world. So if that sounds good to you, Mr. Collins, take me to see Mr. O'Hare...if it doesn't...I'll be on my way."

I gave him the ole boxer's stare, contemplating his words. He wasn't much older than me, and he seemed to have an easy way about him, except when it came to the ring. *What could it hurt?* I thought. Besides, Pappy would not be happy if I sent him on his way, and the last thing I needed was Pappy upset. "I'll take you to see Pappy, Mr. Riley, and in time I'll let you know what I think of *you* as a man!"

"Fair enough, Mr. Collins." A sly smile crossed his face. "Lead the way." Joe became my cornerman that day, and eventually the best friend I ever had.

"Hey, Jack?" Joe called out, taking me from my nostalgia. "Do you remember Will 'the Hit-man Hinterman?"

"Yeah, of course I do, Joe. How could I forget my first semipro fight? Will's the only guy who ever left his mark on me. Why do you ask?" I spat out shower suds.

"Well, I ran into him the other day. He donates his time training kids over at the Lincoln Center."

"The Lincoln Center?" I stepped from the shower, a look of repulsion on my face.

"Yeah...the Lincoln Center." Joe disregarded my look of distaste. "Will was wondering if you might be willing to come by sometime and give his boys a few pointers. Unless of course you're still upset with him for messing up your pretty face."

"Upset? Why should I be upset?" Wiping the steam from the bathroom mirror, I examined the scar above my right eye. "The ladies love this scar, Joe, and you know how much I love the ladies."

"Everybody knows how much you love the ladies, Southpaw. So what do you say?" He analyzed his own semi-handsome features in the mirror. "You want to mentor some kids?"

"Sure, Joe, why not. If it's for the kids. Besides, you can't help but respect the guy. He found a way to stay in the fight game, even though his career ended."

"I hoped you'd feel that way, Southpaw. So I set it up for later today...after your training. Shit, Jack, look at the time! We've got to go, or we're going to be late. It's almost seven thirty, and you know how Pappy feels about being late."

"Relax, Joe. Take a breath." I grabbed my keys from the dresser. "I'll get us to the gym on time."

"How are you gonna do that, Jack? It takes twelve minutes to get to the gym, and it's seven twenty-eight. Pappy's gonna have our ass." He slammed the car door shut.

"Calm down, Joe...it's gonna be fine." I turned over the ignition.

"I am calm, Southpaw." He squirmed anxiously in his seat. "Come on; let's go!"

"Okay, Joe...okay...we're going." I accelerated the car toward O'Hare's. "You know, Joe?" I said, grumbling in imitation of ole Pappy. "A tardy man is a lazy man, and a lazy man will miss the knock of opportunity every time." I gave him the ole boxer's stare with a grin.

"Ha-ha, Southpaw. Make all the fun you want, but we both know you can't take it when you disappoint the ole man either."

Visions of Pappy's disappointment began to play out in my mind, causing my cocky smile to disappear. Hitting the gas pedal hard, I sped toward O'Hare's, hoping against time that we weren't too late.

"You're late, Jack," Pappy yelled from across the gym. "Where's your buddy Joe? He's supposed to have you here by seven thirty. The clock on the wall says seven forty. Get your hands wrapped, Jack, and get ready to hit the heavy bag. I've got Sanchez coming in later to spar with you." He shook his head in disappointment.

"Sir, yes, sir…Pappy, sir. Joe is getting the equipment as we speak, sir." That was my desperate attempt to lighten Pappy's mood.

"Shut the lip, Jack, or we can be done right now!"

"Yes, Pappy," I said, nodding solemnly. Joe walked toward me, gauze and tape in hand.

"Let's get you wrapped, Southpaw." Joe's voice was empathetic.

"Pappy's calling me Jack." I looked to the ground in shame. "He only does that when I've really disappointed him."

"He's disappointed in you, Southpaw, and upset with me. The look Pappy shot me when I came through those doors. Well, let's just say if looks could kill, you'd be looking for a new cornerman right now. You'd better get over to the heavy bag, Southpaw." He pushed on my left glove. "You don't want to keep Pappy waiting today."

"You're right," I said, looking at Pappy's disgruntled face. I threw a few shadow punches in preparation.

"I want fifteen solid minutes." Pappy took hold of the heavy bag. "Okay, tardy man, let me see what you've got." Hoping to take the disappointment from his eyes, I threw a few solid jabs and my best combination. "That it?" he grunted.

Responding to his challenge, I hit the bag with a hard, solid left hook, causing Pappy to stumble. "Not bad, tardy man." He retook his stance. "Now let me see some body shots." Nodding in understanding, I hit the heavy bag low and hard. Stepping back, pleased with myself, I wiped the sweat from my brow. "That's it? No more?" Pappy grumbled. "That's all you've got?"

Feeling shame and Pappy's disillusion, I began to beat the heavy bag. Right jab, right jab, combination. To the ribs, to the stomach, to the kidneys. Sweat poured from my body. Pappy desperately tried to hold on as I mercilessly hit the bag. "Enough!" Pappy grumbled, shoving the heavy bag hard in release. Breathing heavily, nodding my head in understanding, I looked to him for some form of approval or forgiveness. "Get over to the ring, tardy man," he ordered "Sanchez is waiting for you."

"Yes, Pappy." Nodding in obedience, I walked toward the ring with a heavy heart.

"Hey, Southpaw?" Joe called out from our corner in the ring. "Sanchez here...says he's ready to show you how it's done. Says he's been waiting for the chance. His chance. To take the great Southpaw Slugger down." He lifted the ropes, allowing me to enter. "What do you think of this guy, Southpaw?" He massaged my shoulders to keep me loose.

"I think Sanchez made a big mistake coming in here today." I stretched my neck, hearing its cracks, fueling my fire.

"Okay, boys, let's go." Pappy pulled himself up by the ropes, standing outside the ring.

Tapping my gloves together to start, I looked at Sanchez. He was cocky and confident, bobbing and weaving his way around the ring. I did a couple of quick steps, giving him a little of my own boxer dance, looking for his weakness. *Where is it, Sanchez? Come on,* my mind muttered. *You can show it to me.*

Sanchez waved me in with his left, keeping his right high to protect his jaw. A smirk flashed across his face as he threw what he believed to be a few threatening punches. *There it is.* I watched Sanchez drop his shoulder, exposing his jaw. Quickly I moved in, turning Sanchez into my personal punching bag, hitting him with one combination after another. One body shot after another. To the ribs, to the kidneys. Showing no mercy.

"Enough!" Sanchez's trainer threw in the towel. "Enough!"

Ignoring his pleas, I continued to pummel Sanchez, turning his body into a limp rag doll. "Southpaw?" Pappy commanded from outside the ring. "Enough." Nodding in obedience, breathing heavily, I backed away from Sanchez and returned to my corner.

"What were you trying to do out there, Southpaw?" Joe said, removing my headgear. "This is a sparring match…not a title fight."

"I was trying to square things Joe," I answered, breathing heavily. "Trying to take the disappointment from Pappy's eyes. Show him I wasn't lazy. That I could work hard."

"Well, I don't know about Pappy, but Sanchez is gonna remember your hard work. Today, tomorrow, and probably well into next week." Shaking his head, he removed my gloves.

"Good work today, Southpaw." Pappy gave a nod of approval. "Roadwork this afternoon…ten miles, nothing less."

"You'll get it, Pappy. Ten miles." I nodded happily, feeling euphoric at being back in his good graces. "I'm gonna grab a quick shower, Joe; then we can head over to the Lincoln Center."

"Sounds good, Southpaw. I'll take the time to see if I can make my own amends with Pappy."

"Good luck with that, buddy. I just had to practically kill a guy to get him to forgive me."

"Well, let's hope an apology for being late is enough." He walked toward Pappy's office and entered as if it were a lion's den.

Letting the warm water run down my body, I turned my thoughts to my upcoming fight against Jimmy the Irishman. I had yet to discover his weakness, and his strengths were all too apparent. Joe said the Irishman was just a stepping-stone on my way to the belt, but I'd been in the fight game long enough to know there was no such thing.

"Hey, Southpaw, speed it up in there. Will's expecting us around noon." Joe interrupted my thoughts.

"I'll be right out, Joe. Were you able to make amends with Pappy?"

"Not quite. He wants me to come back later this afternoon. To discuss my responsibilities as a good cornerman."

"A private meeting with Pappy?" I stepped from the shower. "That can't be good."

"You're telling me." His voice was consumed in sadness. "I really hate disappointing the ole guy."

"I know what you mean, Joe; disappointing Pappy is like a wound to the soul…it cuts deep."

"Real deep, Southpaw. Not to mention that ole man can scare the shit out of you when he wants to."

"Yeah, he can be a scary ole cuss, but don't worry, Joe; you and Pappy will work it out. Come on, buddy. We need to get moving."

"You're right, Southpaw. We don't want to disappoint the kids." He fell in step beside me.

The Lincoln Center

The Lincoln Civic Center was a small, run-down gym located in a not-so-great part of town. Why it was given such a grand name that implied so much more was a mystery to us, as well as everyone in the neighborhood. The only thing grand about the Lincoln Center was the many steps that led to its entrance.

The center was originally intended to keep young boys out of trouble and off the streets. But as time went on, it became a haven for boys between the ages of twelve and fifteen who were interested in taking their fighting skills from the streets to the boxing ring.

"Doesn't look like much, does it, Southpaw?" Joe took a parking spot next to an old white pickup. "Got any change to feed the meter," he asked, checking his own pockets.

"Yeah, I've got a couple of dimes." I shook them loosely in my hand.

"Look at all those steps, Southpaw. You'd think they led to a grand museum instead of an old, ratty gym."

"Yeah, they are deceiving, Joe." Dropping the dimes, I watched the meter register four hours.

"Hey, aren't you the Southpaw Ssslugger?" a young voice squeaked out from behind.

"Why, yes, I am, young man, and who might you be?" I looked down into a smiling face full of freckles. Both front teeth were missing, which seemed to be the cause of the slur on his S-Ls.

"My name is Petey O'Donovitch. I'm gonna be a boxer here one day…when I'm older. I'm only seven, but the Hit-man lets me hang out whenever I want. My brother's Davey O'Donovitch. He's a boxer here right now. He's fifteen! What you doin' here, Mr. Ssslugger?"

"Well, Petey…me and my buddy Joe here have come to help you kids out today. If that's okay?"

"It's okay with me, Mr. Southpaw, but maybe…" Concern filled his voice. "You and your friend should let me take you in."

"Why's that, Petey?" I asked, feeling his apprehension.

"Well, Mr. Ssslugger, the Hit-Man just don't like strangers in his gym. I once saw him drag a guy out by his collar and throw him straight down the steps. All twenty-five of them! Bounce, bounce, bounce, he went all the way down. With the Hit-Man yelling never to come back. I've never seen a guy so scared."

The devilish look on Joe's face told me some friendly teasing was about to begin, and it was going to be at little Petey's expense. "All twenty-five you say, Petey?"

"Yep. Seen it with my own two eyes, Mister."

"Hmm," Joe grunted, stroking his chin. "Petey? What makes you think Mr. Ssslugger and I are strangers?"

"Well, Mister, a stranger is a person you don't know...and, well, I don't know ya, Mister."

"Well, what about Mr. Southpaw Ssslugger, Petey? You seem to know him."

"Everybody knows the Southpaw Ssslugger, but that don't mean he's not a stranger."

"So, let me get this straight, Petey. What you're telling me is you can know *of* someone, but they would still be considered a stranger?"

"Yep, that's what I'm tellin' you, Mister."

"Huh," Joe said, sounding dumbfounded.

"Hey, Mr. Ssslugger." Petey cupped his hand in a whisper. "Is your friend here a little slow?" He eyed Joe with empathy.

"Nah, Joe's all right, Petey." I gave him a wink of reassurance.

"If you say so, Mr. Ssslugger." Turning to Joe once again, he tried to explain the dire consequences. "Look, Mister, I've seen the Hit-man when he's mad, and believe me, you don't want no part of it.

"You hearin' this, Southpaw? Petey here is concerned for our well-being. Our personal safety."

"Maybe we should listen to him, Joe." I gave him a wink. "For safety reasons."

"Well, Petey, I guess it's decided then. There's only one safe way for me and Mr. Ssslugger. You're going to have to take us in."

"That's what I've been trying to tell you all along, Mister." Petey groaned. "Follow me." He turned to start the long climb and quickly turned back around. "And whatever you do," he added, looking straight at Joe, "stay close!"

"Yes, sir." Joe saluted and then matched Petey's climb step for step.

"Hey, Mr. Southpaw?" Petey said, disregarding Joe on his heels. "Did you know the Hit-Man used to be a boxer just like you back in the day?"

"You don't say, Petey?"

"Yep, some say he could have been as good as you—maybe better—but I don't believe it, Mr. Southpaw. Nobody's as good as you."

"Well, thanks for the vote of confidence, Petey, but I guess we'll never know."

"Guess not, Mr. Ssslugger." Reaching the top of the steps, Petey pulled on the heavy doors, allowing the smells of sweaty bodies and dirty towels to make their escape.

"Can you smell that, Petey?" I asked, inhaling deeply. "God, I love that smell."

"The stink, Mr. Ssslugger?" Petey wrinkled his nose in disgust.

"That's not stink, Petey. That's a boxer's road to success." Inhaling once again, I sighed in satisfaction.

"The road to success?" Petey closed his eyes, inhaling deeply, his face becoming distorted. "Still smells like stink to me, Mr. Ssslugger." Opening his eyes, he got back to the business at hand.

"Now I'm gonna need you two to stay here. Where it's safe. While I go talk to the Hit-Man."

"Rest assured, Petey"—Joe's eyes were wide with fear—"we'll stay right here."

We watched as Petey made his way across the gym to where the Hit-Man held court. He seemed nervous taking his place in line, fidgeting behind several other boys. The Hit-Man called them forth one by one; he looked intimidating standing tall with a full brace on his left leg.

"Watch this, Southpaw. Petey? Hey, Petey?" Joe quickly ducked behind me as Petey's head snapped in our direction. Joe peeked out from behind me in playful terror. A look of irritation covered young Petey's face, and he sent Joe the evil eye before returning his attention to his place in line.

"Maybe Petey's right, Joe. Maybe you are a little slow." I felt sympathy for our new little friend. We continued to watch with intrigue as Petey was called forth. He seemed uncomfortable, stammering out his concerns before cautiously pointing to me and Joe across the gym. The Hit-Man looked at us before nodding his approval.

"It's okay," Petey yelled, giving a big, toothless smile.

"We're in, Mr. Ssslugger." Joe gave his new little friend the thumbs-up.

"Jack." Will limped his way over. "I'm so glad you could make it. You being here today will mean so much to my boys."

"No problem, Hit-Man. Glad to do it. You remember my buddy Joe here?"

"Sure do; thanks for getting him here, Joe."

"Wasn't a problem, Will. Southpaw was happy to do it."

"Hey, kids, gather 'round. I've got a surprise for you today all the way from O'Hare's gym. Jack Collins, the 'Southpaw Slugger,' and Joe Riley, his cornerman. They're here today to help you kids out with anything you might need to improve your boxing skills."

"Wow! It really is the Southpaw Slugger, but who's Joe Riley?" a few boys said, gathering around.

"You boys don't know who Joe Riley is?" I looked at the circle of boys in disbelief.

"No, Mr. Southpaw," one of the boys replied courageously, giving Joe a second glace for recognition.

"Why, Joe Riley knows more about boxing than anyone in the fight game. He can slice a welt or close a cut in a matter of seconds. Believe me, when the going gets tough—it's Joe Riley you want in your corner. Heck, I wouldn't be the boxer I am today if it wasn't for Joe Riley!" A few boys stated their apologies, while others nodded their respects.

"Thanks, buddy." Joe gave me a quick wink. "Now who's got a question for the Southpaw Slugger?"

"I do, I do," several boys shouted eagerly. The younger ones jumped up and down in excitement.

"Okay, kids, one at a time." The Hit-Man commanded their attention. "The Southpaw is gonna be here all afternoon, plenty of time for everyone to get their chance. Davey, you first." He pointed to a young man whom Petey stood next to proudly.

"Mr. Collins, how old were you when you knew boxing was in your blood?"

"That's a good question, Davey." I thought back to the first day I walked into O'Hare's. "I was twelve, Davey, and I knew it the minute I threw my first punch."

"So it's a feeling then, Mr. Collins?"

"No, Davey, it's more than that. It's more like a desire that can't be squelched."

"Yeah, a desire." Davey nodded in understanding.

"Who's next?" Looking at a sea of waiting faces, I fielded a few more personal questions, while Joe explained the mechanics and importance of a good cornerman.

"Enough with questions," a young boy whined. "Let's box!"

"Yeah!" Joe and I agreed along with a few other boys.

"Okay, boys," the Hit-Man commanded, taking center stage. "You all know your assignments for today. Now get to it, and let me see some hard work and determination."

The boys quickly dispersed to their designated areas. Some shadowboxed, working on their agility. Some sought out the speed bags to increase their rapidity. Others hit heavy bags that were hung sporadically throughout the gym to measure impact and accuracy. But whatever their assignment…their choice…they were all in their glory.

Joe and I walked the gym together, addressing each boy's need or concern. They seemed to come alive with each and every suggestion. Their young minds absorbed all the information, filing it away, to be critiqued and brought out when the time was right. Most seemed hungry and determined to become great boxers one day, while others were just looking to be a part of something. Joe and I had been there most of the afternoon when he reminded me of my promise to Pappy and the roadwork I'd yet to run.

"Boys, gather 'round, and pay your respects." Will waved them in. "It's time for Southpaw and Joe to leave."

"Aw, already?" the boys moaned collectively.

"Do you have to go, Mr. Southpaw?" Davey O'Donovitch wiped the sweat from his brow. "I could still use a little help with my left hook."

"I'm afraid I do, Davey, but you've got a great trainer here in Will. I'm sure the Hit-Man can help you with any of your concerns."

"That's okay," Davey muttered. "I just thought, with you being the Southpaw and all." He returned to the heavy bag. I caught the dispirited look in Will's eyes as Davey practiced his left hook alone.

"Gather 'round, boys," I shouted, waving them back in. "Before I go, I'd like to tell you boys about the toughest fighter I ever fought."

"There's nobody tougher than you, Mr. Southpaw," a few boys shouted. Every boy took his place inside the circle, every boy except Davey O'Donovitch. He chose to ignore my call, hitting the heavy bag with one weak left hook after another.

"Come on, Davey!" Petey called out, waving his brother in. Davey ignored his call. "Go 'head, Mr. Ssslugger," Petey said, taking a seat down front. "We're listening."

"Thanks, Petey." I gave him a wink of gratitude. "Well, boys, it was about three years ago, early in my boxing career. I had prepared for this fight long and hard…or so I thought, until my opponent entered the ring. His presence alone was intimidation enough, cloaked in a dark, forbidding robe. But when he removed the hood that concealed his face, I knew at a glance he was a fighter to be reckoned with! There was pure determination in his eyes, and he wasn't one that was going to go down easy." Slowly scanning the circle of young boys, I gave their minds time to envision and absorb. I caught the eye of Davey, slowly moving in intrigue toward the circle.

"Now, this fighter!" I locked eyes with Davey. "He could match me blow for blow. If I threw a right hook, he threw a right hook. If I threw a jab, he threw two. He never wavered…never backed off… regardless of what I threw his way. In fact, this scar!" I pointed above my right eye. "It came from him. He's the only fighter who's ever left his mark on me."

"Who was it, Mr. Ssslugger?"

"The fighter, you ask, Petey?" I locked eyes with him.

"Uh…huh." Petey leaned in close, eyes wide in suspense.

"The toughest guy I ever fought Petey was your trainer…Will 'the Hit-Man' Hinterman."

"The Hit-Man did that to you?" Petey moved in close, inspecting the scar.

"He sure did, Petey." I turned my head slowly, giving him a good look. "My buddy Joe here can back me up; he was there."

"It's true, Petey," Joe confirmed. "The Hit-Man is the only fighter that ever left his mark on the Southpaw."

"Wow!" Petey looked from me to the Hit-Man and back again.

"Well, kids, I want to thank you all for allowing me and my buddy Joe in your gym today. Keep your gloves up. Stay out of trouble, and don't ever give up on your dreams."

"We won't, Mr. Southpaw…thanks for coming, Mr. Southpaw… come back anytime, Mr. Southpaw" rang throughout the gym.

"I want to thank you myself, Jack." Will said. "You really made an impact on these kids today, and the toughest fighter story… ahhh, maybe a little embellished?"

"Not at all, Will, and I have the scar to prove it. You're doing a good thing here, Hit-Man, and you've got a few kids with some real talent. That Davey O'Donovitch? I wouldn't be surprised if we saw him in the ring one day."

"Yeah, Davey and a couple of other boys seem to have the right combination of heart and talent. I just need to keep them off the streets and out of trouble long enough to develop their skills. Well, I won't keep you, Jack; I know you have roadwork. Thanks again for coming."

"Anytime, Will." I felt empathy for the once-great boxer.

"Joe? I want to thank you too. You made my boys realize how important conditioning is to maintain their stamina and duration in the ring."

"No thanks needed, Hit-Man—anything I can do to help."

"Well, I better get back, fellas; you can't leave these boys unattended for too long. If you do, chaos tends to break out."

"We were all little hellions at that age," Joe said, defending the boys. "Just young boys, trying to find our way. It's the nature of the beast." He sighed.

"Yeah…I guess." Will curiously looked at Joe, as if he had just said something profound. "Well, thanks again, fellas." He limped back.

"Look at him, Joe." I watched the Hit-Man stop to adjust his leg brace. "One minute you're a contender…the next you're a cripple."

"Maybe so, Southpaw, but you have to admire the guy. He's been dealt some bad cards, but he stays in the fight game anyway."

"I do respect the guy, Joe, but these kids? They seem to have no idea who their trainer is…was. The Hit-Man could've been the middleweight champion of the world."

"They're just kids, Southpaw. You can't expect them to know. Besides, you told them the scar story; if that didn't impress them, nothing will. Come on, buddy. You still have roadwork this afternoon."

"I know; I'm coming, Joe." I looked at the floor, hesitant to leave.

"Hey, Hit-Man," a voice called out from across the gym. "Do you think you could help me with my left hook? There doesn't seem to be much power in the delivery."

"Power comes from the shoulder, Davey…not the arm." Will limped his way over, taking a stance. He threw a solid left hook into the heavy bag. "Now you try." Davey took only a moment before delivering a solid left hook straight from the shoulder.

"Yeah, that feels good, Hit-Man." Davey nodded in appreciation, delivering another solid left hook.

"Hey, Mr. Hit-Man?" Petey came to their side. "Show my brother the punch that gave the Southpaw Ssslugger his scar."

"Surprisingly enough, Petey…it was a left hook." He threw it once again, causing the heavy bag to wince in pain.

"Can you show me some punches, Mr. Hit-Man?" Petey chirped in excitement.

"Sure, Petey." Will gave a genuine smile. Petey took a stance next to Will, raising his small fists proudly, imitating Will's every move. Punch for punch. Jab for jab. Bobbing and weaving next to his newfound hero. Joe and I left the gym that day in high spirits, taking the steps of the civic center two by two.

"Ten miles, Southpaw…ten miles," Pappy's voice echoed in my ears. Entering the gates of Brookston Park, I was in full stride when, off in the distance, I spotted a couple of hot numbers sitting on a park bench. The blonde was trying hard to look like a long-haired Veronica Lake—with little success. But the brunette? Now, she had the look of a real beauty. A cross between Ava Gardner and Rita Hayworth. With my natural interests piqued, I slowed my pace, contemplating my approach.

"Well, hello, pretty ladies." I brought my jog to a stop.

"Well, hello, handsome!" The blonde took a stance, striking her sexiest pose. "My name's Mandy Taylor, and who might you be?" she purred.

"Jack." I looked past the Veronica Lake wannabe, enticed by the beautiful brunette sitting behind. "What might your name be, pretty lady?"

"Elizabeth...Elizabeth Dawson, but my friends call me Liz," she shyly replied.

"Well, hello, Liz. I'm Harry Decker, a.k.a. Jack Collins, the Southpaw Slugger, but you can call me Jack."

"It's very nice to meet you, Jack." Liz got up from the bench, displaying a voluptuous body to go along with her beautiful face. "So you're a boxer?" Her voice was soft and warm.

"Yes, ma'am, I've got a fight coming up on the twenty-sixth at the Paramount. Maybe you and your friend would like to come watch me knock a guy out in the first round."

"Knock a guy out," Mandy interrupted. "In the first round? You're pretty sure of yourself, Harry Decker, a.k.a. Jack Collins. Besides, I don't think Liz and I can make it. We have an invitation to a party that night."

"We do, Mandy?"

"Yes, Liz. We do!" It was then I realized that if I wanted to see this beauty again, I'd have to sweet-talk her friend. Stepping in close, I gently took her hand.

"Mandy? Sweetheart?" I softly caressed her hand. "What party could be more fun than watching me in a boxing match?" I looked deeply, seductively into her eyes.

"Well, we haven't actually accepted the invitation, Jack." She was feeling my sexual prowess. "So we're not committed to the party...just yet." I could sense her knees weaken.

"Great, then you girls can make it." I dropped her hand, breaking the sexual tension.

"I didn't say that, Jack." Mandy quickly recomposed herself. "Two weeks is a long time off...and, well...we just can't commit this early."

"Oh, come on, baby," I pleaded. "If you girls can make it, there'll be two ringside tickets awaiting your arrival at the box office."

"We'll consider it, Jack, but I can't promise anything."

"Well, I've said all I can say. It was very nice to meet you ladies, but my roadwork awaits." Tipping an imaginary hat, I started a slow jog. "Remember, ladies, Saturday the twenty-sixth." I ran off deep into the park.

"So what do you think, Liz? Do you want to go to a boxing match?" Mandy gazed off in the distance. "Oh yeah, we're going to a boxing match," she said, answering her own question.

"But, Mandy, if we've received an invitation to a prior engagement, it would be rude not to attend."

"Liz, you can be so naive sometimes. There is no prior engagement."

"Then why did you tell Jack there was, Mandy?"

"Because you always want men to believe you have other options, Liz. No one wants an available girl. Besides, even if we had a prior engagement, we would change it, if it meant seeing that sexy specimen of a man again."

"I have to admit, Mandy, he is very charming, and awfully cute."

"Cute enough to charm the panties right off a girl," Mandy purred.

"Mandy, the things you say sometimes." Liz blushed.

"Hey, look at the time, Liz; we've gotta go. I start my new job at the Safari Club tonight." Grabbing her pocketbook from the bench, Mandy struck a seductive pose. "Cigarettes, gum, or Mandy…I mean, or candy." Both girls burst out in laughter, walking arm in arm out of Brookston Park toward home.

The Next Day

"It can't be seven?" I moaned, pulling the blankets up over my head, attempting to drown out the screeching alarm.

"It's seven a.m., Southpaw." Joe burst into my bedroom, silencing the alarm and beginning his riddle. "What do you call a guy who is in the best shape of his life, is quick on his feet, can jab, punch, and knock a guy out in the first round?"

"I don't know, Joe." I took my head from under the blankets. "Me?"

"Right as usual, my friend. Get up, Southpaw; we can't be late today. Pappy chewed me a new one for bringing you in ten minutes late yesterday. He said we are all part of a team, and if I couldn't do my job, he would get someone who could."

"Pappy's not gonna get rid of you, Joe; you're the best cut man in the business. He's just using that gruff bark of his to get you in line."

"Well, it's working, Southpaw, so let's get moving. I don't want to be late two days in a row."

"Don't worry, Joe; we won't be late. Just let me grab a quick shower, and we'll be on our way."

"You've got less than ten minutes, Southpaw." He checked his watch.

"Hey, Joe?" I called out over the noise of the shower. "I met a couple girls on my run yesterday in Brookston Park…invited them to the fight on the twenty-sixth. A blonde and a brunette. If they show, the brunette's mine." I stepped from the shower, wrapping a towel around my waist.

"They'll show, Southpaw; the ladies can't resist you, with your green eyes, square jaw, perfect white teeth. You know, a boxer's not supposed to be pretty. Look at you, Southpaw. You don't even use a comb."

"What can I say, Joe." I ran my fingers through my hair. "Except you forgot to mention my mannish charm." Giving a wink, I dropped the towel.

"Okay, Casanova," Joe said, chuckling. "Let's get you and all your mannish charm to the gym."

"Right behind you, buddy." I fell in step beside my best friend.

"Nice to see you boys can tell time," Pappy called out from the ring. "Sanchez's trainer called. Sanchez has the flu, so he won't be back. So I got Martinez here"—he slapped him on the back—"to spar with you today."

"Flu," Joe snickered. "More like Sanchez caught the Southpaw-whooped-his-ass bug." Dropping my gym bag, I threw a few shadow punches Joe's way, making imaginary contact. "I think I have the flu." Joe fell to the floor, pretending to lose consciousness.

"You boys stop playing around," Pappy barked. "We've got a big fight coming up, and the Irishman would like nothing more than to give you the flu, Southpaw."

"Pappy's right." Joe picked himself up from the floor. "Let's get your hands wrapped, Southpaw, and get you in the ring."

Martinez was getting some last-minute instructions from his trainer when I entered the ring. He gave me his best intimidation stare, nodding his respects, but I sensed his fear. The rumors of what I had done to Sanchez the day before still lingered in the gym. Never taking my eyes from Martinez, I shadow punched my way over to my designated corner.

"How's he looking to you, Southpaw?" Joe gave me a quick shoulder massage. "You think this guy's got anything?"

"We'll soon find out." I stretched my neck, hearing the tendons crack, preparing my mind to fight.

"Okay, boys, let's go!" Pappy stood outside the ring.

"You know, Joe. I got a feelin' flu season is comin' early this year." Giving him a quick wink, I slapped my gloves together and made my way to the center of the ring. Eyeing Martinez from under my brow, I contemplated my strategies of destruction.

CHAPTER FOUR

Saturday, September 26, 1941
Boxing Match: Jack Collins versus Jimmy "the Irishman" O'Leary

"The cab's here. Come on, Liz; we gotta go." Mandy gave a light touch-up to her lipstick.

"I'm ready, Mandy." Liz gave herself a final check in the mirror. "Wait." She ran the brush through her hair once again.

"What is with you tonight, Liz? You act like you've never been on a date before."

"I don't know, Mandy. I just feel so nervous tonight. What if Jack doesn't remember us? What if we get to the arena and there are no tickets at the box office?"

"Are you kidding me, Liz? That guy had his charm in high gear. Don't worry; he'll remember us. I just hope he's smart enough to bring a friend along. The man may have good looks and charm, but not enough to handle two women." She gave herself a final look of approval. "Come on, Liz; we've gotta go," she said, hearing the horn of the cab once again.

"Okay. Okay, Mandy, I'm ready." Liz grabbed her coat, giggling with excitement.

"The Paramount Arena, and step on it!" Mandy said, closing the cab door.

"Yes, ma'am!" The cabbie hit the gas pedal hard.

"Isn't this exciting, Liz?" Visions of Jack's sweating, muscular body ran through Mandy's mind.

"Yes, it is, Mandy." Visions of Jack's green eyes and charming smile ran through Liz's mind.

"We're here, ladies." The cabbie interrupted their thoughts. "The Paramount Arena."

"Liz, look!" Mandy's eyes were wide with excitement. "Jack's the headliner. Jack 'the Southpaw Slugger' Collins versus Jimmy 'the Irishman' O'Leary. Pay the cabbie, Liz." Mandy jumped from the cab.

"Thank you. Keep the change." Liz caught up to Mandy at the box-office window.

"Excuse me? Excuse me?" Mandy said in a tone of entitlement. "We're friends of Jack Collins; I believe you have two ringside tickets awaiting our arrival."

"Tickets?" the clerk asked, confused. "Ringside?"

"Yes," Mandy said, her assertive tone turning hopeful. "There should be two tickets."

"Well, I don't seem to have any tickets, Miss." The clerk looked around his booth in dismay. "Hey, Bob?" he called over to the next booth. "Did the Southpaw leave any tickets with you for this evening?"

"Yeah, Marv, I told you earlier; the Southpaw left a couple of tickets." He held them up for inspection. "They're for a Mandy and an Elizabeth...Liz?"

"That's us," Mandy squealed. "That would be us. I'm Mandy, and this is Liz, Elizabeth." Grabbing Liz by her coat sleeve, she pulled her closer to the window.

"Enjoy your evening, ladies." Bob handed over the tickets.

"Yes, ladies," Marv chimed in with a devilish smile. "Enjoy your evening."

"Thank you, Bob. Come on, Liz." Mandy gave Marv a glance full of loathing.

"So Jack's got two new broads, eh, Bob?"

"Guess so, Marv, but I'm not surprised. You know the ladies love the Southpaw."

"That they do, Bob. I wonder where Marilyn is tonight. She's usually Jack's first pick when he's coming off of a fight."

"Don't know, Marv, but looking at the dark-haired beauty? Marilyn has got some serious competition."

"That she does, Bob." Marv nodded in agreement. "That she does."

"Our tickets are row one, seats E and F," Mandy said. "That's got to be right up front, Liz. Excuse us, excuse us…we're guests of Jack Collins. We need to get to our seats." Mandy pulled Liz by her coat sleeve, pushing her way through the crowd, oblivious to the disruption she was causing. "Here, here they are, Liz." Taking her seat, she pulled Liz down next to her. "This is so exciting! Don't you think this is exciting, Liz?" She scanned the arena.

"Very exciting, Mandy. I've never been to a fight before." Looking at the bloodstained canvas, Liz suddenly felt an overwhelming queasiness. The intro music blasted, announcing the fighters' arrival.

"Here he comes, Liz. Jack! Jack! We're over here." Mandy jumped up and down in a frenzy. "Jack? He didn't even look in our direction." She fell back into her chair in a pout.

"It's so noisy in here, Mandy; he probably just didn't hear you."

"Whether he heard me or not, Liz, he knows where we're sitting; after all, he got us the seats."

"Yes, Jack was gracious enough to give us these tickets, but he has a fight to be concerned with. He needs to focus on that…not us."

"Don't defend him, Liz! We're just as important as this fight. He invited us! He pursued us! Not the other way around!

"I'm not defending him, Mandy; I just…"

"Shush, Liz…the fight is starting."

"Let's get ready to rumble." The MC's voice echoed, causing the crowd to go wild. "In this corner, weighing in at one hundred seventy-seven pounds in the red trunks…Jimmy 'the Irishman' O'Leary." Cheers and whistles filled the arena. The Irishman bobbed and weaved his way around the ring, taking center stage. He waved to his fans before returning to his corner.

"In this corner, weighing in at one hundred seventy-five pounds in the white trunks…Jack 'the Southpaw Slugger' Collins." Jack stepped from his corner, doing a little boxer's dance of his own, acknowledging the roaring crowd with a nod and a wave.

"Yeah, Jack!" Mandy squealed, trying once again to gain his attention.

"Bring it in, boys." The ref gestured to join him center ring. "No hitting below the belt. No biting, and absolutely no late punches. When I say break, the fighting stops…understood?" The fighters nod in understanding. "Okay, boys, let me see a good, clean fight." Tapping gloves, the boxers both took the opportunity to give their best intimidation stare before returning to their designated corners.

"God, he's handsome," Mandy sighed.

Ding, ding! "That's the sound of the first round, folks," the broadcaster proclaimed. "Both fighters quickly leaving their corners, bobbing and weaving their way around the canvas. The Irishman throws the first punch. It's a right hook landing squarely on the Slugger's left jaw, causing his head to toss back from the force. The Irishman throws another punch; it's a quick jab, opening the scar above the Slugger's right eye. Blood has begun to flow here tonight, folks."

"Jack?" Liz sighed, stomach churning.

"Take him down, Jimmy," a voice yelled from behind. "Show him how the Irish do it!"

"I can't watch anymore." Liz covered her eyes, shaking her head, desperately trying to block out the sound of debilitating punches echoing in her ears.

"Right jab, right jab, combination, left hook," the commentator yelled in a frenzy.

"Liz? Liz? Open your eyes." Mandy pulled on her hands.

"Stop it, Mandy. I can't watch!" She pulled from her grip.

"He's out!" the commentator announced. "The Southpaw Slugger has knocked the Irishman out!"

"What?" Liz peeked through her fingers and saw the Irishman's lifeless body lying out on the canvas.

"The winner by a knockout…Jaaaack 'the Southpaw Slugger' Collins," the MC's voice echoed. Cameras flashed as the crowd went wild. "Southpaw, what can you tell us about your strategy this evening? You looked to be in a little trouble the first few minutes of the round."

"A boxer doesn't give his fighting strategies," I replied, breathing heavily. "Just let me say the Irishman was a worthy opponent, but the gods were smiling on me tonight."

"Well, there you have it, folks…a great boxer, yet a humble man. Don't forget about our exhibition fight tomorrow night, folks, when Louie Sanchez takes on Gorge Martinez."

"Excuse me? Excuse me, ladies?" a young boy shouted over the disbanding crowd. "Are you ladies Liz and Mandy?"

"Why, yes, we are." Liz smiled softly.

"Mr. Collins asked me to deliver this to you." He handed her a folded note.

"He did see me," Mandy said. "What does it say, Liz?"

"Thank you for coming. Please meet me at my dressing room... Jack."

"What are we waiting for? Let's go." Mandy grabbed Liz's arm. Off in chase she pushed her way through the dispersing crowd.

"Mandy, slow down," said Liz, feeling her body ping-pong back and forth. "Mandy, stop it!" She pulled from her grip. "Do you even know where the dressing rooms are?"

"No, but they have to be around here somewhere." Mandy anxiously looked around. "Let's ask this guy up ahead. I think I saw him in Jack's corner earlier. Excuse us; we're looking for Jack Collins's dressing room?"

"Well, you've found it. You must be Mandy?"

"Why, yes, but how did you know?" She batted her eyes flirtatiously.

"Jack told me all about you girls. Excuse me; where are my manners? Hi, my name is Joe. I'm Jack's best friend and your escort tonight, Mandy—if you'll have me?"

"My escort?" The smile left her face.

"Hi, Joe, I'm Elizabeth, but you can call me Liz."

"Well, hello, Liz. Joseph Riley, but you can call me Joe. Very nice to meet you."

"Very nice to meet you, Joe."

"So, ladies." Joe pulled his gaze from Liz. "Jack tells me he met you girls in Brookston Park?"

"Why, yes, Joe." Mandy demanded center stage. "Liz and I were just sitting on a bench enjoying the afternoon when Jack came running by and invited us to his fight. I wasn't sure at the time if I wanted to come. I mean...with Jack being a complete stranger and all, but he insisted that if Liz and I could make it, we would have a great time. We gave up an invitation to a party tonight at Jack's insistence."

"What are you talking about, Mandy...what party?" Liz inquired.

"Oh, don't get me wrong, Joe," Mandy continued. "I was okay with coming tonight, but I think Jack may have brought me here under false pretenses."

"Well, whatever brought you ladies here, I'm glad you could make it. Why don't I just slip inside the dressing room here and see what's holding Jack up?" He opened the door just wide enough to slide inside.

"You better speed it up, Southpaw...I'm feeling a little tension between the ladies."

"Tension? What kind of tension, Joe?" I asked.

"The usual. Until it's established who's getting who...they're fighting for territory. I think Mandy was a little disappointed when she found out I was her date tonight. I think she was foolish enough to believe she had a shot at you. My advice: if she wants the alpha dog instead of the wingman, she better quit hangin' with that beauty out there."

"Alpha dog? Wingman? What are you talking about, Joe?"

"It's the natural order given among men, Southpaw. In our friendship you're the alpha dog, and I'm the wingman."

"Who decided I was the alpha dog?" I said, checking the adhesive bandage over my right eye.

"Society decides. The most desirable male in the pack is always the alpha dog, and his cohorts are wingmen. It's not a position you get to pick, Southpaw, but don't get me wrong—your leftovers are plenty good enough for me. Besides, you know my philosophy on women."

"Your philosophy, Joe?" I replied, satisfied with the bandage coverage.

"A woman is a woman is a woman. One just as good as the next, and thank God for my philosophy, or my feelings could have really been hurt this evening. The disappointment in dear sweet

Mandy's eyes when she found out I was her date was absolutely heartbreaking."

"I think it's going to take a little more than a broad like Mandy to break your heart, Joe."

"Like I said, Southpaw. One is just as good as the next. You ready to go have some fun, buddy?"

"Ready, Wingman. It's been a long dry spell."

"Well then, after you, Alpha Dog." He pulled open the dressing-room door.

"Good evening, ladies," I said, stepping out into the corridor. "I hope I haven't kept you waiting too long. Did you enjoy the fight tonight?"

"I loved it, Jack." Mandy sashayed forward. "Liz couldn't watch most of it. She kept hiding her eyes."

"Liz?" I looked into a pair of beautiful dark eyes. "You didn't enjoy the fight?"

"It wasn't that, Jack. I'm just a little uncomfortable watching men fight, but I do want to thank you for inviting us tonight."

"You're very welcome, Liz." I sensed a strange yet comfortable feeling unlike anything I had ever felt before.

"Well, where should we go tonight, ladies—any suggestions?" Joe rubbed his hands together in anticipation. "Southpaw and I have a whole six weeks off before training starts again."

"Let's go to the Safari Club," Mandy suggested. "The Jimmy Dorsey Band is playing, and they have a great new singer, Ruth Grayson."

"I don't know, Mandy." Joe sounded apprehensive. "I think we need a reservation to get into that club."

"Normally you would, Joe, but I'm their new cigarette girl." She struck her sales pose. "I can get us in."

"Sounds great then, baby. Lead the way."

"We will." Mandy giggled flirtatiously, taking Liz's arm. "Joe's not so bad," she whispered. "In fact, he's kind of cute in a rugged sort of way. Oh, by the way, boys." She looked over her shoulder.

"When we get to the club, let me do all the talking. Fredrick, the maître d', has a little crush on me. He'll do anything I ask." She gave Joe a teasing smile.

"Whatever you say, baby." Joe returned her smile with a wink.

The Safari Club

"Hi, Freddy," Mandy purred, stepping to the podium. "We don't have a reservation for tonight, but I thought you might have an available table for little ole me and my friends."

"Mandy, you know it's reservation only on Saturday nights." Freddy the maître d' seemed preoccupied.

"Oh, come on, Freddy." Mandy lightly stroked his hand. "You sure you don't have a little ole table for your favorite cigarette girl? I know there is always a couple tables set aside for important people, and we're just a small little party of four."

"Sorry, Mandy." Freddy scanned his reservation book. "I don't see anything for at least two hours, and stop calling me Freddy when we're at work!"

"Maybe we should try the Cotton Club over on Stuart Avenue?" Joe said. "You know we can get in there, Southpaw."

"Southpaw?" Fredrick came to attention. "Hey, you're Jack Collins; you had a fight over at the Paramount tonight."

"Yes, he did," Joe interjected. "He knocked the Irishman out in the first round."

"I'm a big fan of yours, Mr. Collins. I tried to get tickets for your fight tonight, but they were all sold out. Mandy, why didn't you tell me the Southpaw was in your party?"

"You didn't give me a chance, Freddy!"

"Give me a few minutes, Mr. Collins. I'm sure I can find a table for you and your party." Freddy quickly left the podium.

"This looks like a great club, baby." Joe smiled. "Thanks for suggesting it."

"You're welcome, Joe." Mandy, slightly embarrassed, returned his smile.

"Right this way, Mr. Collins." Fredrick led the way, applause erupting throughout the club.

"Good fight tonight, Southpaw," a male voice shouted from across the club.

"Yeah, the Irishman never knew what hit him," another voice proclaimed.

"Wow, this is a little embarrassing." I gave a slight wave of my hand.

"Enjoy it, Southpaw. You've earned it." Joe proudly walked in step beside me.

"Here we are. The best table in the house," Fredrick announced with a wave of his hand.

"Thank you, Fredrick. There'll be two ringside tickets waiting for you at the box office for my next fight against Frankie Rocco."

"Thank you, Mr. Collins. Not necessary, but greatly appreciated. Gaston will be your waiter tonight. Take good care of Mr. Collins and his party. Enjoy your evening, folks."

"What can I get you this evening?" asked Gaston, sounding very refined.

"Well, Gaston." Joe leaned back in his chair. "We're celebrating a big win tonight. My buddy Jack here knocked out Jimmy the Irishman tonight. So how about a bottle of your best champagne?"

"Very good, sir. May I suggest a bottle of Dom Pérignon?"

"Oh yes!" Mandy came alive. "Could we have some Dom Pérignon, Joe?" she asked, lightly stroking his hand.

"We can have anything you want, pretty lady. Gaston! A bottle of your best."

"Very good, sir." Gaston gave a slight bow. "Right away."

"I'm sorry, Jack? Liz? Is Dom Pérignon okay with you two?" Joe asked.

"It's fine with me, buddy."

"Sounds wonderful, Joe."

"Great." Joe returned his attention to Mandy. "So you work here, baby?" He looked around. "Pretty swanky club."

"I'm their new cigarette girl, Joe. Cigarettes, gum, or Mandy…I mean, or candy?" She giggled flirtatiously.

"I'd buy everything you're selling, honey," Joe said, giving her the once-over.

"May I fill your glasses, sir?" Gaston had returned with the champagne.

"That would be great, Gaston." I replied. "We settled back to enjoy the night's festivities. Soft music began to play, and the stage curtain opened, displaying Jimmy Dorsey and his band.

"May I present the wonderful Ms. Ruth Grayson?" Jimmy announced, waving his band sticks. "You made me love you. I didn't want to do it," Ruth softly began to sing.

"Oh, I love this song," Liz sighed, swaying romantically in her chair.

"Would you care to dance, Liz?" I asked.

"I'd love to, Jack."

"I should probably warn you, Liz. I taught Fred Astaire everything he knows."

"Thanks for the warning, Jack." She softly smiled, accepting my hand.

As we stepped onto the dance floor and I took her into my arms, the strange, comfortable feeling consumed me once again. Her fingertips lightly touched my neck, feeling like a gentle caress as we glided around the floor. We danced in step, together, as if we had done it our whole lives. *Who are you, Elizabeth Dawson*? I asked myself. *And what is this strange yet wonderful feeling I have for you?*

"Mandy, would you like to dance?" Joe asked. "I'm not the dancer Jack is, but I can hold my own on the dance floor."

"No, thank you, Joe, maybe a little later. So tell me about yourself, Mr. Riley. What is it you do up there in the ring with Jack?"

"I'm his cornerman. I get him prepared to fight. Tape his hands. Get him emotionally psyched. Monitor any cut or welt received during the fight. Watch how the other boxer is fighting. Give him strategies on how to win. How to conquer his opponent."

"So in other words, Mr. Riley," Mandy murmured, moving a little closer, "you're a fighter too, in an indirect sort of way?"

"I guess you could say that, baby." Joe looked deeply, longingly into Mandy's eyes.

"I guess we could," Mandy purred, moving a little closer. "You know, Joe? I've never been with a boxer before." She gave Joe's thigh an insinuating squeeze.

"Is that right?" Joe smiled seductively.

"Joe and Mandy really seem to be hitting it off," I said, looking back to our table.

"I'm not surprised." Liz followed my gaze. "Men have always liked Mandy. Unlike me, she is very comfortable and confident in their presence. I envy her sometimes."

"Envy, Liz? Trust me; you have no reason to envy Mandy." My lips brushed her ear in a gentle caress.

"Jack." Her body stiffened in my embrace. "I'm not like Mandy."

"I know you're not, Liz." I pulled her in with a romantic spin.

"Joe, darling?" Mandy waved around her empty glass. "Mandy girl needs a refill."

"Mandy girl needs to slow down a little." Joe refilled her glass halfway. "We've got a long night ahead of us, baby."

"Why, Joseph Riley." She batted her eyes flirtatiously. "Have you got plans for little ole me tonight?"

"Plans? Let's just say, you lead the way, little lady, and I'll follow."

"Then fill it up this time, lover." Mandy handed back her empty glass.

"So tell me about yourself, Liz." I said. "What do you do when you're not strolling through the parks or sashaying around the dance floor?"

"I'm a sales rep for Macy's. And you, Jack? What do you do when you're not boxing?"

"Well, Liz, boxing takes up most of my time, but I'm a tool-and-die machinist by trade. Someday when my boxing career is over, and I'm hoping that isn't anytime soon, I plan to open my own shop."

"Your own shop, Jack? That sounds very exciting."

"Exciting? I don't know about exciting, Liz, but it will definitely pay the bills."

Ruth Grayson brought the song to an end.

"You're a wonderful dancer, Jack, but I think we should rejoin our friends." Liz lightly applauded.

"Anything you want Liz." Taking her arm, I escorted her back to the table. "You two look like you're having a really good time," I said, helping Liz with her chair.

"We're having a great time." Mandy hiccupped.

"Yeah, a great time, Southpaw." Joe lightly caressed Mandy's bare shoulder.

"I can see that. Liz, may I pour you another glass of champagne?"

"Yes, Jack, please. I would love one." We both watched as two lonely drops fell from the bottle.

"I guess you two really have been enjoying yourselves." I gestured to Gaston to bring another bottle.

"I need to excuse myself." Mandy stumbled slightly getting up from her chair.

"Mandy, are you okay?" Liz steadied her.

"I'm fine, Liz." Mandy giggled. "I just need to use the little girls' room."

"I'll go with you." Liz protectively took Mandy's arm and escorted her from the table.

"I'm about ready to turn this little swore-ay into a private party. What do you say, Southpaw? You ready to go our separate ways?"

"I just ordered another bottle of champagne, Joe. What's your hurry?"

"My hurry, Southpaw? You of all people should know my hurry. My hurry is I'm comin' off a dry spell, and sweet Mandy has been rubbing my leg and anything else she can get her hands on under the table for the last half hour. A guy can only take so much."

"Your leg, and anything else?" I lifted my brows in insinuation. "Like what else, Joe?"

"You know what else, Southpaw." His voice was sarcastic.

"You go ahead, buddy. I think I'm gonna pass on having a private party with this one."

"Why? You're coming off a dry spell yourself, Southpaw. What's it been, seven weeks?"

"Eight, but who's counting?"

"It sounds like you are."

"Yeah, I guess I am." I chuckled in surprise.

"Then what's stopping you? Liz is a beauty, and that body..." He gave a low wolf whistle.

"I don't know, Joe. There's just something different about Liz."

"Something different? She's just a woman, Southpaw...better looking than most, but still just a woman."

"Maybe, but she's not like any of the women I'm used to. She seems like...well...like a nice girl."

"A nice girl! Run, Southpaw."

"Run, Joe? Really?"

"As fast and as far as you can, Southpaw...and don't look back."

"Come on, Joe."

"Come on, nothin'. Let me tell you about the 'nice girl.'" He adjusted his chair and leaned in close. "The nice girl is a different breed of woman. They play by a different set of rules. Nice girls have a way of messin' with your head. They make you do things you thought you'd never do. I've seen a few good men taken down by them. Take it from me, Southpaw...*run!*"

"A few good men, Joe? I think I can handle it."

"Make light of it, Southpaw, but remember, you've been warned."

"Okay, Joe, consider me warned." The girls returned to the table.

"Everything okay, Liz?" I asked.

"Everything's fine, Jack." Liz anxiously glanced to Mandy.

"You ready to get out of here, baby?" Joe murmured. "Go somewhere a little more private."

"Sure, Joe." Mandy seemed a little more composed. "Where would you like to go?"

"Anywhere you want, pretty lady. You lead the way, and I'll follow."

"Anywhere?" Mandy smiled in insinuation.

"Anywhere." Joe naughtily grinned.

"Jack?" said Mandy, not taking her gaze from Joe. "Can I trust you to get Liz home safely? Joe and I are going to go somewhere and get better acquainted."

"Sure, Mandy, you can trust me."

"Ready, Joe?" Mandy grabbed her handbag.

"I've been ready, baby—just waitin' on you," said Joe, not taking his gaze from Mandy. "Liz, it was great meeting you. Jack, I'll see you later." He anxiously escorted Mandy from the table.

"I hope Mandy's going to be all right," Liz said, watching Mandy stumble slightly, giggling her way out of the club.

"She'll be fine, Liz. Joe will take good care of her. Can I pour you another glass of champagne?"

"Please, Jack." She returned her attention to the table so as not to be rude. Her upbringing was ever so present. "How long you been a boxer, Jack?" she asked, smiling softly.

"Three years now, Liz. I started boxing fresh out of high school, but I've been training since I was twelve."

"Twelve! Really, why the interest at such a young age?"

"Well, there was this guy…Big John. He used to bully me. Bullied most of the kids that went to my school."

"Bullied! You, Jack? I find that very hard to believe."

"Well, it's true. Big John used to scare the hell out of me…until Pappy taught me how to box."

"Well, that explains learning how to fight. You needed to defend yourself. But what draws a man into the ring? Why would someone purposely want to engage in a fighting match?"

"That's a good question, Liz. I've never really thought about the why. I just know that I've had the desire to be one of the best from the moment I threw my first punch."

"So it's a desire then?"

"It's really more than that, a man gets an indescribable feeling of euphoria when he goes toe-to-toe against his equal and triumphs."

"A euphoria, Jack? I don't understand."

"I'm sure there's some scientific explanation, Liz. Something in the male's DNA, but for me…I just truly love the sport. It's a part of me. My one true passion, and like I said—I knew it years ago that first day inside O'Hare's gym."

"Passion? Now, I do understand having a passion, Jack, but fighting? It just seems so barbaric and brutal, and when your scar opened up, and the blood ran down your face…" She shook her head in torment. "Well, I just couldn't watch it anymore."

"You were worried about me, Liz?" I touched her hand, feeling a warm sensation.

"I wasn't worried, Jack." She shifted uncomfortably. "I just found it difficult to watch."

"Well, what can I say, Liz?" I let go of her hand, breaking the tension. "I love the sport, but enough about boxing. Tell me about you. How long have you and Mandy been friends?"

"A few years. We met at Macy's. She was working in the perfume department then. We became quick friends and now share an apartment together."

"An apartment? You seem to be very different women to become friends."

"I know Mandy can come off as being a little forward and offbeat sometimes, but she would do anything for me. We're really more like sisters than friends."

Watching this exquisite woman, I was truly enthralled. For the first time, I was truly interested in something a woman had to say. She was funny, shy, and beautiful, and she gave me feelings of comfort. We shared stories of our pasts and hopes for our futures as I desperately searched for her weaknesses, her flaws, but there were none to be found. "Liz, would you care to take another spin around the dance floor?"

"I would love to, Jack, but I didn't realize it was getting so late. Do you mind if we leave? It's almost midnight. My father always said nothing good happens to a single girl after midnight."

"Your father sounds like a smart man." I gestured to Gaston for the check. "Come on, Cinderella; let's see if I can get you home before midnight." I escorted her to an awaiting taxi. "There'll be two stops tonight." Shutting the cab door, I looked to Liz for direction.

"Three Forty-Two Parkway Terrace, please." Her voice was soft and warm.

"You got it, lady." The cabbie pulled away from the curb.

"I had a wonderful evening tonight, Jack. Thank you so much for inviting me."

"You're welcome, Liz." I put a gentle arm around her, and we sat in a comfortable silence. The fifteen-minute cab ride seemed to take only moments.

"Three Forty-Two Parkway Terrace," the cabbie announced, pulling alongside the curb.

"We're here, Liz," I murmured, taking my arm from her shoulder, breaking our blissful comfort.

"So we are, Jack." There was a sound of disappointment in her voice.

"Keep the meter running, buddy. I'll only be a minute." I shut the cab door. "I had a great time tonight, Liz," I said, standing outside her apartment door. "Do you mind if I kiss you good night?" Without a word, she closed her eyes, tilting her face in permission. As I lightly brushed my lips against hers, a tenderness, a gentle intimacy, consumed me. A feeling unlike anything I had ever felt before.

"Thank you, Jack." Liz slowly opened her eyes. "For a wonderful evening."

"You're welcome, Liz." I gazed into her warm, dark eyes, unable to turn away, hypnotized.

"I should probably go inside," she murmured. She turned reluctantly, putting her key in the lock. "Thank you again, Jack." Glancing over her shoulder, she gently pushed open the door.

"Hey, Liz?"

"Yes, Jack?" She hastily turned to me.

"Tomorrow's Sunday. Would you like to do something with me?"

"I would love to, Jack." She quickly pulled pen and paper from her handbag. Blushing, as if she was embarrassed by her eagerness, she held the small paper containing her phone number.

"Okay then—until tomorrow." I gently pulled the paper from her hand.

"Until tomorrow, Jack." Liz stepped inside, quietly closing the door. Tiptoeing through the darkness, she slipped into bed. Sensuous sounds of Joe and Mandy's lovemaking seeped through her bedroom walls. "Jack?" She softly sighed, gently caressing her inner thighs, in unknown ecstasy.

"Six Eighty-Seven Center Street." I shut the cab door and leaned back, too wired to relax. My thoughts turned to Liz. Joe's warnings echoed in my ears. "Nice girls are a mistake; they mess with your head." *He's right; what am I doing? I've got a fight coming up. I need to stay focused. The last thing I need is to get emotionally tied up.* "Change of plans, buddy. Take me to Five Thirty-Six Chenille Drive."

"Whatever you say, Mister; it's your dime." He made a quick U-turn.

Relaxing back, confident in my decision, I went over the events of the day. I was euphoric about my win over the Irishman, and I became aroused thinking of the many ways to celebrate with Marilyn.

"Five Thirty-Six Chenille. That'll be three seventy-five."

"Keep it." I handed him a five through the cab window.

"Well, hello, lover." Marilyn greeted me at the door wearing sexy black lingerie. "I was beginning to think I wasn't going to see you tonight."

"I'm sorry, baby; things ran a little late." I swept her into my arms.

"Late? Late how, Jack?" Her tone was untrusting.

"Late, like celebrating with Pappy and Joe." I nuzzled her neck.

"You could've at least called, Jack. You knew I'd be waiting."

"Come on, baby…be nice. I'm here now; isn't that what's really important?" I brought her in for a kiss.

"I guess?" She kissed me reluctantly.

"You guess?" I said, pulling her in close. I kissed her deeply, passionately, feeling her body respond to my touch.

"Let's go, Jack," she moaned. She took my hand, leading me to her bedroom, letting her negligee seductively fall to the floor.

The Next Morning

"*Mmm*," Liz moaned, waking to find her hands still nestled under her gown. Teasingly she ran her fingertips down her stomach to her inner thighs. "Jack?" She rolled out of bed with a blushing, sexual sigh.

"Well, good morning, Liz." Mandy turned down the flame under the iron skillet. "I'm just making Joe some breakfast; would you like some?"

"No, thank you, Mandy, just coffee this morning." She poured herself a cup and took a seat at the kitchen table across from Joe.

"You and Southpaw have a good time last night?" Joe lifted his brows in insinuation.

"We had a wonderful time, Joe. In fact, we're doing something later today."

"You don't say?" Joe sounded a bit surprised. He realized his warnings had not been heeded.

"Liz, you sure you don't want any breakfast? I'm making eggs, sausage, and biscuits. Joe just loves a big breakfast. Don't you, baby?"

"A guy has to regain his strength somehow, sweetheart." Getting up from the table, Joe came up behind Mandy and nuzzled her neck.

"Don't talk like that, Joe." Mandy giggled. "You're embarrassing Liz."

"Just stating the facts, baby." He gave her butt an affectionate squeeze.

"I think I'll finish my coffee in the other room." Liz left the kitchen unnoticed. Mandy and Joe were engrossed in the morning-after sexual play.

"Good morning, baby." Yawning, I took a big contented stretch and snuggled up to Marilyn.

"Good morning, lover." Marilyn relaxed back into my embrace.

"What's the chances of giving your man a little send-off this morning?" I nuzzled her neck, softly moaning. "Something to remember you by?" I lightly caressed her beautiful naked body.

Marilyn answered with her tongue, lightly traveling down my body in a sexual caress, causing my body to spasm in eagerness.

"Relax, Jack," she purred. "Let Marilyn work her magic." She reached her destination.

"Work your magic, baby." I groaned, responding to her gentle, teasing touch.

"You like that, don't you, baby?" Marilyn moaned in a sexual whisper. "Tell Marilyn you like it, Jack." Her nails pressed deep into my stomach, causing pleasurable pain.

"You know I like it, baby." I was breathing spasmodically "Nobody takes care of me quite like you."

"And no one ever will, Jack." She tightened her grip, causing my body to spasm in delight, bringing me to total, utter completion.

"You're the best, baby," I moaned breathlessly, feeling exhausted but fulfilled.

"You're welcome, lover." Marilyn came up the bed on all fours. Proud and sleek, she looked like a panther that had just devoured its prey. Laying her head on my chest and purring, she cuddled in close. "What should we do today, Jack?" She ran her fingertips sensuously up and down my body.

"Hey, look at the time!" I jumped from the bed, causing Marilyn to catch herself. "I didn't realize it was so late. Baby, could you call me a cab while I take a quick shower?"

"You're leaving, Jack?" A confounded look crossed her face.

"I have to, baby...just for a little while." I quickly made my escape to the shower, hearing Marilyn mumbling her objections.

"The cab is on its way, Jack," Marilyn shouted over the shower. "So...am I at least going to see you tonight?"

"I wish I could, baby, but I'm meeting Pappy and Joe. We're going over some fight footage of Frankie Rocco. I don't know how long it's going to take."

"You know I stay up late, Jack. You could come over after."

"What, baby? I can't hear you over the water."

"You could come over after, Jack?" she repeated, raising her voice.

"You know how Pappy can be, sweetheart. The meeting could take all night. I don't want you waiting around on a possibility." Stepping from the shower, I said, "Go out with some of your friends. Have some fun."

"I don't want to go out with any of my friends." Her bottom lip formed a pout.

"Oh, come on, baby. Don't be like that; we'll get together again real soon...I promise. Come on—the cab's here. Give us a kiss," I cajoled her. Marilyn reluctantly gave me a quick peck on the cheek. "That's all I get, baby?" I gave her a heartbroken look.

"You know I can't stay mad at you, Jack." Marilyn caved in, kissing me deeply, passionately, slowly, provocatively grinding her body against mine.

"You make it hard for a man to leave, baby." Giving her butt a hard squeeze, I made my exit.

"Call me, Jack?" Marilyn called out from her doorway.

"Sure, baby." I gave her a quick wave and disappeared inside the cab. "Take me to Six Eighty-Seven Center Street." Relaxing back into the cab, I closed my tired, bloodshot eyes. I made a mental note to tell Joe: *If anyone asks, we were watching old footage with Pappy.*

"Six Eighty-Seven Center Street, buddy," the cabbie announced, taking me from my slumber.

"Thanks, buddy, keep the change." I made a beeline to my apartment in search of my comfortable bed and closed my weary eyes for a much-needed sleep.

"Where are you and Jack going tonight, Liz?" Mandy asked, coming into the living room.

"Jack hasn't called yet, Mandy." Liz sighed.

"Don't worry, Liz; he will."

"It's two thirty, Mandy." Liz sadly looked at the clock on the wall.

"It's early. I'm sure he'll call." Mandy grabbed the newest *Stargaze* magazine from the pile on the coffee table, fuming inside.

"*Mmmm.* Just what I needed." Taking a good stretch, I rolled over and adjusted my eyes to the clock on the nightstand. I picked up the bedside phone. *Don't do it!* Joe's words echoed in my ears. "Nice girls are a different breed. They mess with your head." *Maybe I should go for a jog first?* I set down the receiver. *Yeah, a jog always clears my head.*

Jogging past Brookston Park, my ego was fully in charge. *What's there to be afraid of? Liz is just a woman. Lord knows you've had plenty of those. You just beat a middleweight contender, and you're afraid of a five-foot-two, hundred-pound woman? You're a grown man! You're the Southpaw Slugger*! Feeling confident, I made a U-turn and headed for home.

"Jack's not going to call, is he, Mandy?" Liz's voice was solemn.

"It's still early, Liz." Mandy tried to sound upbeat.

"It's four thirty, Mandy. He's not calling, and why should he? He can have any woman he wants; why would he want me? I can't even stay out past midnight. He probably thinks I'm a child."

"Trust me, Liz. Jack doesn't think you're a child."

"Then why hasn't he called? I should have never cut the date short, but Jack makes me so nervous. He makes me want to do things I know I shouldn't be doing."

"Really?" Mandy's voice filled with intrigue. "Like what kind of things?"

"It really doesn't matter now, does it?" Her eyes misted with tears. "Because I'm never going to see him again."

"Oh, come on, Liz. Don't be sad; be grateful—grateful you found out early, before you wasted your time and got..." Mandy stopped in midsentence, hearing the phone ringing. Liz came to attention.

"Do you think that could be him, Mandy? Do you think it could be Jack?"

"There's only one way to find out." Both girls ran toward the phone, coming to a quick halt. The phone rang several more times. "Answer it, Liz." Mandy anxiously shouted.

"Yes...hello, Jack?" Liz quickly uttered into the receiver.

"Well, hello, Liz. How did you know it was me?"

"I didn't; I mean, I thought, maybe...how are you, Jack?" she stammered.

"I'm fine, Liz, and you?"

"I'm fine too, Jack." Eyes bright, she tried to contain her excitement.

"Sorry about not calling earlier, Liz, but my meeting with Pappy ran later than expected. So if you could find it in your heart to forgive me, I would love to take you out this evening."

"Well, I don't know, Jack." Mandy encouraged her to stay calm. "It's kind of late in the day to be asking for a date."

"Come on, sweetheart, please? Your choice. Anywhere you want to go."

"Well...all right!" She gave in to her excitement. "Yes, Jack, I would love to see you again. I hear there's a new Fred Astaire movie playing at the Capitol?"

"Then the Capitol it is. Maybe I can pick up a few new dance moves from my old pal Fred."

"Maybe." Her voice filled with light laughter.

"Then it's a date. I'll pick you up at seven."

"See you then." Liz sighed gently hanging up the receiver.

"I knew he would call, Liz. So, what's the plan? When is he picking you up?"

"Seven. He's picking me up at seven." Liz suddenly became aware. "That only gives me two hours, Mandy. What am I going to wear? I have nothing to wear!"

"Relax, two hours is plenty of time to knock the socks off Mr. Jack Collins."

"Then you'll help me?"

"Of course I will. Come on, Liz." She ran toward the bedroom. "We only have two hours." Liz followed in uncontrollable happiness. "Nope...nope...nope," Mandy said, searching Liz's closet with the eye of a predator, dismissing one dress after another. "This one." Her voice confident as she selected a form-fitting emerald-green dress. "And these suede heels."

"Are you sure, Mandy?"

"Trust me, Liz—you'll look beautiful."

"My hair! What about my hair? How should I wear my hair?" She sat down at her vanity.

"Down and flowing. Men find long hair to be very sexy. It goes back to the caveman days, when men would grab us by our hair, pull us into their caves, and have their way with us."

"Cavemen? Pulling hair? What are you talking about, Mandy?" Liz looked at her friend's reflection in the vanity mirror.

"Nothing." Mandy shook her head as if trying to rid visions of cavemen. "So it's a movie tonight?" Picking up the hairbrush, she ran it through Liz's long, dark, lush hair.

"Yes!" Liz sighed contentedly. "We're going to the nine o'clock. There's a new Fred Astaire movie playing at the Capitol. Jack's hoping to pick up a few new dance moves tonight." She chuckled lightly.

"If I know Jack—and believe me, Liz, I know the type—he'll be looking for more than a few new dance moves tonight."

"Don't be ridiculous, Mandy; this is only our second date, and Jack's been nothing but a gentleman. Why would you even say something like that?"

"I'm sorry, Liz. Don't pay any attention to me. I guess I'm just a little jealous that you have a date tonight, and I don't. I thought after last night...I mean, I felt like Joe and I really made a connection."

"I'm sure there's a very good reason why you haven't heard from Joe, Mandy."

"Well, I don't know what it would be." Mandy sighed in discontent and then applied a finishing gloss to Liz's hair. She stepped back to admire her work. "Perfect! Your hair's perfect. Your dress is perfect. You look absolutely beautiful; don't change a thing."

"You don't think it's a little too much?" Liz pulled the straps of her emerald dress onto her shoulders. "After all, we're just going to the theater."

"There's no such thing as too much, Liz." Mandy pulled the straps back down. Both girls were looking into the mirror, critiquing the look, when they heard a knock on the door.

"That must be him, Mandy. He's ten minutes early!"

"I'll get the door, Liz; you compose yourself. And *do not* under any condition come out of this bedroom until seven fifteen—understand?"

"But, Mandy, I'm dressed. I'm ready now." "Trust me, Liz; a man never appreciates anything he gets too easily. Seven fifteen… not a minute before." Closing the bedroom door, Mandy gave herself a quick once-over in the hallway mirror before answering the door.

"Hi Jack, come on in and make yourself comfortable," Mandy said. "Liz will be out in a few minutes. Can I get you something to drink?" She poured herself a glass of wine.

"No, thank you, Mandy, nothing for me." I took a seat in the corner chair. "Did you and Joe have a good time last night?"

"Oh yeah, Joe's great. We had a really nice time."

"Well, I could tell he really enjoyed meeting you."

"Well, if he enjoyed meeting me so much, Jack"—a tone crept into her voice—"why haven't I heard from him today?"

"I'm sorry, Mandy. Where's my head these days? Joe asked me to let you know he's working with Pappy tonight on strategies for my upcoming fight against Frankie Rocco."

"Oh." Mandy's voice softened. "I knew Joe must've gotten tied up with something unavoidable, or surely I would have heard from him after last night."

"Of course, Mandy." I tried to make my voice reassuring. "I'm sure you'll be hearing from Joe again…real soon."

"Well, if you see him first, Jack, you tell him I had a wonderful time and to call me."

"Will do, Mandy." Looking at my watch, I realized I was on the fifteen-minute wait.

"Seven fifteen. Here I come, Jack Collins. I hope I'm ready." Liz took a deep breath opened the bedroom door and sashayed apprehensively into the living room.

"You look beautiful, Liz." I stood up in awe, hat in hand. "And that dress."

"Thank you, Jack." She blushed, nervously adjusting the sleeves.

"I thought we could go for a drink before the movie. There's a new place on Dakota Drive I'd like to check out."

"Sure, Jack, a drink sounds wonderful." Her voice was uneasy. "If you think we have the time."

"Plenty of time, Liz. The movie doesn't start till nine, and the club is right on the way."

"Go already." Mandy ushered us toward the door. "Don't do anything I would do, Liz." Giving a devious smile, she closed the apartment door as Liz shot Mandy a quick, agitated glance. "You okay this evening, Liz? You seem a little, well, uncomfortable."

"I'm fine, Jack—just a little nervous. You tend to have that effect on me."

"Really! I'm flattered, but you have no reason to be nervous around me, Liz." Feeling my own anxieties, I opened the car door.

The sweet, clean smells of a nice girl invaded my nostrils as she glided past me into the front seat.

What are you doing, Jack? my mind stammered. *You need to walk away from this one.*

I can handle it! my ego replied as I slid into the driver's seat. "Ready, Liz?" I said, turning over the ignition.

"Ready, Jack." She smiled softly.

I turned on the radio, and a romantic ballad began to play. A strange swooning sensation washes over me once again. *You're in trouble,* my mind uttered.

The Following Morning

"You were out late last night, Liz," Mandy said; seated at the kitchen table, reading the morning paper. "Did you have a good time with Jack?"

"I had a wonderful time, Mandy." Pouring herself a cup of coffee. "Jack is just so thoughtful and romantic." Liz smiled dreamily and glided her way over to the kitchen table.

"Okay, Liz. I'll bite. What did Mr. Collins do last night to put such a smile on your face this morning?"

"Nothing. Everything." She softly sighed.

"And what does 'nothing, everything' mean?" Mandy sighed in imitation.

"I'm not really sure, Mandy. I just know that when I'm with Jack, everything's wonderful, and when I'm not?" She sighed sadly.

"Liz?" Mandy's voice was apprehensive. "I'm glad you're having a great time with Jack, but you've got to know, Liz. He's a love 'em and leave 'em kind of guy—a ladies' man."

"I don't believe that. Besides, you don't know him. Not like I do."

"Maybe not, but I know the type, and Jack Collins has all the earmarks of a ladies' man. I just don't want to see my best friend get hurt."

"Jack would never hurt me, Mandy."

"All I'm saying is protect yourself. Don't fall in love too fast."

"It's too late. I'm already over the moon for him."

"And Mr. Collins?" Mandy asked, realizing her defeat. "Does he feel the same way about you, Liz?"

"I don't know, but we're going out again this weekend. So I believe that's an indication he likes me too. I'm famished. Would you like some breakfast?" She sashayed her way to the refrigerator, refusing to have her spirits dampened.

"Sure, Liz." Mandy watched her friend waltz around the kitchen, using their breakfast foods as dance partners. She hoped against all odds that Liz wasn't just another girl in the long line for Jack Collins.

CHAPTER FIVE

Four Weeks Later

"Good morning, Southpaw, just thought I'd give you a call to make sure you're still alive and kickin'. What's it been now—three, four weeks?"

"Sorry, Joe, I meant to give you a call a few times, buddy, but the days just got away from me. I've been spending a lot of time with Liz."

"So I've been informed. I've taken Mandy out a few times, here and there, just enough to keep her on the line. So you didn't heed my warning, eh, Southpaw? Decided to play with the nice girl after all. Well, how's that workin' out for ya?"

"Well, I have to admit, buddy—I'm definitely in uncharted waters."

"I tried to warn you, Southpaw…the nice girls? They play by a different set of rules."

"So you did, buddy, so you did. Hey, Joe? Do you think you could meet this afternoon at the Irish pub on South Saginaw? I feel like I need to relax a little—get some male perspective."

"Sure, Southpaw, how's three o'clock sound?"

"Sounds great, buddy; I'll see you then." Hanging up the phone, I realized I missed my friend.

Later That Afternoon

"Hey, Jack, long time no see," Mick called out from behind the bar. "What brings you to the pub this afternoon?"

"I'm meeting Joe, Mick; you seen him?" I looked around the dark bar.

"Not yet, Southpaw. Can I get you something to drink while you're waiting?"

"Just a beer, Mick. Make it a draft."

"One draft beer coming right up. Saw your fight against the Irishman last month. Thought you were in a bit of trouble there for a minute, till you hit him with that famous left hook."

"Ah, Mick, you know how fights go. They're never over till they're over."

"Well, you impressed the hell out of me with that comeback. Beer's on me, Southpaw." He set down the cold draft.

"Thanks, Mick, appreciate it." Taking a big slug, I anxiously looked at the door as light flooded the bar. I was disappointed to see two men entering, neither one Joe.

"You okay, Jack? You got something heavy weighing your mind?"

"Just a little woman trouble, Mick."

"Woman trouble, you say? Draft beer's not nearly strong enough for that kind of trouble, Southpaw." He set down a shot of Kentucky's finest.

"You're right, Mick…thanks." I took the shot, feeling its burn. Light flooded the bar once again; Joe was standing in the doorway. "Hey, Joe, buddy, over here."

"Hey, Southpaw. How've you been?" he said, adjusting his eyes to the dimly lit bar.

"I've been good. It's good to see you, Joe. Take a seat." I nodded to the empty barstool next to me.

"Hey, Joe." Mick nodded. "What can I get you?"

"I'll take one of those, Mick." Joe pointed to my half-empty draft. "So what's up, Southpaw? What do you need some male perspective on? As if I don't know."

"Well, you know I've been seeing a lot of Liz lately, and we have a great time when we're together."

"So what's the problem? Thanks, Mick." He accepted the draft. "Liz is a great-looking woman; enjoy it while you have her."

"That's the problem, Joe. I can't enjoy it. She won't let me. Liz is a virgin and intends to stay that way until she's married."

"What? Huh…I figured Liz for a nice girl, but hanging out with a girl like Mandy…how nice could she be? A virgin, you say? That is a problem for a guy who's used to getting it on the regular."

"Now do you understand my dilemma, Joe?" I gestured to Mick to bring another shot.

"Well, sort of, but if it's just sex you're looking for, there's plenty of women who would be willing. Shit, give Marilyn a call. She's always up for the Southpaw ride."

"I've thought about that—giving Marilyn a call. I've even picked up the phone and started to dial a couple of times, but then I'd start to feel guilty. Liz would never understand that one relationship has nothing to do with the other, and Marilyn…well, Marilyn is Marilyn."

"And a man has his needs, Southpaw, and that's a fact!"

"Come on, Joe. That not an excuse any woman would buy."

"Maybe not, but look at you, Southpaw. You're sexually frustrated! Chewin' on that straw like a hungry dog. Where did you even get that straw?" Grabbing it from my mouth, he threw it to the floor. "Look, Southpaw, the way I see it, you've got a woman that isn't willing to give it up. So unless you're planning on getting married real soon, you've got one choice. You get it on the down lowww." Joe's voice trailed off as sunlight flooded the bar, revealing the shapely silhouette of a woman standing in the doorway. "Don't look now, Southpaw, but I think your *de*stressor just walked through the door."

"What?" I swung around on my stool to a vision of Marilyn standing in the doorway looking sexier than ever.

"Hey, Mick? You better bring Southpaw here another shot." Joe chuckled. "I have a feeling he's going to need it." He watched Marilyn sashay her way over, coming to rest between my thighs.

"Hi, Jack, long time no see," Marilyn purred. "Doesn't Jack want to play with Marilyn anymore?" She moaned seductively.

"I do, if Jack doesn't want to," said Joe, giving Marilyn the once-over.

"Go away, Jack's little friend." She snuggled in closer between my thighs. "Well, Jack?"

My mind began to race. Liz's angelic face pulled me to one side, while Marilyn's devilish ways pulled me to the other. I felt my resistance began to wane as Marilyn lightly stroked my inner thigh, reminding me of her many talents.

"Why don't you let me buy you a drink, baby? With my apologies." I pulled her in close. "I've been a real bad boy."

"Yes, you have, Jack." She pushed her voluptuous backside into Joe, taking his barstool.

"I guess I'll just move down one?" Joe pulled his draft from in front of Marilyn.

"You still drinking dirty martinis, baby?" I asked, feeling her hand massage the inside of my thigh.

"Yes, lover, the dirtier the better." She lightly dragged her nails over my groin area.

"Hey, Mick?" I said, not taking my gaze from Marilyn. "Could you bring this pretty lady a dirty martini?"

"Sure, Jack. Coming right up."

"So what do you say, baby; after we have a couple of drinks, maybe we go somewhere and catch up on lost time?"

"I don't know, Jack; are you deserving?" She gave me a sensuous glance.

"I don't know about deserving, baby, but I'd sure be appreciative."

"I don't mean to interrupt your sexual foreplay, Southpaw, but I think I'm gonna take off," Joe said.

"Sure, buddy. See you later." I nodded, acknowledging his leaving. "So what do you say, baby?"

"Sure, lover. Why not? I've got no plans for the evening."

"Great, another martini, baby?" I looked at her half-empty glass. Marilyn gave an appreciative nod. "Hey, Mick? Another drink for the lovely lady."

"Sure, Jack." Mick slyly smiled. "Coming right up."

"So, baby, how've you been? It seems like ages since we spent some time together."

"It has been a while, Jack, but whose fault is that? Thanks, Mick." Marilyn accepted the fresh martini, giving it a quick stir with the olive pick.

"Oh, come on, baby. Let's not go there. What's important is we're here now. Together."

"I guess you're right, Jack." She relaxed back into my light embrace.

"So what do you say, pretty lady?" My lips lightly brushed her earlobe. "We go somewhere a little more comfortable?"

"I think that could be arranged, Jack. Shall we go back to my place?"

"I have a better idea, baby. The Sunset Motel is just around the corner, and…"

"You know I hate motels, Jack," she said, cutting me off. "The clerks always look like little trolls with their condescending, all-knowing look. Like they know just why you're there."

"Oh, come on, baby," I moaned. "Please? It's just around the corner, and I've missed you so much. I just don't think I can wait. Please—for me?" I gave her a sad face.

"Okay, Jack. We can go to the Sunset, but one of these days I'm going to learn how to say no to you."

"Now, why would you want to do that, baby?" I gave her a charming smile. Marilyn disregarded the question, downing the last of her martini.

"Let's go, Jack." Sliding off her barstool, she sauntered her way toward the door.

"Right behind you, baby. Night, Mick." I tossed a few bucks on the bar.

The Sunset Motel

"Can I help you, sir?" The clerk at the Sunset grinned mischievously.

"We'd like a room, please."

"For how long, sir?" He winked, giving Marilyn the once-over.

"For as long as it takes, you little troll," Marilyn snapped. "Just give us the key."

"Yes, ma'am." He anxiously cleared his throat. "Room 402. You can take the elevators. Will there be anything else this evening, sir?"

"No, I think we have everything we need this evening," I said. Accepting the room key, I escorted Marilyn, who was obviously upset, toward the elevators.

"I told you, Jack." Marilyn was fuming. "Just like little trolls!"

"Oh, come on, baby—don't let that little man get to you." I stepped inside the elevator and pushed button four. "He doesn't know what we have together. The passion we feel."

"You're right, Jack; I'm not going to let that little troll ruin our night together." Her lust for me returned, and she pushed me hard against the elevator wall.

"You never cease to amaze me, baby." We made out like two starving adolescents who had been thrown a few crumbs. Kissing deeply, passionately, we groped and explored each other's willing bodies as the elevator whisked us to the fourth floor.

"Hurry up, Jack." Marilyn's patience was waning as she groped me from behind.

"I am hurrying, baby," I said, fumbling with the key outside our room.

"I've just missed you so much, Jack." She pushed me forward as I felt the key release the lock.

"Why don't you show me how much, baby?" I moaned in anticipation. Groping her voluptuous body, I stumbled toward the bed as we removed each other's clothing in a frenzied embrace. I quickly entered her, demanding that my needs be satisfied.

"Oh, Jack." Marilyn moaned in pleasure. "I've missed you so much." She responded to my every thrust. As I closed my eyes, consumed with my own desires, visions of Liz entered my mind, causing my sexual urgency to soften. My hands began to slowly explore the beautiful vision my mind had produced. My lips gently nuzzled Liz's neck as she moaned in ecstasy, responding to my touch. Whispering sweet sentiments, we made slow, passionate, intimate love. Both of us reached an explosive climax before collapsing together on the bed in fulfilled exhaustion.

"Sweetheart," I moaned, reveling in complete, utter sexual satisfaction.

"Jack!" Marilyn snapped. "Open your eyes."

"Huh?" As I blinked several times, Marilyn came into focus.

"Get off of me, Jack." Marilyn pushed me hard.

"What's the matter, baby?" I watched her scurry around the room, picking up her clothes in a frenzy. "Marilyn!" I lightly grabbed hold of her arm.

"Don't touch me, Jack!" She slapped my hand away.

"Baby...please...tell me why you're so upset."

"Why?" Her eyes welled with tears. "You really have no idea?"

"No, I really have no idea." I was completely dumbfounded.

"Lover!" she said, hurt changing to anger. "It's one thing for a woman to know her relationship with a man may be just sexual. It's something else when she knows the man is making love to another woman, and using her body to do it. I don't know who you were just screwing, Jack, but it wasn't me."

"What?" I shook my head in confusion. "What are you talking about, Marilyn?"

"Do me a favor, Jack, and lose my number." Marilyn trembled, giving me a look of complete sadness and betrayal before running from the room.

"Marilyn, wait!" I grabbed a sheet to cover myself. "Marilyn?" Standing in the doorway, I watched her push the elevator buttons in a heightened panic, wiping the tears from her face. "I'm sorry." Suddenly I realized how deeply I'd hurt her. She gave me a quivering smile in response to my apology before bravely stepping inside the elevator and letting the doors close behind her. "Liz, what have you done to me?" I closed the motel door with a heavy sigh.

I awoke the next morning in my own bed to the sounds of Joe's clapping hands and riddle. "What do you call a guy whose twelve-week dry spell has ended?"

"Not this morning, buddy." I rolled over with a sigh.

"Oh, is Southpaw tired?" he teased. "Did Marilyn wear you out?"

"Oh yeah, she wore me out all right. She told me to do her a favor and lose her number."

"What? Lose her number?" Joe was flabbergasted "Why?"

"I don't know, but it's got me confused. I always thought Marilyn understood we were just a sexual thing. She always acted like she was okay with our arrangement."

"Women are never okay with just a sexual arrangement, Southpaw. They always act like they are, but in the end, they always expect it to turn into something more."

"Maybe so, but I thought Marilyn understood. She always seemed...well, savvy to the ways of the world."

"Don't try to figure out women, Southpaw; you'll just be wasting your time. But do tell me, what got you the ole heave-ho?"

"Well," I began, reflecting back, "after you left the pub, we had a few more drinks. Then I suggested we go over to the Sunset Motel. She wanted to go back to her place, but I knew if we went there, I'd be hard-pressed coming up with a reason to leave. It took a little coaxing, but I talked her into the motel. Things were going along fine until Liz entered my mind. Then I don't know what happened. Apparently my lovemaking style changed. Marilyn accused me of using her body while thinking of another woman, and next thing I knew, she slammed out the door."

"Well, there you have it. There's your mistake, Southpaw. You never bring another woman into the bedroom, even if she is just in your mind."

"I know that, Joe, but in my defense, it wasn't my intent to bring Liz into our love session. I don't even know how it happened. It just did."

"It the nice-girl hex, Southpaw. I've heard about it but never really seen it. Liz has reeled you in, locked you down, and she doesn't even know it."

"What are you talking about, Joe? Locked me down!"

"She's put the nice-girl spell on you."

"The nice-girl spell? Really, Joe?"

"Okay then, Southpaw—you explain it."

"I'm in big trouble here, aren't I, buddy?" I sighed heavily. "Any suggestions?"

"Don't look at me, Southpaw. You know my motto, love 'em and leave 'em. I don't need the emotional drama or heartache that comes with the love game."

"So you're gonna leave me out here, hangin'...all alone. You're supposed to be my wingman, remember. The guy I want in my corner when the going gets tough."

"I am in your corner, Southpaw, when we're fighting a fair opponent. But against a woman who's beautiful, stacked, and a virgin to boot? Forget it! Who'd a thought, the Southpaw Slugger, taken down by a woman? His first technical knockout." He shook his head sadly.

"Well, you have to admit, Joe. In my defense, she is exceptional."

"That she is, Southpaw." He nodded in agreement. "That she is."

CHAPTER SIX

December 7, 1941

"We interrupt your musical program...breaking news just in...Pearl Harbor has been attacked."

"What?" I pulled back the shower curtain.

"At 7:53 this morning, Japanese bombers flew over the shores of Hawaii, dropping their bombs, leaving our military base in devastation. The attack came in two waves. The first at 7:53 a.m., the second at 8:55; by 9:55 it was all over. We will continue to bring you updates as we receive them throughout the day. We now return you to your regular programming."

"What the hell?" Grabbing a towel, I jumped from the shower, ran to the phone, and dialed Joe's number. I let it ring several times before hanging up; then I dialed Mandy's apartment.

"Who would be calling this early on a Sunday?" Joe moaned, holding his head, feeling it pound. "Somebody, please...answer the phone."

"Liz?" Mandy called out. "Will you please answer the phone?" She was feeling the signs of her own hangover.

"I've got it, Mandy. You and Joe go back to sleep. Hello?"

"Liz! Is Joe over there? Do you have the radio on? Did you hear the news report?"

"No, I haven't heard any news, Jack. Yes. Joe is here. Why? What's going on?"

"We've been attacked, Liz! The Japanese have bombed Pearl Harbor."

"Oh my God, Jack! No!" She squeezed the phone tightly. "Joe! Mandy! We've been attacked!"

"What?" Joe looked at Mandy through glazed eyes. "Did Liz just say we've been attacked?"

"I think so." Mandy blinked in confusion. Joe jumped from the bed, hastily put on his pants, and ran from the room. "Wait for me, Joe!" Mandy grabbed her robe, running behind.

"It's Jack." Liz handed Joe the phone.

"Jack! What the hell is going on?"

"The Japs have done it, Joe. They've bombed Pearl Harbor. Turn on the radio, buddy. I'm on my way over."

"What's going on, Joe? Liz?" Mandy nervously looked back and forth. "Somebody!"

"The Japanese have bombed Pearl Harbor." Joe's voice was solemn. "Turn on the radio."

"New updates just in. *'Air raid, Pearl Harbor...this is not a drill'* were the words booming from the PA as sirens blared and bombs exploded on the island of Hawaii this morning. The attack came as a complete and utter surprise, for there was no formal declaration of war given by the Empire of Japan. Our country waits with bated breath as to how President Roosevelt will respond to this attack on American soil. We return to your normal programming and will bring you further updates as they are received...may God help us." The radio crackled.

I pounded feverishly on the apartment door.

"Southpaw!" Joe's eyes were wide and determined. "We have to do something. They can't get away with this. We're Americans. The strongest country in the world."

"We will, Joe." I joined my circle of friends, gathered around the radio.

"Everything is going to be okay, isn't it, Jack?" Liz's eyes were welling with tears.

"I don't know, sweetheart." I put a protective arm around her.

"I'm scared, Jack." She buried her face into my chest, tears flowing. The radio crackled its next interruption...

Later That Day

"Come on in, Southpaw." Pappy answered the door. "I've been expecting you."

"Thanks, Pappy." Taking the door, I allowed myself in. I nervously cleared my throat. "There's no easy way to say this, Pappy, so I'm just going to say it: the fight's off. I'm joining the army first thing in the morning. I'm going to serve my country, and you can't talk me out of it."

He gave me the ole boxer's stare, not speaking for what seemed like forever, but I'm sure it was just moments.

"You're not going to get an argument from me, Southpaw. I would expect nothing less from you, son. I'm just sorry you have to put your boxing career on the back burner to do it. You're one of the greats."

"Thanks, Pappy, but we both know it could be more than just the back burner. My time in the ring is now, but I can't ignore what has happened. I can't just go on with my boxing career and pretend our country isn't in turmoil. So I have to accept..." I blinked back the tears. "And so do you...that this could very well be the end of my boxing career."

"I don't know that, boy, and neither do you," Pappy grumbled. "But I will tell you what I do know. A man has got to do what's in his heart, Southpaw, or his life will never be right. Follow your heart, son."

"Thanks, Pappy, it means a lot that you understand." My voice became melancholy. "But I'm really going to miss being Jack Collins, the Southpaw Slugger."

"What are you talking about, boy?" he stammered. "You'll always be the Southpaw Slugger; nobody can take that from you." There was a glint of sadness in his eyes. "Besides, we're the strongest country in the world. No one has the strength and fighting power we possess. We're going to go over there and kick their Jap asses, and you'll be back in the ring by next summer. You'll see."

"You're right, Pappy." I nodded in reassurance. "Besides, what's a few months in the fight game?" I chuckled lightly.

"Nothin', Southpaw!" Walking me to the door, he seemed to feel my uncertainty. "Southpaw? Son? Look at me." His eyes searched mine. "Everything's going to be all right." We locked eyes.

"I know." I nodded. Each of us conveyed our unspoken concerns.

"Okay, then." Pappy broke free. "You take care of yourself over there, boy." He retrieved a kerchief from his back pocket.

"You okay, Pappy?" I looked into his sad, moist eyes.

"I'm fine, Southpaw...it's just these damn allergies." He roughly wiped his eyes. "They flare up on me every now and then. Now get out of here, boy, and get ready to fight the biggest fight of your life."

"Will do, Pappy." Standing tall, I smiled confidently, preparing to fight the good fight.

December 9, 1941

"What do you call a guy who gives up a great boxing career?" Joe solemnly walked into my bedroom. The alarm screeching 7:00 a.m.

"I don't know, Joe—a fool?" I turned the radio alarm to light music.

"No! We call him a soldier in the United States Army." He gave a salute. "Pappy told me you went by to see him the other day... called off the fight."

"I had no choice, Joe. Our country's been attacked. It was the right thing to do."

"You don't have to convince me, Southpaw; joined the army myself, bright and early this morning. I report to Fort Bragg December twenty-first. That gives me about ten days to enjoy being a civilian. How about you, buddy? Received your orders yet? More importantly, have you told your pretty lady?"

"I leave for Fort Hood on the twenty-third, and no, I haven't told Liz. I'm not sure how. Do I ask her to wait? Do I tell her not to wait? Do I ask her to marry me?"

"What are you looking at me for?" Joe's eyes were wide. "Those are questions only you can answer, but I think the real question is...do you love her?"

"I know I want her in my life. I know I don't want to lose her."

"That not what I asked you, Southpaw. *Do...you...love...her?*"

"You know, Joe, I think I might." My mind reminisced. "When I was fifteen, my father told me it was time to have the talk. Naturally I assumed it was going to be about the birds and the bees, but I was wrong. It was the talk of women.

"He said, 'Son, there are two kinds of girls. Girls you have fun with and girls you marry, and you'll need to know the difference. Now the fun girls, they'll be easy to spot, but the marrying kind of girl—she'll be a little harder. The marrying kind of girls are considered good girls, nice girls. They'll let you get to first base, maybe second, but second base for a good girl will only come with time. Now, I'm sure, son, you'll come across a few good girls before you marry, but the only way to know you've got the right good girl—the girl for you—is that she'll make you feel not only lust but also comfort and love.'

"So of course, Joe, I asked the obvious question. 'How do I know if it's love, Dad?'"

"How?" Joe uttered, eyes filled with intrigue.

"'Well, son,' he said. 'Throughout your life, good and bad things are going to happen. When the good things happen, you'll want to share them with someone, and when the bad things happen…well, let's just say you'll need to share them with someone. Now, when you've found the woman that brings you both these comforts, then you've found the right one, son—you've found love."

"So do you, Southpaw? Do you look for Liz? Have you found the right one? Have you found love?"

"Well, that's my dilemma, buddy. When I heard our country had been attacked, my first thoughts were of you."

"Me?" Joe was taken aback, shifting uncomfortably.

"Yes, of you, but after giving it some thought…I'm sorry, buddy; I think I'm gonna have to go with Liz on this one." I gave him a stupid grin.

"Thank God, Southpaw." He sighed in playful relief. "You had me worried there for a minute. I thought you'd turned soft on me."

"So what about you, Joe? Any thoughts toward Mandy?"

"Mandy's one of the fun girls, Jack; I think we both know that. Besides, you know my motto—love 'em and leave 'em. Hey, turn that up, Southpaw," he said, hearing the radio crackle.

"Ladies and gentlemen, your president…Franklin D. Roosevelt." Cheers and applause erupted over the airwaves before becoming silent. "December 7, 1941, a date which will live in infamy," President Roosevelt's voice echoed. Joe and I listened with bated breath. Concern filled our eyes, and we contemplated our futures, as President Roosevelt declared war!

"Why the sad face, Liz?" Mandy glanced up from her *Stargaze* magazine, sprawled out on the floor.

"Jack leaves for boot camp in a few days, and I'm just so confused, Mandy."

"Confused, about what?" She turned the magazine page.

"Jack? My life? Everything? I wish I could be more like you, Mandy; you're always so comfortable and confident when it comes to men, always knowing just what to do."

"I didn't use to be, Liz. Believe it or not, there was a time I was naive and unsure—until I got wise to their ways."

"Their ways, Mandy?"

"The ways of men." Mandy closed her magazine, sitting up on the floor. "Men are not complicated creatures, Liz. In fact, there are only three things a woman must do to keep a man, and every woman has the power and ability to do them."

"What are they? Please tell me."

"Well, first and foremost, you must keep him happy in the bedroom. A man must know you desire him as a man. Second, feed his ego. Tell him he's wonderful, even when he's not, and he will strive to be wonderful. Third, take care of him like his mother did. Make his dinner, clean his house, do his laundry—these things give him feelings of security and comfort. Understand, Liz?"

"I think so." Liz hesitant.

"It's really quite simple, Liz. If you take care of them, they will stay; if you don't, they will stray. Hey, that rhymes, stay, stray. But the most important thing, Liz—the thing that makes all this work—is timing. Your timing has to be perfect."

"Timing? What does timing have to do with anything, Mandy?"

"Your timing is absolutely vital! You must know exactly when he feels he has earned your love, and that's when you give it to him—unconditionally. If you give your love before he feels he has earned it, then he may feel that you are not worthy of him, and if that happens, he will never completely trust that you love him, and only him. If a man gets a woman's love too easily, he will question her value—because a man will never believe he is her exception."

"How will I know when that is, Mandy?"

"That's the tricky part, Liz. It's the part I've yet to master."

"Do you think I should tell Jack I love him? Do you think I should give him my love?"

"I don't know. Like I said, the timing is tricky, but I do know men aren't real intuitive creatures. They have to be told our wants and desires. So, if I had to guess, you're either going to have to tell Jack or show him."

"You're right, Mandy. How's Jack supposed to know how I feel if I don't tell him? Thank you, Mandy. Thank you for always being there for me. For helping me understand the ways of men. Is there any way I can help you?"

"Well, now that you mention it, Liz, there is something." Mandy poured herself a glass of wine.

"What is it, Mandy? Anything."

"Men have never looked at me in quite the same way I've seen them look at you. If I could figure out why, figure out the difference…"

"What are you talking about, Mandy? I've seen the way Joe looks at you. He adores you."

"Oh yeah, he adores me all right. That must be why I haven't seen or heard from him in a week. I'm so disgusted with Joseph Riley right now I can't see straight." She downed her glass of wine.

"I'm sorry, Mandy; I guess I've been so preoccupied with Jack I hadn't noticed. I just assumed things were going well between you and Joe. I know he has spent many a night here."

"That's just it! We spend the nights together, but we don't talk about any kind of future. Sometimes I think Joe is only interested in me for sex."

"I don't believe that, Mandy. If you're having sex, there has to be love."

"Oh, Liz, you can be so naive sometimes. Believe me, with men sex can exist without love. In fact, I think they'd prefer it that way."

"I could never have sex without love, Mandy. I'm not even sure I could have it before marriage."

"Don't worry, my naive little friend; you're the type of girl a man is willing to wait for—the type of girl a man is willing to marry."

"Do you think Jack will ask me to marry him, Mandy?" Her eyes filled with hope.

"Maybe. Who knows, Liz?" Feeling the effects of the wine, Mandy was distracted by the ringing of the phone. "Hello…oh, hello, Jack…yeah, Liz is here…okay, I'll tell her." She hung up the phone. "Jack's on his way over."

"What? Now? Tonight?"

"Oh, I almost forgot the last rule, Liz. Always look beautiful when you're talking to your man. He can never think logically or clearly if he's looking at a woman he desires. Now I suggest you go and put on that sexy emerald dress that Jack loves so much. Go…shoo." She waved her hands in dismissal. "He'll be here any minute."

"You're the best friend a girl could hope for, Mandy." Liz gave her a quick hug and ran from room.

"Remember that, Liz," Mandy called out. "Guys may come and go, but I'll always be your friend." Pouring herself another glass of wine, she softly murmured, "Your forever single, unattached friend."

"Mandy's not going to be real happy to see me, Southpaw. Tell me again why I'm here?"

"Moral support, Joe! I need my wingman with me tonight. To give me the courage to make the right decision. Whatever decision that may be." I firmly rapped on the girls' apartment door.

"Well, if isn't Jack and his disappearing sidekick," Mandy snipped, giving Joe a dismissive glance. "Come on in, Jack. Liz will be right out. Would you like something to drink? A beer or maybe a glass of wine?" She waved her half-empty glass.

"No thanks, Mandy." I took a seat on the living-room sofa.

"I'll take a beer," Joe uttered.

"I don't remember asking you, Mr. Riley!" Mandy stomped off toward the kitchen.

"Mr. Riley?" Joe muttered. "You see now why I didn't want to come over here, Southpaw." He walked toward the kitchen, preparing himself for what every man knows to be the most vicious, ruthless, unforgiving attack: the attack of a woman scorned. Taking a deep breath, he hesitantly entered.

"Pssst, Jack?" Liz called out from her bedroom doorway—taking my attention, leaving my wingman alone and unprotected inside the scorned woman's cave. "Come here, Jack." She softly waved me over.

"Liz?" I was taken aback, mesmerized by her beauty. "What is it, sweetheart?" Confused, I stepped inside her bedroom.

"I love you, Jack," she whispered, taking the emerald straps from her shoulders.

"What, sweetheart?" I remained utterly confused.

"I love you, Jack." Slowly, hesitantly, she unzipped her dress, letting it fall to the floor.

"Liz? Sweetheart?" I was unable to take my eyes from her, shivering nervously before me. Her half-naked beauty was breathtaking, leaving me speechless...

"I'm sorry, Jack." Her eyes were beginning to mist. "I thought I could do this." She slouched to the bed in defeat. "I love you with all my heart, but I can't do this." She took her emerald dress from the floor, covering herself. "All I can hear is my mother's voice: 'A lady waits, and a gentleman will wait for her.'"

"Your mother's right, sweetheart." Dropping to one knee, I took a small box from my pocket. "Elizabeth Earlene Dawson—love of my life—will you marry me?" I opened the small jeweler's box. Liz was speechless, looking at the square-cut diamond engagement ring. Her sad tears were replaced with joyful, happy ones. Her eyes shone bright.

"Then it's a yes?" I lifted my brows in anticipation.

"Oh, yes, Jack, yes, yes, yes, yes, yes…a thousand times yes." She threw her arms tightly around my neck.

"Come on, Liz." I grabbed her hand. "Joe, Mandy?" Happiness consuming me. "You two made up yet?" We entered the kitchen.

"I think we have, Southpaw," Joe said. "Have we, baby?"

"No!" Mandy crossed her arms in a pout.

"Well, you two need to make up for at least a day. Liz is going to need a maid of honor, and I'm going to need a best man."

"We're getting married," Liz squealed, flashing her engagement ring.

"Oh, my God," Mandy squealed, running to Liz and examining the ring.

"Congratulations, Southpaw." Joe came to my side.

"Thanks, buddy." I smiled confidently, knowing I had made the right decision. "Come here, future wife." Taking Liz into my arms, I felt that wonderful comfort only she could bring.

"I love you, Jack," she whispered into my ear. "I'll love you the rest of my life."

December 12, 1941

"What do you call a guy who is marrying a girl he's only known for a few months?" said Joe, entering my bedroom with no fanfare.

"I would call him a very lucky man, Joe." I gave him my most charming smile.

"Then I need to ask you a question, Southpaw." He was unimpressed by my charm. "Do you truly love this woman, or are you just afraid to leave her behind? I'm only asking because as your wingman and best friend, it's my job." There was a conviction in his voice I'd never heard before.

"Liz is the girl for me, Joe. I think I knew it the first time I saw her in the park."

"You're sure, then?" He gave me the ole boxer's stare.

"Surer than I've ever been about anything in my life, Joe."

"Well then, in that case, my friend, it's my job as your best man to get you down to city hall before Liz changes her mind. Do you have the marriage license and ring?"

"Yes," I said, double-checking my pockets.

"Then let's get you down to city hall, Southpaw, and get you married!"

"Mandy, can you help me with the last few buttons on my dress?" Liz anxiously smiled. "I seem to be all thumbs today."

"Sure, Liz, turn around." Mandy's voice was soft and distant.

"I feel so lucky today, Mandy, marrying Jack. Confident in knowing we will love each other through it all. No matter what comes our way." She sighed in contentment.

"I'm sure you will, Liz." Mandy's voice quivered.

"Mandy?" Liz turned around to find a sad face. "Honey?" Her voice was soft and warm. "What's wrong? Why are you so sad?"

"I'm sorry, Liz; this is supposed to be your day." Her eyes were misting. "A happy day, and I'm ruining it."

"Nonsense, Mandy, you're my best friend. I love you. Please tell me why you're so sad."

"It's stupid, Liz. It's just that...well...I feel like I'm losing my best friend." She sniffled. "You're getting married today, and soon you'll forget all about me." Tears began to flow.

"Mandy. Honey, that's nonsense. We're friends for life. The fact that I'm getting married is not going to change that—you'll see. Now dry your tears." Liz handed her a Kleenex. "What about you and Joe? You two seem to be getting along well again."

"Joe leaves for boot camp in less than a week, and he hasn't mentioned anything about a future together," Mandy whined, her tears returning.

"Mandy Taylor, you stop it!" Liz stammered. "Stop it right now! You're a wonderful girl, and if Joseph Riley can't see that...then... well, then...he doesn't deserve you!" Mandy's tears stopped suddenly. Both girls burst out in laughter at Liz's attempt to be bold.

"You're a good friend, Liz, and you make a beautiful bride." Mandy sniffled, wiping the last of her tears.

"I do. Don't I, Mandy?" said Liz, seeing her bridal reflection in the mirror, eyes becoming misty.

"Now you stop it, Liz, or I'll start crying again," Mandy demanded. "Come on. Let's get you to city hall so you can marry the man of our dreams. I mean, the man of your dreams," she said, realizing her blunder.

City Hall

"Harry Marvin Decker, do you take Elizabeth Earlene Dawson to be your lawfully wedded wife...to have and to hold from this day forward till death do you part?"

"I do." I looked into a pair of warm, beautiful dark eyes.

"Elizabeth Earlene Dawson, do you take Harry Marvin Decker to be your lawfully wedded husband..."

"I do, and I promise to love him forever." Liz sighed.

"To have and to hold." The justice smiled. "From this day forward till death do you part?"

"Sorry." Liz blushed. "I do."

"We can now have the exchanging of the rings. Harry?" The justice nodded to me.

"With this ring I wed the beautiful Elizabeth Dawson." I slid the gold band onto Liz's left-hand ring finger. "The woman I will love for eternity."

"Elizabeth?" The justice nodded in permission.

"With this ring I wed Harry Decker. The only man I will ever love. Now, and for the rest of my life." She slid on the gold band, eyes misting in complete, utter happiness.

"Harry Decker!" Mandy muttered. "Joe, what happened to Jack Collins?"

"Shush, Mandy," Joe reprimanded. "You know Harry is his given name."

"I now pronounce you man and wife. You may kiss your bride." I took my wife into a warm embrace, shutting out the world around us, and we consummated our vows with a long, tender kiss.

"Should I call you Jack or Harry?" Mandy interrupted. "I much prefer Jack. Harry is just so…I don't know." She shook her head in distaste.

"Whichever you prefer, Mandy," I answered, not taking my eyes from Liz. "They're both me."

"Well, if it doesn't matter to you, I'm going to call you Jack. It's much sexier than *Harry*!"

"I'm going to call you Harry," Liz softly whispered. "Jack Collins belongs to the world, but Harry Decker is all mine."

"That I am, Mrs. Decker, and always will be," I said, feeling that same wonderful feeling.

"Congratulations, Southpaw…Liz. Shall we go?" Joe was trying to contain his excitement.

"Go? Where to, buddy?"

"That's for me to know and for you to follow. After you, Mr. and Mrs. Decker." He gave a chivalrous wave.

"Love of my life." I extended my arm. "Shall we?"

"Yes." Liz softly smiled, graciously accepting my arm.

"What's going on, Joe?" Mandy asked. "Where are we going?" Joe disregarded her question and quickly ran ahead to open the courthouse doors, revealing my once-sleek blue Ford, now decorated.

"Compliments from the young boys in the neighborhood." Joe proudly looked at their handiwork. "Just married" had been scrawled in large white letters covering both the passenger and driver doors. The back windows were whitewashed for our privacy, as well as Joe's secrecy of destination. Several empty cans had been tied to the rear bumper to announce the approach of a wedded couple inside. "Your chariot awaits, Mr. and Mrs. Decker." Joe took the steps of the courthouse two by two and opened the back passenger door.

"This is so exciting." Liz slid into the backseat.

"Thank you, buddy. This is great." I gave him a warm, genuine smile, sliding in next to my bride.

"You haven't seen nothin' yet, Southpaw. The celebration is just beginning." Closing the car door, he quickly ran around and took his seat behind the wheel. "Come on, Mandy! Get in." He pushed open the front passenger door from the inside.

"Well, I never!" Mandy slid inside, closing the car door. "You still haven't told me where we're going, Joe." She looked at him, upset.

"You'll see." Joe stepped on the gas. "You'll all see." He smiled to us through the rearview mirror.

"I trust you, buddy." I returned his smile with a wink.

"Where do you think he's taking us, Harry?" Liz murmured in quiet excitement.

"Does it matter, my love?" I took her into a warm embrace.

"Not at all, my love." She snuggled in close. "Not at all."

"We're here!" Joe pulled alongside the curb.

"Why did you bring us here, Joe?" Mandy moaned in disappointment. "I'm here five days a week."

"Sir...madam." Joe gallantly opened the back door.

"It's the Safari Club, Harry." Liz sighed. "How perfect."

"You couldn't have picked a better place, buddy." Taking my wife's arm, I helped her from the car.

"Thanks, Southpaw, your approval means a lot to me." Joe opened the doors of the club and ushered us inside.

"Right this way, Mr. and Mrs. Decker." Fredrick stepped from the reservation podium, leading us to the best table in the house and then signaling Jimmy Dorsey of our arrival.

"This song goes out to Harry and Elizabeth Decker in honor of their marriage. 'You Made Me Love You.'" Jimmy signaled the band.

"Oh, Harry." Liz sighed. "Thank you, darling, for remembering."

"I wish I could take the credit, sweetheart, but anything that happens tonight is all Joe."

"The song's perfect, Joe." Liz turned to find that Joe and Mandy were no longer standing behind us. "Now where did those two disappear to?"

"I don't know, sweetheart. Joe disappeared with Mandy in tow when he handed us off to Fredrick. They'll be back, but in the meantime, my love...may I have this dance, Mrs. Decker?"

"You may, Mr. Decker." She smiled and curtsied. We glided around the dance floor in a style that would make even Fred Astaire take notice. We were oblivious to the world around us, inside our cocoon of love.

"Congratulations, Mr. and Mrs. Decker, on your wedding nuptials." Jimmy took us from our private world, bringing the song to an end. "May this war end quickly, safely returning all our servicemen."

"Yes," Liz murmured. "May it end very quickly."

"Southpaw...Liz. Over here," Joe called out, gesturing us back to our table. It was now beautifully adorned with candles, flowers, and a bottle of Dom Pérignon champagne.

"The table's beautiful, Joe—everything's beautiful." Liz's eyes were soft, sending a message of gratitude.

"The night is just beginning, Mrs. Decker. A toast." Joe raised his glass. "To the bride and groom. May your days be filled with happiness, your nights filled with passion, and may you always remember tonight, because tonight, you are surrounded by love. I'm going to miss you, Southpaw." He locked eyes with me. "I'm gonna miss being in your corner."

"I'm gonna miss you too, buddy." I raised my glass, feeling our bond of brotherhood.

"Hear, hear." Mandy downed her champagne. "Liz, I need to freshen up. Come with me while these boys say their sentimental good-byes."

"Hurry back, sweetheart." I let go of Liz's hand.

"I'll be back so fast, darling, you won't even know I was gone." She gave a loving smile over her shoulder.

"Can you believe Joe and his speech?" Mandy rolled her eyes. "I thought for a moment back there he was going to cry."

"Don't make fun of Joe, Mandy." Liz's voice was sympathetic. "I feel sorry for him."

"Sorry for Joe? Why?"

"Because he didn't have a very easy life growing up. Did you know he was raised in a state orphanage? Harry and Pappy are the closest thing to a family Joe has ever known."

"No, I didn't know, but I'm mad at Joseph Riley right now, and he doesn't deserve my sympathies. I haven't seen or talked to him since the day Jack proposed. And this afternoon? Not opening my car door! I'm probably only seeing him tonight because I'm your best friend and maid of honor. He had to invite me!" She rummaged through her handbag in discontent.

"I'm sorry, Mandy. I'm sorry things haven't worked out between you and Joe."

"It doesn't matter, Liz. Besides, I didn't take you from the table to talk about Joseph Riley. I took you from the table to talk about your big night tonight. Aren't you excited? You're going to finally lose your virginity. Lord only knows how you held on to it this long."

"Mandy, please." Liz's eyes darted around the ladies' room.

"Don't worry, Liz; it's empty. I've got more class than that... than to tell the world your private business. So?" She smiled in anticipation. "Are you excited?"

"Excited? More nervous than excited. I just don't want to disappoint Harry."

"I don't think you have to worry about your sexual abilities, Liz. Rumor has it Jack's a great lover. From what I understand, all a girl has to do is lie back and enjoy the Southpaw ride," Mandy purred.

"My husband's name is Harry, not Jack, and I'd appreciate it if you'd keep the rumors about his past to yourself. He's a married man now, and the past is just that, Mandy: the past."

"I'm sorry, Liz. I didn't mean to offend you. I just wanted you to know there's nothing to be nervous about. Jack...Harry...whoever...is known to be a very skillful man when it comes to the bedroom. When it comes to pleasing a woman...that's all."

"I'm sorry too, Mandy. It's just...I've thought of making love to Harry so many times, playing out the scenes of our wedding night in my mind. But now that the time has come, and I'm about to consummate my marriage, I just don't know, Mandy. Regardless of how wonderful my husband is known to be, what if I'm just not any good at lovemaking?"

"Oh, honey, you'll be fine." Mandy chuckled in adoration. "You love the guy. The guy loves you. It'll all work out—you'll see."

"I just want our first night together to be perfect, Mandy."

"Then it will be, Liz. You, Jack, Harry, whoever," she said. "The two of you love each other, so perfect is the only way this night can turn out. Besides, if Jack Collins ever hurts you, he'll have me to reckon with. Now let's get back to the table and celebrate your nuptials."

"What took you two so long? I was just getting ready to send out a search party." I helped my wife adjust her chair.

"Relax, Jack, just a little girl talk." Mandy adjusted her own chair. "No need for concern." She poured herself a glass of champagne.

"Mr. and Mrs. Decker, would you please return to the dance floor?" a voice echoed over the microphone.

"What's going on, Harry?" Liz looked at an empty dance floor.

"I'm not sure, sweetheart." I curiously looked at Joe.

"The dance floor awaits, Mr. and Mrs. Decker." Joe gave a sly grin.

"So it does, buddy." I escorted my wife to the dance floor, and the lights dimmed, a spotlight hitting us. "Here Comes the Bride" began to play. A three-tier wedding cake was being pushed out of the darkness.

"Congratulations, Southpaw...Liz," Joe called out from the table.

"Joseph Riley?" Mandy gave a light punch to his arm. "Just when I've decided you're not a very nice guy, you go and put on a night like tonight."

"The Southpaw is like my brother, Mandy. I'd do anything for the guy." He whistled in jubilation.

"So I see." Mandy looked at Joe in adoration.

"Never underestimate the wingman, little lady," he said, applauding along with the other patrons.

"Wingman? What's a wingman, Joe?"

"Nothing you need to concern yourself with, Mandy girl. Shall we join them?" He extended his arm.

"Sure, Joe." Mandy smiled, accepting his arm and proudly walking onto the dance floor.

The four of us savored what came to be known as our wedding reception, enjoying each and every moment, cherishing them. Liz and I were consumed with love for each other. Mandy and Joe were lusting for each other. Champagne poured freely as we told funny stories from our pasts and hopes for our futures. We danced the night away Fred Astaire style.

"I can't thank you enough for tonight, buddy," I said as we brought the evening to an end.

"Glad to do it, Southpaw. That's what wingmen are for." He smiled in satisfaction.

"Well, you've been a great one, Joe." My voice filled with gratitude. "Shall we go, Liz?"

"Yes, my darling. Thank you so much for tonight, Joe; everything was wonderful, just wonderful."

"Think nothing of it, Liz. See you before I leave for Fort Hood, Southpaw?"

"You bet, Joe." I escorted my wife from the Safari Club, anxious for the wedding night to begin, yet surprisingly nervous at the same time.

"Good evening, sir, madam. Welcome to the Hilton. How can I help you this evening?"

"We have a reservation for Mr. and Mrs. Harry Decker," I said, smiling proudly.

"Oh, yes, Mr. Decker. The honeymoon suite." He motioned to the bellhop.

"There must be some kind of a mistake." I felt slightly embarrassed. "I didn't reserve the honeymoon suite."

"There is no mistake, Mr. Decker. A Mr. O'Hare came in this afternoon and upgraded your reservation. He also asked if I would please give you this note."

"What does it say, Harry?" Liz looked over my shoulder.

"'Congratulations, Southpaw, on your marriage to Elizabeth. May the two of you live a long and happy life together.'"

"That was nice of Pappy." Liz smiled.

"Yeah, ole Pappy's got a loud bark, but he's just a sentimental softy underneath it all." I read the rest of the note silently. *P.S. Take care of yourself over there, Southpaw. Remember to stay off the ropes, and keep your gloves up...as you continue to make me proud, protecting our great country.*

"Follow me, please, sir." The bellhop picked up the bags. Liz and I followed, giddy with happiness. Standing silent inside the elevator, we conveyed our love through amorous eyes as it took us to the top floor. "Here we are, sir, the honeymoon suite." The bellhop unlocked the door and stepped aside.

"Where do you think you're going, young lady? It's customary for the groom to carry his bride over the threshold." I swept her into my arms. Liz blushed, burying her face in the crook of my neck.

"Congratulations again, Mr. and Mrs. Decker." The bellhop quietly closed the door.

"Oh, Harry. The room...it's beautiful." She smelled the bouquet of roses. The fireplace crackled romantically.

"Would you like a glass of champagne, my love?" I popped the cork of the Dom Pérignon.

"I'd love one, Harry." She picked up her overnight bag. "I won't be long, darling." Quietly she closed the bathroom door.

"Take your time, sweetheart." I poured two glasses of champagne and quickly changed into my bedtime attire in anticipation of the evening that lay ahead. After about twenty minutes, my anticipation turned to apprehension. "Are you okay in there, sweetheart?"

"I'm fine, Harry." Liz timidly stepped from the bathroom in a semi sheer white negligee.

"You're beautiful, Mrs. Decker." I handed her a glass of champagne.

"Thank you, Harry." Taking a small sip, she looked nervously toward the bed.

"Everything is going to be wonderful tonight, sweetheart."

"I just don't want to be a disappointment to you, Harry." Her eyes searched mine.

"There's no way you could disappoint me, sweetheart." Taking the glass from her hand, I led her to our honeymoon bed.

"I love you, Harry." Her voice was soft and warm, drawing me in.

"I love you too, sweetheart." Laying her back, nuzzling her neck, I explored her body inside a warm embrace.

"Harry," she softly murmured. "This is exactly how I hoped it would be." Her dark eyes filled with love.

Kissing her ever so tenderly, lingering over her lips, I was amazed by the love I felt. I was consumed with an intimacy unlike anything I'd ever felt before, making love for the first time in my life to a woman whom I would love for the rest of my life.

December 21, 1941

"Hey, Pappy." I was standing on his front porch. "I just wanted to come by and thank you for the upgrade to the honeymoon suite. That was really great of you, and Liz loved it."

"Think nothing of it, Southpaw; consider it a wedding gift." Stepping aside, he allowed me into his home. "You must be leaving for boot camp soon?"

"Two days, Pappy. I board the bus for Fort Hood on Tuesday."

"You ready to show them what the good ole US is made of, son?"

"I'm gonna try my best, Pappy. I think you've prepared me to be a good fighter."

"Good, good." Pappy gestured to me to sit across from him. "Are you scared, Southpaw? I hope you're scared; a little fear is the only way to stay sharp. You need to look at those Japs like any other opponent. Never underestimate, never go in overly confident, and always treat every time like it's the first round. Look for their Jap weakness, and when you've found it, move in and conquer those sons of bitches." He threw a quick right hook.

"I will, Pappy." I chuckled at his intensity. "I'll remember everything you taught me. I promise."

"Good...good...Southpaw." He poured two shots of brandy.

"You okay this morning, Pappy? You seem a little preoccupied. Something on your mind?"

"I'm fine—just a little worried about Joe."

"Joe? Why? Didn't he come by to see you? He told me you were going to be his last stop before boarding the bus to Fort Bragg."

"He came by." Pappy's voice was somber. "We had a long talk. He told me things, Southpaw. Things I didn't know. Things about his childhood."

"Like what kind of things, Pappy?" I felt his upset.

"Like he lost his parents in a house fire when he was three and lived out his childhood in a state orphanage. Did you know he has no photos of his parents? Just a recurring dream of a man carrying him on his shoulders...a man he believes to be his father."

"He believes to be his father, Pappy? He doesn't know?"

"Apparently he's unable to see the man's face, but he can hear his voice. It's gruff like mine. So he always thought his father would have been a lot like me. What do you say to a boy who's just given you the highest honor, Southpaw? Just compared you to the memory of a father he never knew?"

"I don't know, Pappy. I mean...Joe told me about being raised in an orphanage, but he's never mentioned anything about a recurring dream or any memories of his father."

"Well, I didn't say anything, Southpaw, and I'm ashamed of myself. I mean, a boy comes to you..." His eyes misted, and his voice trailed off in dishonor.

In that moment I realized how much Pappy had grown to care for me and Joe. Pappy had always been a man's man—a hardnose. A guy who didn't show his feelings, but in spite of it, we had become his sons. The sons he never had. Just as Pappy had become the father Joe never knew. "You gonna be okay, Pappy?" I was unsure how to console him.

"I'll be fine, Southpaw." He regained his composure. "It's just these damn allergies; they keep flaring up on me." Taking a kerchief from his back pocket, he dabbed his eyes hard.

"Joe's got a good head on his shoulders, Pappy. He'll be fine. You taught him more than you know."

"I hope you're right, Southpaw. I would hate to see anything happen to the boy." He shook it off. "A toast," he said, raising his glass of brandy high. "To you and Joe. May you both come back safe and unharmed, and may those Jap sons of bitches regret the day they ever came on our shores."

"Hear, hear." Raising my glass, I looked at the man I had grown to love and quickly took the shot. "Well, I guess I better get going, Pappy. I'm a married man now. My wife will be waiting."

"Sure, sure. Let me walk you out. Well, I guess this is it for a while, eh, son?"

"Yeah, Pappy. I guess it is."

"You take care of yourself over there, Southpaw." He gave the ole boxer's stare for longer than usual.

"I will, Pappy. I promise." I threw a few shadow punches his way before turning and walking to my car.

"Hey, Southpaw," Pappy called out. "If you see Joe over there, you tell him I'd be proud to be his honorary father."

"Will do, Pappy." Shutting my car door, I adjusted my rearview mirror to get a last look at the man who had taught me so much. I gave the horn a few taps in his honor before slowly pulling away from the curb. Pappy returned my honks with a few quick shadow punches before reaching to his back pocket and retrieving his handkerchief.

December 23, 1941

"I love you, Harry; I'll miss you," Liz shouted over the diesel engine of the bus destined for Fort Hood.

"I love you too, Liz." I let go of her hand as I felt the bus moving from the curb. "Take good care of my wife, Mandy."

"I will, Jack; don't worry."

"Good-bye, darling." Liz waved, eyes misting, as the bus rounded the corner and disappeared from sight.

"He'll be fine, Liz." Mandy's voice was reassuring. "Jack knows how to take care of himself. He's a fighter, after all."

"I know, Mandy, but I'm going to miss him so." She sadly looked at the empty street. "Let's take in a movie or something. I don't feel like going home just yet, and the theater is just a few blocks down."

"Sound good to me, Liz. *Penny Serenade* is playing at the Regal, and I could look at Cary Grant all day." She took Liz's arm, and they strolled toward the theater. "So tell me, Liz. How was it?"

"How was what, Mandy?"

"Don't play coy with me, Elizabeth Decker. You know exactly what I'm talking about...your wedding night? If your husband is half as good as the rumors, your honeymoon must've been fabulous!"

"The wedding night, Mandy." Liz smiled in reminiscence. "Our wedding night was wonderful."

"And the honeymoon?" Mandy was giddy for details.

"The honeymoon...well..."

"Why am I sensing displeasure, Liz?"

"I wouldn't say displeasure, actually. It's just, well...some of the nights that followed our wedding night were—"

"Were what, Liz?" Mandy was getting impatient.

"Well...let's just say...less than wonderful."

"And what does 'less than wonderful' mean?" Mandy asked, lifting her brows curiously.

"Nothing, Mandy," Liz said dismissively. "It's just me being insecure."

"Come on, Liz; you can tell me. I'm your best friend."

"Well, you know I don't have much experience when it comes to lovemaking."

"Any," Mandy corrected. "Any experience."

"Okay, any experience, but Harry…he has this…this appetite… this—"

"So the rumors are true," Mandy interrupted.

"Mandy!" Liz stammered. "I'm trying to tell you."

"Sorry, Liz. Go on."

"Harry has this sexual appetite…that I'm just not sure I can satisfy."

"What do you mean, can't satisfy?"

"Just that, Mandy. It's not lovemaking; it's something different."

"I'm not understanding, Liz. It's just sex. How different can it be?"

"Just different, Mandy." Her eyes were welling with tears.

"Oh, honey, it can't be worth tears." Opening her handbag, Mandy handed her a Kleenex. "Now dry your tears, and tell me how Jack's sexual appetite is different."

"My husband's name is not Jack," Liz sniveled. "It's Harry."

"My mistake. Tell me how Harry's appetite is different."

"Well…" Liz's voice was soft as she lightly dabbed her eyes. "Most of the time, Harry is gentle and tender in our lovemaking, but then there are these other times." Her voice hardened. "When he's forceful and demanding."

"What's wrong with a little variety, Liz? Give it a chance; you might like a little force and demand on occasion." Mandy gave a devious wink.

"I've tried to relax and just go with it, Mandy, but when I do, I just feel cheap and dirty. Isn't lovemaking supposed to be romantic? Something intimately shared between two people who are in love? I almost feel like Harry is two different people sometimes—like he's two different men."

"Well, I think you're worried over nothing, Liz. It may take some time and practice, but I'm sure everything will work out for you two in the lovemaking department. At least you have a relationship to work on. Joe left for boot camp the other day, and he didn't even bother saying good-bye."

"Oh, Mandy, I'm sorry. Here I am going on about myself. How are you doing?"

"I'm fine, Liz. Que sera, sera; there are plenty of Joes out there." She forced a light smile. "Oh, look at the time, Liz. We need to hurry, or we're going to miss the beginning of the movie, and Cary Grant waits for no woman." She picked up the pace.

CHAPTER SEVEN

March 1942

"Are you okay, Liz?" Mandy lightly knocked on the bathroom door.

"Yes...no...I don't know."

"Well, can I help you with anything?" Mandy pleaded through the bathroom door.

"No, I'm fine, Mandy. Just feeling a little nauseous this morning. I'll be right out." Liz flushed the toilet and put a cool washcloth to the back of her neck. Mandy, unmoving, heard the water turn on and off several times before the lock clicked and the door opened.

"You sure you're okay, Liz?"

"I'm fine, Mandy." Liz passed her by, heading to the kitchen.

"Well, you don't look fine. You look a little green. This is the fourth time this week you've woken up nauseous. You're tired all the time. You're craving really weird foods, and...oh my God!" She stopped dead in her tracks. "Liz, you have all the signs of being pregnant."

"Mandy, don't be ridiculous; I can't possibly be pregnant. I've only been married a few weeks."

"What difference does that make, Liz? You could be married for one day and be pregnant. Heck, you could be pregnant and not be married. We need to make you a doctor's appointment. What's your doctor's name, Liz?" Mandy took the phone book from under the phone stand.

"Dr. Midland. You don't really think I could be pregnant, do you, Mandy?"

"There's only one way to find out, Liz. Midland, Midland." Mandy dragged her finger down the yellow pages.

"Wouldn't that be wonderful, Mandy? A little boy or little girl?" Liz's voice was dreamy. "That looks just like Harry?"

"A little Jack? Yes. That would be adorable, but the female version of him?" Mandy rolled her eyes.

"You're right." Liz chuckled fondly. "Harry wouldn't make a very pretty girl, would he?"

"Not unless you like square-jawed and muscular in a female. It's ringing, Liz." She handed her the phone.

"Hello? Yes, I'd like to make an appointment with Dr. Midland for a pregnancy test. Mrs. Elizabeth Decker. Yes, Tuesday at eleven thirty would be fine." She looked at Mandy, bright-eyed. "I'll see you then." She hung up the phone.

The Following Tuesday

"Well, Doc, give us the news; is she pregnant or not?" Mandy chirped, seated inside the exam room.

"Congratulations, Mrs. Decker..."

"I knew it," Mandy squealed.

"Excuse me, miss, but I'm trying to have a conversation with Mrs. Decker."

"Sorry, Doc." Mandy zipped her lip.

"As I was saying, Mrs. Decker, you're approximately twelve weeks pregnant. I'm writing you a prescription for iron pills; your blood count was a little low. That's probably why you've been more tired than usual. I'm also a little concerned with your cholesterol levels. So watch your diet, but otherwise everything looks good. I'll want to see you again in two months. You can pick up your prescription on your way out."

"Thank you, Dr. Midland." Liz smiled.

"You're welcome, Mrs. Decker. Congratulations again." He quietly closed the door.

"I knew it!" Mandy squealed the moment the door was closed. "I mean, what else could it be? When does Jack, Harry, whoever... when does your husband get back from boot camp? I can't wait to see his face when you tell him the news."

"In a few days, Mandy." Liz's voice was solemn. "We'll have two weeks together before he's deployed to active duty."

"What's wrong, Liz? Why aren't you excited?"

"I am excited, Mandy; it's just everything is happening so fast. What if Harry isn't ready for a baby? After all, we've just gotten married, and with him being in the service and all, I'll be raising this baby alone."

"Excuse me? Alone! I don't think so. I'll be with you every step of the way, and your husband? Well, he's going to be ecstatic!"

"Do you think so, Mandy?"

"I know so, Liz. You'll see. Jack loves you more than anything in the world...I mean Harry." She gave an apologetic smile.

Harry's Return from Boot Camp

"What time do you expect Jack today?" Mandy flopped on the bed.

"I expect *Harry* in about an hour. His bus is due in at eight o'clock, but who knows? They're so unpredictable. Can you help me with my zipper, Mandy?" Liz turned around, inhaling deeply.

"Sure, Liz." Mandy zipped it with ease. "Good move on the emerald dress. You look beautiful. Pregnancy agrees with you."

"I was actually a little surprised I could still wear it."

"Sure you could, Liz; you've still got a few good months before you have to start wearing those horrid maternity clothes." Mandy wrinkled her face in disgust.

"They're not so bad, Mandy." She sat down to her vanity. "What do you think…up?" She pulled her hair into a weak French twist. "Or down?" She let it fall softly around her shoulders.

"Down, Liz, always down. I have to admit, I'm a little envious, Liz. You've got Jack, and now a baby on the way, and I've got? Well?" She sighed in discontent.

"You mean I have Harry," Liz chuckled, attempting to lighten Mandy's mood.

"I mean Harry," Mandy uttered Liz's attempt falling flat.

"It will happen for you one day, Mandy—you'll see." Her voice was soft and encouraging. "What is it you always say? 'So many men…so little time.' Your time will come. Just you wait and see."

"That's not exactly what that saying means, Liz, but thank you." Mandy chuckled. "I get the drift of what you're trying to say."

"Well, what does it mean then, Mandy?"

"It's not important, Liz." She shook her head in dismissal.

"Hello, is anybody here?"

"It's Harry!" Liz softly shrieked.

"Well, what are you waiting for, Liz? Go to your husband!"

Liz happily ran from the bedroom.

Mandy looked at her reflection in the mirror, melancholy consuming her.

"Harry…darling." Liz ran into my open arms.

"Sweetheart, I've thought of this moment so many times." I took her into a warm embrace.

"Me too, darling. I've missed you so."

"Not as much as I've missed you, my love." I kissed her passionately, unable to control my longing.

"Harry, please. We're in the living room." Liz blushed, pulling from my embrace. "Come, I've got some exciting news." She led me to the couch.

"What kind of news, sweetheart?" I hugged her passionately once again, nuzzling her neck.

"Please, darling." She broke from my passionate grip. "I'll tell you all about it, but first I want to hear all about you. How was boot camp? Were you able to see Joe while you were there?"

"Boot camp was fine, and no, I didn't see Joe, sweetheart." I smiled at her innocence. "Joe is stationed at Fort Bragg; I was stationed at Fort Hood." I lightly ran my fingertips over her exposed knee.

"Oh, how foolish of me, Harry." She blushed in embarrassment. "Harry, did you know Joe left for boot camp without even so much as a good-bye to Mandy?"

"No, I didn't, sweetheart, but I don't want to talk about Mandy, or Joe, or boot camp. I only have a two-week furlough, sweetheart, and I want to spend that time with my wife. Dancing with my wife. Going to the theater with my wife. Making love to my wife." I lifted my brows in innuendo. "I've just missed you so much, sweetheart." Taking her in my arms once again, I kissed her deeply, passionately, exploring her body, unleashing all my pent-up sexual frustration.

"Harry? Darling? Please, slow down. We have plenty of time for that. Besides, Mandy's in the next room," she whispered. "She'll hear us."

"Who cares if she does?" I nibbled her earlobe. "Come on, sweetheart. I've been such a good boy for such a long time." I slid my hand between her thighs, my fingers teasingly working their way, playfully attempting to remove her panties.

"All right, Harry, but not here." She pulled my hands from under her dress. "Let's go into the bedroom, and be quiet. I don't want Mandy to hear us."

"I'll be as quiet as a mouse, sweetheart." Tiptoeing impishly behind her, I closed the bedroom door. "Come here, my love." My voice was full of yearning as I kissed her deeply, eagerly tugging at her dress.

"Harry, stop it! You're going to rip it." Liz pulled away. "I'll do it." Slowly, hesitantly, she removed her dress, revealing all her beautiful assets.

"I'm sorry, Liz. I've just missed you so much."

"I've missed you too, Harry, and I understand your yearnings; I have my own."

"Then what are we waiting for, sweetheart?" Quickly removing my uniform, I pulled her onto the bed. My asset came to full alert, searching for a destination.

"Harry…please?" She pulled herself once again from my embrace. "Do you have to be so forceful?" Her voice trembled.

"I'm sorry, Liz." I lightly caressed her back. "I've just missed you so much, sweetheart."

"I've missed you too, Harry. It's just…" Her eyes searched mine. "I'm just a little uncomfortable when your desires are so demanding."

"I'm sorry, sweetheart. It's just been so long," I said apologetically. "Please?" Gently laying her back, I kissed her ever so softly, ever so tenderly.

"I love you, Harry," she whispered, timidly responding to my touch. Keeping my lustful passion at bay, I made sweet, gentle, romantic love to my wife, bringing myself to an unsatisfied completion.

"Harry?" Liz said, basking in her coziness. "I haven't told you my surprise yet." She gently stroked my arm.

"What's the surprise, Liz?" I asked, preoccupied with my lack of sexual fulfillment.

"We're going to have a baby, Harry." She sighed softly.

"What?" I came out of my haze to full attention.

"You're going to be a father." She smiled.

"A father?" The news hit me like a blindsided left hook, but it could also be the explanation for her sexual reserve. "A baby, Liz? How's that possible? I mean, I know how it's possible…when?" I felt like I'd just been TKO'd.

"In about six months." She beamed. "Are you happy, Harry? I hope you're happy."

"Of course I'm happy, sweetheart." Taking her in my arms, I gently kissed her forehead.

"I'm so happy…you're happy, Harry." Liz snuggled into me.

"Liz?" Mandy gently knocked on the bedroom door. "Is everything okay? I've got the late shift at the club tonight, so I won't be home until after two."

"Everything's wonderful, Mandy." Liz snuggled in deeper. "Have a good night at work, Mandy. I'll see you in the morning."

"Okay, see you in the morning, Liz. Welcome home, Jack, and congratulations on becoming a daddy." Mandy giggled, leaving the doorway.

"Daddy." I pulled my wife in close, attributing her sexual reserve to the news of her pregnancy. Feeling the wonderful comfort of Liz washing over me, I drifted off to a happy, blissful sleep.

The Next Morning

"Liz, my love?" I reached for her, only to find an empty bed. Then I heard my wife's soft voice singing in the shower, and visions of her naked, soapy body caused my manhood to become aroused. Leaving my warm bed, guided by this heat-seeking missile, I followed my urges. "Good morning, my love." I pulled back the shower curtain.

"Harry! You scared me," she said, trying to cover her voluptuous breasts with a tiny washcloth.

"No reason to be scared, sweetheart. It's just me, your husband." Letting my pajama bottoms fall to the floor, I stepped into the shower.

"What are you doing, Harry?" Her voice was anxious.

"Relax, sweetheart." I gently removed the tiny washcloth and suckled her right breast, my fingers gently playing between her thighs.

"Harry?" She moved away as if in slight discomfort.

"Yes, sweetheart?" Moaning in desire, I kissed her deeply, passionately, hungrily. Pushing her beautiful body against the shower wall, I used my knees to open her legs, allowing myself full entry.

"Harry, please?" Ignoring her pleas, becoming fully aroused, I thrust myself deep inside her, ravaging her body. I released all my longing, all my pent-up sexual frustrations, moaning in desire. My body spasmed in delight, as it brought me to complete, total sexual satisfaction. Breathing heavily and coming down from my desires, I felt her rigid body against the shower wall. "Forgive me, sweetheart." I released her, confused by her inhibition. "Forgive me." Returning her washcloth, I stepped from the shower.

"Good morning, Liz," Mandy chirped, coming into the kitchen. "Where's your handsome husband this morning?"

"My handsome husband went out for a run because I'm a terrible wife," Liz muttered sadly.

"Terrible wife? What are you talking about, Liz? You're not a terrible wife." Mandy poured herself a cup of coffee.

"Yes, I am, Mandy." Her bottom lip quivered.

"No, you're not, Liz. Now come and sit down." Mandy took a seat at the kitchen table. "And tell me all about this terrible tragedy you believe has happened."

"It was just awful, Mandy." Liz quickly took a seat. "Harry came to me in the shower this morning, to make love, but it wasn't love, Mandy; it was something else. He took me, Mandy, quickly, forcefully. It was like he was driven by this uncontrollable desire, and when it was all over, I didn't feel love. I felt used. Like I was fulfilling a need—his need." Her eyes welled with tears. "Lovemaking is supposed to be intimate and romantic." She began crying softly.

"Oh, honey." Mandy's voice was consoling. "Making love has no one way. It can be soft and romantic, forceful and demanding, or even a combination of both. It just depends on the circumstances. The desires of the moment."

"I don't understand, Mandy." She dabbed her eyes.

"Look, you and Jack—Harry, whoever—are basically still newlyweds. The two of you are just getting to know each other. You have to learn to negotiate in the bedroom. Talk to him; be honest about your feelings. Tell him your wants, your desires, and allow him to be honest with you."

"My wants, Mandy?" She sniffed. "My desires?"

"Yes, Liz, it's the only way he's going to know. Now dry your tears." She handed her a fresh Kleenex. "I'm going to get dressed and get out of here, so you and your husband can have the place to yourselves. Talk to him, Liz. Find that happy medium. It will all work out. I promise."

"I hope you're right, Mandy. I love Harry more than anything in the world."

"Then get his breakfast started, Liz; he'll be back soon. Remember, cook for him like his mother did. It's one of the three things that keep a man."

"Thanks, Mandy." Liz was feeling more confident. "Now, cooking is something I do." Turning on the radio, she felt as if all her problems had been solved. She grabbed eggs, bacon, and fresh-squeezed orange juice, happily singing along to the romantic ballad on the radio.

"I'm back, Liz." I came through the apartment door, wiping the sweat from my forehead

"Did you have a good run, Harry? I've made breakfast; I hope you're hungry."

"I'm famished, sweetheart." I came into the kitchen. "I'm sorry about this morning, Liz…in the shower? It's just that I missed you so much; I couldn't control my desire for you."

"I'm sorry too, Harry, and you shouldn't have to control your desires. Not when it comes to your wife. All I want is to make you happy, Harry."

"And you do, Liz, but there are many ways a man and woman can make love."

"I know, Harry, and I'm open to finding ways we both can enjoy our lovemaking."

"That's all I ask, Liz." I was consumed with love.

"I'll try, Harry; I promise. Now eat your breakfast before it gets cold," she playfully demanded.

"Yes, ma'am. Aren't you having any breakfast, sweetheart?" I looked at the feast displayed before me.

"I was…till the smell of bacon made me nauseous." She rubbed her queasy stomach and munched on a saltine.

"Oh, sweetheart." Chuckling, I pulled her onto my lap. "Do you know how proud I am to be your husband and how happy you have made me with the news of being a father?"

"Do I make you proud and happy, Harry?"

"Each and every day, sweetheart." I went in for a kiss.

"I'm sorry, Harry." She covered her mouth. "I think I'm going to be sick." Jumping from my lap, she ran to the bathroom.

"I hope you're okay, sweetheart." As sounds of vomit hit the toilet, I pushed away the once-desirable plate of food, smiling at the thought of becoming a family.

Last Day of Leave

"How would you like to spend our last day together, my love?" I snuggled her from behind.

"Whatever you would like to do, Harry, is fine with me." She was looking into her clothes closet, preoccupied.

"What do you say we go shopping and get a few things for the baby, sweetheart? I've seen the longing in your eyes every time we pass a baby carriage on our walks in the park."

"Am I that obvious, Harry?" Leaning back into me, she sighed in blissful comfort.

"You are to me, my love." I gave her a soft peck on the cheek. "Now get dressed!" I said, lightly tapping her bottom. "I want to pick up something special for our last night together."

"Let's go to Macy's, Harry; they have a great baby department, and I would love for you to meet some of my coworkers."

"Sounds like a plan, my love. Now quit lollygagging and get dressed."

"Easier said than done, Harry," she murmured, returning to the task of finding a dress that would allow for the small baby bump protruding from her stomach.

"Wait till you see, Harry." The elevator was taking us to the third floor of Macy's. "They have so many beautiful baby items, darling, from strollers to cribs to the tiniest little sleepers." Her natural instinct was to nest, preparing for her baby chick.

"I'm sure they do, sweetheart." I smiled in adoration. The Macy's elevator dinged the arrival of the third floor.

"You see, Harry!" she exclaimed as we stepped from the elevator. "Everywhere you look…baby."

"Liz?" A blonde haired woman at the cashier's desk called out. " This must be your handsome husband we've all heard so much about!"

"Yes, Bev, this is my very handsome husband, Harry." She lightly touched my arm.

"It's very nice to meet you, Harry." Bev gave an approving smile. "So, what brings the two of you here today? What can I do to help?"

"Well, Bev, if you could help my wife with picking out some baby items while I go do my own little secret shopping, I would greatly appreciate it."

"It would be my pleasure, Harry." Bev smiled flirtatiously.

"I'll be back in about thirty minutes, sweetheart." Liz was already preoccupied with the display of baby sleepers.

"Take your time, Harry. I could look at baby things all day."

"Take care of her for me, Bev." Giving her a quick wink, I headed for the elevators.

"You got it, Harry." Bev returned my wink. "That is one handsome husband you have there, Liz. Does he have any brothers?" She sounded captivated.

"No, Bev, just an older sister—Helen." Liz added another sleeper to her purchase pile.

"That's too bad," Bev moaned sadly. "Oh well." Shrugging off her disappointment, she returned to the business at hand. "What do you say we start with the carriages, Liz? This is our newest model, the Baby-Master. It's top-of-the-line, and with your employee discount, very reasonable."

"It's beautiful." Liz lightly touched the handle, feeling the carriage move with ease.

"Should I put one aside for you, Liz? I've got a feeling they're going to sell out quickly."

"Yes, please do, Bev. I'm not sure where I'm going to put everything, but I'll work all that out by time the baby arrives."

"Liz? You aren't still living in that small apartment with Mandy over on Parkway Terrace, are you?"

"I'm afraid so, Bev, but only until Harry returns for good. He doesn't want me to be alone, especially now—with the baby coming and all."

"Well, store policy is we can only hold your items for up to ninety days, but I've got the power to hold them until you're ready, Liz.

At least this way the apartment doesn't have to be cramped until the baby arrives."

"That would be great, Bev, thank you." She returned to the sleepers on display. "Everything is so small and adorable." She added a yellow sleeper with a quacking duck pattern to the quickly rising purchase pile.

"Liz? Sweetheart?" I called out from across the store, making my way back. "Look what I found!"

"Harry, they're adorable, but what if we have a girl?"

"All the more reason, sweetheart." I was dangling a tiny pair of boxing gloves from my left hand. "If she looks anything like her mother, she's going to have to know how to defend herself."

"Your husband's right," Bev chimed in. "A girl's gotta know how to defend herself." Liz chuckled, adding the tiny gloves to her purchase pile.

"Were you able to find what you were shopping for, Harry?"

"Right here, pretty lady." I waved a small lingerie bag. "Did you find everything you were looking for?"

"Not everything, darling, but it's a start."

"I'll say." Bev rang up the last of the purchases and handed me the large Macy's bag. "Harry? It was wonderful to meet you. Liz, I'll see you on Monday?" She tagged the stroller with a save ticket.

"See you then, Bev, and thanks again." Liz took my arm and stepped to the elevator.

"What do you say we skip lunch and go straight home, sweetheart? With this being our last night together and all, I'd like to spend it at home…alone."

"Whatever you like, Harry." She tightened her grip on my arm.

"I talked to Mandy, sweetheart, and gave her some money for a hotel. So we'll have the apartment all to ourselves for our last night."

"Harry! Would you please stop referring to tonight as our last?"

"Sweetheart?" I chuckled at her assumption. "I don't literally mean our last night."

"Do you promise, Harry? Do you promise you'll return to me?" Her eyes filled with fearful tears.

"Hey, of course I'm coming back." I looked into her watery eyes. "You think a few Japs are going to keep me from returning to you? I'm the Southpaw Slugger, known to knock a guy out in the first round." I gave her chin an imaginary jab. "Come on, sweetheart." I put a protective arm around her. "Let's go home."

"You guys are back early. I was just packing up a few things to take to the hotel," Mandy said.

"Well, don't let us rush you, Mandy, but if there's anything I can do to help?"

"Relax, Jack. I'm going, but you could take my suitcase to the car."

"Anything to hurry things along." Grabbing her suitcase, I quickly exited.

"I think Jack has some big plans for you two tonight, Liz," Mandy said.

"I think you're right, Mandy. He bought some lingerie while we were out shopping that could fit into a bag no bigger than a…a…" She shook her head, at a loss for words.

"Oh, sexy lingerie." Mandy smiled deviously.

"Sleazy lingerie," Liz corrected.

"Does it really matter, Liz?"

"Yes, Mandy—for me, it does."

"Look, Liz, your husband could be going away for a very long time. Don't you want him to have good memories of your last night together?

"Of course I do, Mandy."

"Then give your husband what he wants, Liz. What he desires. Send him away with only fond memories. Memories he can pull from. Memories that will keep him faithful, longing for home… longing for you."

"But, Mandy—"

"But nothing, Liz."

"Suitcase is in the car, Mandy; is there anything else I can do to hurry things along?"

"Just give me a minute, Jack! I'm going…Liz, honey. I'll be back in the morning to take you and Jack to the bus, and remember, Jack, no grandstanding over there; you're going to be a father now."

"Got it, Mandy—no hero stuff." I encouraged her toward the door.

"Okay, Jack! Geez. See you tomorrow, Liz." Mandy gave her an encouraging wink.

"I thought she would never leave, sweetheart." I handed her the small lingerie bag in eager anticipation.

"What could this be?" Liz sheepishly looked into the bag.

"I know they're not really lingerie, Liz." My anticipation was rising.

"Harry?" She took the black bustier and garter from the bag. "There are no panties."

"I know, my love," I said, feeling aroused. "Try them on."

"Okay, Harry, if it's what you want." She hesitantly walked to the bedroom.

"Would you like some wine, Liz?" I popped the cork in anticipation.

"A small glass, Harry." She looked at the sleazy undergarments lying on the bed.

"Do you have them on yet, sweetheart?" I asked eagerly. "Come on out. I want to see you in them."

"I'll be right out, Harry." Looking at her reflection in the mirror, she heard her mother's words. *Respect yourself, Liz, or a man never will. Always be a lady first.* "Be quiet, Mother." She replaced her mother's words with Mandy's. *Always take care of your man in the bedroom. Make him feel desired.* "If a woman in a bustier is what my husband wants, then a woman in a bustier is what he is going to get!" Straightening her shoulders, she walked from the bedroom with all the sex appeal she could muster.

"Very sexy, sweetheart." I handed her a small glass of red wine.

"Thank you, Harry." She quickly gulped the wine. "Another," she said, handing back the empty glass.

"Sorry, Mrs. Decker. One glass of wine is all you get—doctor's orders."

"Do I please you, Harry?" Liz shifted uncomfortably in front of me. "I want to please you."

"Very much so. Come here, my love." I pulled her into a passionate embrace, nuzzling her neck, roughly massaging her voluptuous breasts, unable to control my wanton desires.

"Would you like me to take the bustier off, Harry?" Liz winced in discomfort.

"No, keep it on. I want to take you with it on." I forced my tongue deep into her throat. Quickly turning her around, I entered her from behind, thrusting myself deep inside her. Squeezing her breasts, manipulating her nipples, I moaned in ecstasy with each and every thrust. My body convulsed in hard spasms, bringing me to completion, satisfying my sexual demons. "That was wonderful, Liz." I was breathing heavily, caressing her warm body, basking in total satisfaction.

"I'm glad you enjoyed yourself, Harry." Her body was unmoving.

"Sweetheart?" I lightly caressed her back. "You didn't enjoy yourself?" I grew uneasy, feeling her limp body beneath me.

"It's not that, Harry. I'm just an inexperienced lover. I'm sure in time…" Her voice trailed off, and she quietly started to cry.

"In time? Liz, sweetheart. I don't want you to enjoy our lovemaking in time. Please, talk to me. Tell me what it is you do enjoy."

"Do you really want to know, Harry?" She sniffled.

"Of course I do, sweetheart."

"Well." She looked at me through her tears. "I enjoy it when you kiss me tenderly." She smiled apprehensively.

"And, sweetheart?" I said, encouraging her to go on.

"I like it when you lightly touch my body. When you do that, Harry, your fingertips feel like soft feathers caressing my skin."

"Go on?"

"And when you nibble my earlobes, whispering sweet nothings." Her eyes were smiling. "When you do that, Harry, I just want to melt. It's the intimate lovemaking I enjoy, and the other way, Harry, is just..."

"Yes, the other way?"

"The other way...just makes me feel cheap and unloved, as if you're just taking care of a need. A need that could be taken care of by any woman."

"I'm sorry, sweetheart. I didn't know you felt that way."

"So, you understand, Harry." She snuggled into me.

"Yes, sweetheart, I understand." I lightly kissed her forehead, realizing that the pregnancy was not her reason for sexual reserve but that I had married a good girl in every sense of the word.

Harry a.k.a. Jack Leaves for Boot Camp

"Good-bye, Harry, I love you. I'll write you every day," Liz shouted over the gearing up of the bus.

"I love you too, Liz." I blew her a kiss.

"Good-bye, Jack," Mandy said. "Be careful; be safe. I'll take good care of Liz for you."

"I'm depending on you, Mandy." I waved good-bye to the two women who had become so important in my life: Liz, whom I loved more than life itself, and Mandy, the woman I entrusted with taking care of her.

"Well, you seem happier, Liz, more content. I take it you and Jack had the sex talk?"

"Yes, my husband, Harry, and I discussed our lovemaking."

"And...come on, Liz. Don't make me pull it out of you; how did it go?"

"It went wonderful, Mandy." She smiled contentedly. "I did just what you said. I told Harry that intimate, romantic lovemaking is what I enjoyed, and the other kind of lovemaking, the demanding, forceful lovemaking, really wasn't lovemaking at all."

"And Jack was okay with that?"

"Yes. He said he loves me and wants nothing more than for me to enjoy our lovemaking."

"Really?"

"Yes, Mandy." Liz sounded proud and satisfied. "We've had nothing but intimate, romantic lovemaking ever since."

"Well, that's great, Liz. I told you everything would work out in that department if you just gave it time."

"I know, and you were right. You always seem to be right, Mandy, when it comes to the ways of men."

"Yeah." She exhaled sharply. "Sometimes I think understanding the ways of men can be a curse."

"Why would you think it's a curse, Mandy?"

"Don't pay any mind to me, Liz. What should we do today?"

"Whatever you would like." Liz's voice giddy. I'm just so happy that Harry and I were able to work things out before he left. I would enjoy anything."

"Well, in that case, Liz, if you're up for anything, let's go to the movies so I can drool all over Clark Gable. Some of us girls still have to get our action on the big screen."

"Well, he's no Harry Decker, but I can see the attraction. Hey, wait a minute. Wasn't it Cary Grant you were just drooling over a few weeks ago?"

"That was a few weeks ago, Liz. A girl's got a right to change her mind." Mandy gave a devious smile and a wink.

CHAPTER EIGHT

July 1942

"I got a letter from Harry today." Liz rubbed her very pregnant belly.

"Good news, I hope?" Mandy was spread-eagled on the floor, reading her *Stargaze* magazine.

"He's going to try and be here for the birth of the baby. He can't promise anything, but he wants us to keep our fingers crossed."

"You got it, Liz." Mandy waved her crossed fingers in the air.

"Harry can be so romantic," Liz sighed. "I miss him so much, Mandy."

"I'm sure Jack misses you too, Liz, and I'm sure he'll do everything in his power to get to you when it's time for his baby to be born."

"I know he will, Mandy." Liz took a restless breath, kicking off her shoes.

"My God, Liz! Look at your feet! They're so swollen. Have you been watching your salt intake, young lady, like the doc ordered? You know your blood pressure can get out of control, and that's not good for you or the baby...here." She sat up. "Give me your feet."

"That feels wonderful, Mandy." Liz relaxed back into a foot massage "I don't know what I would do without you. You've been such a great help to me over these last few months."

"That's what friends are for, Liz. Taking care of each other in their times of need."

"I know, Mandy, but you've been really wonderful. Harry and I are very lucky to have you as a friend, and my baby is going to have the best aunt in the world."

"Aunt? Thank you, Liz." Mandy softly smiled.

Susie Mae Decker: September 1942

"Mandy," Liz called into the darkness.

"Liz?" Mandy was half asleep. "What is it?" She turned on her bedside lamp.

"I think it's time, Mandy. I think the baby's coming." Liz winced in pain. "I can't have the baby yet, Mandy. Harry's not here."

"Your husband may not be here, Liz, but your best friend is." Jumping from the bed, Mandy threw on a blouse and a pair of jeans. "Come on, honey...we can do this." She gently led her to the car.

"Please hurry, Mandy," Liz moaned. "The pain is getting worse."

"Don't worry, Liz; we're almost there." She stepped hard on the gas.

"I want my husband, Mandy. Harry!" Liz cried out in pain.

"It's gonna be okay, Liz. Hang on!" Mandy took a quick right into the hospital parking lot. "We need some help here," she said as they burst through the emergency doors, Liz doubling over in pain.

"Orderly, bring a wheelchair. Quickly!" A nurse came to their aid.

"Everything's going to be fine, Liz. Don't worry." Mandy helped her into the wheelchair.

"We'll take it from here, Miss." The nurse took hold of the wheelchair handles. "You can wait in the waiting room."

"I'll be right here, Liz," Mandy anxiously shouted from behind. "Right here." She looked at the signs for directions. One pointed to the waiting room, but she followed the one to the chapel.

She opened the doors, quietly took a seat, and dropped to her knees. "Dear Lord, you're probably a little surprised to hear from me, as I'm not a religious woman, but if you could please watch over my friend in her time of need, it would be greatly appreciated. And if you could get Jack back here in time for the birth, that would be great too, Lord…amen." She slowly got up, only to quickly drop back down. "Make that Harry, Lord." She looked at the crucifix. "I meant to say Harry. Get Harry back in time. I'll be in the waiting room, Lord. Thanks for listening."

"Decker family?" An orderly was scanning the waiting room. "Family for Elizabeth Decker?"

"Yes!" Mandy came to attention. "That's me. Is Liz okay? How's the baby?"

"Mrs. Decker and her daughter are fine. They're in room 322," the orderly said dryly, looking at his chart.

"I'm an aunt," Mandy squealed, giving the orderly a quick peck on his cheek.

"Miss? Please." He lightly touched his cheek. "This is a hospital!"

Mandy, oblivious of her actions as usual, happily ran down the hall.

"Liz?" She lightly tapped on the hospital-room door.

"Come in, Mandy." Liz softly smiled. "Come in, and meet your niece."

"My niece?" She stepped lightly toward the bed. "Oh, Liz, she's beautiful, absolutely beautiful," she said, looking at the perfect little dark haired bundle nestled in her friend's arms. "Have you decided on a name yet?"

"No." Liz sighed sadly. "I'd always hoped Harry would be here and we would decide on a name together, but I guess that's not going to happen."

"Who says that's not going to happen, sweetheart?"

"Harry!" Liz's voice filled with surprise and happiness. "You made it."

"Thank you, Lord." Mandy looked to the heavens, giving a quick wink.

"Of course I made it, sweetheart. Nothing could keep me from you. I came straight from the train station." I said removing my uniform cap, while smoothing my rumpled uniform.

"Come, Harry, and meet your daughter." Liz extended her hand.

"My daughter?" I came to her bedside, peering down at the tiny bundle. "She's beautiful, Liz, and her eyes…they're so dark. Dark like the center of a black-eyed Susan."

"Yes, they are." Liz peered deep into them. "What should we call her, Harry?"

"I think it's obvious, Liz." I took the perfect little bundle from my wife's arms. "Susan. We should call her Susan. No…wait." Gazing into my daughter's dark eyes, I fell in love for the second time in my life. "Susie! Her name should be Susie—Susie Mae Decker."

"Susie," Liz softly repeated. "Susie's perfect, Harry."

"You're going to be Daddy's black-eyed little Susie." I christened her forehead with a gentle kiss. The charge nurse came through the door.

"I think it's time for our new mother to get some rest. You can visit again tomorrow," she said dismissively, taking Susie from my arms.

"No," Liz softly pleaded. "Just a few more minutes. Please."

"We have rules for a reason, Mrs. Decker." The nurse gave a stern look. "Visiting hours are over."

"She's right, sweetheart," I said. "You need to get some rest."

"But I missed you so, Harry." Her sad eyes were weary.

"I'll be back tomorrow, sweetheart." I lightly brushed the hair from her forehead. "When they let you out of this place, I'll have a big surprise waiting for you."

"I don't need any surprises, Harry; all I need is for this war to end, and you to come home to me safe and unharmed." Her tired eyes fluttered.

"Oh, but you're going to love this surprise, sweetheart. Just you wait and see."

"Okay." She softly murmured. "Whatever you say, Harry." Drifting off to a much-deserved sleep.

Three Days Later

"Where are we going, Harry?" Liz perked up in the front seat. "This isn't the way home."

"There's more than one way to go home, sweetheart." I turned the radio to a soft ballad.

"You're right, Harry." She pulled our daughter in close. "It really doesn't matter which way we go home. The important thing is you're home."

"The important thing is we're together, sweetheart." I pulled into the drive of Twelve Forty Leland Street.

"Who lives here, Harry? I really don't feel like visiting anyone. Please, Harry, let's just go home."

"What do you think of this house, Liz? Isn't it quaint? Doesn't it look cozy?" I gazed through the windshield at the white house surrounded by a white picket fence. A cobblestone walkway led to its entrance. Beautiful pink roses lined the driveway.

"Yes, Harry, it's beautiful."

"Perfect! Don't you think, Liz? Perfect for a young couple just starting a family."

"Yes, Harry, it's perfect. Can we go now?"

"Surprise!" Mandy suddenly appeared in the doorway.

"Mandy? What's she doing here? What's going on, Harry?"

"Surprise, sweetheart. Welcome home. I signed the papers a few days ago and moved most of your things in yesterday."

"Home? But how, Harry? When? When did you have the time to house hunt?"

"Mandy did all the work, sweetheart. She met with the realtors and had everything ready for me to sign upon my return. I have to admit she did a great job. Shall we go in, Mrs. Decker?" Taking Susie, I helped Liz step from the car.

"Hold on a minute, Liz." Mandy ran down the steps of the front porch. "Let me help you." Putting a protective arm around her, she helped her walk up the steps leading to our new home.

In that moment I knew I had everything a man could ever ask for: a beautiful wife, a precious new daughter, and a confidante who would do everything in her power to take care of them both until my return. Liz had found a friend in Mandy, and for the life of me, I couldn't understand why. She was flamboyant, brash, and promiscuous, the total opposite of my wife. But they had an undeniable love for each other, and for that I was grateful.

"Come on, Jack," Mandy bellowed. "What's holding you up? It's not like you had the baby."

"I'm coming." Holding my daughter tight, I quickly took the steps and joined them on the porch.

"Are you ready, Liz?" Mandy's eyes were bright.

"Ready." Liz was giddy with excitement.

"Voilà!" Mandy pushed open the front door, and Liz stepped inside. "Well, what do you think, Liz? Isn't it the home you've always dreamed of?"

"It's beautiful, Mandy." She looked around the house in awe. "Absolutely beautiful. A quaint cottage filled with love."

"Wait till you see the backyard, Liz. You're going to love it!"

"What's in the backyard?" Liz's eyes darted back and forth between me and Mandy.

"There's only one way to find out, sweetheart—go and see." Mandy and I scurried behind her in anticipation.

"Oh, Harry, Mandy," she gasped. "I feel like I just stepped into the Land of Oz." She followed the stone pathway leading to a glider nestled inside a tall bouquet of flowers.

"Aren't they beautiful?" Mandy spun around in happiness. "The flower's official name is the black-eyed Susan, but in honor of your daughter, Jack's renamed them." She pointed to the small sign: "Garden of the black-eyed Susie."

"That was supposed to be my surprise, Mandy."

"Sorry, Jack." She gave an apologetic look."

"It's all right, Mandy," I said, seeing the happiness in my wife's eyes. "It doesn't matter."

"Come, Harry." Liz patted the seat next to her on the glider. "You and Susie, come. Sit with me."

"I've got it all worked out, sweetheart," I said, quickly taking a seat. "Mandy is going to move in and help you with Susie. When I return, I'm opening my own tool-and-die shop. You know, a man can make a good living in the trades."

"Just return to me, Harry." She placed her head on my shoulder. "That's all I need."

"I'll return, my love." I pulled her in close, basking in pure contentment.

"So the house is perfect then?" Mandy was giddy for approval.

"Yes, Mandy." Liz softly smiled. "Perfect, but how were you able to keep the house a secret? We tell each other everything."

"It wasn't easy, Liz, but I can keep a secret when it's important. Besides, your husband wanted to be the one to show you the house."

"So much for that idea," I murmured.

"Well, the house is perfect, Mandy. Everything's perfect. Thank you both. I have a wonderful husband, a wonderful friend, a beautiful new baby, and a beautiful new home. I don't think a girl could ask for more." She gave a small yawn. "I didn't realize how tired I would feel." She lightly shook her head as if trying to regain some energy.

"Of course you're tired, Liz," Mandy said. "You just had a baby! Why don't you and Susie take a little nap, while Jack and I get the last few things from the apartment?"

"I have to admit, a nap does sound good. What do you say, Susie; you want to take a little nap with Mommy?"

Susie gave her own little yawn in reply.

"Well, it's unanimous then, sweetheart." I helped my wife and daughter back to the house.

"There's one last surprise, Liz." Mandy threw open the bedroom door, grinning from ear to ear.

"Mandy insisted the baby have a bed of her own, sweetheart."

"It's beautiful, Mandy," said Liz, admiring the lacey white bassinet. "Did Mandy also insist on hanging boxing gloves from the mobile?" She chuckled softly.

"No, my love, that was all my idea, but you have to admit, it does give the bassinet a certain something."

"That it does, Harry." She gently laid Susie inside. "It gives it her father's Southpaw charm."

"Get some rest, sweetheart," I said, tucking my wife into bed. "We won't be long, an hour or so."

"Okay, Harry." She softly sighed, asleep before we left the bedroom.

"Jack Collins, the Southpaw Slugger! Why don't you drive, Jack?" Mandy tossed me her car keys.

"The Southpaw Slugger," I said nostalgically. "I haven't been called that in so long, Mandy. I didn't realize how much I missed him until now."

"Liz hates it when I call you Jack, but I think it fits you. Jack is so much sexier than Harry, and Lord knows you're a sexy man, Jack."

"Mandy, are you flirting with me?"

"I flirt with all men, Jack, but would you like it if I were?"

"I'm a married man, Mandy, and you're best friends with my wife. I don't think it's appropriate—do you?"

"Relax, Jack. I'm just trying to have some fun with a sexy boxer I used to know."

"I am relaxed, Mandy." I suddenly felt discomfort. "How much is left at the apartment?"

"Not much, Jack, just a few boxes. So how have you been, Jack? We really haven't had any time to talk."

"What do we have to talk about, Mandy?"

"Do you think I'm pretty, Jack?" Dropping the visor, she looked at herself in the mirror. "I know I'm not the beauty Liz is, but I have my qualities—don't you think, Jack?"

"You're fine, Mandy. What's this all about?"

"Nothing...just conversing, Jack."

My instinct as a man told me there was more than conversation going on. Mandy was up to something, but for the life of me I couldn't imagine what.

"We're here." I pulled into the complex. "Come on, Mandy. Let's get this done. I don't want to leave Liz and the baby for too long."

"It shouldn't take too long." Mandy sidestepped me into the apartment. "Those boxes there against the wall can go, and then there's just a few things left in the bedroom to pack up."

"Great, I'll just take these to the car." I collected the packed boxes.

"Sure, Jack." Giving me a playful glance, she sashayed her way back to the bedroom.

As I took the boxes to the car, my mind processed Mandy's strange behavior. *I have to be misinterpreting what's going on here. There's no way she's coming on to me, but there's definitely something odd going on, and it can't be good.* "You about ready, Mandy?" I said, returning to the apartment. "I want to get back."

"Just about, Jack. Can you come back here and help me? These boxes are really heavy."

"Anything to hurry things along." I stopped dead in my tracks.

"Hello, Jack," Mandy purred, sexually posed in a red bustier and garter. "See anything you like?" She strutted toward me, her plump breasts and bare bottom calling out. "What's the matter, Jack? Cat got your tongue?"

"Get dressed, Mandy," I said, feeling aroused.

"Come on, Jack. Nobody has to know," she provocatively moaned.

"Stop it, Mandy."

"Are you sure that's what you want, Jack?" She looked at the bulge forming in my pants. "It doesn't look like that's what you want," she said, slowly unzipping my pants.

"Stop. Yes...please." Grabbing her hands, I held them against me, frozen in temptation.

"I knew it!" Mandy yanked her hands from me in disgust. "A leopard never changes his spots."

"Get dressed, Mandy." Regaining my composure, I zipped my pants. "I'll meet you in the car."

"Yeah, meet you in the car, Jack." She sounded repulsed as she pulled on her slacks over the garter.

Sitting behind the wheel in Mandy's black sedan, I desperately tried to process what had just happened. I grew more and more frustrated, upset with Mandy for trying to seduce me, and upset with myself for almost allowing her to do it.

"Why did you do that, Mandy?" I heard the car door close but was unable to look at her. "You're Liz's best friend—she thinks of you like a sister."

"That's exactly why I did it, Jack. I love Liz, and I don't want to see her hurt."

"So you think trying to seduce me is showing your love?"

"I wasn't seducing you, Jack. I was testing you, and you failed miserably."

"Failed? I don't think my wife would quite see it that way. You were the one half naked trying to remove my trousers."

"Is that really what happened in there, Jack? Are you really that unaware of your sexual desires?"

"What would you know about my sexual desires, Mandy?"

"That's not important, Jack. Your wife, my best friend, will never be comfortable with any kind of lovemaking that isn't romantic and intimate."

"I don't think you need to tell me how to satisfy my wife's desires, Mandy."

"Maybe not, but what about your wants? Your desires? Your needs?"

"What about them? I'm perfectly satisfied with my wife."

"Satisfied for now, but we both know your demons will come to call."

"My demons?"

"Your sexual demons. The demons that enjoy forceful sex, demanding sex. Sex that is filled with lust and unbridled passion. Your demons will become famished again, Jack, and you'll have no choice but to quench their hunger."

"You're being ridiculous, Mandy. You make me sound like some kind of animal. Like I can't control my wants and desires."

"Aren't you? I saw the response in your pants. The hunger in your eyes. I think the only thing stopping you from taking me right there on the floor was the fact that it was me, but even then, you were contemplating my offer."

"I have no intentions of defending myself, Mandy, for a natural bodily response."

"Look, Jack. I know you love Liz. I think you loved her the first time you saw her in the park, but you need to know and understand yourself. You will always be a man that desires unbridled sex. A sex Liz is incapable of giving. So let me be that woman, Jack. The woman that will make no demands. The woman that will take care of your needs and protect your wife—my friend—from being hurt."

"This is a ridiculous conversation, Mandy, and I'm done talking about it."

"Not talking about it isn't going to make it go away. You need to realize and understand that romantic love and your sexual desires do not, cannot, live in the same place. You also need to admit that you need both, and eventually you will seek out what you are not getting at home. Your sexual demons will come calling again, Jack, and you will be powerless against them. Think about what I'm saying, and accept the type of man you are." She flipped her hair provocatively. "I can protect you and Liz both."

"I don't need to think about it, Mandy, and I sure don't need your protection." I pulled into the drive of our new home. "I'm not an animal. I can control myself."

"I think you're wrong, Jack, but I've said my piece." She slid over into the driver's seat. "Tell Liz I love her, and I'll call her later." Putting the car in reverse, she pulled from the drive.

"Sexual demons," I muttered under my breath. "Coming to call?" I watched her car disappear from sight.

"Harry?" Liz called out from the porch. "Where's Mandy going? I thought she was joining us for dinner. She made a chicken casserole."

"She didn't say, sweetheart." I picked up the boxes. "She just said to tell you she loved you, and she would be back when my leave was over."

"That's odd, Harry. Where is she going to stay? She doesn't have any girlfriends outside of me."

"Beats me, Liz; I guess she just wanted to give us some time to ourselves. Technically we're still newlyweds, sweetheart." I gave her a quick peck on the cheek. "Do I have time to take a quick shower? I'd like to freshen up before dinner; all this moving has made me feel a little grungy."

"Sure, Harry, dinner is in the warmer."

"Great, sweetheart, I won't be long." Dropping the boxes, I escaped to the shower.

"Harry?" Liz called out over the shower. "You didn't make Mandy feel unwelcome, did you?"

"No, sweetheart. I didn't make Mandy feel unwelcome." I scrubbed my head in silent frustration.

"Well, it wouldn't be the first time you encouraged her to leave, Harry."

"Believe me, Liz; it was all Mandy's idea to leave. I had nothing to do with it."

"I don't mean to sound accusatory, Harry. It just that Mandy has done so much for me—for us—in your absence. She's been a really great friend. I just hope she didn't feel like she was intruding."

"I don't think that was it, sweetheart. Mandy's a wise woman; she knows when a man and a woman need some time alone. I just think she wanted to give us a few days to get reacquainted and enjoy our new daughter."

"You're probably right, Harry. Mandy is very wise. Dinner's ready whenever you are, Harry."

"I'll be right out, sweetheart." I gave myself a final rinse, determined to keep my sexual demons at bay, vowing to prove Mandy wasn't as wise as everyone thought she was.

"So, where do you go when you report back for duty, Harry?" "I'm being sent to Pearl Harbor, sweetheart," I said. I washed down a bite of Mandy's dry casserole with water. "They need my expertise as a machinist to help rebuild."

"Will you be safe there, darling?"

"I'll be as safe as I can be when our country's at war, sweetheart."

"Harry! You don't think the Japanese would bomb us again?"

"Anything's possible, sweetheart, but they could never hit us again. Not with a surprise attack anyway. Do you think we could talk about something else, sweetheart? My leave is over in a few days, and I would like to spend those days enjoying my wife and new daughter."

"I'm sorry, Harry. I just worry about you. I don't know what I would do if anything ever happened to you."

"Nothing's going to happen to me, Liz. The good ole US of A will figure out a way to defeat our enemies and win this war. Don't worry, honey; pretty soon I'll be around so much you'll be sick of seeing me."

"That could never happen, my love." She softly touched my hand. "Come, darling, you must be tired. It's been a long day."

"What about the dishes, sweetheart?" I picked up my half-empty plate.

"Leave them, Harry. I'll get them in the morning." Taking my hand, she led me to the bedroom. "I'm sorry I can't make love to you tonight, Harry; it's too soon after the baby."

"You don't have to be sorry, sweetheart. Just being home with you and Susie is enough."

"I love you, Harry." She snuggled into me, exhaling slowly.

"I love you too, sweetheart." Lying in the darkness, I listened to the quiet breaths of my family. My thoughts turned to that afternoon and Mandy's accusations. *I can control myself. If anyone has a sex problem, it's Mandy; after all, what kind of woman offers herself up in that way?* Dismissing her accusations, I pulled my wife in close and drifted off to a blissful, contented sleep.

Susie's soft cry jolted me from a sound sleep.

"Susie?" Liz sounded exhausted.

"Let me, sweetheart." I gently got out of bed.

"Thank you, Harry." Yawning, she snuggled deeper into the blankets. "Her bottle's in the refrigerator. Just warm it a bit."

"Shhh, little lady." I lifted my daughter from her bassinet and quietly tiptoed from the bedroom. Taking the premade bottle from the refrigerator, I placed it inside the warmer. "Just a little longer, sweetheart," I said, hearing her cries. I tested the bottle and returned it to the warmer. I rocked back and forth to sooth her as her cries started to become inconsolable.

"Gonna take a sentimental journey," I softly began to sing. "Gonna set my heart at ease...gonna take a sentimental journey, to renew old memories." Her cries softened. "Do you like this song, my little dark-eyed Susie? Should this be our song?" Her cries turned to a sniffle.

"I'll take that as a yes, little lady." I took the bottle from its warmer. "Gonna take that sentimental journey, sentimental...journey...home." My voice became softer as I returned to the bedroom. "Sentimental...journey...home."

"Harry?" Liz, half asleep, looked around the bedroom in confusion.

"Everything's fine, Liz; go back to sleep." I took a seat in the rocker. "Would you like to hear a bedtime story, Susie? Yes? Well, let me see, my love." I gently rocked her back and forth in the darkness.

"There once was a gladiator king named Jack, who had a beautiful black-eyed princess daughter. Now, the princess was so beautiful that all the king's men vied for her hand in marriage, and all the women were envious of her beauty, except the queen. Elizabeth was beautiful in her own right, and the king loved her very, very much. Unfortunately, the king had several enemies that wanted to take over his kingdom, and his enemies knew there was only one way to destroy the gladiator king. The only weakness the king had was the love he felt for his family. He was indestructible on his own, but if they could harm his family, they could destroy him.

"What's that you ask, my little Susie? Was the king scared? *Never*! For when the king was just a prince, he was trained to fight. He was known throughout the land as the Southpaw gladiator—the gladiator that could take down any man with one swift swing of his fist."

"Thank you, God," Liz sighed contentedly. "Thank you for sending me Harry." She snuggled deeply into the covers.

October 1942: Love Letter to Liz

It's after midnight, and I'm having trouble sleeping once again, my love. I take your letter from under my pillow, along with the photograph of you and our beautiful baby daughter. I'm nostalgic looking at the photo, feeling it was a lifetime ago, yet knowing it was just last week that I was home and in your arms.

The island of Hawaii is slowly becoming beautiful again. There are only a few signs left of the devastation that occurred almost one year ago. The guys here are great. The only way it could be better is if my buddy Joe were among them. Speaking of Joe, I got a letter from him yesterday, postmarked Europe. All seems to be well with him. He's been promoted to staff sergeant. The army seems to agree with him. Well, my love, I'm going to try and get some shuteye; reveille comes early. I kiss your photo every night and count the days until I can return to you.

Your loving husband, Harry

September 1943

Dearest Harry,

I miss you so much, my love; my heart aches. Susie loved the birthday card you sent of the little girl holding up her finger, showing she was one year old today. In fact, our daughter held up her own little finger to Mandy before blowing out her one birthday candle. The time seems to go by so quickly, darling, in terms of our daughter growing up, yet it moves ever so slowly in waiting for your return.

I foolishly watched the door today, my love, in hopes that you would surprise me with your presence, the same way you did a year ago today when our little girl was born, but to no avail. I think our daughter sensed my sadness, because she did the most incredible thing, Harry—she took her first steps. She walked three steps over to your photograph before falling on her little bottom. "Da-Da," she said, pointing to your photograph. It brought tears to my eyes, Harry; somehow she knows the man in the photograph is her father.

I've enclosed a recent photo of your daughter, and I'm sending you a piece of birthday cake. The cake is probably a foolish gesture, but I'm a foolish girl in love when it comes to you, Harry. I long for your return and hope this godforsaken war will end soon.

Love always, Your loving wife

June 1944

Dearest Liz,

This war continues to drag on with no end in sight. I'm still here on the island using my expertise to make the parts our country so desperately needs. To hopefully, finally end this war. My mind tells me I am doing my part, doing what my country needs, but my heart tells me I'm a fighter. I belong out on the battlefield, not in a warehouse bunker. I know you want me safe, Liz, but I've requested a transfer to active duty, to fight side by side with my military brothers.

I received a letter from Joe the other day; he's not the same. There's something different in his words. The tone of his letters. This war needs to stop! It's gone on long enough. I walk the base and see the faces of the guys who have received their Dear John letters—their eyes, filled with loneliness, longing for their past, longing for the lives they once had, before this god-awful war started.

Regardless of what happens, Liz, wherever this war takes me, always know I love you more than anything in the world. I thank God every day for you and Susie. I trust in your love and know you will wait for my return.

Love always, forever yours, Harry

CHAPTER NINE

Pearl Harbor, August 1944

"Atten…hut!" Snapping to attention, I turned to see a sergeant major in full dress, his chest peppered with medals. He was leaning on a cane, and the right side of his face was slightly disfigured. "What do you call a guy who's a sight for sore eyes and makes you long for home?" I stood there in awe, speechless. "I asked you a question, soldier!" the officer bellowed.

"I'd call that guy Joe—my best friend."

"Right as always, soldier." He grinned wide, eyes smiling. "How ya doin', Southpaw?"

"Good, Joe." Feeling surreal, I anxiously came to his side. "How are you doing, buddy?"

"Good now." Both hands leaned on his cane. "I'm just passing through, Southpaw. I have about an hour before my flight leaves."

"They're sending you home, Joe?" I was unable to take my eyes from him.

"For a few weeks of R and R, Southpaw. Get my leg strong again. Get rid of this thing." He slightly lifted his cane from the floor. "Then I'm headed overseas to rejoin my company, the fighting Thirty-First! The body may be a little banged up, but it'll heal. Pappy's picking me up from the bus stop." He wobbled slightly.

"That's great, Joe." I grabbed a chair and pulled it close. "What's it been now…three years?"

"Pretty damn close, Southpaw." He took a seat, adjusting his bad leg.

"Impressive, buddy." I eyed the Silver Star and several other commendations pinned to Joe's chest.

"I owe a lot of them to you, Southpaw." He gave the medals a dismissive glance.

"To me, Joe?"

"I took your fighting techniques onto the battlefield. Assess your opponent, find his weakness, move in, and conquer. The battleground became my boxing ring, and these medals became my championship belt."

"I'm glad I could help, Joe, but you earned every one of those," I said, dismissing his praise. "Do you mind if I ask what happened?" I looked at his scars. "How you got hurt?"

"We had some new recruits come in, Southpaw—young kids, green kids, with no more fighting experience than what they got in boot camp. There was this redheaded kid, Tommy, barely eighteen. He reminded me of that kid Petey we met over at the Lincoln Civic Center a few years back. You remember Petey, don't ya…Mr. Southpaw Ssslugger."

"Sure, Joe, I remember Petey." Visions of the freckle-faced kid with no front teeth filled my mind.

"Well, the kid reminded me so much of our little friend Petey that I had no choice but to take him under my wing. We were on a recon mission, search and seizure. I told the kid to stay behind me, but he got nervous and came up quick. Just as his foot was about to come down on a land mine, I yelled for my men to take cover and pulled him behind what was left of an old, abandoned shelter. The edge of his boot must have caught the pin. He didn't take a direct hit, but the poor kid blew off a part of his foot, and as for me? Well, as you can see, I got the fallout."

"I'm sorry, Joe."

"Guess what else, Southpaw?" he continued, disregarding my sympathies. "The kid ended up being Pappy's nephew. What's the odds of that?"

"Nephew? I didn't even know Pappy had a nephew. How did you find out he was Pappy's nephew?"

"A few months after it happened, I got a letter from Pappy, thanking me for taking care of the kid. I wasn't surprised to get a letter. Pappy wrote every month or so encouraging me to fight the good fight, but this letter, Southpaw—this letter was different. He wrote that when life is at a point when it becomes fragile, and things can change on the turn of a dime, a man has to be able to say his feelings, without pride. He wanted me to know how proud and honored he was, the day I compared him to my father. Because only a good man could produce such a courageous son. You have no idea what reading those words meant to me, Southpaw."

"They're more than words, Joe; we're family. You, me, and Pappy."

"Thanks for that, Southpaw." His voice was soft and appreciative. "Well, enough about me. How are you and the beautiful Elizabeth doing?" He smiled wide.

"Well, I'm good, as you can see. Liz is fine, beautiful as ever. I'm a father now. I have a beautiful baby girl named Susie." I proudly showed her picture.

"A father, you say, and a girl to boot? Now that's karma, Southpaw. The gods are going to have fun with you, but congratulations." He chuckled.

"Thanks, Joe, but I'm not understanding why the thought of me being a father brings you such humor."

"Really, Southpaw? No idea why *you* having a daughter would be funny?"

As I thought about his words, they became clear. Both of us burst out in laughter as snippets of me raising a girl played out in our minds. Our laughter eventually subsided, returning us to the somber realities of our lives.

"I've never seen any action, Joe. I've been stationed here on the island my whole tour. They tell me my expertise is needed here—that the building and repair of wartime equipment is where my service is needed—but I'm a fighter, Joe. I believe my country would be better served if I were on the battlefield. I've put in for a transfer to active duty, several times, only to be denied."

"The fighting, Southpaw? The battlefield? It's not like the ring. It's ugly and unfair. I can't remember the last time I felt relaxed, let alone safe. Your mind, your body, it's always on constant alert. Always waiting for the next attack. Never knowing when or where it's going to come from. You have a wife and daughter, Southpaw; when this war is over, run home to them as fast as you can, and never look back. Once you have seen and felt the effects of war, you can never be the same...the eyes have seen too much."

"Excuse me, sergeant major? Your Jeep is here to take you to the airport."

"Thank you, Private; I'll be right out. Well, I guess this is it, Southpaw—for now anyway." Wobbling slightly on his cane, he extended his hand.

"For now, Joe. Take care of yourself." I accepted his hand, pulling him in close. "I love you, buddy; don't ever forget that." I felt his body weaken, relaxing into the safety of my arms, his brother's arms. I probably held him a little longer than I should have, but for some reason I couldn't let go.

"You've been a good friend, Southpaw." He regained his composure, standing tall. "My only true friend, and I thank you for that."

Proudly we walked side by side to his awaiting Jeep. Joe sensed my reluctance to say good-bye.

"Let's go, Private," Joe grumbled, head high, blinking back the tears.

"Take care, my brother. It's been an honor and a privilege." I stood in full salute till the Jeep taking my brother and best friend disappeared from sight.

Joe's Return: August 1944

Pappy waited a few feet away from a small crowd that had gathered at the Gladwin bus stop. There was a general feeling of excitement in the crowd eagerly waiting for the bus that would return their soldiers. The younger women giggled with anticipation, making last-minute touch-ups to their hair and makeup, in hopes of impressing their soldiers. The older women anxiously wrung their gloved hands, their eyes exuding worry along with unconditional love, awaiting the return of their soldier sons.

"I see it! I see the bus," one of the younger women squealed.

Smiles and light cheers erupted throughout the crowd. The bus came to a stop, exhaling the sound of reaching its destination. As the soldiers began to step from the bus, it was apparent that for a few of the boys, this would be their last stop...they would not be returning to the war. For others, it was a jubilation—a time to catch up with their loved ones before returning to their posts and once again defending our great country. Joe was the last soldier to step off the bus. It was immediately apparent that he fit neither category. His persona was of a seasoned soldier. A man who had been humbled by the horrors of war and carried the scars.

"Welcome home, Joe." Pappy gave the ole boxer's stare. His eyes looked at the cane before coming to rest on the scars covering the right side of Joe's face.

"It's good to be home, Pappy." Joe adjusted his uniform cap in an attempt to conceal his scars.

"I've got your room all ready, son. It isn't much, but—"

"I don't want to put you out, Pappy," Joe interrupted. "Just take me to a hotel. I'll be fine there."

"Nonsense, boy." He grabbed Joe's duffel bag. His eyes becoming misty, and he turned from Joe in embarrassment. "The car's this way."

Joe fell in step behind his honorary father. He sensed a different Pappy, a softer Pappy, as if the war had also taken its toll on him.

"You've got a lot of medals there, son." Pappy pulled into traffic. "The Silver Star." He nodded to the gold star with a superimposed silver star inside, hanging from a red, white, and blue striped ribbon. "Do you mind telling me?"

"My squad was being barraged by artillery." Joe's voice was grave. "Several of my men were wounded, some severely, lying out on the battlefield. The enemy had us pinned down. No way to get any medical help in. No way to safely pull them out. They said what I did was courageous, gallant—that I put myself in the line of fire, exposed myself to personal harm. But all I did was pull my wounded brothers to safety—nothing more."

"It was a noble thing to do, son."

"Maybe so, Pappy." Joe shifted uncomfortably, looking out the window, remaining silent the remainder of the ride home.

"We're here, son." Pappy turned off the ignition of his old blue pickup. "Let me get that," he said, grabbing Joe's duffel bag from the truck bed. "I thought you could just rest up for tonight, Joe. Tomorrow we'll head over to the gym. I've still got a few fighters this godforsaken war hasn't taken, but mostly the gym's filled with young boys looking for the guidance their fathers aren't here to give. I thought afterward, we could go over to the pub for lunch. Mick would love to see you." He set the duffel bag inside his guest room.

"Sounds good, Pappy." Joe looked around the room that would be his home for the next few weeks.

"There's fresh towels in the bathroom, son. Get some rest." Pappy quietly closed the door, feeling an overwhelming need to take care of Joe.

The Next Day

"How you feeling this morning, Joe?" Pappy looked up from his morning paper.

"I feel good, Pappy—a little unsettled. It took me a minute to realize where I was when I first woke up." He gave a hesitant smile. "Do you mind if I help myself to some coffee?"

"You take a seat, son, and let me get that for you." Pappy jumped up from the kitchen table.

"That's really not necessary, Pappy." Joe humbly took a seat. "I can get my own coffee."

"I know you can, boy. Cream? Sugar?" Pappy hovered over him.

"Black." Joe shifted uncomfortably.

"Hungry, son?" Pappy said, setting down a warm breakfast plate.

"Pappy, this really isn't necessary. I can take care of myself."

"I know you can, boy." He set down fresh silverware.

"Really, Pappy." A slight annoyance crept into Joe's voice. "I'm fine."

"I know you are, boy. Just trying to help out." He sliced off a pat of butter and spread it over Joe's toast. "Now eat up before it gets cold."

"Do you really want to help, Pappy?" Joe asked gravely.

"Sure I do." He hovered over Joe's shoulder.

"Then sit down, and quit coddling me!" Joe snapped. "Be yourself!"

"I don't coddle, boy! You're a guest in my home." Pappy took his seat and snapped open his paper. "When you're done, boy, rinse your dirty dishes, and stack them neatly in the sink!" He grumbled from behind his morning paper.

"Will do, Pappy," Joe said, grateful at the return of cantankerous, demanding ole Pappy, the man he had missed dearly and grown to love. "Hey, Pappy?" Joe said, talking between bites. "I was able to see Southpaw in Hawaii on my return to the States." Pappy turned back the edge of his paper, eyes filled with concern.

"How is Southpaw?"

"He's good, Pappy." There was a genuine tone of love in Joe's voice. "He's doing everything his country asks of him and more."

"He's a good man. You're both good men." Pappy refolded his morning paper. "Well, it looks like you haven't lost your appetite, son." He looked at the empty plate. "You ready to head over to the gym?"

"Ready, Pappy." Joe rinsed the dirty dishes, stacking them neatly in the sink.

"Then let's go, boy. Meet you in the car."

"Right behind you, Pappy." Joe reached for his cane and then stopped suddenly. The words of his doctor echoed in his ears. *Your leg is healed, soldier. You can put down the cane whenever you're ready.*

"Where's your cane, son?" Pappy looked at Joe, sliding into the front seat, shutting the truck door.

"In the trash, Pappy—where it belongs."

"Good for you, boy." Pappy shifted his truck into reverse, feeling more like himself than he had in a long time.

"I can't tell you how good it is to be home, Pappy. Everything's exactly the way I remember." Joe filled with excitement looking out the window. "There's Cunningham's Hardware...Dailey's Drugstore. Do they still have those great burgers, and is that little beauty Celeste still working behind the counter?" He smiled in reminiscence.

"Yes and yes." Pappy turned into the gym parking lot.

"And then there's O'Hare's." Joe said. Memories and snippets of yesteryear flooding his mind.

"You coming, boy?" said Pappy, pulling Joe from his nostalgia.

"Yeah, I'm comin', Pappy." Joe happily exited the truck and caught up with Pappy, feeling like a giddy schoolboy. The smells and sounds of O'Hare's flooded his senses. The stench of sweat filled his nostrils. The rhythmic, fluttering sound of someone pummeling a speed bag echoed in his ears. Trainers shouted direction and encouragement to their fighters sparring in the ring."God, I missed this place, Pappy." Joe scanned the gym, regaining a sense of himself.

"Well, don't just stand there, with your mouth watering. Get in there, and help these boys become fighters!"

"Sure thing, Pappy." Joe walked up to a young boy whose attempts to jump rope kept ending in failure. "What's your name, son?"

"Henry...Henry Hinterman," the boy stated proudly.

"Hinterman? By chance are you any relation to Will 'the Hit-Man' Hinterman?"

"He's my uncle," Henry declared.

"I know your uncle Will. He's a good man, but I'm curious, Henry; why aren't you training over at the Lincoln Center with the Hit-Man?"

"My mom won't let me ride my bike that far." He attempted the rope once again, moaning in frustration at his failure.

"You know, Henry, when I first started using the speed rope, I had a lot of trouble with it too. Do you mind?" Joe extended his hand.

"Nah." He handed Joe the rope.

"Now if I remember right, Henry, with the rope you need to find your rhythm, your natural rhythm. The wrists do all the work; your hands are just for control." Joe turned the rope slowly, testing his leg, falling into a slow two-legged rhythm. "You see, Henry? Rhythm—that's the key."

"Yeah." Henry nodded his head. "I think I do see."

"Good. Now you try." Joe handed Henry back the rope. "Keep a firm grip on the handles, Henry; use only your wrists."

"Like this?" Henry slowly fell into his own natural rhythm.

"Just like that, Henry. Now pick up your speed…faster…faster… you've got it, Henry!" Joe exclaimed. "Can you do one leg at a time?"

"I'll try." Henry quickly, easily switched to a one-legged jump. "What's a one-legged jump for?"

"The one-leg jump is for strength and balance, Henry. You catch on quick, kid."

"What's your name, Mister?" Henry slowed his speed, catching his breath.

"Joe, Joe Riley. Sorry about that, Henry; I guess I didn't introduce myself."

"No problem, Joe. I've been looking for a trainer, and you seem to know a little about the fight game. Is there anything else you can show me?"

"Well, what else would you like to see, Henry?" Joe straightened his shoulders.

"Anything, Joe. Everything."

"Well, let's take a look at your natural stance, Henry. This is mine." Joe took a fighting stance. "Now show me yours."

"How's this, Joe?" Henry quickly took a boxer's stance.

"Not bad, Henry. Throw a few shadow punches for me." Joe sensed a natural ability.

Henry threw a quick jab and a right combination.

"My dad showed me a few things before he joined the army. He said there might come a time when I'd have no choice but to fight, and he didn't want me to be afraid to answer its call."

"Your dad's right, Henry. Even if you never engage in a fight. A man should always know how to defend himself."

"I think you'll do, Joe. You can be my trainer." Henry sounded confident in his decision. "But I've got to go now." He looked at the clock. "My mom wants me home by twelve."

"Well, thanks for the job, Henry, and the vote of confidence. See you tomorrow?"

"Tomorrow, Joe." Henry ran for the door. "Bright and early."

"I'll be here, Henry—bright and early."

"I see you met Henry." Pappy joined Joe at the heavy bag. "His dad's overseas right now. His mother brought him in a few days ago. You know his uncle's the Hit-Man?"

"Yeah, I figured out the bloodline, but he seems like a good kid. Willing and determined…a little young?"

"He's eight and a half, almost nine, or so I was informed by young Henry. The kid just wouldn't take no for an answer, so I figured, what the hell? You about ready for some lunch, Joe? The gym always clears out about this time. The pub's just around the corner. We could walk?"

"Sounds good, Pappy. I'd love to see Mick." Falling in step with Pappy, Joe felt a calmness he hadn't felt in a long time.

"Hey, Mick! Got a surprise for ya." Pappy walked proudly into the pub, Joe by his side.

"Well, I'll be god damned. Joe, good to see you, son." Mick shook his hand, trying not to stare at his scars.

"What the hell?" a voice slurred from a few barstools down.

"Be quiet, Scooter," Mick chastised. "Mind your business. Joe, Pappy, take a seat. I'll draw you a couple drafts."

"Thanks, Mick." Pappy took the barstool between Joe and Scooter.

"Pretty slow today, Mick?" Joe looked around the empty, quiet pub.

"Been this way since the war started…all you young guys…pretty much nonexistent in this town."

"Hey, Mick, when you're done talking to Scarface, I'll take another." Scooter tapped his empty glass.

"You might want to mind yourself today, Scooter." Mick poured him another shot as light flooded the dim bar.

"What can I get you ladies?" Mick said, setting down two fresh coasters.

"I'll take a dirty martini," the redhead replied.

"Me too." The brunette glanced flirtatiously in Joe's direction.

"He might look pretty from that side, sweetheart, but from this side..." Scooter sadly shook his head. "Come on down here, sweetheart, and let ole Scooter take care of you." He tapped the seat next to him.

"No, thank you." The brunette snubbed him.

"Your loss, sweetheart." Scooter downed the last of his whiskey.

"Order me a sandwich, will you, Pappy, while I go wash up?" Joe got up from his barstool.

"Sure, Joe. I'll take care of it. You go on, son."

"Where you going, Scarface?" Scooter taunted. "How'd you get those scars anyway?" Joe walked past, ignoring him. "Hey, I'm talking to you, boy! Where's your manners?" He watched the restroom door swing shut.

"Where's his manners?" Pappy grumbled. "Scarface?" He snatched Scooter up from his barstool. "He's a goddamn war hero, you drunk son of a bitch."

"Don't hit me." Scooter's eyes filled with fear as he raised his hands in protection.

"You're not worth hitting." Pappy pushed scooter hard in his release. "Get the hell out of here, you worthless, sad sack of shit!"

"You gonna allow this, Mick?" Scooter picked himself up from the floor.

"I tried to warn you, Scooter."

"I said get the hell outta here!" Pappy stepped forward, threatening.

"Okay, okay. I'm going." Scooter pushed the pub door open. "This is no way to treat a customer, Mick."

"Sorry, ladies, Mick." Pappy returned to his stool.

"No apologies necessary, Pappy. What can I get you and Joe for lunch?"

"How's about a couple of Reuben sandwiches and couple orders of fries, Mick."

"Sure thing, Pappy."

"You take care of it, Pappy?" Joe said, returning to his barstool. "Get us some lunch ordered?"

"Yeah, I took care of it, son." Pappy took a big slug of draft.

"I thought you might." Joe took a big slug of his own.

The Following Week

"Hey, Joe." Henry whistled a happy tune coming into O'Hare's, an oversized pair of boxing gloves hanging from his shoulders.

"Hey, Henry. What you got hangin' there?"

"They're boxing gloves, Joe. My uncle Will gave them to me a few years back."

"Don't you think they might be a little big, Henry?"

Henry disregarded Joe's question, seemingly unaware. He pulled on the oversized gloves, tightening the strings with his teeth.

"Where should we start today, Joe?" He slapped the gloves together in anticipation.

"Well, Henry, seeing as you already have your gloves on, what do you say we start with the heavy bag? Show me a few jabs and a combination."

"Will do, Joe." Henry delivered the punches with the confidence of a warrior.

"That's not bad, Henry. I thought you might look like a sad sack…considering."

"It's the gloves, Joe." Henry admired the oversized heirlooms. "When my uncle Will gave them to me, he said they contained family strength and power and to put them on when I was ready. Big enough, strong enough, to wear them. What else do you want to see, Joe?" Henry took a fighting stance.

"How about I just hold the bag, Henry, and you show me your fighting style?"

"Sure, Joe, but you might want to hold on tight. This is the first time I've had the family gloves on, and I'm not sure just how much power and strength they have. I wouldn't want to hurt ya, Joe."

"Thanks for your concern, Henry." Joe tightened his grip.

"No problem, Joe." Henry delivered a solid left hook.

"You weren't kidding, Henry," said Joe, pretending to stumble from the impact.

"I tried to warn you, Joe. A fighter's blood runs through these veins." Henry continued to hit the heavy bag with all the power and strength he could muster.

"So you did, Henry." Joe was thoroughly enjoying his newfound little friend.

The Final Few Days

"Hey, Pappy," Henry sadly muttered, coming through the door of O'Hare's. "Is Joe around?" A melancholy look covered his face.

"He'll be here shortly, Henry. He had a few things to take care of this morning. Where's your gloves, son?"

"In my locker, Pappy." Henry's voice was solemn.

"Well, get 'em on, boy! Your trainer will be here shortly." Henry glumly walked to his locker, retrieved his gloves, and reluctantly put them on. "Get over to the heavy bag, Henry. Joe's not gonna like it if you lollygag today." Henry slowly stepped to the bag, throwing halfhearted punches.

"Got my orders, Pappy." Joe announced coming through the doors of O'Hare's. "I board the bus Monday, for Fort Bragg. Then I'll be rejoining my unit overseas. Somewhere in Europe."

"Good." Pappy sounded apprehensive. "That's good, Joe."

"We knew this was temporary, Pappy—that my leave would end and my country would call upon me once again. Everything's going to be okay, Pappy; you'll see."

"I know. I know, Joe." Pappy solemnly shook his head in understanding. "There's something up with Henry today," he said, getting back to the business at hand. "He seems out of sorts, and he's carrying a nice shiner." Both looked at Henry halfheartedly hitting the heavy bag, with one weak punch after another.

"Why you hittin' that heavy bag like a sad sack, Henry?" Joe came to his side. "You're not a slacker, Henry. Hit that bag like you mean it!"

"I have to quit training, Joe," Henry sadly muttered. "School starts in a few days, and my mom said there would be no time for boxing." He threw another weak punch. "Plus, she's mad at me for getting into a fight." He pointed to the shiner below his left eye. "She doesn't understand, Joe. I tried to tell her it's in my blood. That boxing is my destiny. She told me to find a new destiny, Joe. Can you believe it!" Sadness filled his eyes.

"How did you get that shiner, Henry?" Joe lifted his chin to get a good look. His cornerman skills taking over, he assessed that it was no more than just that: a black eye.

"Just helpin' out a buddy, Joe." Henry threw another punch. "It was two against one. I had no choice but to help."

"You're a good man, Henry, but there'll be no training today." Joe pulled the oversized gloves from Henry's hands.

"No training, Joe?"

"Come on, Henry. Let's take a walk."

"Where to?" Henry quickly fell in step beside him.

"To the pub for a couple of beers."

"But Joe, I'm not nearly old enough to drink beer."

"I know, Henry." Joe looked down with a warm smile at the young innocent face. "A root beer for you and a draft for me."

"Okay, Joe." Henry smiled, walking proudly next to Joe.

"A couple of beers, Mick." Joe and Henry took their seats at the bar. "A root beer for my friend Henry, and I'll take a draft."

"Right away, Joe." Mick grabbed two chilled glass from the cooler.

"I've never been in a pub before, Joe." Henry timidly looked around the bar.

"There's a first time for everything, Henry," Joe said.

"What's wrong with him, Joe?" Henry nodded to a man passed out at the end of the bar.

"That, Henry, is a man who never found his destiny—his true destiny." Joe looked at Scooter, eyes filled with empathy. "You see, Henry, sometimes what we think is our destiny is really just an opportunity to prepare for our real, true destiny."

"What do you mean, Joe?" Henry took a slug of root beer.

"Well, Henry, take your uncle Will, for example. He believed his destiny was to be a professional fighter, and he went after that destiny with a vengeance, fulfilling the call. In fact, your uncle Will was a contender for the title, but what happened? A little fender bender changed his destiny. Something most people would've walked away from altered your uncle Will's life. Now he's a mentor for young boys who need help finding their purpose, their destiny. You see, Henry, I believe your uncle Will's true purpose was to be a mentor, but he needed the skills of a boxer to fulfill his true destiny. Just like I believe my purpose, my destiny—for now, anyway—is to be a soldier."

"So you think I might be the same, Joe? That boxing isn't my true purpose?" Scratching his head, Henry contemplated Joe's words. "It's just something to lead me to my real destiny?"

"I believe it's possible, Henry. I also believe if you don't move on when life's purpose calls, your destiny will leave you behind, and you'll end up like Scooter down there—lost, never to find or fulfill your true purpose."

"So you think it's time for me to move on, Joe?" Henry's voice was solemn.

"Maybe, Henry; besides, my time here, for now, is done."

"You're leaving, Joe?"

"I'm afraid so, Henry. I board the bus Monday, Memorial Day, and you start school Tuesday. So you see, it all works out; we've fulfilled our time together, and now it's time to move on."

"I see, Joe, but I'm really gonna miss you." Sadly, Henry slurped down the last of his root beer. "And O'Hare's."

"I'm gonna miss you too, Henry, but who knows? Maybe we'll meet again. Another root beer, Henry?"

"Sure, Joe," Henry said sadly.

"Hey, Mick, another round for me and my friend," said Joe, feeling his own sense of sadness.

Monday…Memorial Day

A small, somber crowd gathered at the Gladwin bus stop to say good-bye to their soldiers. Mothers hugged their soldier sons ever so tightly, saying their final good-byes. Fathers stood proud, giving words of encouragement, keeping their fears to themselves. Young women whispered their promises to wait. Soldiers vowed to return. Joe stood tall among them in full dress, belonging to neither category.

"You have everything you need, son?" Pappy looked at Joe through proud, sad eyes.

"Yep, all set. I guess this is good-bye, Pappy." Joe extended his hand. "Thanks for everything."

"You're welcome, son." Pappy pulled him in close for a manly hug. "You take care of yourself over there, and remember you have a home to come back to when this godforsaken war is over."

"Thanks, Pappy, that means a lot." Joe's eyes were as misty as Pappy's.

"Joe? Hey, Joe?" a young voice called out. "Wait!"

"It's Henry!" said Pappy, seeing young Henry off in the distance pedaling his bike as fast as his legs would move.

"Joe?" Henry was breathless. "I came to say good-bye."

"You rode your bike all this way, Henry?" Joe's voice was stern, yet he was unable to contain his smile. "Does your mother know?"

"She knows, Joe." Henry assured dropping his bike.

"Glad you could make it, boy." Pappy smiled.

"Wow!" Henry looked at the medals covering Joe's chest. "Being a soldier really is your destiny."

"It is for now, Henry." Joe looked down at the young boy he'd come to care for.

"What's that one for, Joe?" Henry pointed to a green ribbon with a gold embossed eagle hanging from it.

"This one, Henry?" Joe unpinned the medal from his chest. "This is commendation medal. It's given for good conduct. For always delivering—rising above and beyond the call." He pinned the medal to Henry's tank top, causing the neckline to droop from its weight.

"Good conduct, Joe?" Henry eyed the medal hanging from his chest.

"That's right, Henry. You always gave a hundred percent. Never sad sacked. Even your judgment of me was based on my actions, not the scars I carry on my face. That makes you a stand-up guy in my book, Henry." Joe stood tall, giving a salute.

"I'll wear it proud, Joe," Henry said, looking at his scars.

"I got these scars, Henry, the same way you got your shiner—just helpin' out a buddy."

"I knew it would be something like that, Joe." Henry smiled proudly.

"Well, Henry, I guess this is good-bye for now." Joe took his place in line.

"See you next summer, Joe?" Henry asked, his voice hopeful.

"Maybe, Henry. We'll just have to see where life leads." Joe boarded the bus.

"Good-bye, Joe," Henry called out, standing tall in salute. Joe nodded to him through the bus window before looking straight ahead, eyes misting. Pappy put his thick arm around young Henry. Both watched as the bus exhaled a puff of smoke, rounded the corner, and disappeared from sight.

"Let's go, Henry." Pappy was somber, picking up Henry's bike with one hand.

"I'm feelin' like a sad sack today, Pappy." Henry sluggishly walked toward Pappy's old blue pickup. "I know that would disappoint Joe." He kicked a small stone in depression.

"You're not a sad sack, Henry. You're just a guy who's gonna miss his friend." Pappy put his bike inside the truck bed. "What do you say we go by the pub and get a couple of beers? I know I could use one."

"Sure, Pappy," Henry said, soberly closing the truck door. "You do know, Pappy, I'm not old enough to drink beer?" His voice was sad and somber.

"I know, Henry. A root beer for you and a draft for me." Pappy turned over the ignition and shifted the truck gears. Henry and Pappy rode in silence, missing their friend.

CHAPTER TEN

Pearl Harbor, September 1944

Dear Liz,

I have finally gotten what I've longed for since this dreadful war started. My request for transfer has been granted. I received my orders just a few hours ago, my love. I'm being sent overseas, probably somewhere in Europe.

Please understand, Liz; I had no choice but to request the transfer. I'm a fighter, Liz. The battlefield is where I belong, not in some warehouse bunker. Always remember, I love you and Susie more than anything in this world, and I promise to return to you both. Take care, my love. Give Susie a kiss for me.

Forever yours, Harry

Dear Harry,

I just received your letter announcing your deployment. I'm so mad at you right now I can hardly write. How could you, Harry? How could you do this to me and Susie? How could you do this to us? I'm desperately trying to understand why you would purposely put yourself in harm's way. How will I write to you, Harry? Where will I send the letters? I love you, Harry, but I just don't understand. Why?

Your very upset wife, Liz

"Mandy, will you please mail this for me on your way to work today? It's a letter to Harry."

"Sure, Liz." Mandy's voice was hesitant. "Has something happened? You seem upset."

"My foolish husband is being sent overseas, and by his own doing," Liz stammered. "That letter is going to let him know exactly how I feel about what he's done!"

"Liz?" Mandy pulled at the seal of the envelope.

"That's private, Mandy!" Liz grabbed for the letter. Mandy pulled it from her.

"You can't send this, Liz," Mandy quickly scanned the letter. "What if this is the last letter your husband ever reads? Are these really the last words you want him to hear?"

"Yes…no…I don't know. I'm just so scared, Mandy." Her eyes filled with tears "When is this dreadful war going to end?"

"I don't know, Liz, but you have to be strong now. For your husband. For your family. Now sit down, and write another letter," she commanded. "Tell him how much you miss and love him. Tell him how much his daughter is looking forward to meeting her daddy. Tell him you'll be waiting with open arms for his return. That is what's going to get your husband through this terrible war and back to you. Now dry your tears, and write another letter, Liz." Crumpling the letter, Mandy threw it into the wastebasket.

Liz took out a fresh piece of stationery from the desk, misting it with perfume.

"Dear Harry." She sniffled. "I love you more than words can say, and count the days until you return…"

"That's more like it, Liz," said Mandy, looking over her shoulder.

"Let's go, soldier! Get on the truck," Captain Freeman growled. "Have you been on the island so long you've gotten soft, soldier?"

"No, sir." I jumped into the back of the army truck.

"Let's go!" Captain Freeman commanded, pounding the tailgate. The army truck jumped into gear as ordered. Soldiers were sitting straight and silent, moving only to the beat of the pavement as they were bumped and jostled inside the truck on their short ride to the transport ship.

"We're here, boys," the captain announced, pushing down the tailgate. "Get aboard, men, get your gear stowed, and make yourself comfortable, ladies. It's gonna be a long, bumpy, rough ride."

Grabbing my gear, I took my place in line to board. I watched as one army truck after another unloaded soldiers. All were here to board the *Bismarck,* a transport ship known for taking men overseas to far-off destinations. It took several hours for all to get boarded and the gear stowed, but finally we were underway, and I couldn't help feeling eager to finally be joining this war.

"A letter from your girl?" a soldier seated across from me inquired.

"My wife." I gave a wave of my left hand.

"You might want to treasure that." He nodded to the letter. "I got a feelin' wherever we end up, they won't be delivering mail."

"That's okay; this letter has everything I need." Inhaling its aroma, I tucked it safely inside my shirt. "Harry, Harry Decker." I extended my hand. "You got a girl, soldier?"

"Had one when I joined, but I got my Dear John about a year in...Francis O'Sullivan." He returned my handshake. "But my friends call me Sully."

"Irish?"

"Born and bred." He kissed the shamrock that hung from his neck.

"Get some shut-eye, soldiers; you're going to need it," the captain barked snuggling into his own corner.

"Yes, sir." Settling in, I said a quick prayer for protection and guidance. I closed my tired, excited eyes and rested my hand atop Liz's letter safely tucked inside my shirt, allowing the waves of the transport ship to rock me into a deep, blissful sleep.

November 1944

Dear Liz,

We've walked now for days; our objective is to meet up with the Seventh Army, the Lucky Seven, in the town of Sicily. Most of the guys in my division are like me, new to the fighting, with the exception of Francis O'Sullivan, Sully. We met onboard the transport ship and had an instant bond. I'm not surprised, for Sully is Irish, born and bred, as he's proud to say—the same as Pappy and Joe.

I'm exhausted, Liz, but I feel more alive than I have since this war started. I read your letter nightly, inhaling its sweet perfume before tucking it inside my shirt next to my heart. It helps me sleep, my love. Thank you, Liz, for understanding, for being my wife, for making me a father, for just loving me. Your love sustains me when I'm tired and weary.

Good night, my love.
Your loving husband

"Wake up, ladies…we're moving out!" the captain demanded walking through the cluster of exhausted soldiers sleeping on the ground. The rustling sounds of fatigued soldiers donning their helmets and grabbing their knapsacks and rifles filled the air.

"How close are we, Sully?" I asked, stepping in line with him.

"By my estimations?" Sully looked at his worn, torn map. "We're about four klicks out, Decker. Four klicks away from hot coffee, warm food, and if we're lucky, a few friendly ladies looking to accommodate a soldier." He smiled contentedly. "Unless the Seventh has worn them out. Those greedy sons of bitches."

"Not interested in the ladies, Sully; I'm a married man, remember? Got a beautiful woman waiting for me at home. But the hot coffee and warm food…" I rubbed my hands in anticipation.

"I remember, Decker, but we're at war. A soldier needs to stay sharp out here. Having our manly needs taken care of every now and again? Absolutely necessary. No different than food, water, or sleep. All equally necessary."

"I understand the need and desire, Sully, but you're a free man. Not bogged down with the rules of matrimony. Besides, I have Rosie Palmer and her five sisters taking care of me." I wiggled the fingers of my right hand.

"Rosie's okay in a pinch, Decker, but there's nothing like the flesh of a real woman. Besides, married rules don't apply out here. Getting your needs taken care of isn't much more than a business transaction. A little bit of sweet talk. Maybe a chocolate bar. A silk pair of nylons—if you're holdin'." He tapped his pack with an insinuating smile.

"Sweet talk I've got, Sully. Always had the charm. But the chocolate bars and silk nylons? Fresh out."

"Lucky you have Rosie and her sisters then, Decker, because pure charm won't even get you a hand job out here." He picked up the pace, seeing the town of Sicily off in the distance.

"Fall out, men. Coffee and warm chow in the canteen," Captain Freeman bellowed, making his way to the officer's bunker to check in with the Seventh.

"What are those soldiers doing, Sully?" I nodded to two men cowered in a corner. One was dictating, the other taking notes. "William Stevens...private...Robert Washington...private second class."

"Those poor bastards, Decker." Sully nodded to the men in empathy. "They have the unfortunate job of recording our fallen brothers."

As we stepped inside the canteen, the aroma of hot coffee and warm food made my mouth water. Living on cold canned rations can take its toll. Grabbing a plate and filling it with warm beans and rice, I was unable to shake the images of the two soldiers outside the tent huddled in the corner. "Mind if we sit outside, Sully?"

"Makes no difference to me, Decker—for now." He eyed the women flirtatiously working the tent. We took our seats across from the unfortunate soldiers wiping blood from the dog tags so as to clearly read the imprinted names.

"Tags from the Thirty-First." An incoming soldier tossed the two men a fresh bag.

"Just what we need." The soldier giving dictation moaned, opening the drawstring bag. "Mark Conner, private. Martin Sheers, private first class. Harold Daugherty, private. Joseph Riley, sergeant major." The words echoed in my ears, causing my mind, body, and heart to ache. "Ryan Bennet, private."

"Wait a minute. Wait a minute," my voice demanded as I came to my feet. "What name did you say?"

"Ryan Bennet?" The dictating soldier looked at me. "Do you know him?"

"No!" I stammered dismissively. "The name before Bennet! What was the name before?"

"Joseph Riley?"

"Do you know the guy, Decker?" Sully coming to my side. "He a friend of yours?"

"More than a friend, Sully. There has to be some kind of mistake. Let me see those tags." I snatched them from the dictating soldier. "Joseph Riley, sergeant major." My body slumped. Visions of my cornerman, wingman, best friend, and brother flashed through my memory.

"Sorry, buddy." The soldier took another dog tag from the bag. "James Monroe, private second class."

"Sorry, Decker." Sully uttered.

"Me too." I felt a deep sense of sadness.

"Here, these should get you a nice one." Sully took the silk nylons from his pack. "Take 'em, Decker. It'll make you feel alive again." He pushed them into my hand. I nodded my head in dazed, disbelief and walked into the canteen feeling surreal, scanning the accommodating women. Looking for one who most reminded me of Liz, I selected a shapely brunette seated in the corner.

February 1945

Dear Pappy,

This is the saddest letter I ever had to write. Your son, my brother and best friend was killed last week serving his country. I won't go into the details of his death, because it is unimportant and will not change the fact that we have lost our Joe. I prefer to remember how he lived; he was a great cornerman before becoming a noble and courageous soldier.

His remains are being sent back to Gladwin, to be buried in the veterans' cemetery, as his final wish was to return home. I have enclosed Joe's Silver Star and a letter addressed to you, which were found among his personal possessions.

Take care, Pappy...Southpaw

"Joe?" Pappy sadly sighed, turning the letter back and forth in his hand. He was curious as to what it contained, yet knew it would be Joe's last letter. Preparing himself, he took a quick shot of whiskey and opened Joe's final letter with a quivering hand.

Dear Pappy,

I have never been good at telling people how I feel. Somehow, even though I know it's impossible, I feel it's a trait I've inherited from you. So please, let my actions speak in place of my words. May I present to you the Silver Star, my honorary father, as a small token of my gratitude for being chosen to be your honorary son.

Love, your son, Joe

"The honor was all mine, son." Pappy proudly pinned the medal to his chest, eyes misting. "Damn allergies." He took his kerchief from his back pocket and dabbed his tear-filled eyes. Regaining his composure, he retrieved the silver keepsake box containing all of Joe's letters from its place of safety inside his desk drawer. "I hope you know you were loved, son." He placed Joe's final letter inside the silver box and poured himself another shot of whiskey.

"To you, my son." Holding his glass high, he quickly took the shot. Consumed with loss and grief, he took a seat slowly he rocked back and forth, hugging the medal to his chest, consoling himself as well as his son. His eyes welled with tears, and for the first time he didn't blame his allergies, openly grieving for the loss of Joe.

March 1945

"I'm home, Mom," Henry bellowed, coming through the front door.

"How was school today, Henry?"

"It was okay." Henry made a beeline to the cookie jar and poured himself a big glass of milk. His eyes came to rest on the Gladwin newspaper laid out on the kitchen table. "Hometown Hero Laid to Rest," Henry read from its front page, immediately recognizing the soldier in full dress, chest laden with medals. "Joe?" Henry sadly picked up the paper in disbelief, reading the attached article.

> Joseph Riley, Silver Star recipient, was laid to rest this morning at the Gladwin veterans' cemetery. There was a short memorial service and a twenty-one-gun salute in honor of the young war hero. Prior to his honorable war service, he was active in the boxing world as cornerman/assistant trainer to the great Jack Collins, "the Southpaw Slugger," who is currently serving in our military.

"Veterans' cemetery?" Visions of the old cemetery on Catkin's Road flooded young Henry's mind. Leaving his cookies and milk behind, he quickly changed into his blue Sunday suit, pinning the commendation medal to his breast pocket. He ran to the bathroom, grabbed the Brylcreem from the vanity, and squeezed out a handful, plastering his hair in a desperate attempt to tame his cowlick.

"I'm leaving, Mom." Henry slammed the front door, jumped on his bike, and pedaled toward the old cemetery, cowlick waving in the wind.

Entering the hallowed gates, Henry slowed his bike, overwhelmed by the number of white crosses peppering the holy ground. Off in the distance, he saw a man kneeling before one of the white crosses, slump shouldered. Henry slowly, carefully, respectfully walked through the sacred grounds, quietly coming to rest by Pappy's side.

"Henry?" Pappy stuttered, quickly wiping the tears from his face.

"So it's true?" Henry looked at the white cross. "Sergeant Major Joseph Riley" was etched in stone.

"Yeah…it's true." Pappy softly touched the engraved cross, his eyes misting once again. "I'm sorry, Henry. I'm acting like a sad sack today." He dropped his hand from the cross in misery.

"You're not a sad sack, Pappy. You're just a guy who's gonna miss his friend." Henry put his small arm around Pappy's wide shoulders. "I'm gonna miss him too, Pappy." Unpinning the commendation medal, he gently set it on the white cross.

"What are you doing, boy?" Pappy stammered. "That's your medal. Joe gave you that medal."

"I know, Pappy." Henry's eyes were misting. "But it's Joe's medal, and under the circumstances…"

"Under no circumstances." Pappy seized the medal. "Joe wanted you to have it." He repined the medal to Henry's breast pocket. "He recognized you to be a man of honor. Someone who rises above. Now it's your duty not to disappoint him." He gave the ole boxer's stare.

"I won't, Pappy. I won't disappoint him." Henry stood tall, wiping the mist from his eyes.

"I know you won't, boy." Pappy got to his feet. "What you say we go over to the pub, Henry, and get a couple of beers in honor of Joe?"

"Sure, Pappy." Henry looked at the white cross, whispering his good-bye.

"You ready, Henry?" Pappy turned to leave.

"Yeah, I'm ready." He stepped in line with Pappy's stride. "You do know I'm still not old enough to drink beer, don't you, Pappy? I'm nine and a half now, but still not nearly old enough."

"I know, Henry. A root beer for you and a draft for me." He tossed Henry's bike in the back of his old blue Chevy pickup. "Hop in, Henry."

"Do you think Joe dying in the war was his destiny, Pappy?" Henry somberly closed the Chevy's door.

"I don't know, Henry, but I do believe a man chooses how he dies. Joe would've chosen to die nobly and with honor. So maybe dying for his country was Joe's fate."

"I think you're right, Pappy." Henry nostalgically touched his commendation medal.

The Pub

"Hey, Pappy, Henry," Mick called out from behind the bar with a welcoming nod. "What can I get you boys today?" He set down two fresh coasters.

"A draft for me and root beer for Henry." Pappy glanced at Scooter seated at the end of the bar. "I'll be right back, Henry. Need to use the restroom."

"Okay, Pappy." Henry took his seat at the bar.

"What you all dressed up for, boy?" Scooter slurred. "Is that your Sunday suit? Don't you know it's Tuesday, boy?" Scooter snickered.

"I know," Henry mumbled.

"And your hair, boy!" Scooter snorted. "Do you know you got a piece sticking straight up? Whoop!" Scooter tugged on a piece of his own hair, indicating a cowlick. Henry felt the top of his head, desperately trying to flatten the protruding hairs.

"Leave the boy alone, Scooter." Mick refilled Scooter's shot glass.

"I'm just talkin' to the boy, Mick; ain't no crime in that. So tell me, boy, what you all dressed up for?"

"I went to my friend Joe's funeral today," Henry said.

"Joe?" Scooter looked at Henry through glazed eyes. "You mean ole Scarface?"

"Don't call him that." Henry shifted uncomfortably.

"So Scarface didn't make it back." Scooter wobbled on his barstool. "Mick, bring me another shot so I can toast ole Scarface." He tapped his empty glass on the bar.

"I said," Henry repeated, giving him a stern look, "don't call him that!"

"Scarface, Scarface, Scarface," Scooter slurred disrespectfully.

Feeling the weight of the medal, Henry looked at his refection in the bar mirror. Visions of Joe flashed through his memories, and his father's words echoed in his ears: *A man never looks for a fight, son, but he must never back down when he hears its call.* Standing tall, Henry bravely, timidly walked toward Scooter. "I said," He uttered through clenched teeth, raising his fists, taking a boxer's stance, "*don't call him that*! Call him by his name! Call him Joe!"

"Or what?" Scooter snickered. "You gonna fight me, boy?"

"If I have to." Henry nervously readjusted his stance. Scooter caught a glimpse of Pappy's disgruntled face behind him.

"Calm down, boy. There's no need to fight…to Joe!" Scooter respectfully lifted his glass.

"Everything okay out here, Henry?" Pappy took his seat at the bar.

"Everything's fine, Pappy." Henry dropped his fists, returning to his stool.

"You wear that medal proud, son…to Joe." Pappy raised his glass.

"To Joe." Henry respectfully raised his root beer, taking a big gulp.

CHAPTER ELEVEN

August 27, 1945

"It's been almost four years, my love." Liz refolded the last letter and tucked it inside her apron pocket. Shaking her head, clearing her thoughts, she returned to the chores of the day. Turning up the radio, she sang along with Doris Day's "Secret Love" as she folded her freshly dried laundry.

"We have breaking news." The radio crackled, stopping Liz midsentence in her sing-along. "Just in from Washington: a nuclear bomb, code name 'Little Boy,' carried by the US aircraft the *Enola Gay*, was dropped on the city of Hiroshima, Japan, on August sixth. A second bomb named 'Fat Man' was dropped August ninth on the city of Nagasaki, also in Japan. Due to the intensity and devastation of these two bombs...Japan has just announced their surrender!"

"Oh my God!" Liz screamed, dropping her freshly folded laundry.

"What is it, Liz?" Mandy ran to the laundry room, Susie in tow.

"Why are you screaming, Mommy?" Susie chimed in.

"The Japanese have surrendered, Mandy. The war is over!"

"Oh, my God," Mandy squealed, eyes wide in exhilaration.

"Your daddy is coming home, Susie." Liz picked up her daughter, giving her a quick spin. Susie hugged her mother's neck tightly. Both cheered and danced in delight.

"Shhh, you two…quiet!" Mandy waved her hand to silence them, turning up the radio.

"There are a few political amendments that need to be done between our countries, but our servicemen are coming home! The war is unofficially over!" The sound of sirens began to blare; people rejoiced in the streets in celebration of America's victory. On September 2, six days after the Japanese surrendered, an official instrument of surrender was signed, and the war was officially over.

October 1945

"Which one, Mandy?" Liz swished two dresses still on hangers back and forth in front of her. "The blue or the pink?" Mandy looked from one to the other.

"They're both pretty, Liz."

"You're not helping, Mandy." Liz dismissed both dresses, selecting two more from the pile.

"Which one? The purple or the turquoise?"

"I like this one, Mommy." Susie picked the famous emerald dress from the pile on the bed.

"Like father, like daughter." Mandy gave her niece a quick hug.

"You two are not helping," Liz said, dismissing both the turquoise and the purple.

"Wear the emerald, Liz. Your daughter likes it, and if I remember correctly, your husband loved it. Besides, do you really think it matters what you're wearing? Jack, Harry, your husband…has missed the first four years of his daughter's life, and most of the beginning of your marriage. I don't think what you're wearing is going to be that important to him. Do you?"

"Probably not, Mandy. It's just that it's been so long since we've seen each other. I just want to look pretty for him."

"Then put on the emerald, Liz." Mandy took the nostalgic dress from the pile.

"Can I wear my pink dress, Mommy? I want to look pretty for Daddy too."

"Of course you can, Susie, but we've got to hurry," Liz said, taking the emerald dress from its hanger.

"Can I wear my gloves too, Mommy?" Susie pleaded.

"Yes, Susie. Now run and get dressed. Hurry, sweetheart; if we don't leave soon, we'll be late for the arrival of your daddy's bus." Liz turned to look at her reflection in the mirror. "I don't know, Mandy. Maybe this dress is a little too much for a Sunday afternoon," she said, smoothing the front of the famous emerald dress.

"There's no such thing as too much when you want to impress a man. The dress is beautiful, Liz, and you look beautiful in it. That's all that matters."

"How do I look, Mommy?" Susie gave a quick spin in her favorite pink dress, her hands adorned with pristine white gloves.

"You look beautiful, sweetheart."

"Absolutely beautiful," Mandy chimed in. "Now you two better get going." Liz started to return the unchosen dresses to their hangers.

"Leave those, Liz. I'll hang them back up. Now you and Susie go!"

"Thank you, Mandy." Liz gave her a quick hug, looking at the sea of discarded dresses.

"Go, Liz," Mandy stammered. "Go!"

"Good-bye, Aunt Mandy," Susie called out, taking her mother's hand.

"Good-bye, Susie." Mandy rehung one of the discarded dresses feeling bittersweet. Happy for Liz having her husband returned to her, safe and unharmed…happy for Susie getting the return of father she so longed for…yet, lonely for herself wondering when her day would come—if her day would come. Her thoughts turned to Joe and the sadness of him passing washed over her once again.

The Bus Stop

"Let's hurry, sweetheart." Liz took hold of Susie's hand, maneuvering their way through the anxious crowd waiting for the bus that would bring home their returning soldiers. Excitement and longing filled the air.

"We're here to pick up my daddy," Susie said, looking at an older woman standing just outside the crowd. "He's coming home today. From the war. He hasn't seen me since I was a baby. I'm a big girl now. I'm almost four." She held up four small gloved fingers.

"Well, I'm sure your daddy will be very happy to see you." The older woman softly smiled. "I'm here to meet my son. He is also returning from the war, and may I say you look very pretty in your pink dress."

"Thank you." Susie smiled proudly, smoothing the front of her pink dress with her gloved hand.

"Here it comes!" one of the younger girls squealed, seeing the bus round the corner.

"Your father is finally home," Liz murmured, giving Susie's hand a gentle squeeze.

The crowd stood in silent anticipation. The bus pulled alongside the curb, exhaling its arrival. One by one the passengers disembarked: Soldiers, sailors, airmen, and marines. Susie anxiously searched the faces of the disembarking soldiers, looking for the man in the photograph she knew to be her father.

"Hank!" a young girl squealed, running into the arms of her returning soldier.

"Bobby!" squealed another young girl, jumping into the arms of a broad-shouldered marine as he spun her around in delight.

"Stephan!" the older woman softly called out. Her soldier son stepped from the bus, his uniform sleeve pinned up, waving in the breeze.

"Mom." The young soldier sighed in relief.

"Welcome home, son." Her eyes welling with tears, she gave him a gentle hug. Susie watched intently as the woman took her one-armed son and protectively, proudly walked from the bus stop.

"Where's my daddy, Mommy?" Susie impatiently returned to the DE boarding soldiers.

"He'll be coming, sweetheart." Liz felt a tug to her heart as the last soldier, her soldier, stepped from the bus. "Harry?" she softly called.

"Liz, sweetheart." I took her into my arms. "I've missed you so much." Nuzzling her neck, I felt that familiar, wonderful comfort only Liz could bring, melting my heart.

"Have you missed me too, Daddy?" Feeling a tug on the bottom of my uniform jacket, I looked down into a pair of beautiful dark eyes, and my heart melted for the second time. "Do you know who I am, Daddy?"

"I would recognize those beautiful dark eyes anywhere." I scooped her up into my arms. "You're my little black-eyed Susie," I said, squeezing her tight.

"Daddy, you're crushing me." Susie giggled, smoothing the front of her dress like a proper little lady.

"May I say you look very pretty in your beautiful pink dress, sweetheart?"

"Thank you, Daddy. I wore it to look pretty for you. Mommy tried on a lot of dresses to look pretty for you too, Daddy."

"Susie Mae Decker!" Liz blushed.

"Well, you did, Mommy," Susie replied innocently.

"You've never looked more beautiful, Liz." I pulled her in close with my free arm.

"Thank you, Harry," she said, snuggling into me.

"Shall we go home?" I gave my girls a gentle hug. My heart filled with happiness and love.

"Yeah." Susie raised her little arms in cheer.

"Yes, Harry, let's go home." Liz gently exhaled.

The crowd slowly dispersed from the bus stop, grateful to have their husbands, sons, and fiancés home once again, regardless of the condition they were returned. The war was over, and America had triumphed. Life could begin once again.

My Return to Twelve Forty Leland Street

I awoke the next morning to the smell of fresh coffee and the light sounds of a radio playing off in the distance. "Daddy?" Susie gently knocking on the outside of the bedroom door. "Daddy?" A pair of beautiful dark eyes peeked around the door.

"Good morning, sweetheart." I sat up in bed. "Would you like to come in?" Slowly nodding her head, she cautiously tiptoed around the bedroom door and walked hesitantly toward my bed.

"I've never had a real daddy. Just one in a picture, but I think I'm really going to like it."

"Susie Mae Decker!" Liz scolded, coming into the bedroom. "What are you doing in here, young lady? Didn't I tell you to let your father sleep?"

"He was awake when I came in, Mommy." Susie batted her eyes innocently.

"Are you sure, young lady?" Liz gave her a stern look. Susie turned away from her gaze.

"I really was awake, Mommy." I Pulled my wife playfully onto the bed, and gave Susie a pardoning wink.

"All right," Liz playfully chuckled. "I can see how this is going to work. Come on, you two; breakfast is ready, and I hope you're hungry. We've got steak, eggs, and pancakes." She climbed off the bed.

"Good, because I'm starved." I patted my wife's behind. "How about you, little lady?" I asked, scooping up my daughter.

"I don't know, Daddy." Susie giggled. "What does starved mean?"

"It means you're really, really hungry, sweetheart." I gave her a happy peck on the cheek.

"Then I'm starved too, Daddy." Susie giggled contentedly, hugging my neck tight.

"Everything looks delicious, Liz." Dropping my daughter gently into her seat, I sat down to the small feast.

"I want everything Daddy's having." Susie scooted her chair closer to mine. "I'm starved."

"Steak, eggs, and pancakes it is for the little lady." I filled her plate, grateful to be home, grateful to be safely tucked inside Twelve Forty Leland Street. "I thought I might go by O'Hare's after breakfast, Liz, and see how ole Pappy's doing. Do you mind, sweetheart?"

"Not at all, Harry. I'm sure Pappy would love to see you. I phoned him once after receiving the news of Joe's death and asked if I could help with any of Joe's final arrangements. He told me that wouldn't be necessary. That he would be taking care of Joe. He sounded so sad and lost, Harry. I didn't realize Pappy and Joe had become so close."

"Joe and Pappy bonded during the war, Liz—we all did." Sadness consumed me. "Do you mind if we talk about something else? The thought of Joe just—"

"I'm sorry, Harry; of course we can." She gave my hand a gentle squeeze.

"Daddy, are you sad?" Susie's sweet, innocent little face peered into mine.

"Just a little, sweetheart."

"Why are you sad, Daddy?" She climbed onto my lap.

"I was just thinking about my friend Joe, sweetheart, and how much I'm going to miss him."

"Don't be sad, Daddy." Her voice was soft and comforting.

"I'll try, sweetheart." Susie slid off my lap. Within seconds, the sounds of "Sentimental Journey" echoed throughout the house.

"Daddy?" Susie returned to my lap. "Whenever I was sad and missing you, Mommy would play this song for me. She said wherever you were, no matter how far away, you would hear it and know I was thinking of you. Maybe your friend can hear it too, Daddy, and know you're thinking of him?"

"Thank you, sweetheart, but this is our song."

"Mommy said you should always share, Daddy." Lightly cupping my face inside her tiny little hands."Gonna take a senmenal jorney." She began to sing. The words were mispronounced, but they had never sounded sweeter. They brought me a sense of happiness, and filled me with nostalgia.

"Never thought my heart would be so yearnin'." She continued to serenade me, pulling on my heartstrings. "Gonna take a senmenal jorney…senmenal jorney home. You don't have to be sad anymore, Daddy. I sang real loud to make sure your friend could hear."

"Thank you, sweetheart." I Pulled her in close, inhaling her beautiful innocence.

"Mommy, can I go and play with my dolls now? I'm all finished with breakfast." She slid off my lap, her breakfast barely touched.

"Sure, sweetheart, go and play. You okay, Harry?" Liz took Susie's place on my lap.

"I'll be fine, Liz. Nothing a visit to Pappy won't fix. The old guy has always been able to put things in perspective for me."

"Take as much time as you need, Harry." She got up from my lap. "Your family will be here waiting for you, whenever you return."

"You have no idea, sweetheart, the comfort that brings," I said, giving her a grateful smile.

Pulling into O'Hare's parking lot, I was greeted by a big "SOLD" sign pasted to the side of the building. *There must be some kind of mistake.* My mind was spinning. *Pappy would never sell the gym.* Quickly exiting my car, feeling confused, I opened the doors of O'Hare's. The smells hit my nostrils, telling me I was home.

"Can I help you?" an unfamiliar voice called out. My eyes adjusted to the dimness of the gym.

"Yes, I'm looking for Pappy O'Hare." An unfamiliar face of a middle aged, dark haired man came into view. "The owner of this place."

"Mr. O'Hare is no longer the owner. He sold me the gym right after the war ended. My name is Dave Bradley." He extended his hand. "And you are?"

"An old friend of Pappy's." I returned his handshake. "Harry Decker."

"Well, Mr. Decker, we start demolition today and renovation at the end of the month. You're looking at the future Bradley Pharmacy and Soda Shoppe."

"O'Hare's gym…a drugstore, soda shop? I can't believe it."

"You can't believe it? My family has been after this property for years, but we could never get Mr. O'Hare to sell. He called a few months ago, out of the blue, and said, 'Make me an offer I can't refuse.' We drew up the papers a week later, and he handed me the keys, along with a letter. He said a guy named Southpaw would be by sometime and asked if I would give it to him, but the guy hasn't shown up yet." He shrugged his shoulders.

"That's me! I'm Southpaw! Harry Decker, a.k.a. Jack Collins, the Southpaw Slugger, or at least I used to be."

"Great." He seemed taken a little aback by my enthusiasm. "The letter is in my office, but it could take me a few minutes to find it; as you can see, things are a bit of a mess around here."

"Take your time, Mr. Bradley. Do you mind if I look around the place while you track it down?"

"Feel free, Mr. Decker." He walked toward Pappy's old office. "The demolition crew isn't due till eleven."

"Thanks." I looked around the place that held so many memories. Climbing into the ring, I did a quick boxer's dance, throwing a couple of combinations and a quick left hook as the memories came flooding back.

"Hey, Southpaw...Sanchez here thinks he can take you. What do you think about that, buddy?"

"Joe?" My eyes became moist.

"Let's go, Southpaw." Pappy's image stood outside the ring. *"Let's see what you've got."* My heart was consumed with sadness as the ghosts of O'Hare's made me yearn for the past.

"I found it, Mr. Decker." Dave interrupted my nostalgia. "It was under a pile of papers."

"Thank you." I climbed down from the ring, a little embarrassed.

"A lot of memories here for you, Mr. Decker?" He handed me the letter.

"More than memories, Mr. Bradley. This place was my life before the war. Mine, Pappy's, and Joe's." Slowly I looked around the gym that had meant so much to us all.

"Well, if there's nothing else I can help you with, Mr. Decker..." His voice was dismissive. "Demolition's here."

"No, nothing else, Mr. Bradley." Feeling my emotions begin to rise, I quickly headed for the exit doors.

"Okay, fellas, take it down." The words echoed in my ears, stopping me dead in my tracks. Closing my eyes, I inhaled deeply, savoring the smells I'd come to cherish. With the sounds of the ropes hitting the canvas floor, I pushed open the doors with an overwhelming sense of sadness and exited O'Hare's for the last time.

Sitting behind the wheel of my sedan, my heart ached as I stared at the unopened letter. "Southpaw" was written in Pappy's chicken scratch along its front. I was afraid to open it, afraid of the heartache it contained. The turmoil Pappy must have felt to sell his beloved gym. Taking a deep breath for courage, I opened Pappy's letter and slowly began to read.

Dear Southpaw,

If you are reading this letter, then my prayer has been answered. Welcome home, son. I'm sure the selling of O'Hare's has left you in a state of confusion.

"You got that right." Shaking my head in disbelief, I returned to the letter.

I've always lived by the rules of the ring, Southpaw: assess your opponent, find his weakness, move in and conquer. Living by this philosophy has always allowed me to handle whatever life threw my way—until now.

Life threw me up against an opponent I wasn't able to defeat, wasn't able to understand. No matter what I did. No matter what retaliation was used. My opponent refused to show weakness, continuing to take from me without warning or reason, crushing me in its wake. This unyielding opponent was the war...taking my boys from me...one never to return.

The pain I felt receiving your letter telling me of Joe's death was—well, let's just say my spirit died that day. Without you and Joe, the gym no longer held a place in my heart. It became just a building with too many memories. The war left me on the ropes, Southpaw; that's a bad place for a fighter to be, but I'm not ready to throw in the towel just yet—not quite ready to surrender.

I've decided to go to Europe and see some of the places Joe wrote me about in his letters. He talked of France, Italy, and Germany, each place containing its own beautiful splendor Some places torn by war, but their beauty was there all the same. He said he felt at peace in Europe, as if each country was doing its part, leading him to his destiny, helping him fulfill his purpose in this life. Who knows,

Southpaw, maybe I'll get lucky—find my peace, find my new purpose, find my new destiny. Never lose sight of what's important to you, Southpaw; take the time to enjoy your life and your family while you have it.

Take care of yourself, son.
Love, Pappy

"Godspeed, Pappy. I hope you find your peace, your happiness." Returning the letter to its envelope, I wondered how so many lives had been altered with just one event. As I put the car in reverse, my thoughts turned to Joe, and I knew what I needed to do. Where I needed to go. To find my peace. To put my mind at rest.

Walking slowly, cautiously, taking care to respect each grave, I read the perfectly lined military crosses in search of my best friend. General, sergeant, captain, corporal, private, all buried side by side. Taking care of each other, even in death.

Sergeant Major Joseph Riley…1919–1945, the marker read. It was a standard white cross given to all military personnel, but Pappy's son, my cornerman, deserved so much more. My thoughts went back to the last day I saw Joe, the turmoil he had felt. The agitated unrest that serving his country had brought him, but also the sense of privilege he had felt being called upon to protect it.

I fell to my knees, trying to understand the loss of my friend, my brother. It was there I saw it, surrounded by a patch of overgrown grass: a tribute to Joe's legacy and a recognition of a family. A pair of cement sculptured boxing gloves were firmly embedded in the earth. "Son" was engraved on the right glove, representing Pappy; "Brother" was engraved on the left, representing me. The gloves were intertwined, positioned in protection of Joe. Tears filled my eyes as I pulled the overgrown grass, thanking Pappy for allowing me, along with him, the privilege of protecting our honorary son and brother so he might rest unafraid, in peace.

Taking the scenic route home, I said good-bye to the past and contemplated my future, grateful to have one. I realized what gifts I had been given throughout my life, the gifts I still had: my beautiful wife, my sweet daughter, my life itself. I accelerated my sedan in a hurry to get home. In a hurry to start my life at Twelve Forty Leland Street.

CHAPTER TWELVE

August 1947

"Sorry I'm late, Liz." Mandy came through the front door. "You two ready to go school shopping?"

"Just about, Mandy." Liz sounded frustrated. "I can't find Susie's other shoe. How many mornings are we going to have to do this, young lady, before you start putting your Mary Janes by the back door?"

"I don't know, Mommy." Susie was sitting atop the dining-room table, swinging her shoeless foot.

"Is this the lost shoe, Liz?" Mandy waved the black Mary Jane.

"Yes," said Liz, relieved. "From now on, Susie, your shoes are to be put at the back door. Do you understand, young lady?"

"Yes, Mommy. I'm sorry, Mommy." She lightly hugged her mother's neck.

"I'm sorry too, sweetheart." Liz returned her hug.

"You okay, Liz? You seem a little tense today. Did you take your blood-pressure pill?"

"Yes, Mandy, I took my pill!"

"Then why the attitude? You're being short with me. You're mad at your daughter for misplacing her shoe. She's five, Liz; kids do things like that."

"I know; I'm sorry, Mandy…it's Harry. He just seems so unhappy lately. When he first came back from the war, everything was wonderful. He seemed so grateful every day to be home. To be with me and Susie. He threw himself into opening the tool-and-die shop, but now, lately…"

"Maybe he's just tired, Liz; opening a new business can be exhausting."

"It's more than that, Mandy," said Liz, shaking her head. "It's more than that; something's missing."

"Like what, Liz?"

"I don't know. I know he misses Joe and Pappy. He misses the fight game. He misses being Jack Collins. I don't know, Mandy; maybe it's not the boxing. All I know is Harry's unhappy. I want him happy, Mandy. How can I make my husband happy again?"

"You know what, Liz? I read in the paper the other day they're looking for trainers for the Gladwin Police Silver Gloves."

"Silver Gloves? What's that, Mandy?"

"It's an organization for young kids interested in becoming boxers. They have boxing tournaments and win trophies, belts, everything. Just like professionals, but they're not."

"Oh, Mandy, Harry would be a wonderful trainer." She sounded like all her problems had been solved.

"I'll bring the article over to you tomorrow, Liz. Can we enjoy our day now?" Mandy teased. "Now that we found a way to make Jack—Harry—your husband happy again."

"Yes, Mandy," said Liz, feeling a sense of relief.

"Okay then. Let's go get my niece some beautiful new school clothes!"

"Yeah," Susie squealed. "I want everything pink!"

September 1947: Susie's First Day of School

"I'm home, sweetheart," I said. "Sorry I'm late."

Susie greeted me at the front door. "I've got so many things to tell you about my first day at school, Daddy."

"In a minute, sweetheart." I gave her a quick pat on the head. "First let me go say hello to Mommy; then you can tell me all about your first day at school."

"Okay, Daddy." She followed on my heels into the kitchen.

"Harry, I really wish you would call when you're going to be late," Liz reprimanded. "I've been holding dinner. That's twice this week."

"I know, sweetheart; I'm sorry." I gave her an apologetic kiss.

"Now can I tell you about my school, Daddy?" Susie fidgeted in anticipation.

"Yes! Harry, please! Take your daughter into the other room. She's been waiting for you since she got home from school. Now both of you, shoo, get out of my kitchen so I can finish dinner."

"Come on, Daddy." Susie sighed, pulling me from the kitchen and leading me to the couch. "Miss Baker, that's my teacher, Daddy. She said we could draw a picture of anything we wanted, because it was the first day of school. My friend Emily drew a picture of her cat, Milo. She didn't do a very good job, Daddy." She shook her head sadly. "My friend Noah drew a picture of his dog, Frisco. He's got a *really* big dog, Daddy!" Her eyes grew wide. "My friend Huck..." Susie giggled.

"What did you say, sweetheart? Your friend who?"

"*Huck*! I thought his name was funny too, Daddy, but he's so nice." She smiled softly. "I think I like him the best, Daddy."

"What did you draw, sweetheart?" I realized if I didn't intervene, I was going to hear about every drawing in the class.

"Here it is, Daddy." She pulled it from behind her back. "Isn't it pretty? It's Twelve Forty Leland Street!"

"So it is, sweetheart." I chuckled at the realization that my daughter had picked up my habit of always referring to our home as Twelve Forty Leland Street. "I see some real talent here, Susie," I said, admiring the misshapen white cottage tucked securely behind a white picket fence, several pink circles representing the roses lining the driveway. "Where shall we hang up this great masterpiece?"

"Right here, Daddy." She pointed to the front door. "So everyone can see it when they walk by."

"The front door it is. So what do you think, sweetheart?" I stood back, admiring the masterpiece.

"Good, Daddy." She nodded her head in approval.

"That looks really pretty there, sweetheart. Now both of you come and sit down. Dinner's ready," said Liz, setting the roast on the dining-room table.

"Daddy will you read me a story tonight?" Susie said toying with her broccoli.

"Don't I read you a story every night, sweetheart?"

"There'll be no bedtime story tonight, Susie, unless you finish all your vegetables." Liz nodded to the untouched broccoli still on her plate.

"Do I have to, Daddy?" Susie batted her dark eyes.

"Harry?" Liz gave a stern look.

"Yes, sweetheart, I'm afraid so. No story unless you eat all your vegetables."

"Okay, Daddy." She took a bite of broccoli, swallowing as if it were poison.

"Have you thought anymore about the Silver Gloves, Harry?"

"I'm not a trainer, Liz; I'm a boxer."

"I know that, Harry, but how different can the two be? I'm sure the kids would be ecstatic to have the great Southpaw Slugger as a trainer. I know you miss the boxing world, even if you don't, and I know it's not the same without Pappy and Joe, but if you would just give it a chance, Harry." She lightly touched my hand.

"Maybe I will, Liz." I gave her an encouraging smile. "When things slow down at the shop."

"Whatever you feel is best, darling. Bath tonight, Susie. Finish up your vegetables if you want a story tonight."

"Okay, Mommy." Susie wrinkled her nose in disgust eyeing the last few pieces of broccoli. "Can we read *Cinderella* tonight, Daddy?"

"Not *Cinderella* again." I moaned in pain. "Wouldn't you like to hear a different story, sweetheart?"

"But it's my favorite, Daddy. I'm going meet a prince one day, live in a castle, and ride around in a pumpkin carriage. Do you think we could get some mice, Daddy, and turn them into coachmen?"

"Not on your life, young lady," Liz interjected. "There'll be no rodents running around in my house."

"But, Mommy, how can I have coachmen without mice?"

"There will be no mice in my house, Susie. Now finish your broccoli, or there will be no story either."

"Daddy?" Susie sighed in defeat.

"Sorry, sweetheart, I can't override your mother on this one."

"Let's go, Susie. Finish up." Liz took some of the dirty dishes into the kitchen.

"I'll take care of the dishes tonight, sweetheart." I stacked my plate atop Susie's, hiding the uneaten broccoli.

"Thanks, Daddy," Susie whispered, melting my heart.

"Okay then, young lady, let's go." Liz ordered. "Bath time."

"Can I have bubbles and bath toys tonight, Mommy?"

"Bubbles but no toys tonight, Susie. It's past your bedtime already."

"Okay, Mommy. I'll be quick, Daddy." Susie happily skipped toward the bathroom. Scraping the uneaten broccoli into the garbage guilt and shame consumed me as I reflected back on the events of the day.

"Liz," I moaned entering our bedroom. "How many times can a child listen to the same story. Every night it's '*Cinderella*, Daddy; read *Cinderella*!'"

"She does love her *Cinderella*." Liz smiled, looking at my reflection in her vanity mirror. "Is she asleep, darling?" She brushed her long, lush hair.

"Almost, sweetheart. She's waiting for you to come in and say good night." I muttered, gently moving her beautiful hair, I caressed the back of her neck with a kiss.

"You know, Harry, we're very lucky." She turned to me. "We have a lovely home, a beautiful daughter; your business is taking off. We have a very comfortable life. Everything you need for happiness is right here, darling, but all that doesn't seem to be enough for you. You don't seem happy, Harry."

"I'm happy, sweetheart."

"Mommy," Susie called out from her bedroom. "I'm waiting for my kiss good night."

"I'm coming, sweetheart," Liz softly called back. "Harry, promise me you'll go down to the center when things slow down and give the Silver Gloves a chance."

"Mommy...my kiss good night." Susie was getting impatient.

"On my way, sweetheart." Liz got up from the vanity. "Promise me, Harry. I want my husband happy again."

Nodding my head in promise, I looked at my reflection in the vanity mirror, feeling pangs of remorse. My wife was interpreting my guilty conscience as unhappiness and longing for the boxing world. In truth, without Pappy and Joe, I felt no desire for the fight game. Mandy had turned out to be right: my sexual demons had come to call, and I was powerless against them.

A Visit to Joe

Carrying a small American flag and flowers, I made my way to Joe's grave site. "Hey, buddy, sorry I'm a little late this year." I replaced the worn flag with a new one. "These flowers are from Susie's garden. When I told her I was going to visit my friend, she picked them from the backyard. A gift from her, she said in her innocence, so you would have something pretty to look at. I've got a great family, Joe: a loving wife, a beautiful daughter that steals my heart every time I look into her dark eyes. So what's the problem, you ask?

"I've got demons, Joe, that I can't seem to control. I have these desires, sexual urges that Liz is uncomfortable fulfilling, so I seek out other women to satisfy them. I know…I know…it's wrong, and I feel guilty every time I do it, saying this will be the last time. But I know even as I speak the words they're a lie.

"I miss you so much, buddy. You, Pappy, my life before the war. I knew that life. I understood that life. This life I lead now…I'm just not sure. I love my wife and Susie, an unconditional love that holds no bounds. I would lay down my life for either of them, so why do I do it, Joe? Why do I betray my family? Why do I take the chance of destroying what I love so much? Mandy told me years back my demons could not live in the same place as my life, and she was right. So what should I do, buddy; any suggestions?" Sadness consumed me as the flag waved in the gentle breeze.

"I know, Joe; you're a love 'em and leave 'em kind of guy. I should have probably listened to you years ago and stayed away from the nice girls, but the heart wants what the heart wants, and I do love Liz with all my heart." I inhaled deeply with a sigh.

"Thanks for listening, Buddy." I stood up brushing the dirt from my trousers. "It feels good to just to talk. See you soon." The small American flag caught a light breeze, causing it to wave slowly, sadly.

A Few Weeks Later

"Susie, you've got to hurry; the bus will be here shortly."

"I'm almost ready, Mommy. I just need to find my other shoe."

"Susie! How many mornings are we going to do this? I keep telling you, put your shoes at the back door!"

"I know, Mommy," Susie said, looking under the living-room chair.

"If you know, Susie, then why are we looking for them again?"

"Good morning, ladies. What seems to be the problem this morning?" I said, knowing full well Susie had misplaced her shoes once again.

"It's your daughter, Harry! The bus will be here any minute, and she can't find her shoe, again; and there goes her bus." Her voice sounded powerless.

"It'll be fine, sweetheart. I can drop Susie off this morning."

"Thank you, Harry. When you get home this afternoon, Susie, your shoes are to be put by the back door. Do you hear me, young lady? This missing the bus has got to stop. You keep telling me you're not a baby anymore; you're a big girl—well, big girls know where their shoes are every morning."

"I found it, Mommy." Susie pulled the lost Mary Jane from under the couch, buckling it to her right foot. "I'm ready, Daddy." Her soft voice said from behind my morning paper.

"So you are, sweetheart." I flipped down the edge of my morning paper and looked into a pair of dark eyes. A wave of love washed over me.

"Okay, you two, let's go." Liz encouraged us toward the door. "Susie, here's your Cinderella lunch box. Harry, your coffee thermos."

"Bye, Mommy." Susie waved from the car window as I gave a few quick taps on the horn.

"Good-bye, sweethearts." Liz waved from the front porch as Mandy pulled into the drive.

"Hey, Liz. Susie miss the bus again?"

"Yes, I'm beginning to believe Susie and her father are in cahoots on this whole missing-the-bus thing."

"Susie definitely loves her daddy, but you can't blame her, Liz—Jack's a charming guy."

"Yeah, maybe too charming."

"What's that supposed to mean?"

"Nothing. Everything. I don't know, Mandy. Things still seem to be off between me and Harry. I thought it was the boxing, but I've encouraged him several times to go down to the Silver Center, which he still hasn't done." She sounded frustrated. "It's nothing I can pinpoint. I don't know; maybe it's me? Everything happened so fast between me and Harry. Getting married, starting a family, and I've never been quite sure if I satisfy him in the bedroom. Maybe I don't, Mandy. Maybe he is having an affair. Do you think that could be it? He's having an affair?"

"Jack's not having an affair." Mandy's voice was dismissive. "A one-night stand, a sexual romp maybe, but never an affair." She chuckled.

"What's the difference, Mandy?" Liz's eyes saddened.

"Oh, honey, I was just kidding, but believe me; there is a difference. A one-night stand, a sexual romp? You get your needs taken care of, and it's done…over. But an affair? That's where emotions come into play. That's how marriages get destroyed. But your husband, Harry? He loves you with all his heart. And Susie—well, Susie means the world to him. I may not be able to keep a man, Liz, but I do know the creatures. So you can believe me when I say Jack will never be anyone's husband but yours."

"You're right, Mandy." Liz sighed. "I'm just being foolish. Harry did say he would go down to the Silver Gloves when things slowed down. I know how much he misses the boxing world. How much he misses Joe and Pappy. Don't mind me, Mandy. I'm just feeling a little insecure today. Let me just go grab my pocketbook, and we can be on our way."

"Sure, Liz." Mandy's mind sent up a flag of suspicion.

CHAPTER THIRTEEN

February 1948

Pulling open the doors of the Silver Gloves Center, I felt my adrenaline start to pump. As I walked through the gymnasium, my senses were flooded by the sights, sounds, and smells of the boxing world, and I found I could hardly contain my excitement.

"Mr. Slugger?" a voiced called out from behind one of the heavy bags hung sporadically throughout the center.

"Petey?" I looked into a smiling face that had lost its freckles and now revealed two front teeth, which had corrected the slur on his S-Ls.

"Yeah, it's me, Mr. Slugger. What are you doing here?" He wiped the sweat from his brow.

"I thought I might start doing some volunteer training, a few days a week. If that's all right with you, Petey?" I smiled in jest.

"It's all right with me, Mr. Slugger." He chuckled, clearly remembering our first meeting so many years ago at the Lincoln Center.

"How's your brother, Petey? How's Davey? Still boxing?"

"Nah, Mr. Slugger." He sounded disheartened. "A few years back, Davey started hanging out with a bad crowd. Dropped out of the fight game. The Hit-Man tried to help him, but my brother was just too pigheaded to listen."

"That's too bad, Petey. Davey had some great potential."

"He sure did, Mr. Slugger." Petey gave a halfhearted punched the heavy bag. "I read about Joe in the papers; it's too bad what happened to him."

"Yeah, Joe was a good man, Petey." Both of us took a few minutes to reflect. "Come on, Petey. Enough of the nostalgia; we're here to train. Here to box. Joe would be the first one to call us out for sad sackin'. Let me see what you've got, Petey. Let me see your best combination."

"Sure, Mr. Slugger." He threw a quick left jab and a right uppercut, following with a powerful left hook.

"You're a southpaw, Petey." I gave a sly smile.

"That I' am, Mr. Slugger." He proudly smiled. Digging in, he threw another left hook, causing the heavy bag to wince in pain. "I trained at the Lincoln Center with the Hit-Man till I was fifteen. Then he set me up with one of his old trainers—Lou Armando? Lou's brother, Gus, is Gladwin police, so they let me train out of here."

"Yeah, I know Lou. He's a good man. Tough, but he knows the fight game."

"Petey? You're supposed to be training, not jackin' your jaws," a voice shouted from behind. Turning, I saw Armando, gruff as ever. His face looked like an old English bulldog's, but his body and mind were pure pit bull—strong and unrelenting. And he trained his boxers to be just that: pit bulls.

"I'll let you get back to it, Petey." Petey gave a respectful nod and returned to his training, hitting the heavy bag without mercy.

I felt euphoric leaving the center that day. Renewed. My contender days may have been over, but the fight game was still in my blood, and its call was stronger than ever. I now understood the Hit-Man's desire to train, to mold. To be a part of the greatest sport in the world. My wife was right. I did miss the fight game, and I couldn't wait to get home and tell her all about my day.

A Few Days Later

"Ready for our weekly excursion, Liz?"

"Ready, Mandy." Liz was smiling from ear to ear.

"Well, you're in a good mood this morning. What's going on?"

"I'm in a wonderful mood, Mandy. I have Harry back, and he's happy. He finally went down to the Silver Gloves last week and started training with the young boys. In fact, he ran into an old friend, Petey—a young boy he and Joe had met a few years back at the Lincoln Center. Apparently Petey's training to go pro. He's Golden Gloves or something right now, but he trains at the Silver Center, because his trainer, Lou something, is related to a Gladwin police officer. I think they're cousins. No, brothers. I'm not really sure, but Harry's happy, and that's all that matters." Her smile big and happy.

"That's great, Liz. I met a new man." Mandy happily squealed. "I really think he may be the one!"

"That's wonderful, Mandy. You can tell me all about him over lunch." Liz grabbed her coat and handbag.

"His name is Charlie, but everyone calls him Buck. He's so handsome and charming. I'd really love for you to meet him."

"How about Sunday? You and Charlie could come over for dinner."

"Buck, Liz," Mandy laughingly teased. "My man's name is Buck, not Charlie."

"I stand corrected, Mandy. We could have you and Buck over for dinner this Sunday. I feel like a girl today, Mandy." Liz's voice ecstatic. "So happy and content."

"Me too, Liz. Isn't it funny how we, as women, can only enjoy our day when all is right with our men?"

"Yes, it is. Why is that?" Liz smiled happily.

"Don't ask me. I have a hard enough time understanding the ways of men, but why we as women do what we do? I'm not even sure we know." Both chuckled, feeling euphoric, as all was right with their worlds.

Sunday Dinner

"Which tie, Liz?" I held one in each hand.

"The blue, Harry," she said, glancing up as she struggled to get the seam of her nylons straight.

"You know this guy's going to be a loser too." I threw the unselected tie on the bed.

"Probably, Harry, but Mandy really seems to think he's the one."

"Wasn't Chet the one, and Bill, and Jerry? And let's not forget the Rock Hudson look-alike. What was his name—Ted?"

"Tab. Like the movie star, Tab Hunter? Please, Harry, be nice?" Liz's soft dark eyes pleaded.

"I'll be good, sweetheart—for you." I heard the doorbell chime.

"That must be them, darling." Liz dropped and smoothed the front of her skirt. "Shall we go greet our guests?"

"Yeah, the sooner we get started the sooner I can show Burt to the door."

"Buck, darling," Liz corrected. "His name is Buck." She opened the door. "Good evening." Liz's voice was warm and welcoming.

"Liz, Jack, I'd like you to meet Buck." Mandy gave him an adoring smile. As I gave Buck the ole boxer stare, my gut told me, *Loser.* Just how much of a loser was yet to be seen.

"Please come in." Liz and I stepped aside, allowing our guests to enter.

"Buck? Can I get you something to drink before dinner?"

"Sure, Jack, or should I call you Harry?"

"Either or Buck," I answered, thinking, *You won't be around long enough for it to matter.* "Martini?" I took the cheap gin from the bottom shelf. Liz and Mandy joined us at the bar.

"Buck, tell Jack about your business idea." Mandy took his arm possessively. "Jack's a business owner; maybe he could give you a few pointers."

"No business talk tonight, baby," Buck said, "but that reminds me—I'm going to need your car for a while tomorrow. We should gas it up on the way back to your apartment tonight. You just got that new Phillips 66 card. Didn't you, baby? Got any more in the shaker, Jack?" Buck handed back his empty martini glass.

"Sure, Buck." Refilling his glass, I gave Liz a sideways "*loser*" glance.

"Buck?" Liz always looked for the good. "Mandy tells me you two met at the Safari Club."

"Yeah, Mandy was sashaying around the club selling her wares. What is that pitch line you use again, baby?"

Mandy struck her sexy sales-pitch pose. "Cigarettes, gum, or Mandy...I mean, or candy," Mandy purred.

"That's it, baby, and I love Mandy's candy." Buck gave her a seductive once-over.

"Oh, Buck," Mandy gushed.

"Shall we sit down? Dinner's ready," said Liz, always the gracious host.

"Sure, I'm famished." Buck took his seat, oblivious to the custom of women sitting first. "Mandy tells me you're a great cook, Liz. Looks good." Buck was salivating, eyeing the feast set before him. Roast beef, mash potatoes, steamed broccoli, and fresh rolls.

"I do my best, Buck." Liz took her seat as I helped adjust her chair.

"Hey, Jack, before you sit down." Buck lifted his half-empty martini glass.

"Sure, Buck, another martini coming right up." I was silently fuming.

"Mandy has told me so many nice things about you, Buck," Liz said. "Do you know how lucky you are to have Mandy? She's a wonderful woman."

"Sure, Mandy's a great broad." Buck helped himself to a large slice of roast beef. "Hey, Jack, just bring the whole shaker back with you; it'll be easier, buddy." Buck downed the last of his martini, holding his empty glass to be refilled.

Remembering the promise I had made to my wife to be nice was proving to be difficult. Buck was on a quest to drink my bar dry, and I was running out of the cheap gin. Mandy was once again oblivious to the flaws that ran rampant in the man seated across from her. Liz was desperately trying to soften Buck's rough edges, in hopes of finding the good. The dinner seemed to drag on, but the night finally came to an end.

"Well, the food was great, and the drinks? Wonderful!" Buck was slightly hammered, standing with Mandy by the front door. "You make a great martini, Jack, but they're always better when you use the good stuff."

"Nothing but top shelf for Mandy's friends," I said, smiling wide.

"Thanks for dinner, Liz. I'll call you tomorrow." Mandy seemed euphoric, under Buck's spell, as they took the steps that led from our home.

"I'll talk to you tomorrow, Mandy. Nice meeting you, Buck," Liz called out, waving from the front door.

"Loser, just like I said, sweetheart." We watched Mandy and Buck pull from the drive. "How long do you think this one will last, Liz? I give it two weeks, or until the Phillips 66 card taps out."

"You're probably right, Harry," Liz said, sighing sadly. "I just wish she could find someone that truly cares for her. She's really a great girl. I just don't understand why men can't see that."

"Mandy gives too much of herself, and too quickly, for anyone to ever appreciate her, sweetheart. Until Mandy thinks more of herself, she'll probably just continue to collect one loser after another."

"I hope you're wrong, Harry. Mandy's a wonderful girl, and someday, someone is going to recognize that!"

"I hope you're right, sweetheart—for your sake. I know how much you love your friend."

"Yes, I do, Harry. I just wish someone else would love her too."

CHAPTER FOURTEEN

May 1955

"See you tomorrow." Susie said stepping from the junior high school bus. She adjusted the heavy load of school books, taking the steps of twelve forty Leland street. "Mom, I'm home." Susie set her schoolbooks on the dining-room table. "You're not going to believe what happened at school today. We had one fire drill after another…Mom, are you home?" Susie heard a soft moan coming from the kitchen. "Mom?" Making her way to the kitchen she found her mother lying on the floor, disoriented, with a small gash to her forehead. "Mom!"

"Call dad…," Liz mumbled. "Tell him…come home."

"Mom, what is it?" Susie took her hand. "Please, you're scaring me."

"I need your father," Liz moaned.

"Hello," Mandy called out, coming through the front door. "I was just in the neighborhood. Where is everybody?"

"Aunt Mandy!" Susie voice anxious. "We're in the kitchen. Something is wrong with Mom!" Mandy ran to the kitchen and saw Liz lying on the floor.

"I'm here, Liz." Mandy knelt down next to her. Distress filled Liz's eyes as she tried to speak.

"What's wrong with her, Aunt Mandy?" Susie started to cry.

"We need to get her to the hospital. Take her arm, Susie. Help me get her to the car."

"She's going to be all right, isn't she, Aunt Mandy?" Fear consumed her as she helped lift her mother.

"Of course she is, sweetheart; we just need to hurry." Mandy was struggling to keep Liz upright, gently taking the porch steps. "Susie, open the back car door and get in. I need you to hold your mother's head." Susie quickly jumped into the backseat. Mandy gently laid Liz inside.

"Mandy?" Liz moaned.

"I'm right here, Liz." Mandy glanced through the rearview mirror, fear gripping her heart. She hit the gas pedal hard, honking the horn, running the red lights. "Almost there, Liz." Taking a quick right, she pulled into the emergency entrance. "We need some help here!" she shouted, jumping from the car. "You! Both of you!" She pointed to two orderlies smoking just outside the entrance. "Now!"

"Please help my mom." Susie anxiously watched the orderlies place her mother on a gurney, whisking her through the emergency doors. "She's going to be all right, isn't she, Aunt Mandy?"

"Of course she is, sweetheart." Mandy put a comforting arm around her. "Let's go find a pay phone and call your father."

"Yes." Susie sounded relieved. "Daddy will know what to do."

"Excuse us. Where can we find a pay phone?"

"Just down the hall, to your left." The admissions nurse directed them with her pencil.

"There's no answer, Aunt Mandy. Where can he be?" Susie let the phone continue to ring.

"I'm sure he's there, Susie. He's probably just got so many machines running he can't hear the phone."

"Mom's going to be okay…isn't she, Aunt Mandy?" Susie hung up the phone.

"Of course she is, sweetheart. The doctors will figure out what's wrong with her, and she'll be home with you tonight. You'll see." Mandy smiled in reassurance. "Come on, sweetheart; let's go to the waiting room. We'll try your father again a little later."

"What's taking so long, Aunt Mandy?" Susie tossed the magazine onto the table. "It's been over an hour. They must know something by now."

"I'm sure when they know something, they'll be out to tell us. Just relax, sweetheart."

"Decker family?" a nurse announced, scanning the waiting area.

"Yes." Susie and Mandy quickly jumped to their feet.

"You can see Mrs. Decker now. Please follow me."

"Is my mom okay?" Susie anxiously followed on the heels of the nurse.

"The doctor is with her now. He will answer all of your questions. Here we are." She pulled back the curtain.

"Mom!" Susie ran to her bedside and gave her a gentle hug.

"I'm okay, sweetheart." Liz returned her hug.

"Doctor, how is she?" Mandy was no longer able to keep the fear from her voice.

"Mrs. Decker was very lucky this time. She had what we call a minor infarct, a mild stroke, due to high blood pressure. She needs to watch her diet and take her medication as instructed." He gave Liz a stern look.

"Liz, you haven't been taking your medication?" Mandy looked at her in disbelief.

"I get busy, Mandy, with Susie, Harry, the house. Besides, outside of today, I've been feeling fine."

"Regardless of your busy schedule, Mrs. Decker," the doctor interjected, "Your medication is absolutely necessary. I can't stress this enough. Next time you might not be so lucky."

"I understand, Doctor. When can I be released? When can I go home?"

"Soon, Mrs. Decker. Rest now." He walked from the room, pulling the curtain.

"Susie, here's a dime. Go call your father, and tell him to get down here! I'll stay here with your mother." Mandy pulled up a chair.

"Mom?" Susie was reluctant to leave.

"I'll be fine, sweetheart. Do what your Aunt Mandy says, and go call your father."

"Okay, Momma." Susie quickly ducked outside the curtain.

"You really scared her, Liz. You scared us both. Susie still needs her mother, and I still need my best friend." Mandy took her hand.

"I'm sorry, Mandy." Liz gently squeezed her hand. "Forgive me?" she asked, smiling softly.

"Hello, Daddy? Where have you been?" Susie's voice was quivering. "I've been trying to reach you for hours."

"What's wrong, sweetheart?" I said, feeling the fear rise in my body.

"We're at McClellan Hospital." Susie started to cry. "Mommy had a mild stroke, and I couldn't find you, Daddy." Breaking down, she let the tears flow.

"My God, honey…is your mother all right?" Heart pounding, I feared the answer.

"I think so, Daddy," Susie sniffed. "Just come pick us up, and take us home."

"I'm on my way, sweetheart. Don't worry; everything's going to be fine. I'll be there shortly." I hung up the phone.

"Get dressed," I said, turning to the naked woman lying on the cot in my office. "You have to leave." I handed her a fifty-dollar bill.

"Are you sure?" she purred. "I haven't earned all this yet." She gave my hand a gentle stroke.

"Get dressed, and get out!" Grabbing her clothes from the floor, I shoved them toward her.

"There's no reason to be nasty." The sexiness left her voice, and she slipped back into her dress.

"I'm sorry, but you have to leave. Let's go." I impatiently stood by the door.

"What's your hurry all of a sudden, lover?" Ignoring her question, I locked the shop door and hurried to my car. "Hey, wait a minute!" The woman was hot on my heels. "How am I supposed to get back?" She grabbed my car door, holding me hostage.

"You'll have to take the bus." I nodded to the bus stop at the corner.

"I don't do buses, honey." Her tone was direct and unwavering. "I'm a cab kind of girl."

"Then take a cab." I tossed a five out the window, hitting the gas pedal hard. My mind riddled with worry, I sped toward McClellan Hospital.

"Nice doing business with you, sweetheart," She called out loudly tucking the money inside her bra as she walked to the bus stop.

"I got hold of daddy he's on his way." Susie said returning to the room. "Everything's going to be all right now. You were right, Aunt Mandy. Daddy was at work all the time." She contentedly smiled; looking to her mother whom appeared stronger, sipping a cup of water.

"I'm sure he was," Mandy muttered.

"Excuse me? Excuse me?" Maneuvering my way around two orderlies, I made my way to the nurse's station. "Excuse me; I'm looking for my wife, Elizabeth Decker."

"And you are?"

"I'm her husband, Harry Decker. I just told you she was my wife!"

"No need to be rude, Mr. Decker." She looked at her paperwork. "Mrs. Decker has been taken to room 305. Take the elevators to the third floor, and turn right."

"Thank you." I gave an apologetic smile and ran to the elevators. "Come on!" I impatiently tapped the elevator button, fear gripping my heart. "Forget it." Pulling open the door to the stairwell, I ran up the steps to the third floor. My heart pounded as I searched the corridor for room 305. Pushing open the door, I felt a sigh of relief, seeing her beautiful face. "Liz, sweetheart, are you okay?" I came to her bedside. "Please tell me you're okay."

"I'm fine now that you're here, darling." Liz softly smiled.

"What did the doctor say, sweetheart?" Fear, guilt, shame—all the emotions—gripped my heart.

"He said Mom has high blood pressure, but she's okay now, Daddy." Susie came to my side.

"No! She's not okay, Jack." Mandy aggressively stepped toward the bed. "It was her carotid artery. The main artery in the neck, which controls blood flow to the brain."

"Mandy's making it sound worse than it is, darling." Liz gave Mandy a look of reprimand. "I'm fine! Now go find the doctor, and see when I can get out of here, Harry. You know I hate hospitals."

"Come on, Jack." Mandy stepped toward the door. "I'll take you."

"I'll be right back, sweetheart." I gently kissed Liz's forehead. "Susie? You take good care of your mother while we're gone."

"Okay, Daddy." Susie gently took her mother's hand.

"Where were you, Jack?" Mandy uttered sternly, the moment we were out of earshot.

"I was at the shop, Mandy. Working. Where else would I be?" I searched the halls for a nurse or doctor.

"Susie called the shop several times, Jack. What, or should I say who, was keeping you from answering the phone? Look me in the eye, Jack, and tell me you were working."

"You're being ridiculous, Mandy," I said, ignoring her request.

"You were with another woman, weren't you, Jack?" Mandy's tone was accusing, causing my back to stiffen. "You were...you bastard!"

"Calm down, Mandy, and lower your voice," I said, scanning the halls.

"The sexual demons have returned. haven't they, Jack? They've come to call, just like I said they would. Who is she, Jack?"

"She isn't anybody, Mandy. I'm not seeing another woman—at least, not in the way you think. My women are professionals. They understand my situation."

"Your situation, Jack? Just what is your situation?"

"A married man in love with a woman incapable of fulfilling all his needs. There's nothing personal between me and the women. Just sex. A business transaction, if you will."

"Just sex? A business transaction? Stop kidding yourself, Jack. It's a betrayal. A betrayal Liz would never understand if she ever found out."

"She's not going to find out." I gave her a cutting look. "Is she, Mandy?"

"Oh, you don't have to worry about me, Jack. I'm not going to be the one to break her heart. Your secret's safe with me."

"Good, because if she ever does finds out"—I said in my most threatening voice—"she might also find out about your little offering to me in the apartment that day."

"Jack, you know that wasn't an offering. It..." Mandy stuttered, "it was a test."

"I don't think Liz would see it that way, Mandy. I think she would see it as a betrayal," I said, returning her words.

"Jack...you wouldn't."

"I think we both have our secrets, Mandy. Where the hell is everybody around here?" I eyed a nurse just up ahead in the hallway. "Excuse me. Excuse me, nurse, maybe you could help me? I'm looking for the doctor in charge of my wife's care—Elizabeth Decker."

"Oh yes, Mr. Decker, I'm your wife's attending nurse. That would be Dr. Thomas. That's him right over there." She pointed to a man in a white coat, standing next to a coffee-vending machine.

"Thank you." I gave a nod of appreciation. "Excuse me, Dr. Thomas?"

"Yes, how can I help you?"

"I'm Harry Decker, Doctor. Elizabeth Decker is my wife. When can she come home?"

"Mr. Decker, your wife was a very lucky woman today. High blood pressure is a condition that needs to be taken seriously."

"I understand, Doctor. When can she come home?"

"If your wife doesn't start taking better care of herself, Mr. Decker, she could have serious complications in the future."

"I understand that. When can she come home?"

"Go back to your wife's room, Mr. Decker. The nurse will be down shortly with the list of instructions and release forms. Then your wife is free to go."

"Thank you, Doctor." I shook his hand in gratitude.

"Yes, thank you very much, Doctor." Mandy gave an appreciative nod.

"You're both welcome." He returned to the coffee machine, making his selection.

"This conversation isn't over, Jack." Mandy followed on my heels as we made our way back to Liz's room.

"Yes, it is, Mandy." I pushed open the door of room 305. "We're all set, sweetheart. The nurse will be in shortly with the release forms and instructions." I took a seat on the edge of her bed.

"Great." Liz softly smiled. "I can't get out of here fast enough, darling."

"I told you Daddy would fix everything," Susie chirped.

"You have to promise me, Liz, that you'll follow the doctor's instructions. I can't take another phone call like the one I got today." I laid my head in her lap. "I don't know what I would do if anything happened to you, sweetheart," I said, my voice cracking with emotion.

"I'm okay, darling." She gently stroked my hair.

"Liz, honey." Mandy's voice was soft. "I'm going to take off. I have to work tonight, and you're in very capable hands now."

"Okay, Mandy. Thank you so much for being there today." Liz reached out for her.

"You're welcome, Liz." Mandy gave her hand a loving squeeze. "You take care of yourself, young lady," she playfully demanded. "I don't want any more drama like this. I still need my best friend."

"I will, Mandy. I promise." Liz released her hand.

"Thank you, Aunt Mandy." Susie gave her a hug.

"You're welcome, Susie. You take good care of your mother for me." Mandy looked into her dark eyes.

"I will, Aunt Mandy." Susie released her, and Mandy quietly left the room.

"I don't know what we would have done, Harry, if Mandy hadn't showed up today. I wasn't expecting her," Liz said, watching the door close behind her best friend.

"I'm just grateful she did, sweetheart. I will never again complain about Mandy just popping over."

A nurse came through the door, clipboard in hand. "Mrs. Decker, I have discharge papers and instructions. I just need a few signatures, and you can be on your way."

"Great." Liz quickly signed.

"I'll take those," I said, intercepting the doctor's instructions and putting them inside my jacket pocket.

"Take me home, Harry." Liz sighed. "Take me to Twelve Forty Leland Street."

"Right away, sweetheart." I smiled, pleased that my wife now also referred to our home as Twelve Forty Leland Street. We drove in silence, feeling the tension of the day leave our bodies, letting go of the fear that had consumed us. Ever so grateful to still have each other. Ever so grateful to be going home to the sanctuary of Twelve Forty Leland Street.

Memorial Day: Visiting Joe

"Hey, buddy." Taking a seat on the grass. I replaced the small, worn American flag. "Got a great surprise yesterday—a postcard from Pappy. I recognized his chicken scratch right away. He's in Tuscany, Italy." I showed Joe's gravestone the postcard of a quaint little town.

"'Dear Southpaw,'" I read aloud. "'Hope all is well with you and yours. I've met a woman, Francine. She's a widow. Her husband and son were both taken by the war. She calls me Pa'pae, and she makes me smile…Take care, Pappy.' Can you believe it, Joe? Pa'pae has found a woman." I shook my head in disbelief. The small American flag rippled in the wind.

"Finally went down to the Silver Center. I'm a trainer now, Joe, and it's great! I understand the Hit-Man now. Training the young boys keeps you in the fight game, and that's something. Ran into Petey while I was there; remember, our young friend from the Lincoln Center? Well, he's got his two front teeth now, Joe, and he's going pro, and he's a southpaw! Can you believe it? Where does the time go?" I shook my head in reminiscence. "Remember Davey, Joe? Petey's older brother? The kid with great potential? Well, he's no longer boxing. Apparently he fell in with a bad crowd and runs the streets—a real badass, according to Petey. The Hit-Man tried to help him, bring him back to the ring, but Davey wasn't interested.

"Mandy brought by loser number...I'm not sure what number. A real charmer, Buck something or other. The guy almost drank my bar dry, Joe. And Mandy was oblivious as usual to his loser ways. I think he and Mandy lasted about a month. Two weeks longer than I gave him. I wish Mandy could find a decent guy for Liz's sake. For reasons I don't understand, my wife loves that woman.

"Liz gave me a real scare a few weeks back. High blood pressure. Put her in the hospital for a few hours. She's home now, and everything seems to be okay. I don't know what I would do if I ever lost her, Joe." My voice became solemn and thoughtful. "Hopefully I'll never have to find out." I sighed. "Well, I guess that's all for now." Standing tall, I brushed the dirt from my trousers. "See you soon, buddy." I stepped carefully, respectfully. The small American flag waved in the breeze.

CHAPTER FIFTEEN

Susie, October 1957

"Mom, where are you?" Susie's voice filled with excitement as she let the front door slam.

"I'm right here, Susie, and what have I told you about slamming the front door?"

"Sorry about the door, Mom, but Johnny O'Brien, the dreamiest guy in school, just invited me to the movies Saturday night. Can I go, Mom?" Her eyes were pleading. "Please, please?"

"I don't know, Susie; you're a little young to be dating."

"Mom, I'm fifteen! Almost a grown woman. Most of my friends have already been dating—Ellen, Katie. Connie Caine's been dating since she was fourteen!"

"Susie, you know I don't care what your friends are doing. Your father and I will have to meet this boy, and if he seems like a nice young man, then maybe you can go to the movies with him on Saturday night."

"Does he have to meet Daddy?" A look of dread covered her face.

"Of course he has to meet your father, Susie. Don't be ridiculous."

"But, Mom, you know how Daddy can be."

"How's that, Susie? Loving? Caring? Protective of his daughter?"

"Okay, Mom." Susie knew arguing with her mother was pointless once she had made up her mind. " I'll bring him by tomorrow after school, if that's okay?"

"Tomorrow after school would be fine. Now come and help me with dinner, and you can tell me all about this new young man."

"His family just moved here from California, and all the girls think he's the dreamiest, with his dark hair and blue eyes. They moved into that big house over on Newport Street. I think they might be rich, because Johnny has his own car, a red Thunderbird." Her eyes were wide with delight. "Daddy just has to let me go on Saturday, Mom, or I'll just die."

"Don't be so dramatic, Susie; you're not going to die. I'll talk to your father, and if Johnny seems like a nice enough young man, I'm sure a matinee or early-evening movie will be fine."

"Where is Daddy anyway? Shouldn't he be home from work by now?"

"It's Wednesday, Susie. He's down at the Silver Center. The Silver gloves tournament is next month."

"That's right; I saw the posters. Petey O'Donovitch is turning pro. He's doing an exhibition fight after the Silver Gloves tournament—some sort of fundraiser."

"That would be it." Liz turned down the flame under the potatoes.

"Mom, did I tell you Johnny had beautiful blue eyes?" Susie dreamily sighed.

Johnny O'Brien

"Mom, Daddy, this is Johnny O'Brien," Susie proudly announced.

"Mr. Decker, Mrs. Decker." Johnny's voice nervously cracked. "Very nice to meet you both."

"Nice to meet you, son." I gave him the ole boxer's stare. "Take a seat. Susie, why don't you and your mother get us some ice tea, while Johnny and I have a talk?"

"Okay, Daddy." Susie was hesitant, shooting her mother a fearful look.

"Do you take sugar in your ice tea, Johnny?" Liz's voice was soft and comforting.

"No, ma'am. Unsweetened is fine."

"I'll be right back, Johnny," Susie promised, following her mother to the kitchen.

"How old are you, son?" I said, beginning my interrogation.

"Uh, sixteen, sir." Johnny nervously cleared his throat.

"And your intentions, son?" I asked, using Pappy's tone.

"My intentions, sir?"

"Yes, your intentions. You do know what intentions are—don't you, son?"

"Yes, sir." He shifted uncomfortably. "My intentions, sir, are to take Susie to the movies on Saturday night."

"Hurry, Mom. You know Daddy's out there right now interrogating him."

"Your father's just asking the necessary questions, Susie." Liz dropped ice into the glasses.

"Necessary questions, Mom?" Susie's tone was patronizing. "I'm not a baby anymore."

"I know you're not a baby, Susie, but it's our job as parents to make sure we do everything we can to keep you safe."

"Keep me safe? It's just a date, Mom."

"Yes, Susie, and you're a young lady." She picked up the tray of ice tea. "Here we are," she said as they breezed their way back into the living room. "Johnny?"

"Thank you, Mrs. Decker." Johnny selected a glass from the tray.

"Are you a respectful young man, Johnny?" I asked, disregarding my wife and daughter's entrance.

"Yes, sir." He sat up a little straighter. "Very respectful."

"Harry?" Liz held the tray of ice tea in front of me.

"Thank you, sweetheart. Okay, Johnny, you seem like a nice enough young man. Saturday night, but you better stay respectful. Don't make me come looking for you, son."

"I won't…I will…I'll stay respectful, sir," he stuttered, working his way toward the door. "Susie, I'll pick you up at seven on Saturday." He slipped out the door, leaving behind his untouched glass of ice tea.

"See you at school tomorrow, Johnny." Susie waved from the front door as Johnny pulled from the curb.

"Well, I think I got my message across." I contentedly snapped open the evening paper.

"Thank you, Daddy, for allowing me to go, but did you really have to interrogate him like that?"

"Your father did no such thing, Susie," Liz corrected. "You're a young lady who needs to be treated accordingly, and your father was just making sure that happened."

"Mom, it's not like it was when you and Daddy were growing up. Times are different."

"Times may be different, but boys? Young men? They are exactly the same. Always demand respect, Susie."

"I know, Mom. If I've heard it once, I've heard it a thousand times. A lady waits, and a gentleman will wait for her. And let's not forget the old standby: a lady always knows when to leave."

"Show your mother some respect, young lady." I flipped down the edge of my paper in reprimand.

"I'm sorry, Mom." Susie's voice was apologetic. "I know you and Daddy only want the best for me."

Saturday Night

"Susie, your date is here." I tapped lightly on her bedroom door, Liz opened it just a crack. "Tell Johnny she'll be right out, Harry."

"I'm getting a strange vibe off the kid tonight, Liz. He doesn't seem like the same insecure kid that was sitting on our couch two days ago, nervously twitching in his seat. It's not too late to kick him out the door, Liz. Just give me the nod, and it's done."

"Harry, don't be ridiculous. Get back out there, and offer Johnny a soda or something." Liz quietly closed the bedroom door. "Your father hates this, Susie. The thought of his little girl going out on a date does not sit well with him."

"I'm almost sixteen, Mom. I'm not Daddy's little girl anymore." She tucked her favorite pink blouse into her jeans.

"You'll always be your father's little girl, sweetheart, no matter how old you get." Liz held up a tube of lipstick with a permissive smile.

"Lipstick…really, Mom?"

"You're fifteen now, Susie. A light shade is acceptable."

Susie meticulously applied the lipstick the way she had seen her mother do hundreds of times.

"Mom, could you please go out there and protect Johnny from Daddy?" Grabbing the brush from the vanity, she ran it through her beautiful dark hair. "I'll only be a few minutes more." She pulled her hair up into a ponytail, looking at her vanity mirror in frustrated dissatisfaction.

"Leave it down, sweetheart. You look beautiful with it down." Liz felt a bit nostalgic, reminiscing back.

"Thanks, Mom." Susie released the band holding the ponytail. "Now, please?" Her eyes were pleading. "Go save Johnny?"

"Okay, sweetheart, have fun tonight." Smiling softly, Liz quietly closed the bedroom door and quickly proceeded to the living room to save Johnny. "Good evening, Johnny, did my husband offer you something to drink?"

"Yes, he did, Mrs. Decker." Johnny sounded relieved to have someone else in the room. "Is Susie about ready?"

"I'm ready, Johnny." Susie grabbed her coat from the hall closet.

"You look just like your mother standing there, sweetheart," I said.

"Thank you, Daddy." She handed Johnny her coat for assistance.

"Good girl." Liz quietly sighed.

"I'll have her back early, sir. How's eleven sound?"

"Make it ten, son, and no funny business tonight."

"No, sir."

"Good-bye, Mom, Daddy." Susie waved from the window of the flashy red Thunderbird.

"I don't trust that guy, Liz," I said, watching Johnny drive off with our daughter. "He's too good-looking and too damn charming, and did you see that smile he gave me there at the end? It was downright sinister."

"There was nothing sinister about his smile, Harry, but you're right! He is good-looking and quite the charmer. Remind you of anyone?"

"Karma." Joe's words resonated in my ears.

"I think we're far enough away." Johnny pulled the red Thunderbird over. "Your dad is something else, Susie." He retrieved the Brylcreem from the glove box. "He thinks his daughter is still a little girl," he said, combing his hair into a perfect DA. "Apparently he doesn't see what I see, a beautiful grown woman with everything in all the right places." He grabbed his leather jacket from the floor of the backseat.

"My dad's just being protective, Johnny. I don't necessarily think that's a bad thing."

"Maybe not, Susie, but the guy needs to come out of the stone ages. I couldn't believe it when he started asking me about my intentions. This is 1957; things are different between men and women today. A woman needs to take care of her man."

"Are you my man, Johnny?" Susie timidly smiled.

"Sure I am, baby." He gave her a wink. "Why don't you slide on over here next to me?" His charm was in high gear.

"Okay, Johnny," she said, shyly sliding over.

"Closer, baby," he said, giving a charming smile. Susie moved closer, mesmerized, entertaining what life was going to be like as Johnny O'Brien's girlfriend.

Next Morning

"Susie, it's time to get up. Come on, sweetheart." Liz lightly shook her awake. "Your aunt Helen came in last night from Port Hope—a surprise visit—and she would like us all to go to church with her this morning."

"Do I have to, Mom?" Susie pulled the covers over her head. "Sundays are the only days I get to sleep in."

"Susie, you know I was never one to push religion on you, but it's important to your aunt, and you know how your father feels about his sister."

"Aggh." She threw off her covers, knowing it was a waste of time to argue, and made her way to the kitchen.

"Good morning, Susie. How was your date last night, sweetheart?" I looked up from my Sunday paper, hoping it was a complete disaster.

"It was wonderful, Daddy." Her eyes filled with bliss. "The movie was wonderful. Johnny was wonderful...everything was just wonderful." She grabbed a piece of toast from the breakfast table.

"I hope Johnny didn't do anything to make me put my gloves back on."

"No, Daddy, he was a perfect gentleman. Just like you warned him to be. I'm really tired this morning, Daddy. Do you think maybe"—she made a sad little face—"I could skip church?"

"No can do, Susie. We're going to respect my sister's wishes and all go to church this morning. Now go get dressed, young lady." Susie left the kitchen slump shouldered. "It's only an hour, sweetheart," I called out behind her, returning to my morning paper.

"Is everyone ready?" Helen said entering the kitchen adjusting her pristine white gloves.

"Just about, sister dear," I said, refolding the morning paper.

"And Susie? Where is she?" Helen not waiting for an answer made a beeline to Susie's bedroom. "Susie, dear, it's your aunt Helen." She lightly tapped on her bedroom door. "You need to hurry, dear. It's not acceptable to be late for church, and you wouldn't want us to leave without you."

"Yes, I would," Susie lowly muttered. "I'll be right out, Aunt Helen."

"Please hurry, dear. We'll be waiting in the living room."

"I'm ready." Liz breezed into the living room looking beautiful as ever. "Where's Susie?" She looked from me to Helen seated on the couch.

"She's still getting ready, and we really do need to leave." Helen's voice was anxious. "You know I'm never late for Mass."

"We won't be late, dear sister." I got up from the couch in pursuit of my daughter. My sister, Helen, was an elementary-school teacher and a spinster, a no-nonsense woman who lived by a strict moral code, her religion. God was her guide, and the Catholic faith was the compass that directed her life. "Let's go, young lady." I sternly knocked on my daughter's bedroom door.

"I'm coming, Daddy!" There was a slight annoyance to her voice. "I'll be right out."

"Make it quick, young lady," I demanded. "We'll be in the car." A couple minutes later, Susie reluctantly slid into the backseat next to her aunt.

"I'm here." She moaned shutting the back door of my new Cadillac.

"I don't believe giving an hour to the Lord is asking too much—do you, dear?"

"No, it's not too much to ask, Aunt Helen, but do you mind if I sit up in the cry room? I feel closer to God there."

"Of course, dear." Helen patted Susie's hand. "The fact that you're paying your respects to the Lord is what's important. Not where you sit in his house."

"Thank you, Aunt Helen." Susie smiled. "I feel the same way." Looking out the window, her thoughts turned to Johnny and her date last night.

"See, sister, plenty of time," I said, pulling into the church parking lot. Most of the congregation was still milling around outside. "If anything, we're early."

"You're never too early for the Lord, brother." Helen stepped from the car.

We took our place in line among the congregation, waiting patiently to enter the church. Helen, Liz, and I took a seat in the front-row pew. My sister never felt more at home than in a Catholic church. Susie made a beeline to the cry room, found on the upper level. Seating herself in a back pew, she took a pad and pencil from her purse and doodled "Mrs. Johnny O'Brien" over and over as the choir began to sing, "Holy God, how great thy name."

Silver Gloves Exhibition Fight

As I opened the arena doors, the sights and sounds of the night's festivities filled me with a sense of exhilaration. I was excited for the boys who had trained so hard in hopes of taking home the trophy. But I was also sad that I'd lost the people who for me represented the sport: my beloved Pappy and Joe.

"How you doing tonight, Mr. Slugger?" Petey nodded, gear in hand.

"Good, Petey, and you?" I shook the nostalgia from my shoulders.

"It's just an exhibition fight, Mr. Slugger. Lou says you can't get hurt in those." Petey raised his headgear and extra-padded gloves.

"Maybe not, Petey, but remember, son, there is no such thing as an easy fight in the fight game."

"I know, Mr. Slugger." He nodded in remembrance. "Assess your opponent, look for his weakness, move in, and conquer. You sticking around to watch me take down Tommy thunder?"

"Wouldn't miss it, Petey. Good luck tonight." I pushed open the locker-room door to a roomful of excited boys. Billy Barnes one of my youngest fighter sat away from the rest of the boys. He seemed to be in deep thought. "You ready for tonight Billy?" I took a seat next to him on the bench. "You drew a tough fighter Danny boy Dougin.

"I'm ready Mr. Slugger." His eyes were focused and determined. "Don't worry I'll make you proud.

"I have no doubt son." I stood and called the young fighters to order. Billy was as good as his word. Danny boy Dougin didn't know what hit him. A technical knockout was called two minutes into the first round as Danny boy struggled to get up from the canvas. Petey had a little tougher time that night against Tommy Thunder. It took him to the third round before Tommy lay on the canvas floor.

December 1957

"Susie, let's go, sweetheart," Liz said. "I've got just enough time to drop you off at school before my hair appointment this morning."

"I'm ready, Mom." Susie buttoned her winter coat. "You know, Mom, the Christmas dance is just around the corner." She followed in step behind her mother through the freshly fallen snow.

"Yes, Susie, I know. It's on Friday, and everybody who's anybody is going to be there."

"Well, do you think…maybe…just maybe, Mom…I could get a new dress?"

"Susie, you have plenty of beautiful dresses in your closet," Liz said, preoccupied with pulling from the drive.

"I know, Mom, but it's the Christmas dance, and everyone I know is getting a new dress. Jillian Clark, Janette Larson, Cindy Burger—all my friends."

"Susie, you know comparing your life to your friends' has never been a good argument with me. So unless you can come up with a better reason, the answer is no."

"Okay, Mom, it's Johnny. I want a new dress so I can look beautiful for Johnny."

"You really like this young man, don't you, sweetheart?"

"Oh, I do, Mom," she gushed. "We've been exclusive now for six weeks. I think he loves me, Mom, and I know I love him."

"Now, sweetheart, you and Johnny are both too young to be in love, but if you're starting to have special feelings for each other… are you starting to have special feelings, Susie?"

"I feel wonderful when I'm with him, Mom, and I think he feels wonderful when he's with me."

"That's not what I mean, sweetheart. Has Johnny started to make advances toward you?"

"What do you mean by advances, Mom?"

"Has he tried to do things with you, Susie—beyond kissing?"

"Beyond kissing, Mom?"

"Yes, Susie, beyond kissing." Becoming frustrated, Liz gave her daughter an insinuating look.

"Of course not, Mom." Susie blushed. "We're in love, but not in the way you're talking about. You have to be married for that kind of love."

"I'm glad you understand the difference, Susie. A lady waits, and a gentleman will wait for her." She pulled up to the school. "You better hurry now; that sounds like the first bell."

"Mom...about the dress?" Susie's eyes were pleading.

"Okay, sweetheart, if it's that important to you, we can go shopping this weekend."

"Thank you, thank you, thank you, Mom. I've found the perfect dress in the Macy's catalog." Giving her mother a quick peck on the cheek, Susie jumped from the car and ran toward the school in delight. Her heart did a flip as she saw Johnny waiting outside her first-hour class, only to flop as she saw Sara Nelson standing there with him. "Johnny?" Susie called out, making her way to him.

"Hey, Susie." Johnny smiled. "You know Sara, don't you?"

"Of course, Johnny. How are you, Sara?"

"Fine." Sara gave her a dismissive glance. "See you later, Johnny." She batted her eyes flirtatiously.

"Later, Sara...have you thought about what we talked about the other day, Susie?"

"Yeah, I've thought about it, Johnny." Susie watched as Sara Nelson strutted her way down the hall.

"And?"

"And I'm just not sure if I'm ready Johnny." Her mother's words echoed in her ears. 'A lady waits and a gentleman will wait for her.'

It's what couples do when they're in love. You do love me. Don't you, Susie?"

"Of course I love you, Johnny. With all my heart."

"Then what's there to think about?" The final bell rang. "See you after class, Susie." He gave her a quick kiss on the lips and ran down the hall.

"See you after class, Johnny." Solemnly she walked into her homeroom and took her seat. Mary Peachier poked her from behind. Susie turned to face the school busybody.

"Jane Rainey told Betty Kinder, and Betty told Lynn Belmont, and Lynn told me, that Sara Nelson has eyes for Johnny."

"Johnny's not interested in Sara." Susie's voice was curt and dismissive.

"Don't get mad at me, Susie Decker. I'm just the messenger. But if I were you, I'd keep my eye on Sara Nelson. You know how she gets her boyfriends."

"Those are just rumors, Mary."

"They're not rumors, Susie. Sara took Jake Reiner from Denise Belmont right before the Christmas dance last year, and she did it by giving out. My boyfriend told me, and Jake told him."

"I'm not worried about Sara. Johnny loves me. We have something special."

"That's what Denise thought too, about Jake, and look what happened to her."

"Well, that's not going to happen to me." Susie turned back around in her seat, sadness gripping her heart.

"Just warning you, Susie. I'd hate to see you sitting with the wallflowers. The same way Denise was, all dressed up without a date. Watching Sara sashay around the dance floor in her boyfriend's arms." Susie didn't respond. Mary's words were breaking her heart.

May 1958

"I don't feel well, Mom." Susie moaned, holding her stomach.

"This is the third day in a row you haven't felt well, Susie." Liz put her hand to Susie's forehead. "I'm going to call Dr. Midland and see if I can get you an appointment for today."

"I don't think I need to see a doctor, Mom. I'm just feeling a little nauseous, and it's usually gone by the afternoon." Liz disregarded her daughter's objections, picked up the phone and dialed Dr. Midland's number.

"Yes, I can hold." Liz put her hand over the receiver. "All the more reason to see a doctor, Susie, because the symptoms keep reoccurring. Yes, I'm here. Ten o'clock. Thank you. We'll see you then, good-bye. "Get dressed Susie." Liz hung up the phone suddenly feeling anxious. Maybe her daughter's aliment wasn't an illness at all, but something that would cure itself in time.

"Susie?" Liz said hesitantly while pulling into Dr. Midland's parking lot and turning off the ignition. "Is there anything you would like to tell me before we go in? We have a few minutes yet, sweetheart." She looked at her watch.

"No," Susie softly muttered, gazing out the car window.

"Nothing…sweetheart?"

"No." Susie shook her head sadly.

"Susie." Liz's voice was soft and warm. "Look at me, sweetheart."

"He told me he loved me, Mom." Susie turned toward her, eyes filled with tears. "And it's what people do when they're in love."

"Oh, Susie." Liz sighed, realizing her suspicions had been right.

"He said we would get married after graduation." Susie sobbed, collapsing into her mother's arms. "So it was okay to practice being a married couple. I'm sorry, Mom." Crying harder, she buried her face in her mother's chest.

"Susie. Stop crying, sweetheart." Liz gently lifted her chin, looking into her tearstained face. "Maybe it is just the flu." She gave an encouraging smile. "Now dry your tears, sweetheart, and let's go see what Doctor Midland has to say."

"Okay, Momma." She sniffled, her voice childlike. Wiping the pink lipstick off along with her tears, she said, "I'm ready, Momma. Hold my hand?"

"Of course, sweetheart." Liz took her hand in loving reassurance.

"I'm sorry, Momma." Susie gripped her mother's hand tight. Liz pushed open the door and protectively led her daughter to a seat in the waiting room.

"Susie Decker?" the nurse announced, opening the admittance door. "Follow me, please."

"Momma?"

"It's okay, sweetheart. I'm here." They followed the nurse to exam room four.

"Please take off all your clothes Susie and put this gown on. The doctor will be with you shortly." The nurse quietly closed the exam-room door.

"Everything, Momma?" Susie's voice soft and hesitant.

"Everything, Susie. Here, sweetheart, let me help you." Tying the gown, Liz heard a light tap on the door. Doctor Midland entered the exam room.

"Good morning, Susie, Mrs. Decker. What seems to be your concern today?"

"Well, Doctor." Liz held her head high. "My daughter seems to be nauseous a lot in the morning, and it seems to go away on its own by the afternoon."

"Hmm." Dr. Midland looked at Susie. "How old are you now, Susie?"

"Fifteen. I'll be sixteen in September."

"Are you dating, Susie?" He crossed his arms as if starting an interrogation.

"Yes, I have…had a boyfriend," Susie muttered.

"And are you sexually active, Susie?" Dr. Midland lifted his brows inquisitively.

Susie shifted uncomfortably.

"Susie, the doctor has asked you a question. Answer him, sweetheart."

"Yes, but only a few times," she quickly said. "And only with one boy."

"Well." Dr. Midland uncrossed his arms. "Let's get you examined and see what's going on here. Susie, I need you to hop up on the table and scoot down, putting your feet in the stirrups." Pulling up a stool, he positioned himself at the bottom of the exam table. Susie closed her eyes in discomfort.

Please let it be the flu. Please let it be the flu." Susie prayed.

"Mrs. Decker, your daughter is approximately five months pregnant." He pushed himself away from the exam table, pulling off his gloves. "We have a few options with girls this age."

"Momma?" Susie looked at her mother in fear and shame.

"Thank you, Dr. Midland, but your options won't be necessary. This is a family matter, and we'll handle it."

"As you wish, Mrs. Decker." He took out his prescription pad. "This is for prenatal vitamins," he said, ripping the sheet from his pad.

"Thank you, Doctor."

"You're welcome, Mrs. Decker. Let me know if I can be of any further assistance." He quietly closed the exam-room door.

"Susie, get dressed." Liz put the prescription in her purse.

"Yes, Momma. What are we going to do, Momma?" Susie asked, pulling on her jeans.

"I'm not sure, Susie. I need to think about this."

"Maybe I could get a job, Momma, after school. To help take care of the baby."

"Don't be ridiculous, Susie." Liz taken aback. "You can't keep this baby."

"What do you mean, Momma? It's my baby."

"Susie, you're fifteen years old. This is 1958. Young ladies do not have babies out of wedlock. It will ruin your life."

"But, Momma." Her eyes were misting.

"But nothing, Susie."

"I'll talk to Daddy," Susie murmured. "He'll figure out a way I can keep my baby."

"You're not talking to your father about anything, young lady. He's to know nothing of this. Your father would insist that Johnny do the right thing. He would be on that young man's front porch demanding his daughter's honor be upheld. Oh no, the last thing we need is your father finding out."

"But, Mom, how are we going to keep this from Daddy?" She touched the small bump growing inside her stomach.

"I'm not sure, Susie, but we are."

"Maybe Aunt Mandy can help."

"*No*! The fewer people that know, the better. School is almost out for the summer, and you're hardly showing." Liz was thinking out loud. "So a girdle and some loose-fitting dresses will take care of that problem. Now, where to have the baby?" Her mind searched and then her eyes lit up. "You can go stay with your aunt Helen in Port Hope. She's always asking if you'd like to come up and visit for the summer. You can have the baby there and put it up for adoption. Yes," she said, satisfied with her solutions. "That will work."

"Aunt Helen's? Mom? Please think of another way." Susie's voice was pleading.

"There is no other way, Susie."

"But, Mom, you know how Aunt Helen feels about religion and sin! I would be so embarrassed and ashamed. Please, Mom, there must be somewhere else...anywhere else...please?"

"Susie, you're being ridiculous. Your aunt loves you, and she will understand that you've made a mistake. Besides, your father would think nothing of you going north for the summer. In fact, he would encourage it. Does Johnny know or suspect that you're pregnant?"

"No. He has a new girlfriend, Sara Nelson." Her voice was sad and somber. "He acts like I don't even exist."

"Good. We can at least keep our family pride. No one else is to know about this, Susie. Just you, me, and your aunt Helen. Do you understand, Susie?" She gave her a firm look. "No one!"

"Yes, I understand, Mom...no one else."

Memorial Day: Visiting Joe

"Hey, buddy, brought us a couple of beers this time." I took two cans of Old Milwaukee from the cooler, popping their caps. Taking a long swallow, I poured a big slug over Joe's grave. "Taste good, buddy? Yeah, nothing like a cold beer on a hot summer day." I took another long swallow.

"Got another postcard from Pappy the other day. He's still in Tuscany. Thinking of putting down roots. Apparently dear Francine has turned Pappy's head. I guess we all get taken down by the love of a good woman, if given enough time. Hey, Joe? To Pa'pae, and love." I raised the beer in a toast and poured another long shot over Joe's grave.

"Things are going good at the Silver Center, Joe. Got a few young boys that show some real potential. Petey put on a great exhibition fight against Tommy Thunder. You would've been proud of him, Joe. He took Tommy down in the third round. Did I tell you Lou Armando is his trainer? You remember Armando, Joe—the Hit-Man's old trainer. Well, he hasn't changed, still a hard-nosed pit bull. Don't really care for his training tactics, but they seem to work well for Petey.

"Mandy brought by another loser for dinner the other night. I think his name was Buck. No, that was the loser before. Chet? No... I'm really not sure, Joe, but it really doesn't matter. He's probably moved on by now anyway. Susie had a boyfriend—Johnny O'Brien, a real charmer. I got strange vibes off the kid, Joe. Sometimes he seemed nervous and insecure. Other times confident, almost defiant. Like he's portraying himself one way to me and another to the world. They're broken up now. Can't say it didn't make me happy, but I think the little punk may have broken my Susie's heart. She's going north for the summer to visit my sister. I'm sure some time up north will heal her young heart. Liz says the first love is always the hardest to get over.

"Is this the karma you spoke of, Joe? Were there fathers out there feeling the pangs of sadness from me breaking their daughters' hearts? Is this their revenge? If it is, I guess I deserve it, but in my defense it was never my intent."

I poured the last of Joe's beer over his grave. "Well," I said, standing tall. "Always good talking to you, buddy. See you soon, wingman." I stepped carefully, respectfully. The small American flag adorning Joe's grave site waved as it caught a breeze.

CHAPTER SIXTEEN

1958: Summer with Aunt Helen

The car ride to Helen's up in Port Hope was silent and strained to say the least. Susie and Liz both in their own thoughts as to what lay ahead. Helen was out in the yard working her vegetable garden when they pulled into the drive.

"Welcome." Helen said brushing the dirt from her garden gloves. "Was it an easy drive?"

"It was fine." Liz said stepping from the car grabbing Susie's suitcase from the back seat."

"Would you like a cup of tea Liz or a soft drink before you head back?"

"No thank you Helen. Harry is expecting me back. Susie?" Liz opened her arms. Susie quickly stepped inside her mother's safe embrace. "It will all be over before you know sweetheart." She whispered hugging her tight.

"She'll be fine Liz. Don't worry I will take good care of her. Have a safe trip back.

"Thank you again Helen." Liz slowly, sadly pulled from the drive.

"Come on Susie, let's get you settled." Helen picked up Susie's suitcases from the driveway. "Then I think it would be a good idea for the two of us to go to church and ask the Lord for some guidance in your time of need."

"Yes, Aunt Helen." Susie sighed, watching her mother's car disappear from sight.

"You can have the room at the top of the stairs, Susie; it gets a good cross breeze. The summers up here can get extremely hot and humid."

"Thank you, Aunt Helen." Susie fell in step behind her aunt, climbing the stairs, preparing herself for the summer that lay ahead.

"Change quickly, dear." Helen laid the suitcases atop the bed. "We don't want to be late for five o'clock Mass. You know how I feel about tardiness. Especially when it comes to the Lord."

"Yes, I know, Aunt Helen. I'll change quickly."

"I'll be waiting downstairs, dear." Helen softly closed the bedroom door. Susie looked around the bedroom that had once made her feel so much joy and happiness when she'd visit as a child; now it only represented loneliness and seclusion. Quickly changing into a pink summer shift, she made her way downstairs to her Aunt Helen, who was waiting with Bible in hand.

"I thought we could walk, dear; it's such a beautiful summer day, and the church is just down the street."

"Whatever you wish, Aunt Helen." Susie followed her aunt onto the path that would lead them to Saint Michael's.

"I think the less said about your condition, Susie, the better." Helen was looking straight ahead, seeing several members of the congregation milling about outside the church entrance.

"Yes, Aunt Helen." Susie nodded, feeling guilt, shame, and embarrassment.

"Good afternoon, good afternoon." Helen nodded to several members of the congregation. The bells of Saint Michael's called them all to Mass inside its sacred walls. "Follow me, dear."

"Yes, Aunt Helen." Following her aunt's lead, Susie dipped her fingertips into the holy water, made the sign of the cross, and genuflected before entering the front-row pew.

"Kneel, dear." Helen gently pulled Susie to her knees, tilting her head in prayer, and giving Susie a sideways glance to cue her to follow suit. Susie bowed her head as instructed, surreptitiously looking around the church, her eyes coming to rest on the crucifixion of Christ.

"Stand, dear." Helen gently tugged on Susie's arm, bringing her to stand alongside her. The choir began to sing "How Great Thou Art." The priest slowly made his way to the pulpit. The parishioners sang along in praise, viewing him as God's emissary.

"Our sermon today is on forgiveness," Father Francis stated in all his holiness. "To forgive someone is to free oneself of the burden and turmoil that keeps our heart and minds captive." Scanning his sea of parishioners, his eyes came to rest on the front-row pew. Susie shifted uncomfortably and looked to her aunt, who seemed to be absorbing the priest's words, tucking them deep in her heart. "For when forgiveness is given, the heart and mind become free of their bondage…to love, and be loved in return."

Susie watched in amazement as Father Francis continued his sermon. Her aunt and the rest of the congregation were mesmerized by Father Francis's holy words. Many of them had blissful looks on their faces, euphoric in their faith. Faith in something more. Faith in something holy.

"Forgiveness." Helen gently squeezed Susie's hand as Father Francis brought his sermon to an end. The congregation stood in honor as the choir sang in praise.

Late July 1958

"Good morning, Aunt Helen, is there anything I can help you with?" Susie asked, waddling her way into the kitchen.

"No, dear, just take a seat; breakfast is ready." Helen set down a warm breakfast plate.

"You know, Aunt Helen." Susie looked at her aunt timidly. "I've heard...that some girls...unmarried girls...keep their babies, and I was wondering if maybe, just maybe, there was a way I could keep mine?"

"Susie, dear, you're only fifteen years old, and—"

"I'll be sixteen shortly, Aunt Helen," Susie quickly proclaimed.

"Regardless, dear. This is 1958; ladies do not have children out of wedlock and keep them."

"Some ladies do, Aunt Helen." Her voice was optimistic.

"You're talking nonsense, Susie. Now finish your breakfast. I don't want to be late for morning Mass."

"If I pray to God for guidance and ask forgiveness of my sin, then could I keep my baby, Aunt Helen?"

"God has already forgiven your sin, but you must still do the right thing by your child. Babies deserve to have a mother and a father, dear. You wouldn't want your baby to carry the stigma of being branded a fatherless child, would you?"

"But, Aunt Helen, I would love my baby enough for both a mother and a father."

"I'm sure you would, Susie, but love is not what we're talking about here, dear. It's the unwritten laws of society. What is and isn't acceptable in their eyes."

"But, how could society not accept an innocent baby?"

"Susie," said Helen, growing irritated, "the decisions for this baby have been made—end of discussion."

"I'm sorry, Aunt Helen. I didn't mean to upset you. I'll go change, and then we can go to church." Susie got up from the table and scraped what was left of her breakfast into the garbage before quietly leaving the kitchen.

"Good girl." Helen's eyes welled with tears as she asked God for her own guidance in helping her niece. Hearing the phone ring, she took a deep breath for composure before picking up the receiver. "Hello? Oh, hello, Liz...yes, Susie's doing just fine. The church has contacted a nice young couple that is incapable of having children of their own. Father Francis and I are meeting with them this weekend. Yes, I think it's best we keep the adoption private. There's no need to thank me, Liz; we're family. With God's help and guidance, I'm sure we'll get through...yes, Liz...Susie's right here...it's your mother, dear." She handed Susie the phone.

"Hi, Momma. Yeah, everything's good...I feel fine, a little homesick maybe." She gave her aunt a hesitant smile. "How are you and Daddy? I miss you both so much." Her voice broke, eyes misting. "It's not your fault, Mom. I made the mistake of trusting Johnny. I thought he loved me." She tried to hold back the tears. "No, Momma, I can't talk to Daddy right now. I'm afraid if I hear his voice, I'll just start to cry...just tell him I love him, and I'll call him later...good-bye, Momma." Hanging up the phone, she wiped the tears from her eyes.

"Come on, dear." Helen put a comforting arm around Susie. "Let's go to Mass and pray to God for some healing and guidance."

August 1958

"Aunt Helen?" Susie called into the darkness.

"Susie? What's wrong, dear?" Helen turned on her bedside lamp.

"I feel funny." Susie moaned. "The baby is moving around a lot, and my stomach's cramping. I'm scared, Aunt Helen." She stepped inside her aunt's bedroom.

"There's nothing to be scared about, dear, but we should probably take you to the hospital. Go and get dressed."

"Okay, Aunt Helen." Susie moaned again. She slowly made her way back to her bedroom and took the white cotton shift dress from the closet. Helen joined her there.

"Let me help you, dear," said Helen, seeing the pain clearly on Susie's face.

"Thank you." Susie pulled the shift dress over her head, wincing in discomfort.

"Come on, dear; we need to hurry." Helen helped her down the stairs and out to the car. "Everything's going to be fine, Susie. Don't worry, dear." Turning over the ignition and saying a silent prayer, she pulled from the drive.

"It hurts, Aunt Helen." Susie moaned in pain, holding her stomach tight. "Please hurry."

"We're almost there, dear," Helen said, trying to stay calm.

"*Aggh.*" Susie tried to contain her scream.

"We're here, dear…we're here." Helen's voice was becoming anxious. "Don't worry; everything's going to be fine." She helped Susie through the emergency doors. "Nurse, please, we need your help." She struggled to hold Susie up. "I believe my niece is in labor."

"When's her due date?" asked the nurse, quickly coming to Susie's aid.

"August twenty-fifth," Susie moaned. "What's happening, Aunt Helen?" She felt a warm liquid run down her leg.

"Orderly, get me a wheelchair—now!" the nurse demanded.

"I'm scared, Aunt Helen." Susie doubled over in pain, another contraction consuming her.

"You'll be fine, dear." Helen helped her into the wheelchair.

"We'll take it from here, ma'am." The nurse took hold of the wheelchair handles.

"Do everything the doctor says, Susie." Helen watched her niece being wheeled through the doors marked "Surgical Area… No Admittance."

"There's a waiting room at the end of the hall, ma'am." The orderly pointed. "You can wait there."

"Thank you, young man, but could you point me in the direction of your hospital chapel?"

"Of course." He softly smiled. "It's directly behind you."

"Thank you." Helen pushed open the chapel doors and knelt before the cross, feeling the same undeniable love and calmness whenever she entered God's sanctuary. "Dear Lord, please watch over my niece at this delicate time."

"Okay, Susie, on your next contraction, I need you to take a deep breath and push as hard as you can. Get ready, Susie. *Now*! Pushhhh," the doctor sputtered. "Good, Susie, you're doing great. You can relax now."

"It won't be much longer, dear, and your baby will be here," a soft female voice said from behind a mask, only a pair of compassionate eyes to be seen.

"Okay, Susie, this is it." The doctor's voice was eager. "On your next contraction, I want you to push as hard as you can." Susie nodded, looking to the kind eyes behind the mask, feeling pain as the next contraction consumed her.

"Push, Susie…push…push," the doctor said energetically. "I can see the head crowning. Okay, Susie, relax…relax…take a few breaths."

"Your baby is almost here," the nurse with the compassionate eyes murmured.

"I need a really big push this time, Susie…now! Give me everything you've got." Susie took a deep breath and gave one hard final push, feeling the baby leave her body.

"It's a boy, Susie." The nurse smiled. "You have a son."

"Nurse!" the doctor shouted urgently. "Scissors, quickly—he's in distress." The compassionate eyes left Susie's bedside.

"Here, Doctor." The soft voice was now direct, professional, as the nurse anxiously watched the doctor cut the umbilical cord that was so tightly woven around the small baby's neck, choking off his breath.

"Get some oxygen on him, stat!"

"Yes, Doctor." The nurse ran from the room, baby in arms.

"What's happening?" Susie looked around the delivery room in fear. "Where is that nurse going with my baby?"

"Calm down, Susie. I need you to relax." The doctor's voice was soft and soothing. "The nurses are doing all they can to help your son. My job now is to get you stabilized." He gave a nod of permission to the anesthesiologist. Susie inhaled deeply, becoming drowsy, relaxed.

"Doctor Schwartz?" said Helen, coming from the chapel. "How's my niece? How's the baby?"

"Susie is fine. She'll be out of recovery in about an hour, but I'm sorry." His voice became grave. "We were unable to save the baby."

"I'm sorry, Doctor?" Helen looked at him in disbelief. "What did you say?"

"I'm sorry, Miss Decker. Somehow during delivery, the umbilical cord became tightly wrapped around his neck, making him unable to breathe for far too long. We gave him oxygen, and he took a few breaths on his own, but I'm sorry; we were unable to save him."

"It's not your fault, Doctor. I'm sure you did your best. It's God's will." She made the sign of the cross. "We are of the Catholic faith, Doctor; I want the baby baptized before burial."

"And Susie?" The doctor's eyes were questioning. "She's asking to see the baby."

"No. Susie is not to see the baby."

"Do you think that's wise, Miss Decker?"

"Susie is a minor, Doctor, and I am her guardian. I would appreciate it if you let the family handle this delicate situation."

"As you wish, Ms. Decker." He bowed slightly. "We have a Catholic priest on staff, or do you wish to call your own?"

"That won't be necessary, Doctor. I'm sure the priest you have on staff is fine. Now take me to the baby. I want to be present when the baptism is performed."

"Nurse Winters?" The doctor gestured.

"Yes, Doctor?" The nurse looked up from her station.

"Will you please contact the priest on staff, then show Ms. Decker to the mortuary holding room?"

"Right away, Doctor." She picked up the phone. "Father McQuean, please. Hello, Father, we have a baptism to be performed...yes, that's correct...as soon as possible. Thank you, Father." Hanging up the phone, she said, "He's on his way, Miss Decker; if you'll follow me, I'll escort you to the holding room."

"Thank you." Helen followed the nurse as instructed, holding her rosary tight.

"Aunt Helen, did you see him?" Susie's voice was soft, filled with excitement. "I only caught a glimpse of him, but he was beautiful. When can I see him?"

"Susie, dear." Helen's voice was gentle. "Shortly after your son was born, he was called back to heaven."

"Called to heaven? What do you mean, Aunt Helen?" Susie looked to her for explanation. "He's going to live a wonderful life with a young couple. That's what you said...I heard you, on the phone."

"I'm sorry, dear."

"No! No! He can't be dead!" Susie was becoming hysterical. "He hasn't lived yet. I have to go to him, Aunt Helen. He must be so scared." Throwing off the covers, she attempted to get out of bed.

"Stop it, Susie!" Helen held her down as Susie struggled. "Stop it, right now! You're in no condition to go running around this hospital. Now calm down, and let me explain what has happened." Susie's eyes welled with tears as her aunt told her the details of her son's death. "They tried everything, Susie…everything." She shook her head sadly. "He just refused to breathe."

"Let me go to my son, Aunt Helen." Susie's eyes were pleading. "He needs me. I need to see him." She gently touched the flat stomach where he used to lie.

"I don't think that's a good idea, dear." Helen adjusted Susie's covers. "Besides, it would serve no purpose."

"Am I being punished, Aunt Helen? Does God hate me for having a baby out of wedlock?"

"No, dear." Helen was taken aback. "God does not hate you. God loves you."

"Then why, Aunt Helen?" Susie's eyes filled with tears.

"It's not up to us to question God's will, Susie." Helen consoled her in a warm embrace. "Mourn the loss of your son, dear. Then move on with your life. It will help no one to stay in the past. You'll have another child someday, Susie. You'll see. God always has a plan." She looked to the heavens without question.

CHAPTER SEVENTEEN

June 1960

"Where is she, Harry? I don't see her." Liz searched the crowd of students adorned in black robes as "Pomp and Circumstance" began to play.

"There she is, Liz. There's our little girl." I pointed down from the bleachers of Central High. "She just sat down, third row, fourth seat in from the right. Do you see her, sweetheart?"

"Oh, yes, there she is. I see her now, Harry. Look at her, darling." She gently took my arm. "I'm so proud of her; she's become such a wonderful young lady."

"You did a great job of raising her, Liz. You're a good mother." I gently patted her hand. "I was a little worried a few years back when that Johnny character broke her heart; she was so unhappy." I shook my head, remembering how devastated she'd been. "I thought sending her to Port Hope for the summer would do the trick, but when she returned she seemed worse, more depressed than when she left."

"The first heartbreak is always tough, Harry," Liz sadly murmured.

"Maybe so, Liz, but you were great with her. Very understanding, always knowing just what she needed when I had no clue."

"Thank you, Harry, but I can't take all the credit. You've been a wonderful father to Susie."

"Thank you for that, sweetheart. Then I guess we're in agreement." I put my arm around her, pulling her in close. "We did a great job."

"Susie Mae Decker," the principal called, diploma in hand. Liz and I proudly watched as our daughter took center stage and accepted her high-school diploma, moving the cap tassel from left to right in recognition of her accomplishment. She waved to us up in the stands, looking happy, beautiful as ever.

September 1961

"Liz, I'm home! Where are you, sweetheart? I've brought someone home for you to meet."

"I'm in the kitchen, Harry," Liz called out.

"Liz, I would like you to meet my new apprentice, Rich Jenkins. I've invited him for dinner, sweetheart." I gave her a quick wink.

"Hello, Rich." Liz smiled warmly. "I hope you like Italian. I've made lasagna."

"Lasagna sounds great, Mrs. Decker. I just hope I'm not an inconvenience."

"Of course not, Rich. You're more than welcome. I've made plenty."

"Where's our daughter tonight Liz? I wanted to introduce her to Rich."

"She has a night class at the college, but she'll be home for dinner." Liz turned off the buzzing timer. "Harry, take Rich into the living room and make him a drink while I finish dinner."

"Good idea, sweetheart." I left the kitchen with Rich in tow. "What can I get for you, Rich?"

"A martini would be great, Harry."

"Martini it is." I grabbed top shelf. "So, Rich, what do you think about the Kirby job? Do you believe it can be completed in three months?"

"Sure, if we keep our nose to the grindstone and don't have too many setbacks."

"That's good to hear. I like your confidence, son. I'll accept the conditions of the contract on Monday, and there'll be a bonus in it for you if we have an early completion."

"Sounds good to me Harry" He accepted his martini.

"Good. Enough about business, Rich. How are you doing? How are you adjusting to a new town?"

"Pretty good." He gave a confident nod. "It's just takes a while to meet new people, establish friendships."

"Well, my daughter knows plenty of people, and I'm sure she would be willing to show you around."

"That would be great, Harry. I'd love to have someone show me the sights. Did your wife say she was in college?"

"Yes, she's going to be a court stenographer; she's in her first year."

"Hi, Mom." Susie walked in the back door and dropped her books on the kitchen table.

"Hello, Susie, how was your class tonight?" asked Liz, arranging yellow peppers atop the antipasto salad.

"Good. We actually got to type a mock court case today." She stole a pepperoni from the salad.

"That sounds interesting, Susie." Liz replaced the stolen pepperoni. "Your father brought his new apprentice home for dinner. Why don't you go in and introduce yourself?" She checked the French loaf in the oven.

"Sure, Mom." Susie stole another pepperoni from the salad on her way out of the kitchen.

"Susie Decker!" exclaimed Liz, seeing the replaced pepperoni gone once again.

"Hi, Daddy," Susie chirped as she entered the living room.

"Here's my beautiful daughter." I smiled proudly. "Rich Jenkins, this is my Susie."

"It's very nice to meet you, Susie. Your father wasn't kidding when he said you were beautiful."

"My father's prejudiced." Susie blushed. "Nice to meet you, Mr. Jenkins."

"Please, call me Rich. When you say Mr. Jenkins, I look around for my father." He smiled warmly.

"Rich it is." She returned his warm smile

"Susie? I thought you might be able to show Rich around. He's new in town, and—"

"That's if it wouldn't be too much trouble," Rich interjected.

"No, no trouble at all, Rich. I would love to."

"Well, I have no plans for this weekend, Susie, or for any weekend, as far as that goes." Rich chuckled.

"This weekend would be great, Rich." Susie's dark eyes were smiling.

"Susie, dear?" Liz called out from the kitchen. "I need your help."

"Kitchen duty calls...if you'll excuse me, Rich?"

"Of course." He smiled with a nod..

"Mom," Susie gushed, entering the kitchen. "Why didn't you tell me Daddy's apprentice was so handsome?"

"Is he handsome, Susie? I hadn't noticed. You know I only have eyes for your father. Could you slice the French loaf for me, sweetheart?"

"Sure, Mom." She took the bread knife from the drawer. "Daddy asked me to show him around this weekend. Where should I take him? What would be fun? Any suggestions?"

"It doesn't matter, sweetheart; when two young people are attracted to each other, just being together is fun."

"Who said anything about being attracted to him? I just said he was good-looking. Besides, I'm doing it for Daddy as a favor."

"That's very nice of you, sweetheart, to do your father a kindness." Liz gave an all-knowing smile. "Now take this salad out to the dining-room table. The men must be starving."

December 1961

"I'm dreaming of a white Christmas...just like the ones I used to know." Sounds of Liz and Susie harmonizing along with Bing Crosby greeted me as I came through the front door of Twelve Forty Leland Street. My not-so-great voice chimed in.

"Where the treetops glisten, and children listen...to hear sleigh bells in the snow."

"How was your day, Harry?" Liz softly smiled.

"It was good, sweetheart." I gave her a gentle kiss on the cheek, feeling the joy throughout the house that only Christmastime brings. Love and satisfaction consumed me as I fondly watched the two loves of my life trim our beautiful Christmas tree.

"Don't you just love Christmastime, Daddy?" Susie was swaying to the music. "There's always such a happy feeling in the air. I was just telling Mom that in the spirit of Christmas, we should probably invite Rich over for Christmas dinner. I know for a fact he's not planning on going home for the holidays."

"That's very thoughtful of you, sweetheart, to worry about a guy you've only seen a handful of times."

"I'm not worried about him, Daddy, but it is Christmastime. It's totally up to you and Mom—just a suggestion."

"What do you think, Liz?" I gave her a wink. "Should we invite Rich over for Christmas dinner?"

"I'm not sure, Harry. Christmas has always been a family holiday. Just the three of us." She put another ornament on the tree.

"Yeah, but it is the holidays, Liz." Grabbing the poker, I gently stoked the fire.

"Well, it's totally up to the two of you, but I think it's the right thing to do," Susie interjected. "After all, no one should be alone at Christmastime."

"You're right, sweetheart; no one should be alone." I gave her a mischievous smile. "That's why I invited Rich a few days ago. He'll be here Christmas Day around noon."

"Oh, Daddy, why must you always tease me so?" Susie stammered, putting her last ornament on the tree. "Dance with me, Daddy." She held out her arms. "Rockin' around the Christmas Tree" began to play.

"I would love to, sweetheart," I said, doing a few quick moves, taking her into my arms.

"Harry, you better stick to the waltz or the fox-trot." Liz lovingly laughed, watching my attempt at the jitterbug.

"I don't know, Liz." I gave my daughter a quick spin. "What do you think, Susie?"

"I think you're a wonderful dancer, Daddy," she said, happily spinning back into my arms.

"Is that the doorbell, Harry? Are you expecting anyone?"

"Not I, sweetheart." I was a little winded.

"It is the doorbell," Liz said, hearing the chimes once again. She set down the box of tinsel. "Well, hello, Rich. What brings you here this evening?"

"Hello, Mrs. Decker. I was just wondering if Susie might be home; and if so, could I speak to her for a moment?"

"Of course, Rich, come in." Liz stepped aside. "Susie is in the front room dancing with her father. Harry has always been under the illusion that he dances as well as Fred Astaire."

"Is he that good?" Rich took off his hat.

"You know, Rich? He is." Lightly laughing, She led the way back into the living room. "Look who's here," Liz called out over the music.

"Hey, Rich." I gave him a wave.

"Hi, Rich." Susie giggled, doing a quick two-step.

"Hello, Harry, Susie."

"What can I do for you this evening, son?"

"Nothing, sir," he said, competing with the music. "I came to see Susie. I was wondering if she wouldn't mind helping me do some Christmas shopping tomorrow. I'd like to send a few gifts back east to my parents, considering I'm not going home for the holidays."

"I would love to go shopping tomorrow, Rich. I still have a little Christmas shopping to do myself."

"Great, Susie. How's about I pick you up around ten—if that's not too early."

"Ten sounds fine, Rich. I'll be ready." She rolled out of a spin.

"Okay then—great." He reluctantly turned to leave.

"What's your hurry, son?" I said as "Rocking around the Christmas Tree" ended and Nat King Cole began. "Stay awhile."

"I'd love too." Rich smiled wide. "Lord knows, I've got no one waiting for me at home."

"Can I take your coat, Rich?" Liz's softly smiled.

"Thank you, Mrs. Decker."

"Would you like a drink, son?" I asked, pouring myself a gin martini.

"I'd love one, Harry."

"Hey, let's play a game of euchre," Susie excitedly suggested. "Do you play cards, Rich?"

"Yeah, I play." He smiled happily, contentedly.

"Great! Mom? You and Daddy can be partners, and Rich and I can be partners. Would you like to be my partner, Rich?"

"I'd love to be your partner, Susie." Rich smiled.

"Great." Susie blushed, opening the deck of cards.

The Next Day

"Mom, can you get that?" Susie called out from her bedroom, hearing the doorbell. "It's probably Rich."

"Sure, sweetheart." Liz rubbed her temples, slowly getting up from the couch.

"Hello, Rich. Come on in. Susie will be ready shortly. It looks like a beautiful winter's day out there." She squinted out at the brightness.

"Yes, ma'am. Sunny skies, freshly fallen snow, really puts you in the Christmas spirit." Kicking the snow from his boots, he stepped inside. Liz inhaled deeply, rubbing her temples, feeling them throb.

"Are you okay, Mrs. Decker?"

"I'm fine, Rich, just a little headache."

"I just need to grab my coat, Rich." Susie came up behind her mother and opened the closet door. "Where would you like to go shopping? I thought because it's such a nice day, we could go downtown. Walk the stores and see the beautiful Christmas decorations." She handed Rich her coat for assistance.

"Oh yes, the decorations are really beautiful this year," Liz interjected. Suddenly feeling woozy, she leaned heavily against the wall for support.

"Mom!" Susie helped her mother steady herself. "What's wrong, Mom?"

"I'm fine, Susie—just a little headache." Liz winced in pain.

"Maybe I should stay home with you today, Mom. We can go shopping another day. Can't we, Rich?"

"Sure, if your mother isn't feeling well." Rich sounded a little disappointed.

"I'll be fine, Susie. There's no reason for you and Rich to cancel your plans." Liz was adamant, recomposing herself.

"Are you sure, Mom?"

"I'm sure, sweetheart. I'll be fine." She gave her an encouraging smile.

"Is there anything we can do for you before we go, Mrs. Decker?" asked Rich, seeing a torn look on Susie's face.

"Now that you mention it, Rich, I would love a fire. Do you mind? Harry usually takes care of that for me."

"Not at all. One fire coming right up." Rich grabbed some logs from the stack and had a fire blazing within minutes.

"Thank you, Rich. Now the two of you go and enjoy yourselves. Get your shopping done, while I lie here in front of this beautiful fire and relax until your father gets home."

"Where is Daddy, Mom? When are you expecting him home?"

"He's over at the shop finishing up an order. He'll be home soon, sweetheart. Don't worry. Rich? Please take my daughter out of here so I can relax."

"You heard your mother. Let's go, young lady." Rich chuckled.

"Okay, Mom, if you're sure." Susie buttoned her coat.

"Good-bye, Susie." Liz gave a playful wave, softly closing the front door.

"I'm sure your mother will be fine, Susie." Rich took her arm, leading her through the freshly fallen snow.

"I hope so." Susie's voice was filled with concern. "Whom are we shopping for today, Rich?" she asked, trying to shake off her apprehension.

"My parents. Perfume and a chenille scarf for my mother. The scarf department is where I need the help. My mother only wears one perfume: Chanel No. 5." His voice was nostalgic.

"And your mother's favorite color?" Susie was taking mental notes.

"She likes blue, but I think all women look pretty in pink."

"I love pink too, Rich, but if you want my opinion? Get your mother blue. Light blue. After all, it is her gift, not yours."

"You're right!" He chuckled. "It isn't my gift. I'm glad I brought you along, Susie; blue it is."

"One parent down." Susie smiled. "And your father?"

"My dad's easy. Tie and cuff links. The man loves his ties." He smiled. "Whom might you be shopping for today, Susie?"

"My shopping's finished," Susie proudly stated. "I just need to pick up a portrait from Professional Designs"

"Great, so here's our game plan." Rich sounded like he was conducting a SWAT team. "We pick up the perfume and blue—light-blue—chenille scarf for my mother at Macy's. The tie and cuff links at Roberto's. They have good quality stuff there. Then we'll pick up your portrait at Professional Designs, and then I'll take you to lunch at that new bistro."

"Sounds like a plan, Mr. Jenkins." Susie cozied into the front seat, letting the enjoyment of Rich's company replace the worry for her mother.

"Just here to please, Miss Decker—destination, Macy's." Turning up the radio, he accelerated the car.

"I think that's the fastest I've ever shopped, Rich." Susie said, waiting in line outside the bistro with all the other Christmas shoppers. "Don't you just love the Christmas crowds, Rich? So full of glee and holiday spirit."

"I have to admit, I love the holidays, Susie—but the crowds? I can do without." He stepped up to the podium. "Two, please," he shouted over the noise of the crowded bistro, "Jingle Bells" softly playing in the background.

"Right this way, sir." The hostess, adorned with a Santa hat, maneuvered her way through the sea of people, Rich and Susie in tow. "Here we are." She handed them both menus. "Enjoy your lunch."

"Aren't the Christmas decorations just beautiful, Rich? I just love the way—" Susie stopped in midsentence, her eyes coming to rest on her father flirtatiously talking to a strange woman in the corner booth.

"Love what, Susie?" Rich looked up from his menu.

"Rich, do you know that woman?"

"What woman?" Rich scanned the sea of people in the overcrowded bistro.

"That woman, there in the corner, with my father."

"No, I can't say I do." He looked at the attractive woman seated with his boss.

"Could she be a business associate, Rich?" Susie felt sick to her stomach.

"It's possible, Susie. I haven't been working with your father long enough to know all his associates."

"Merry Christmas!" The waitress stepped into their view. "Would you care to hear the specials?"

"Rich, do you mind if we just skip lunch? I suddenly feel as if I need to check on my mother."

"Sure, Susie…if that's what you want." He sadly uttered.

"It's what I want, Rich." Susie looked past the waitress to her father engrossed in conversation.

"Thank you, but I guess we won't be having lunch today." Rich handed back the menus.

"Another time, then," the waitress replied, motioning to the hostess that there was an open table.

"Susie, I know it's none of my business, but I'm sure there's a perfectly innocent explanation as to who the woman was with your father," Rich said, pulling out into downtown traffic.

"I'm sure there is, Rich. It's not that. I'm just a little worried about my mother. Do you mind if we don't talk?" She turned up the radio and gazed out the window.

"Sure," Rich solemnly replied. Their fun-filled day had turned to ruin. He drove her home in discontented silence. "We're here, Susie."

"So we are." Susie stepped from the car.

"Thanks again for your help today Susie. I would've bought the pink scarf for sure if you hadn't been with me." Rich chuckled lightly.

"You're welcome, Rich. I'm sorry for cutting the day short. I'm just a little worried about my mother."

"No problem, Susie. Maybe we could go out again sometime?"

"That would be great, Rich."

"Well then, till Christmas Day," said Rich, tipping his hat.

"Till Christmas Day, Rich." Susie stepped inside, closing the door. "Mom, I'm home…Mom?" She looked at the empty couch.

"I'm in the kitchen, sweetheart. Did you and Rich get all your shopping done?"

"Yes, it's all finished. Daddy's not back from work yet?"

"No, he called a little while ago." Liz was preoccupied with searching her cupboards. "The job is taking a little longer than expected. So he won't be home for a couple of hours."

"And what job would that be?" Susie mumbled under her breath.

"What, sweetheart?"

"Nothing. How are you feeling, Mom? You had me a little worried this afternoon."

"Much better, sweetheart." She retrieved the sugar from the cupboard. "I took a blood-pressure pill and a short nap. It seemed to do the trick." Giving Susie a warm smile, she said, "What do you say you put on an apron and help me bake some gingerbread cookies? You know how much your father loves gingerbread."

Daddy doesn't deserve cookies, her mind muttered. "Sure, Mom." She retrieved an apron from inside the closet.

"Turn on some Christmas music, Susie," Liz said, measuring a cup of flour from its canister. "The traditional stuff, sweetheart, something warm and sentimental."

"Okay, Mom." Thumbing through the Christmas albums, Susie selected a collection of Bing Crosby Christmas classics. "Silver Bells" began to play.

"Did you enjoy your day out with Rich, Susie? He seems like a nice young man, and your father really seems to be impressed with him. He says the man knows his business." Liz selected the two gingerbread boys from the box of Christmas cookie cutters.

"Yeah, Rich is a nice guy, Mom." Susie's thoughts were preoccupied with what she had seen at the bistro, her mind desperately trying to explain it away. Maybe it was all perfectly innocent. She hoped it was. But either way, she had every intention of finding out, the moment her father got home.

"Is that gingerbread I smell?" Coming through the front door, I was greeted by the sights, sounds, and smells of the holidays.

"Yes, it is, Daddy." Susie cut me off at the pass.

"Hi, sweetheart, is something wrong?" I shook off the freshly fallen snow. "I thought you and Rich were going shopping today."

"We did, Daddy. We went downtown. In fact, we went to that new bistro on Saginaw Street."

"Oh yeah, sweetheart. I've been there a few times myself. Great food."

"Who is she, Daddy?"

"Who's...who, sweetheart?" I asked, hanging up my coat.

"The woman, Daddy?"

"I don't know what you're talking about. What woman?"

"The woman I saw you hiding with in the corner of the bistro."

"I wasn't hiding in any corner, Susie," I said dismissively. "It's where the hostess seated us."

"That still doesn't tell me who she is Daddy."

"It's complicated, Susie. Just know I love your mother."

"Then try and explain it, Daddy." Her voice was rising.

"Lower your voice, young lady, and remember who you're talking to." I gave her a stern look. "Where's your mother?"

"She's in the kitchen making your favorite cookies. Who was that woman, Daddy?" Susie demanded.

"The woman is no one, Susie. She means nothing."

"Nothing." Her bottom lip quivered. "Daddy, I love you with all my heart, but if you ever hurt my mother—"

"I could never hurt your mother, sweetheart. She's the love of my life."

"Then that woman means nothing?" She whimpered. "She's no one, Daddy?"

"No one, sweetheart. Come on." I put a consoling arm around her. "Let's go have some milk and warm gingerbread cookies." With my daughter nestling inside my arms, I vowed once again to keep my sexual demons at bay. I understood now that Mandy was right once again. It was a betrayal—not only to Liz but to my daughter and the sanctity of my family.

Christmas Day

"Merry Christmas, Daddy." Susie softly smiled, seated in front of the twinkling Christmas tree, still in her pajamas. The picture-window curtains were open, displaying lightly falling snow. "Little Drummer Boy" quietly came from the stereo. An aromatic scent of pine, spices, and cinnamon wafted throughout the house. The sights, sounds, and smells of Christmas were alive and well inside Twelve Forty Leland Street.

"Merry Christmas, darling." Liz came into the living room with a tray of fresh coffee and hot rolls.

"Merry Christmas, sweethearts." I took a minute to capture this precious moment so eloquently laid before me, giving thanks for all the gifts I had received this year, but especially for my most precious: the gift of my family.

"So who's first?" Shaking the nostalgia from my shoulders, I rubbed my hands in anticipation of the day. "Who's ready to see what Santa has left us on this fine Christmas morning? How about we start with you, little lady?" I retrieved the smallest gift from under the tree. "Merry Christmas, my beautiful daughter."

"Thank you, Daddy." Susie tore away the Christmas wrapping and opened the jeweler's box. A delicate necklace replicating the black-eyed Susan flower glittered inside.

"Your father had it made special, sweetheart," Liz murmured. "Just for you. The petals are topaz and the center is a black pearl. He told the jeweler the necklace was beautiful, but not nearly as beautiful as his daughter's eyes."

"Thank you, Daddy; it's lovely." She clasped the necklace securely around her neck.

"You're welcome, sweetheart. And this one is for you, love of my life." I handed Liz the largest gift from under the tree.

"My goodness, Harry. What could this possibly be?" She looked at the large package wrapped in Norman Rockwell Christmas paper.

"Open it, Momma," Susie encouraged. Liz ripped the wrapping paper in delight to reveal a box displaying Ermines on its cover.

"Harry? You didn't." She quickly pulled the lid from the box. Her eyes were wide in awe. "It's beautiful, darling." She ran her hand over the soft fur.

"Try it on, Momma." Susie helped her take the coat from its box. Liz wrapped herself inside the full mink.

"It feels wonderful, Harry. Thank you," she said, rubbing her face gently against the soft fur collar.

"You're welcome, sweetheart." I gave her a soft kiss.

"My gift next." Susie eagerly pulled her gift from behind the tree. "Open it." She fidgeted in anticipation. Liz gently pulled away the paper.

"It seems like yesterday." Liz sighed. Her fingertips lightly touched the portrait in reminiscence.

"Yes, it does, sweetheart," I said, gazing at the portrait of our wedding day.

"I got the picture from Aunt Mandy and had it painted by an artist downtown." Susie beamed. "So you like it?"

"It's the perfect gift. From the perfect daughter. Thank you, sweetheart."

"You're welcome, Daddy."

"Yes, Susie, thank you," Liz said, not taking her eyes from the portrait.

"Oh my goodness!" Susie jumped up from the floor. "Look at the time! It's eleven o'clock! I've got to get dressed. I've only got an hour to pick out a dress and do my hair." She looked at her reflection in the sofa mirror. "And my face. Look at my face!"

"What's wrong with your face, sweetheart?"

"It's a mess, Daddy." She pinched her cheeks for color. "I'm going to need the works this morning. Foundation, blush, lipstick."

"You're beautiful, sweetheart, just the way you are. Applying makeup to that face will only be gilding the lily. Besides, it's just my apprentice, Rich."

"Mom? Please explain to Daddy you should always try to look your best, regardless of the company."

"Let her go, Harry. I still have my gift to give, and I would like to give it to you alone."

"Alone, you say? In that case, my daughter, be off with you." I gave a dismissive wave. Susie was already gone.

"Merry Christmas, darling." Liz handed me a small, beautifully wrapped gift.

"For me, sweetheart?" I ripped the paper away to reveal a beautiful Cartier wristwatch.

"There's an inscription on the back, Harry," she softly murmured.

"You made me love you, but I *wanted* to do it," the inscription read. "You changed the words, sweetheart?"

"Yes, my love." Liz turned up the volume on the stereo. Judy Garland's soft voice came from its speakers. "May I have this dance, darling?" She gently came into my arms. "You made me love you," Liz softly sang along. "I didn't want to do it; I didn't want to do it. Merry Christmas, darling." She nuzzled my neck.

"Merry Christmas, sweetheart." I picked up where she left off. "You made me love you, and all the time you knew it…I guess you always knew it." Feeling the loving comfort only Liz could bring, I glided around our living-room floor with her in a world all our own.

"Mom! Daddy! Can't you hear the doorbell? It rang at least five times." Susie marched past us toward the front door, shaking her head in dismay. "Merry Christmas, Rich. Come in."

"I hope I'm not too early?" He shook the freshly fallen snow from his coat before stepping inside.

"No, your timing is fine, Rich. I'm sorry it took so long to answer the door. I was getting dressed, and my parents? Well, I don't know where my parents were." Hanging his coat, she led him to the living room.

"Merry Christmas, Rich," Liz and I called out in unison.

"Merry Christmas," Rich happily replied. "Mrs. Decker, this is for you." He handed her a large poinsettia plant.

"It's beautiful, Rich. Thank you. How did you know the poinsettia was my favorite winter flower?"

"Just a lucky guess." He blushed slightly. "Susie, this is for you. Merry Christmas."

"Thank you, Rich, but a gift wasn't necessary," Susie said, accepting the beautifully wrapped package.

"It's not much, Susie." He shrugged his shoulders. "I remembered you like pink, and you should always get a girl what she likes. I believe those were your words?" He smiled softly.

"It's beautiful, Rich. Thank you." She took the pink chenille scarf from the box. "But now I feel bad. I didn't get you anything."

"A dance would suffice." He held open his arms in invitation. "I'm no Fred Astaire, but I can hold my own on the dance floor." Dean Martin's version of "Winter Wonderland" began to play.

"I'd love to, Rich." Susie stepped into his arms.

"Shall we, my love?" I opened my arms in invitation. "I am as good as Fred Astaire," I added, giving a wink.

"Let's just watch, Harry...shall we?" Liz relaxed back into my embrace. "She looks happy, doesn't she, darling?"

"That's all I wish for her, sweetheart." I looked at the man who seemed to have captured my daughter's heart. "That the man she chooses brings her happiness."

"Yes." Liz sighed. "Happiness." She snuggled into me, swaying inside my embrace.

"Merry Christmas, sweetheart." I held her close, feeling the holiday spirit, grateful for my many blessings.

CHAPTER EIGHTEEN

Memorial Day 1962

"Where's Daddy off to so early this morning?" asked Susie, coming into the living room.

"It's the week of Memorial Day, Susie. Your father's going to the cemetery."

"That's right. I don't know why I asked. Daddy has done the same thing every Memorial week for as long as I can remember."

"Visiting Joe's grave is your father's way of showing respect and remembering his dear friend."

"I understand Daddy's visits." Susie's voice was sad and somber. "Just because someone is no longer here, doesn't mean they're forgotten."

"I'm sorry, sweetheart. I know you do." She gave her daughter a gentle hug.

Closing the trunk of my car, wreath and flag in hand, I made my way to Joe's grave site, being ever so cautious to respect the graves of the fallen soldiers who surrounded my dear friend. "Hey, buddy." I gently pulled the old, worn flag from its place of honor and replaced it with a new one. It caught a breeze and waved an ever-so-gentle "Hello" back. "It's been another year, my friend, and all is well. Liz is beautiful as ever, and Susie seems to have finally found her way back from her depression. She's dating my apprentice, Rich. I told you about him. He seems to be a good man, but I don't think anyone will ever be good enough for my Susie."

"Excuse me," a male voice said from behind, interrupting my conversation. "Are you a friend of Joe's?"

"Yes." I turned to see a young man standing tall in uniform. "An old friend—and you are?"

"Henry...Henry Hinterman. Joe was my trainer for about six weeks many years ago at O'Hare's gym." He gave a bittersweet smile.

"Henry? Yes. Joe wrote me about you. You're Will's nephew. How is Will?"

"He's doing well. Still training at that ole run-down center they call a gym, but my uncle loves it." He shrugged his shoulders in unbelieving acceptance.

"I'm sure he does." I got a wave of nostalgia. "Harry...Harry Decker, but Joe called me Jack or Southpaw."

"So you're the great Southpaw I heard so much about." Henry smiled. "Between Pappy and Joe, I feel like I know you."

"Good to meet you, Henry." I shook his hand, feeling an instant bond.

"Nice to meet you, sir."

Henry and I talked for hours sitting at Joe's grave site. It felt good talking to someone who had known my friend and mentor. He talked of Pappy's no-nonsense approach to the world of boxing, his intolerance for tardiness, and the fear he had instilled in him as a young boy. He brought me to laughter as he imitated Pappy's grumble, causing young Henry to shiver in memory.

"Then there's Joe." Henry proudly sighed. "He's the reason I'm in uniform today." He lifted the side of his jacket, exposing a medal pinned to his inside shirt. "This was Joe's; he gave it to me before he left...it's a..."

"Commendation medal," I said, finishing his sentence. "Given to those who rise above...for doing the right thing...above and beyond the call of duty?"

"Yes." Henry smiled. Both of us became silent in remembrance of Joe.

"Henry? Do you have any place you need to be?" I asked, breaking the silence.

"No, not till later this afternoon; my mother's having a small picnic. Why?"

"What do you say we go to the pub? Have a beer? I could use a beer." I got up, brushing the dirt from my pants.

"The pub," Henry muttered nostalgically. "I could have a real beer this time."

"A real beer, Henry?"

"Just something between me, Pappy, and Joe." Henry looked at the white military cross and nodded his respects. "Lead the way, Mr. Collins." Both of us stepped carefully, respectfully. The American flag caught a strong breeze, snapping loudly and rigidly in salute.

"Hey, Mick," I said, coming through the front door of the pub. "I brought a friend with me today. Can we get a couple of cold drafts?" We took our seats at the bar.

"Sure, Jack, coming right up," Mick called back from the end of the bar. He mumbled something to the disheveled guy seated there.

"Hey, Mick? Is that Scooter down at the end of the bar?" asked Henry.

"Yeah, it's no-account Scooter. Lookin' for free food and booze. How do you know Scooter?" He eyed Henry suspiciously.

"It's me, Mick—Henry, root-beer Henry." He lifted a piece of hair to represent a cowlick.

"Well, I'll be goddamned," Mick said. "Look at you, Henry, all grown up, able to drink a real beer, and a military man to boot. Jack! This young whippersnapper used to come in with Pappy and Joe, order a root beer, and proudly drink alongside them like it was a real beer."

"So I hear, Mick." I chuckled, thoroughly enjoying the reminiscence of my dear friends.

"Excuse me, Mr. Collins?"

"Sure, Henry." I nodded. Henry got up from his barstool and walked to the end of the bar.

"Mr. Scooter? Do you remember me?" He took the barstool next to him.

"No," Scooter slurred, looking through glazed eyes.

"It's me, Mr. Scooter...Henry."

"I don't know you, boy." Scooter shrank away, eyes filling with fear.

"It's okay, Scooter." Henry's voice was calm and soothing. "It doesn't matter that you don't remember. Get something to eat, Scooter." He tucked some money into his hand. Scooter looked at him, trembling, his mind desperately trying to remember, trying to understand. "Scarface?" His eyes misted.

"Joe," Henry softly murmured. "Call him Joe, Scooter."

"Joe." Scooter's eyes showed remembrance as he nodded respectfully. Henry stood tall and returned to the barstool next to me.

"Joe knew what he was doing when he gave you that medal, son."

"Just helping a man that's lost his way, Mr. Collins." Henry lifted his draft glass. "To Joe,"

"To Joe." I raised my glass with a reminiscent smile.

"To Joe," Mick chimed in, raising a shot of Kentucky's finest.

CHAPTER NINETEEN

Summer 1963

"Did you know this is where my parents met?" Susie said, strolling arm and arm with Rich through Brookston Park.

"Yeah, I think your mother may have mentioned it once or twice…or ten times," Rich teased.

"My mother and Aunt Mandy were sitting on that bench right over there—under that big elm—and my father was running through the park getting in his roadwork. He was a boxer back then, Jack Collins, the Southpaw Slugger." She lovingly smiled. "My Aunt Mandy is the only one who calls him Jack now."

"She's not the only one. The guys down at the Silver Center call him Jack, and the young boxers call him Mr. Slugger."

"How do you know that, Rich?" She gave him a curious look.

"I've been down there a few times with your dad. From what I understand, Harry was on his way to being a contender before the war started."

"So they say. He doesn't talk much about those days," Susie sighed. "It just seems to make him sad."

"I can understand that. Dwelling in the past of bygone days and opportunities isn't something men do well." His voice solemn. "This looks like a good spot, Susie; shall we have our picnic here?" He gestured to a well shaded area next to a lilac tree.

"Here's fine, Rich." She handed him the blanket.

"Isn't it a beautiful day, Susie?" Rich shook out the blanket and laid it down in one motion. "The sun is shining, birds are singing…I'm with my best girl."

"Best girl? I better be your only girl." She gave him a quick, playful jab to the ribs.

"Ouch!" He chuckled lightly, massaging his side. "I stand corrected, little slugger. My one and only girl."

"That's better." Susie gave him an apologetic peck on the lips. Rich relaxed back onto the blanket, Susie nestled her head in the crook of his shoulder.

"How long do you think a couple has to be together, Susie, before they know it's love and not just a phase?" Rich lightly ran his fingers over her bare shoulder.

"I think it depends on the couple, Rich. My parents say they knew right away. They had only known each other for three months before they got married, and they've been together for over twenty years."

"How long have we been together, Susie?" He lovingly stroked her long dark lush hair.

"Almost two years, Rich. Why? What is this all about?"

"Almost two years," he softly murmured, looking into her dark eyes. "That means we've known each other almost eight times longer than your parents did. Which means, if three months equals twenty years"—he did a quick math tally in his head—"we'll be together for one hundred sixty. Susie, love of my life." Taking a knee, he opened a small jeweler's box revealing a square cut diamond surrounded by four baguettes. "Will you be my wife for the next one hundred sixty years?"

"Oh, Rich, yes…yes. I would love to be your wife for the next one hundred sixty years, or longer." Her eyes misted as Rich slipped the engagement ring on her finger.

"Let's not wait, Susie." Rich pulled her in close. "Let's get married right away, in the fall, and start having babies—at least five."

"Five! I've always wanted children, Rich, but five!"

"Okay, maybe five's a little over the top, but what do you think of a fall wedding?" He was unable to contain his happiness.

"The fall sounds perfect, Rich." Her dark eyes filled with love.

"Let's celebrate, Susie." Rich joyfully took a bottle of champagne from the picnic basket.

"Hey." Susie lightly chuckled. "How did that get in there?"

"I'm a man of many talents, my love." He popped the cork, champagne overflowing. "Glasses, glasses, my love. We need glasses," he said, laughing loudly.

"Here they are, my love." Susie happily caught the overflowing champagne.

"To us, Susie. May the love we feel today only intensify as we journey through our one hundred sixty years, and may our babies be as beautiful as you."

"To us, Rich." She clinked his glass in uncontainable happiness.

Susie and Rich's Wedding, 1963

"Who giveth this woman to be married to this man in holy matrimony?" Father Murphy called out.

"I do." I stood proudly next to my daughter inside Saint Paul's Cathedral.

"Do you give her freely and promise to accept this man, Richard Randolph Jenkins, to be her husband?"

"I do," I said, looking at the man who had stolen my daughter's heart. Rich was standing tall, proud, eyes filled with love, gazing upon my daughter, extending his hand. Susie reached for him. I steadfastly held on, unable to let go.

"You have to let go now, Daddy," Susie softly murmured.

"Sorry, sweetheart." Releasing her arm, I looked into the dark eyes beneath the veil, recognizing them to be my little girl's. Yet I saw a full-grown woman standing before me.

"You can sit down now, Daddy." Susie nodded to the pew behind me. Wedding guests giggled in adoration.

"Harry?" Liz softly called out, patting the seat next to her. Everything felt surreal. "It'll be okay, darling," she whispered, taking my arm to comfort me. "You haven't lost your little girl. Susie will always be her father's daughter."

I nodded my head in understanding, consoled by Liz's words, as snippets of my daughter's young life fluttered through my mind. They took me to places I hadn't been in years, bringing me the comfort I so needed on this day—my daughter's wedding day.

"Look at her, Harry," said Liz, taking me from my reminiscence. "She looks so happy. Doesn't she look happy, Harry?"

"That she does, sweetheart." I was consumed with emotion. As Rich lifted her veil, Susie's beautiful, tearful, smiling, happy face came into view.

"Now, with the power vested in me...I now pronounce you man and wife. You may kiss your bride."

"With pleasure," Rich murmured, taking my daughter in his arms and consummating their marriage with a warm, gentle kiss. Applause erupted throughout the cathedral.

That was all it took. Just a few declarations of words, and my little girl was no longer my daughter. She had become someone's wife, and it felt bittersweet.

Summer 1964

"Here it is, sweetheart—room 702." I pushed open the hospital-room door.

"Mom, Daddy?" Susie called us to her bedside. "Come and meet your new granddaughter. Isn't she beautiful?" Susie beamed.

"Beautiful like her mother," Rich happily interjected from the other side of the bed.

"We named her Kayleen Elizabeth Jenkins, Mom, after you." Susie looked at her mother, seeming to transfer some type of motherly code. Liz stood speechless in understanding.

"Kayleen Elizabeth, as it should be." I stammered. "You did real good, sweetheart."

"Would you like to hold her, Daddy?"

"I would love to hold her, sweetheart." Gently taking the precious bundle from my daughter's arms, I fell in love for the third time. "She has your dark eyes, Susie." I reminisced back so many years ago to when it was my daughter safely tucked inside my arms. "Gonna take a sentimental journey," I softly began to sing.

"Hey…wait a minute," Susie playfully stammered in protest. "That's my song, Daddy."

"It's still your song, sweetheart. It's just on lend until we find our own song. Isn't that right, Kayleen?" I nuzzled my precious granddaughter, giving her a slow, gentle spin.

"We need to celebrate!" Rich grabbed a bottle of champagne and paper cups from inside a brown bag.

"I don't think that's a good idea, Rich," said Liz.

"Oh, come on, Liz." Rich popped the cork. "Today's a time for celebration. I became a father. You became a grandmother. Harry a grandfather, and my precious wife became a mother."

"I understand that, Rich, but Susie shouldn't be drinking."

"What's a little sip going to hurt, Liz? It's just champagne." Disregarding her objection, he poured four glasses.

"It's still alcohol, Rich," Liz protested.

"I'm sure a little sip wouldn't hurt anything, Mom," Susie intervened. "Daddy, please take your glass, and celebrate the birth of our daughter—your granddaughter."

"Sure, sweetheart." I accepted two cups and handed one to Liz. "To my granddaughter, Kayleen Elizabeth. May she grow up to be as beautiful as her predecessors." I gave an appreciative nod to my wife and daughter.

"Hear, hear." Rich raised his glass, gulped the champagne, and poured himself another.

"You look tired, Susie," Liz said, setting down her full glass of champagne. "Your father and I are going to leave and let you get some rest, sweetheart."

"Okay, Mom. I am a little tired." Susie yawned, eyes fluttering in fatigue.

"I'll be back tomorrow, sweetheart." Liz lightly brushed the hair from Susie's forehead, giving her a gentle kiss good-bye.

"Okay, Momma." Susie cuddled her daughter contentedly.

"Congratulations on becoming a father, Rich. Take the rest of the week off." I escorted my wife to the door.

"Thanks, Harry...appreciate that...see you on Monday, boss." He lifted his paper cup of champagne.

"Good-bye, Mom...Daddy," said Susie, preoccupied with her new little bundle.

"Good-bye, sweetheart." We let the door close behind us.

"Harry," Liz said, "have you noticed that Rich has been drinking excessively lately?"

"No, not really, Liz." I pushed the down elevator button. "The last few times I've seen Rich, outside of work, there's been reason to celebrate."

"Now you sound like your daughter, Harry, but Rich's drinking is really starting to worry me."

"If it concerns you that much, sweetheart, I'll talk to him on Monday."

"Just ask him to slow down a little, Harry; after all, he is a father now." As she stepped onto the elevator, she gave her temples a quick rub.

"Did you take your blood-pressure pill this morning, Liz?"

"No," she muttered, shaking her head. "With all the excitement of the baby and everything, I forgot."

"Liz! We've been over this. Where are your pills? Do you have them in your purse?"

"No." She winced in discomfort. "They're at home in the medicine cabinet."

"Elizabeth Decker, what am I going to do with you?" My frustration was rising. "Why don't you carry your medication in your purse?"

"I don't know, Harry," she moaned. "Let's just hurry and get home so I can take a pill and lie down." She rubbed her temples harder.

"Elizabeth Decker?" Shaking my head in annoyed frustration, I helped her step from the elevator.

Monday Morning

"Good morning, Rich." I gave a nod looking up from the press machine. "How's my daughter and new grandbaby doing?"

"Doing great, Harry. What's on the agenda for this morning?" He grabbed the protective eyewear from the hook.

"I need you to wrap up the GM job and get it delivered to Truck and Bus."

"Already done, boss—just need your signature to have it delivered." He handed me the clipboard and pen.

"I'm impressed." I signed my John Hancock. "But when did you get this done?"

"I came in for a few hours over the weekend and wrapped it up. Your wife came by on Saturday for a visit, and let's just say, I was encouraged to take some time for myself. I'm starting to get the impression your wife, my mother-in-law, doesn't like me very much."

"She likes you good enough, Rich; it's just...well...she's concerned about your drinking lately. I tried to tell her you have it under control, but—"

"Enough said, Harry. I've been hearing it from Susie too. Personally, I think I handle my liquor very well, but I love your daughter, and I want to make her happy." He shrugged his shoulders indifferently.

"Ah yes." I nodded in understanding. "The things we do for the ladies we love—aye, Rich. I got a new contract order sent over from Delphi. I'd like you to take a look at it and give me your thoughts." Getting back to the business at hand, I rolled out the blueprint.

CHAPTER TWENTY

Summer 1968

"We're here, Grandma," Kayleen's soft child's voice called out. "Where are you, Grandma?"

"I'm in the kitchen, sweetheart." Liz tucked a piece of paper in her apron pocket.

"Hi, Mom." Susie entered the kitchen, Kayleen in tow.

"Hello, sweethearts." Liz looked past her daughter to her granddaughter. "Well, don't you look pretty today in your lilac sundress?"

"Mama bought it for me because I've been a good girl." Kayleen gave a quick spin to show it off.

"Aren't you always a good girl, sweetheart?" said Liz, pulling Kayleen onto her lap.

"Yes, but sometimes, Grandma," Kayleen began to explain, "Daddy comes home, and he doesn't feel well. Mommy likes me to be extra quiet then, so Daddy can take a nap and feel better." She raised her little arms in completion of her story.

"Susie?" Liz shot her daughter a look of disapproval. "Kayleen, take this cookie, and go watch cartoons in the living room. So Grandma and Mama can have a talk." Kayleen slid off her lap and ran into the living room, snickerdoodle in hand. "I thought you said Rich had slowed his drinking down, Susie? From the sounds of it, that's not true."

"He did slow it down, Mom; it's just been lately," Susie confessed. "He says he's under a lot of pressure at work."

"No more pressure than your father, Susie, and you don't see him coming home drunk."

"Rich isn't coming home drunk either, Mom." Susie was defensive. "He's just having a few after work. Besides, I'm handling it."

"Please, daughter, inform me on how you're handling it. By asking your daughter to stop playing? To stop being a child for a few hours so your husband can sleep it off?"

"That only happened a few times, Mom. Please, let me handle my own marriage?"

"I would, Susie, but you don't seem to be handling it very well, and now you're involving my granddaughter. Sit down, Susie. I think it's time we have a woman-to-woman talk."

"Mom?" Susie remained standing in defiance. "I really don't want to have this conversation with you."

"I don't remember asking you, Susie—now sit down."

"*Uggh.*" Susie slumped into the chair. "I'm listening."

"Susie, all men have something that makes them weak," Liz began, sounding more like Mandy than herself.

"All men, Mom? Even Daddy?"

"Even your father. For Rich it's alcohol. For your father? Well, let's just say...he has his own demons."

"What are you talking about, Mom? Daddy doesn't have any demons." Liz reached inside her apron pocket and hesitantly tossed a piece of paper onto the table.

"What's this?" Susie picked up the paper.

"Just what it looks like, Susie. A woman's name and number."

"Brandy…555-3770. Mom? Really?" She tossed it back on the table dismissively. "You know how much Daddy loves his brandy. I'm sure it just a distributor's number."

"Maybe. Maybe not." Liz returned the paper to her apron pocket.

"Well, he's not cheating. My father would never do something like that."

"We're not talking about your father right now, Susie. We're talking about your husband."

"Then why did you bring it up?" Susie stammered.

"I'm sorry, sweetheart. I shouldn't have." Taking her daughter's hand apologetically, Liz continued, "Susie, as women, we are born with a sixth sense. An intuition. It tells us when something is wrong with our family. It alerts us when things aren't quite right with our men or our children, and for you, my daughter, my woman's intuition is on full alert. Rich's drinking is out of control, and at some point, you're going to have to face the fact that your husband has a problem. He may even be an alcoholic."

"An alcoholic, Mom? I think that's a little harsh—don't you?"

"Sweetheart, I don't tell you these things to hurt you, but it's not just about you anymore, Susie. You have Kayleen to consider now, and how Rich's drinking is affecting her. Your daughter is four years old, sweetheart. She shouldn't have to contain herself so her father can sleep it off."

"I know; you're right, Mom. I'm going to talk to Rich about getting some help, but could we please just change the subject for now?" She blinked away her tears.

"Okay, sweetheart, enough for now, but you have to promise me you're going to resolve this drinking issue. This can't continue, Susie."

"I promise, Mom." Susie gave a hesitant smile, having no idea how she was going to keep her promise, hating what her husband was doing to her, doing to her family. She had vowed to love him in sickness and in health, and she intended to keep that vow. She loved Rich with all her heart, and he was such a great husband and father when he wasn't drinking—which she had to admit wasn't very often anymore.

May 1969

"I'm coming…hold on." Susie struggled to unlock the door, juggling a bag of groceries. "Hello, hello?" She picked up the receiver, out of breath.

"Hello. May I speak to a Mrs. Susie Jenkins?"

"This is Susie Jenkins," she said, suddenly fearful.

"Mrs. Jenkins, this is Officer Scott Simpson of the Michigan State Police Department. Your husband was involved in an accident this afternoon, and—"

"Is he okay?" Susie interrupted, feeling sick to her stomach. "Was anyone hurt?"

"Mr. Jenkins was taken to Saint Joseph's Hospital. It was a single-car accident, Mrs. Jenkins. Your husband was traveling at a high rate of speed when he lost control of his vehicle and hit a tree, according to witnesses. Mr. Jenkins appears to be fine, with the exception of being intoxicated. He was taken to the hospital as a precaution due to the severity of the accident."

"I'll be right there, Officer." Susie hung up the phone and ran to the car, adrenaline pumping. "I knew this was going to happen one day; I just knew it!" Her mind was running in several different directions; as she made her way to the hospital. Entering through Saint Joe's emergency she passed a state-police cruiser, lights still flashing. "Excuse me," she said, interrupting the police officer and doctor talking at the admissions desk. "I'm Susie Jenkins. Rich Jenkins is my husband. He was involved in an accident this evening."

"Yes, Mrs. Jenkins. I'm Dr. Evans, your husband's attending. Your husband has a nasty gash above his brow requiring a few stitches, and some severe bruising. He's going to be sore for a little while, but nothing was broken. He should be released within the hour—if Officer Simpson here has no further questions."

"Are you releasing my husband, Officer? Are any charges being made?"

"I've issued your husband a citation for destruction of property, Mrs. Jenkins. There will be a fine and restitution for the damages; otherwise he has broken no laws. Your husband was a very lucky man...this time. In a few days, you can pick up a copy of the accident report for your insurance company. You'll find your husband in bed three, Mrs. Jenkins, just down the hall."

"Thank you, Officer." Susie sighed in relief. Officer Simpson exited the hospital, turned off the flashing cruiser lights, and slowly pulled from the emergency entrance. Susie looked at the numbers painted on the emergency-room wall and pulled back curtain three to reveal a visibly intoxicated husband.

"It's about time you got here." Rich looked at her through bloodshot eyes, reeking of alcohol.

"Rich, this has got to stop! You could have killed yourself...or someone else!"

"Don't be so dramatic, Susie. Anyone can have an accident. Besides, what's a tree doing in the middle of the road, anyway?"

"I doubt very much the tree was the middle of the road." Her voice was sarcastic. "You're lucky it was a tree! What if you had hit another car? What if Kayleen had been with you?" She felt sick at the thought.

"Stop with the dramatics, Susie." Rich moaned in pain.

"Excuse me, Mr. Jenkins?" The nurse pulled back the curtain. "I have your release papers. If you'll just sign here." She pointed to the bottom of the release form.

"What took you so long?" Rich aggressively grabbed the clipboard.

"You're free to leave anytime, Mr. Jenkins." The nurse accepted the clipboard back with a look of disdain.

"Thank you, Nurse," said Susie, giving an apologetic nod.

"You're welcome, Mrs. Jenkins." She pulled back the curtain.

"Something has to change, Rich. You've got to get your drinking under control…or…or…"

"Or what, Susie? You're going to leave? Save your threats, sweetheart. Why don't you go talk to the dumb bastard that planted a tree in the middle of the road? Help me with my jacket, will you? My shoulder's a little sore." Susie helped aggressively. "Don't be so rough," he moaned. "Your husband's been in an accident."

"A self-inflicted accident. Let's go, Rich." Susie yanked back the curtain. "I have to pick up Kayleen from my mother's, and I want to drop you off first. The last thing I need today is a lecture from my mother."

"That's fine with me; all I want to do is go home and crawl into bed." He stumbled his way out of the hospital.

CHAPTER TWENTY-ONE

Visiting Joe

"Hey, buddy." I firmly pushed the spikes into the ground to hold a memorial wreath honoring my dear fallen friend and replaced the small, frazzled American flag. Taking a seat, I pulled the overgrown grass that encircled the firmly embedded boxing gloves protecting our Joe.

"Got a short note from Pappy, Joe." I opened the envelope, Pappy's chicken scratch displayed along its front. "'Dear Southpaw, I hope this note finds you well. I've good news! Francine and I have married and opened a tavern together.'"

I showed Joe a photo of Pappy and Francine standing outside their tavern underneath a sign: O'Hare's Food and Spirits. Francine was smiling happily. Cantankerous ole Pappy was giving his best version of a smile. "He looks happy, doesn't he, Joe?" I chuckled softly, placing the photo against the white military cross marking Joe's grave. Inhaling sharply, I took a moment to bask in the sun, feeling my mentor and friend's presence—if only in spirit.

"I'm getting worried about my Susie, Joe. Rich's drinking is getting worse. He came to work the other day in a rental and had a few stitches in his forehead. He said he hit a tree trying to avoid a dog running out in the road. I believe the tree part, but I sense drinking was the real culprit. I've taken him down to the Silver Center with me a few times, hoping he would take an interest. Help the boys out, maybe mentor a few, clean up his act. But it's not working. I'm just not sure how to help my little girl. It makes me sad to see her so unhappy and torn.

"Liz is beautiful as ever. Still holding out hope for Mandy that someday a man will be found to love her dear friend." I shook my head at her determination. "Would you believe they're trying to drag me into it, Joe? Liz was asking if I knew any good men through my business contacts that Mandy could meet. I told Liz I would keep my eyes open for some single men, but I have no intention of getting into that hornet nest.

"Well, not much to report this visit, my friend, but it's always good talking to you, buddy. Our talks always seem to clear my head, unburden my heart—but that's what wingmen are for, right, buddy? To help guide you through life? See you soon, Joe."

I stepped carefully, respectfully. A gust of wind caught Pappy's photo, wedging it between wreath and headstone, holding it there in a gentle hug. The small American flag caught a breeze, seeming to wave, "See you soon."

September 1976

"Do you have a few minutes for your husband, sweetheart?" I said, nuzzling the back of Liz's neck.

"Sorry, Mr. Decker." She caressed the side of my cheek. "I have a shopping date with our granddaughter."

"I'll be quick, my love." I nibbled her ear.

"I'm sorry, darling; I don't have time. Kayleen's expecting me at ten."

"Ten…ten fifteen? What's a few minutes, sweetheart?" My hands gently explored her voluptuous body, tugging at the zipper of her dress.

"Darling?" Liz playfully wiggled from my embrace.

"Your husband needs some attention too, sweetheart." I collapsed on the bed, realizing my defeat.

"I know you do, darling…tonight." She empathically looked at the full arousal in my pants.

"Promises, promises. I'm holding you to your word, my love," I called out to her.

"Good-bye, Harry." Liz chuckled affectionately, closing the front door.

"Kayleen, your grandmother's here," Susie called out, seeing her mother's car pulling into the drive.

"See you later, Mom." Kayleen ran past her mother and jumped into the front seat. "I thought we would go shopping downtown today, Grandma. My friends told me about this new store, Forever Cool; they have all the latest styles, and I was hoping to get some hip huggers, matching jean jacket, and maybe…" Her voice was pleading. "Some platform shoes?"

"What are hip huggers, dear?" Liz asked, pulling from the drive.

"They're jeans, Grandma, but they're kind of expensive—like, thirty dollars."

"Thirty dollars, Kayleen! For a pair of jeans?"

"They're not just any pair of jeans, Grandma. They're what everybody who's anybody is wearing."

"Well, I wouldn't want my granddaughter to be out of style."

"Thanks, Grandma." Kayleen contentedly settled into the front seat. "I knew if anyone understood style, Grandma, it would be you."

"What do you say we have brunch first, Kayleen? I hurried out the door so quickly this morning I didn't have time for breakfast, and I need to take my blood-pressure pill." She pulled into an open spot in front of the downtown bistro.

"That's fine with me, Grandma." Kayleen shut the car door, feeling the excitement of the day.

"Welcome to the bistro." The hostess smiled. "How many?"

"Two please, and could we have a booth?" Liz softly inquired.

"Of course, follow me. Your waitress will be right with you." She handed them both a menu.

"This is a pretty nice place, Grandma," said Kayleen, looking around the bistro.

"Yes, it's one of your grandfather's favorites. He brings a lot of his clients here." Liz scanned her menu as a short auburn hair waitress approached their table.

"Hello, my name is Mary. I'll be your server today. Were you ready to order?"

"I'll take a salad with Italian dressing and an unsweetened ice tea." Kayleen closed her menu. "In fact, could you put the dressing on the side, please?"

"No problem, and you, ma'am?" The waitress looked at Liz.

"I'll have the same, and could you also bring us an order of your hot rolls?"

"Of course—right away." She accepted back the menus.

"So how are things at school, Kayleen?" Liz opened her linen napkin and placed it gently over her lap.

"School is good, Grandma," said Kayleen, duplicating the gesture.

"Have you met any nice young men, Kayleen?"

"There's one boy, Grandma—Josh Powell." She smiled. "He's really cute."

"And Mr. Powell's intentions, Kayleen—what are they?"

"Grandma, nobody has intentions anymore. You hang out together and see where things go. If you like each other, you start going together."

"Going together?" She sounded confused. "Going where?"

"Not going somewhere, Grandma, just going together. It means you're exclusive." Her grandmother still seemed confused. "That you're spoken for?" Kayleen lifted her eyebrows in explanation.

"Oh, so it's like going steady? Like you've been pinned?"

"Pinned?" Kayleen chuckled. "Yeah, Grandma, it's like being pinned."

"Are there expectations when going steady, Kayleen?"

"Don't worry, Grandma. You and Mom taught me well. I know how to handle boys."

"Glad to hear it, Kayleen…because you know, a lady—"

"I know, Grandma, I know. A lady always knows when to leave," Kayleen said, mocking their words.

"Yes, sweetheart, she does. So how's Rich? How's your father? I haven't seen him lately."

"Daddy? Daddy's okay." Kayleen shifted uncomfortably. "Good, the food's here. Let's hurry and eat, Grandma." She seemed grateful for the distraction.

"What the heck?" said Susie, hearing a commotion she looked out the window. Rich was stumbling his way toward the house.

"Susie," Rich slurred. "Let me in, sweetheart," Dropping his keys, he lightly pounded on the door. Susie yanked open the door eyes glaring.

"The door's not locked, Rich," She stammered. " I thought this wasn't going to happen anymore!"

"What happened? Nothing's happened." He stumbled inside. "I just had a few with the guys."

"By the looks of it," Susie fumed, "it was more than a few."

"Don't start with me, Susie. I'm tired," said Rich, stumbling toward the bedroom.

"Don't start with you, Rich?" Susie followed on his heels. "Just tell me why, then. Why must you drink yourself into oblivion?"

"Quit exaggerating. I don't drink myself into oblivion."

"Okay then. How about a drunken stupor?" Her eyes were furious. "Is that better, Rich?"

"Okay." Rich turned on her. "You want to know why I drink, Susie? I'll tell you why. Because it's the only way I can put up with you and your constant whining."

"Whining?" Susie was taken aback. "What do I whine about?"

"Your father?" Rich glared.

"My father?" Susie was dumbfounded.

"'My father's under a lot of stress too, Rich, and you don't see him drinking,'" he whined in imitation of her. "You have no idea how your father handles his stresses, little girl, and don't get me started on your tight-ass mother."

"My mother? My mother has never been anything but kind to you, Rich."

"Kind? She's in your ear about me all the time. How I'm not good enough for her precious Susie."

"You're being ridiculous, Rich. I can't talk to you when you're like this."

"Who wants to talk?" He crawled onto the bed. "Just get out, and shut the door behind you," he said, pulling the blanket haphazardly over him.

"Rich?" Susie pushed his lifeless body.

"Leave me alone!" He pulled the covers over his head.

"Leave you alone? I'll leave you alone." Susie walked from the room, slamming the bedroom door.

"That's all I want." Rich passed out.

"We're back, Mom," Kayleen announced, coming through the front door. "Grandma bought me some really cool clothes today."

"That's great, sweetheart," said Susie, trying to sound upbeat.

"I'm not so sure they qualify as nice," Liz lightly chuckled. "Hip huggers and platform shoes?"

"It's the new style, Mom." Susie was solemn, attempting a smile. "Kayleen, take your clothes to your bedroom, sweetheart, and then I want you to get started on your homework."

"Okay, Mom. Thanks again, Grandma." She ran off to her bedroom, packages in hand.

"What's wrong, sweetheart? Where's Rich? I see his car is parked crooked in the driveway."

"He's in the bedroom, Mom—sleeping. He stopped and had a few drinks after work."

"A few drinks doesn't turn your car sideways, Susie."

"I know, Mom. I just don't know what to do anymore. What can I do to help him?"

"Unfortunately, Susie, until Rich is ready to admit he has a drinking problem…nothing."

"He's never gonna do that, Mom. Rich thinks he handles his liquor just fine."

"Then quit enabling him, sweetheart. Stop protecting him. If he passes out in the front yard, leave him there. If he's too hungover to go to work, don't call in for him, lying to your father that he's sick. Leave him to his own devices, Susie, and let the chips fall where they may."

"I can't do that, Mom; I've tried. When Rich is sober, he's still the wonderful man I married, but when he's not…" She turned from her mother's gaze. "I'm sorry, Mom. I see the disappointment in your eyes."

"It's not disappointment you see, Susie; it's sadness. I just want what's best for my daughter and granddaughter."

"I know you do, Mom, and I know we can't continue to live this way—anxious all the time, waiting for Rich's next drunken episode. I'll figure out something, Mom; I have to. For my sake, as well as Kayleen's."

"I know you will, Susie. You're a smart girl," Liz reassured her. "I've got to get going, sweetheart. Your father's expecting me home."

"Thanks for taking Kayleen shopping, Mom." Susie forced a smile.

"Don't worry, sweetheart. Things always have a way of working out." Liz gave her daughter an encouraging hug.

"I know," Susie sighed. "Thanks again for everything, Mom. I'll call you tomorrow." She quietly, sadly closed the door.

I heard the door open and close. "I'm home, Harry. Where are you, darling?" Liz called.

"I'm in the bedroom, sweetheart."

"Harry, I really think you need to talk to Rich again. His drinking is really getting out of control, and I'm just not sure what Susie..." She stopped dead in her tracks, seeing me lying seductively on the bed, surrounded by candles.

"Not sure of what, sweetheart?" I smiled.

"Harry, I've just had a horrific day, and I'm worried about Susie." She looked to me with apprehension.

"Later, my love. You can tell me all about it later." I extended my hand in invitation. "It's our turn now." She smiled softly, dismissed her hesitance and accepted my hand coming onto the bed.

"I'm so lucky to have you, Harry." She snuggled inside my warm embrace.

"We're both lucky, sweetheart, to have each other." I kissed her softly, deeply, tenderly. We left the worries of our family behind nestled inside our cocoon of love.

The Next Day

"Good morning, Rich." I looked up from the blueprint. "How you feeling this morning?" I asked, knowing the answer.

"A little rough, Harry, but I can do my job."

"I'm sure you can, son. What do you say we go down to the Silver Center today after work?"

"Thanks, but no thanks, Harry. That's your thing, not mine." He adjusted his safety glasses.

"Are you sure, Rich? The kids loved it the last time you came down."

"They loved you, Harry, the Southpaw Slugger. They were just kind to me out of respect for you."

"That's not true, Rich," I said, realizing his state of mind. "The kids really enjoy all your input."

"No thanks, Harry," said Rich, turning on the press machine, ending the discussion. I decided then and there a visit to check on my daughter would be in order.

Later That Day

I'm gonna take off early today Rich. Lock up the shop for me?"

"Sure thing Harry." Rich nodded adjusting his safety glasses. "See you tomorrow boss."

"Hi daddy, surprised to see you here on a workday." Susie said, opening the front door turning down the radio.

"It's such a beautiful day; I thought I'd get out of the shop for a while and visit my daughter."

"Mom told you, didn't she, Daddy?"

"Told me what, sweetheart?" I said, giving her a look of innocence. "I'm just here for a visit."

"Well, I'm fine, Daddy." Her voice shook.

"You don't sound fine, sweetheart." I gave her the ole boxer's stare. "Come on, Susie. Tell ole Dad what's wrong."

"Nothing's wrong." Her bottom lip quivered. "Everything's wrong, Daddy," she said, breaking down. "It's Rich. He's drinking all the time now, Daddy, and Kayleen—she does everything she can not to come home." Her eyes welled with tears. "Tell me what to do, Daddy...fix it." She sounded like my little girl of yesteryear.

"Sweetheart?" I sighed sympathetically. "You know I don't believe in getting in between a man and a woman. That's something only you women do. Marriage is a private union, and no one knows what goes on behind closed doors. But you're my daughter, and I want to see you happy." I handed her a kerchief to dry her tears. "So, with that being said, I need you to think long and hard about this marriage, and know there is no shame in wanting a better life for yourself."

"I don't want to end my marriage, Daddy." Susie dabbed her tears. "I love Rich. I took a vow."

"Sweetheart, I'm not telling you to end your marriage. I'm telling you to find your happiness. Vow or no vow. Your mother and I will be here to support you. Regardless of your decision."

"I know you will, Daddy." Crying softly, she nodded her head in understanding. "Sentimental Journey" began to play on the radio. "I listen to the oldies." She chuckled lightly, dabbing her tears.

"May I, sweetheart?" I opened my arms in invitation.

"I'd love to, Daddy," she said, stepping into the safety of my arms. "You know, Daddy, you never did give Kayleen her own song." We swayed around the living-room dance floor.

"You're right, honey; I never did." I hummed softly into her ear.

"That's okay, Daddy." She rested her head on my shoulder. "I don't mind sharing. Somehow it feels right that Kayleen and I share this song. Gonna take a sentimental journey," Susie softly began to sing. "Gonna set my mind at ease...gotta take a sentimental journey to relieve old memories." Her words turned to a soft cry.

"Never thought my heart would be so yearny." I picked up where she left off, pulling her in close. "Why did I decide to roam…gotta take a sentimental journey…sentimental journey home…sentimental journey home. It's gonna be okay, sweetheart." I released her from my embrace.

"I know, Daddy," she said, wiping her tears. "It has to be."

"It will be, sweetheart." I smiled in reassurance.

"Thanks for coming by, Daddy, and you can tell Mom she didn't fool anyone." She walked me toward the front door. "I know she had a hand in your visit."

"Believe it or not, your mother had no idea I was coming over today. Good-bye, sweetheart." I gave her a quick peck on the cheek. Humming "Sentimental Journey," I made my way to the car.

"I love you, Daddy," Susie called out.

"Love you too, sweetheart." Giving a gentle wave before closing my car door.

CHAPTER TWENTY-TWO

August 1978

"Where are you off to this morning, Harry?" Liz asked.

"Off to the Silver Center, sweetheart. Got a brand-new batch of kids coming in this morning." I rubbed my hands together in anticipation. "What's your day looking like, Liz?"

"Mandy's coming over; we're going shopping, and then lunch. I think she may have a new beau."

"What number does this loser make? Ten? Eleven?"

"I don't know, Harry. I just wish she could find someone. Someone to love her, for her."

"Well, good luck with that, sweetheart. I'll probably be late tonight. Don't worry about dinner. I'll catch something while I'm out."

"Okay, Harry, have a good day." She picked up the breakfast dishes and set them in the sink.

"Hey, Mandy." Passing her by, I took the steps leading from our house two by two.

"Jack." Mandy nodded, taking the steps one by one. "Hey, Liz," her voice cheerful coming through the front door. "Where's Jack off to in such a hurry this morning?"

"He's off to the center; there's a new group of boys signing up today for the Silver Gloves. What's got you so cheery this morning, Mandy?"

"I think I've met Mr. Right," Mandy squealed, eyes wide in excitement.

"Come. Sit down," said Liz, matching Mandy's enthusiasm. "And tell me all about him."

"He's wonderful, Liz. I met him at the grocery store. Can you believe it? His car had just broken down, and he needed a lift home. Apparently, he's fallen on some hard times. He just lost his job. Is Jack looking for any help at the shop?"

"I don't know, Mandy. I could ask."

"Did I tell you his name, Liz? Paul Neuman. Just like the movie star. Last name spelled different, and his eyes aren't clear blue. They're brown, but I can work with that." Her eyes were shining bright, full of hope.

"He sounds wonderful, Mandy." Liz felt love and compassion for her dear friend.

"Hey, Jack, here's your list of new recruits." Robert Spencer, volunteer trainer and sponsor for the Silver Gloves, handed me the sheet. "They're green, Jack, real green. I don't think half of them even know how to put a glove on."

"That's what we're here for, Bob, to train. To take a novice and start him on the road to becoming a pro. If he has the stuff." Scanning the sheet, my eyes came to rest on a familiar name: O'Sullivan—Francis O'Sullivan III.

"Francis O'Sullivan," I called out, walking into the gymnasium.

"Yes, sir." A young, skinny, knock-kneed boy stepped forward. A gold chain hung from his neck. "I'm Francis O'Sullivan III."

"Where did you get that chain, son?" I asked, looking at the gold shamrock hanging from his neck.

"It was my grandfather's, sir." His eyes glistened "He gave it to me before he died."

"I'm sorry to hear that, son. I'm sure your grandfather was a great man." My mind drifted back to the vision of Francis O'Sullivan the first, kissing the shamrock that hung from his neck so many years ago aboard the transport ship taking us overseas. "Do you mind if I call you Sully, son?"

"I'd like that, sir." He wiped the mist from his eyes, standing proudly. "That was my grandfather's nickname."

"Then Sully it is. Let me see your boxer's stance, Sully."

"Yes, sir." Young Sully quickly took a cockeyed stance. He raised his fists, thumbs tucked inside.

"Thumbs always on the outside, son." Untucking his thumbs, I held his small hands firmly inside mine.

"Yes, sir." Young Sully held his fists upright as I adjusted his cockeyed stance into a proper boxer's stance.

"Now let me see what you've got, son," I said, holding my hands upright, palms out.

"What I've got, sir?" He looked at my palms in confusion.

"Hit 'em, Sully!" I punched the inside of my palms hard. Young Sully let loose with all the power he could muster, throwing several jabs and a combination. "Good, Sully," I said, dropping my palms.

"Thank you, sir." He wiped the small beads of sweat from his brow.

"Drop the sir, Sully. Call me Southpaw or Mr. Slugger." I gave him a wink.

"Okay, thanks, Mr. Ssslugger." Young Sully gave a big, toothless smile.

October 1978

"Kayleen? Over here, honey," Rich loudly slurred, waving from his car window.

"Kayleen, that guy over there is trying to get your attention." Josh pointed to a white Monte Carlo in the high-school parking lot. "Do you know that guy, Kayleen?"

"Excuse me, Josh; I'll be right back." Kayleen quickly made her way over to the car. "Dad? What are you doing here?" She scanned the parking lot in embarrassment.

"I left work early today, honey," Rich happily slurred. "Took a half day. Thought I'd come by and pick you up so you didn't have to take the bus."

"Dad, you're drunk," she quietly scolded. "Mom told me never to get in the car with you when you've been drinking."

"I'm not drunk, Kayleen," Rich slurred. "I just had a few with the boys. Get in the car, sweetheart; I'm fine."

"You're not fine, Dad," Kayleen stammered. "You're drunk!"

"Get in the car, Kayleen," Rich demanded. "Mind your father."

"Is everything okay here?" asked Josh, walking up to the car.

"Everything's fine, boy," Rich slurred, looking at him through bloodshot eyes. "Mind your business."

"Do you want me to get someone, Kayleen?" Josh scanned the school grounds, spotting the janitor raising the new school flag.

"No, it's okay. I'm fine, Josh. Please don't call anyone." Kayleen quickly got into the car. "Let's go, Dad," she said sharply, unable to look at Josh, feeling his gaze. Rich put the car in reverse.

"Who is that kid, Kayleen?" Rich looked at Josh through his rearview mirror.

"His name's Josh Powell. He's my boyfriend."

"Your boyfriend? How come I've never met him?" Swaying into the wrong lane, he quickly adjusted the wheel.

"Because I don't have my friends come to the house." Kayleen's voice trembled.

"Why don't you have your friends come to the house?" He looked at his daughter, who remained nonresponsive, staring straight ahead. "I asked you a question, Kayleen."

"You know why, Dad." Her bottom lip was quivering.

"No, I don't."

"Why did you have to come to my school and embarrass me, Dad?" Her eyes were filled with tears.

"Embarrass you? Oh, now I'm an embarrassment?" Pulling into their driveway, he hit the brakes hard. "You're just like your mother and grandmother." Rich's eyes blazed. Kayleen jumped from the car and ran toward the house. "Where do you think you're going, young lady? I'm not done talking to you yet." Rich ran behind her, stumbling toward the house.

"What's going on, Kayleen?" Susie anxiously met her daughter at the door. Kayleen ran past her, slamming her bedroom door.

"What's going on, Rich?" Susie's voice was panicked. "What did you do?"

"I didn't do anything," Rich mumbled dismissively, stumbling past her.

"You must've done something, Rich."

"I thought I would surprise my daughter and give her a ride home. Apparently she would rather take the bus than ride home with dear old Dad!"

"You went to her school, Rich? Why did you do that? I asked you to never go to Kayleen's school when you've been drinking."

"I don't need your permission to go to my daughter's school," Rich screeched. "I'm her father!"

"Then why don't you act like one?" Susie screamed.

"Oh, now I'm not a good enough father? Who decided that? You or your tight-ass mother?"

"Shut up, Rich," Susie muttered through clenched teeth. "Just shut up." She walked toward her daughter's bedroom.

"Who wants to talk?" Rich fell onto the couch in a drunken slump.

"Kayleen…sweetheart." Susie jiggled the locked bedroom door. "Can I come in, sweetheart? I want to talk to you."

“Go away, Mom,” Kayleen cried. “You’ll just take Daddy’s side.”

“I can’t take anyone’s side if I don’t know what happened. Please, open the door, sweetheart, and let me try to fix this.”

“You can’t fix it, Mom.” Kayleen sadly opened the bedroom door. “Unless you can fix Daddy.” She walked back to her bed and hugged her pillow.

“Just tell me what happened, sweetheart.” Susie sat down next to her.

“He embarrassed me, Mom. Right in front of Josh.”

“I’m sorry, Kayleen,” said Susie, feeling her embarrassment.

“Why can’t Daddy just stop drinking mom?” Her eyes were filled with sadness.

“I don’t know, sweetheart.” Susie took her daughter’s hand.

“Just leave me alone, Mom.” Kayleen threw herself across the bed. “Please.” She cried into her pillow.

“Enough.” Susie calmly got up from the bed. “Enough.” She walked into the living room, where Rich lay snoring on the couch. “Rich?” She nudged his shoulder. “Rich, wake up. We need to talk.”

“About what?” he slurred irritably, blinking his eyes and struggling to sit up.

“I just talked to our daughter about what happened today.”

“Did she tell you how disrespectful she was to her father—embarrassing me in front of some little punk?”

“You embarrassed yourself, Rich.” Susie’s voice was soft and disconnected. “Nobody has to do that for you.” She looked into a pair of bloodshot eyes that she no longer recognized as her husband’s. “I’ve allowed you to treat me badly, but I will not let you jeopardize our daughter’s life. I’ll be talking to an attorney first thing in the morning, Rich.” She calmly got up from the couch.

“Here we go again,” Rich slurred. “The divorce song. I’ve heard that threat too many times, sweetheart, to take it seriously.” He passed back out on the couch, and began to snore loudly.

Visiting Joe

"Hey, buddy," I said, replacing the worn American flag. "Got a postcard the other day from Pappy; all seems to be good with him. The tavern and Francine are both doing well. I wish I could say the same for my Susie. She's filed for divorce. Apparently she's had enough. She says she no longer recognizes the man she married.

"Rich isn't fighting the divorce. In fact, he's moving back east. He gave notice last week. It's probably for the best, but I know ending the marriage truly hurt my Susie. She still loves Rich, and Kayleen…losing her father? I just don't know, but I guess in reality they both lost him to the bottle a long time ago." I shook my head sadly.

"Susie's gotten a job, working for the Sixty-Seventh District as a court stenographer. It seems to give her some joy. We went north for a week to visit my sister. I thought it might help to get Susie away for a while. She always loved Port Hope.

"You remember meeting my sister, Helen? Don't you, Joe? Well, she hasn't changed. Her religion is her life, and attending Sunday Mass is still mandatory while staying in her home. My daughter knows this, Joe. Yet for some reason she was resistant to attending Mass on this trip. Helen, of course, was adamant that Susie attend, to ask God for guidance through her divorce.

"I have to tell you, Joe: a few harsh words passed between the women on the subject of attending church. Susie finally gave in, saying she was only attending out of respect for my sister. Which only agitated my dear sister more. When I asked Susie why she was so upset, why she was fighting the tradition of attendance, she said she wasn't upset—she just didn't feel like going through the charade of attending Mass. Why do women tell you they're not upset, Joe, when clearly they are? It's a mystery, Joe. A mystery I don't think I'll ever understand.

"Kayleen brought her boyfriend, Josh, along. He seems like a nice enough kid. Well-mannered, respectful, and he truly seems to care for Kayleen. Liz and I have been invited to be their dates this Saturday. Some sort of end-of-the-year dance. A fundraiser. Theme—the big band era. It should be fun. Liz and I haven't been out dancing in years, unless you count our living room." I chuckled softly.

"I've been a little worried about my Liz. Her cholesterol's been out of whack, and she's been lax on taking her blood-pressure medication. She worries me, Joe." I softly sighed.

"Well," I stood up and brushed the dirt from my slacks. "It's always feels good to talk, buddy. I have to go by the cleaner's and pick up my suit for the big dance. See you soon." Stepping carefully, respectfully. The small American flag caught a breeze, seeming to wave, "See you soon."

Saturday's Dance

"The kids will be here in a few minutes, Liz; are you about ready?" I said, adjusting my tie in the mirror.

"Almost, Harry, just finishing up." Liz gave herself one last look in the mirror before sashaying into the living room. I smiled approvingly.

"Sweetheart? I can't believe you've kept it all these years."

"I've kept it because it always puts the same look in your eyes, darling. It's there right now."

"You still wear it well, my love." I gave her a gentle spin, admiring the famous emerald-green dress. A horn blasted from the driveway as the grandfather clock chimed seven. "That must be the kids."

"Probably." Liz took a seat on the couch. "Come, sit down, Harry." She patted the cushion next to her. "Josh needs to learn that when he picks up a lady, he comes to the door."

"Sweetheart?" I lovingly smiled. "Things are different now. Kids have changed." I heard a double honk.

"Treating a lady with respect never changes, Harry."

"Didn't you two hear us?" Kayleen anxiously opened the front door, looking at her grandmother seated on the couch. "We've been out in the driveway honking!"

"Yes, we heard the horn, dear, but my dates always come to the door," said Liz, smoothing the front of her dress.

"Grandma, you're not serious? You're going to make Josh come in and get you?"

"I believe he is my date this evening, dear."

"Grandpa?" Kayleen's eyes were pleading for help.

"If you want to get going, Kayleen, I suggest you go outside and tell Josh to come in."

"I can't believe this," Kayleen muttered, heading back out to the car and returning with Josh.

"Mrs. Decker, may I help you on with your coat?" Josh said gallantly, holding open her coat.

"Thank you, Josh, and thank you for inviting me this evening."

"You're welcome, Mrs. Decker." Josh extended his arm.

"So that's how it was done back in your day, huh, Grandpa?" Kayleen watched Josh escort her grandmother from the house.

"Kayleen, sweetheart." I extended my arm. "A lady is a lady is a lady—no matter what the day."

The era of the forties was alive and well inside the high-school gymnasium. Round tables surrounded the dance floor, covered with white linen, adorned with fresh flowers and candlelight. The sounds of a big band playing "Blue Moon" echoed from the rafters.

"It's like stepping back in time, Josh," Liz softly murmured, allowing him to take her coat. Josh handed it to the hat-check girl, further reminiscent of the era.

"Mrs. Decker, would you care to dance?" Josh chivalrously extended his arm in invitation.

"I'd love to, Josh." She accepted his arm as "Sentimental Journey" began to play.

"What about you, Kayleen?" I asked. "Would you care to take a spin around the dance floor with your ole grandpa?"

"You're not old, Grandpa," said Kayleen, falling into step. "Grandma looks beautiful tonight. Doesn't she?" She glanced to her grandmother in admiration.

"Your grandmother has always been a beautiful woman, but when she wears the emerald dress, she's downright magical. You know, that dress is part of the reason I married your grandmother."

"Oh yeah, Grandpa, and what's the other part?"

"I knew she would be the path to having a beautiful granddaughter."

"Oh, Grandpa." Kayleen's eyes were misting over. "You know just what to say to turn a girl's head."

"I only speak the truth, sweetheart." I pulled her close and spun off, humming the sounds of "Sentimental Journey" into her ear.

"Kayleen really seems to like you, Josh, and your feelings toward her?" Liz lifted a curious eye.

"I love Kayleen, Mrs. Decker, and…" Liz began to interrupt, but Josh stopped her. "I know what you're going to say. We're too young to know what love is."

"That's not what I was going to say at all, Josh. I don't think time spent, or age, determines feelings of love. I wasn't much older than you when I said those same words about Harry."

"I'm glad you feel that way, Mrs. Decker, because I intend to marry your granddaughter one day."

"It looks like your grandmother's giving Josh the business." I nodded toward them. Their dance was almost nonexistent. "Do you want me to cut in, Kayleen?"

"Josh can handle Grandma. I'm not worried about him. Let's just enjoy our dance, Grandpa; after all, this is our song."

"You remembered." I smiled in reminiscence. "You know, sweetheart, I always meant to give you your own song."

"I have to confess, Grandpa, I only remember because Mom has told me the story of how we came to share the same song so many times. This song means a lot to her, and I have to admit… whenever I hear it, just like Mom, it brings me comfort. It's something the three of us share. It's private, sweet, and just ours. So it's okay that you never gave me my own song, Grandpa." She rested her head gently on my shoulder.

"I'm glad you feel that way, sweetheart." I held her close, and we shared a moment as our sentimental journey came to an end. We continued to dance the night away, exchanging dates, enjoying our evening back in time. The DJ announced last song, our reminiscent era of the forties coming to an end.

"This will be the last song of the evening, and we would like to thank everyone for coming out and making our fundraiser a success. This song goes out to Elizabeth from Josh: 'You Made Me Love You,'" the DJ announced, dimming the lights.

"Kayleen told me this was your favorite song, Mrs. Decker," Josh said. "May I have the last dance?"

"I'm sorry, Josh, but I only have one partner for this song."

"Love of my life. I believe they're playing our song." I escorted my wife to the dance floor, and we fell in step as if we were one.

"Thank you, Josh, for requesting this song." Kayleen snuggled inside his arms. "Look at them out there; they dance like they're transported back in time. Like they're the only two people in the room. Do you think that will be us one day? So much in love that a song can make us young again?"

"I hope so, Kayleen." Josh held her close as they swayed together in their own romantic bliss.

"You made me love you," I sang softly into Liz's ear. "I love you, sweetheart." I pulled her close with a slow, romantic spin.

"I love you too, Harry." She nestled her head on my shoulder, oblivious to everyone and everything around us. We danced to the music inside our private world.

"Once again I'd like to thank everyone for coming, and for making our fundraiser a success." The DJ lifted the lights as the song came to an end. Liz and I continued to embrace, scarcely noticing the hustle and bustle of chairs being taken down and tables being collapsed.

"Excuse us, Grandma, Grandpa, but the dance is over." Kayleen and Josh stood next to us, coats in hand.

"Oh my goodness." Liz looked around in embarrassment at the almost-empty gymnasium.

"You still got it, Grandpa," Kayleen giggled.

"Shall we, Mrs. Decker?" Josh extended his arm.

"Yes," Liz sighed, accepting his arm and giving him a light kiss on the cheek. "I had a wonderful time tonight, Josh, reliving such wonderful memories—thank you."

"You're welcome, Mrs. Decker." He proudly escorted her from the gymnasium.

"Shall we, sweetheart?" I extended my arm.

"I love you, Grandpa." Kayleen accepted my arm with a gentle hug. Consumed with love, feeling the nostalgia of the night, I proudly escorted my granddaughter from the dance.

"We had a lot of fun tonight," Kayleen said, as Josh pulled into our driveway.

"Would you kids like to come in for some ice tea or hot chocolate?"

"No, thanks, Grandma; we're meeting some friends, but thanks again for being our dates tonight."

"You're welcome, sweetheart," Liz replied. "We had a great time. Didn't we, Harry?"

"We had a wonderful time. You kids be careful tonight." I helped Liz from the car. "Josh, take good care of my granddaughter."

"Don't worry, Mr. Decker; Kayleen will always be safe with me," Josh assured me as I closed the car door.

"What a nice boy, and so mature for his age." Liz waved goodbye from the drive.

"I liked everything about him, sweetheart." I took her arm. "Until he tried to steal my girl by playing her favorite song."

"Nobody could ever steal me from you, Harry." Liz sighed. Walking hand in hand, we took the steps leading to our home, leading us to the comforts of Twelve Forty Leland Street.

"You're sure this is what you want to do, Kayleen?" asked Josh, pulling into parking lot of the Riverside Motel.

"I'm sure, Josh." She closed his parents' car door. "Are you sure they will rent us a room?"

"Pretty sure." He took her hand. "When we get inside, Kayleen, let me do the talking." He pulled on the motel door.

"Okay, Josh." She squeezed his hand tight.

"Excuse me, how much for a room?" Josh looked at the motel attendant.

"Twenty-five dollars, but you have to be eighteen to rent a room." The attendant gave them both the once-over. "Have you got ID?"

"Sure." Josh nervously pushed a fifty-dollar bill toward him.

"That will be room twelve." He handed Josh the key. "And, son…you're gone first thing in the morning." He gave Josh a stern stare. "I don't want any trouble here."

"No trouble here, sir." Josh nervously pulled on the motel door.

"It pushes out, son." The clerk shook his head in dismay.

CHAPTER TWENTY-THREE

May 1981

"Mom, do you have a few minutes?" Kayleen asked. "Josh would like to talk to you."

"Can't you see I'm busy, Kayleen?" Susie glanced at the papers spread all over her kitchen table.

"It's important, Mom." Kayleen was anxiously ringing her hands. Susie noticed her daughter's anxiety.

"Okay, Kayleen, tell Josh I'll be right there." She put a few more papers in their proper pile.

"My mom will be right out, Josh." Kayleen nerverously took the seat next to him on the couch.

"It's going to be all right, babe." Josh took her hand in his.

"Okay, Josh." Susie took the chair across from them. "What is so important it can't wait?"

"Well, Mrs. Jenkins." Josh straightened his posture. "I've been accepted as an intern with General Motors through the skilled-trades program after graduation."

"That's great, Josh. Is that it? I'm really busy."

"Well, that's part of it." Josh shifted uncomfortably.

"And the other part, Josh?" said Susie, encouraging him to spit it out.

"I love your daughter, and we want to get married."

"Don't be ridiculous, Josh. You're both too young to get married. Besides, Kayleen's going into the nursing program after graduation. End of discussion." She started to get up from the chair. Josh cleared his throat.

"Mrs. Jenkins? There's one more part."

"I'm pregnant, Mom," Kayleen quickly uttered, squeezing Josh's hand tight.

"Kayleen?" Susie slumped back into her chair. "We talked about this."

"We used protection, Mom—it just happened," Kayleen said. Josh nodded in agreement, putting a protective arm around Kayleen.

"I love your daughter, Mrs. Jenkins, and I'll have a good job to support her…support us."

"I'm not going into the nursing program, Mom," Kayleen informed her. "I'm going to get my real-estate license. It will be quicker, and I think I could be good at it."

"You kids are so young." Susie looked into their naïve eyes. "And a baby is such a big responsibility. You have no idea what you're getting yourselves into."

"Mrs. Jenkins?" Josh stepped forward. "I love your daughter, and I promise you I'll take good care of her and your future grandchild. You'll never have to worry; you'll see."

"I hope so, Josh," Susie said, looking at his young, determined face.

"It'll all work out, Mom; you'll see." Kayleen was relieved the secret was finally out, and grateful her mother had taken it so well.

Michael Anthony Powell, February 4, 1982

Susie sat anxiously in the waiting room of Hurley hospital. She picked up a magazine and quickly thumbed through it before tossing it back on the table.

"It's a boy." Josh proclaimed proudly, walking into the waiting area just outside labor and delivery. "Michael Anthony Powell has ten fingers, ten toes, and a head full of blond hair."

"And my baby? How's Kayleen?" Susie quickly stood up. Her eyes we're anxious.

"Kayleen's fine. You would have been proud of her, Susie. A real trouper."

"I've always been proud of my daughter, Josh. When can I see them? When can I see my daughter and new grandson?"

"Soon, they were just finishing up when Kayleen demanded I come out and give you the news. They should be wheeling my wife out shortly."

"Wife," Susie muttered. The word sounded foreign. Her baby was now a wife and mother. Her mind flashed back to another day in the hospital so many years ago. Her eyes welled with tears at the memory of the loss of her firstborn.

"Mom, why are you crying? Everything's fine." Kayleen smiled from the gurney, holding her little bundle.

"It's tears of happiness, sweetheart." Susie followed the gurney into room 733 and waited patiently for the nurses to make Kayleen and the baby comfortable before offering their congratulations and quietly closing the door. "Let me see my grandson." Susie gently took Michael from her daughter's arms. "You're beautiful—absolutely beautiful." Her fingertips gently outlined Michael's small face as she reminisced once again.

"I think the word is handsome." Josh smiled proudly. "Handsome like his father."

"Yes," Susie sighed. "Handsome." She shook off the memories of the past.

"When are Mr. and Mrs. Decker coming to the hospital? I have a cigar for Harry." Josh pulled two cigars from his jacket pocket.

"They won't be coming to the hospital, Josh. Michael's first outing will be to Twelve Forty Leland Street." Holding the small bundle close, she remembered how safe she always felt inside the haven.

"Okay then." Josh returned the cigars to his jacket pocket. Taking his son from Susie's arms, he said, "First stop on your release, young man, Twelve Forty Leland Street."

Visiting Joe: July 1984

"Hey, buddy." My voice was grave as I took a seat. "I've got some bad news. I received this letter earlier today. It's from Francine…'Dear Southpaw, our beloved Pa'pae has died. He passed quietly in his sleep a few days ago, and for that I am grateful. There was no pain, no suffering…just a few gasps of breath…then silence.

"'Pa'pae talked of you and Joe often. Entertaining the patrons of our tavern regularly with his tales. Telling them the story of the young boy and Big John the bully. How young Harry cleaned the gym every day after school to learn the skills of boxing to keep his nickel. Taking Big John the bully down with his great left hook, breaking his nose. Growing up to become Jack Collins, the great Southpaw Slugger. The story was told so often that many of the patrons finished the story along with Pa'pae.

"'There were also many stories of Joe, for Pa'pae carried him in his heart. He talked proudly of Joe, when telling how his honorary son won the Silver Star. Pulling his men to safety at the risk of losing his own life. Yet Joe being ever so humble, saying he was only doing his duty, nothing more. The medal was displayed in a place of honor inside our tavern next to the American flag. Pa'pae demanded a toast be made by all our patrons in memory of Joe every Memorial Day. Those not willing to toast were not-so-graciously shown the door.'

"You hear that, buddy? I can just see him…can't you?" I erupted into laughter. "Pappy snatching up some poor schmuck. Grumbling his disappointments, dragging him toward the door." The small American flag rippled in the wind.

My hard laughter subsided, bringing tears to my eyes. The movement of the flag became a slow ripple. "'Enclosed you'll find the Silver Star. Pa'pae wanted it returned to Joe. To be buried with his honorary son. I entrust you, dear Southpaw, with this task… Take care, Francine.'

"It will be an honor." I dug a small hole, placed the Silver Star deep in the soil, and covered it with the soft dirt. I was consumed by sadness at the news of Pappy's passing, yet felt privileged in returning Joe's medal. I stood in salute, eyes misted with tears of honor. The breeze halted, bringing the small American flag to honorary stillness.

February 1986

"Where's my favorite grandson? Where's the birthday boy?" Susie came through her daughter's front door bearing birthday gifts.

"I'm right here, Grandma." Michael ran into the living room and stood proudly in front of her. "The birthday boy's right here." He eyed the wrapped presents. "Are all those for me?"

"They're all for you, sweetheart, and how old is the birthday boy today?" She looked into his joyous little face.

"I'm four, Grandma." Holding up four little fingers, he dropped to the floor, surrounded by presents.

"Four, and such a big boy." Susie tousled his hair, wondering how the time had passed so quickly.

"He-Man!" Michael shouted, grabbing the next wrapped present. "Skeletor!" His eyes were wide as he ripped the paper from the last gift. "Power of Grayskull," he shouted, raising the mighty sword.

"Hi, Mom," said Kayleen, looking up from putting the finishing touches on the birthday cake. "From the sounds of it, Michael's enjoying your gifts."

"That's what birthdays and grandmas are for, Kayleen—getting what you want."

"Dad called." Kayleen was hesitant. "He's in town for the weekend. He asked if he could come by and bring Michael a present. I told him it would be all right if he wasn't drinking, but to be honest with you, Mom, he already sounded drunk."

"Well, don't count on it, Kayleen. You know your father isn't good at keeping his word."

"I'm not, Mom. I don't trust Daddy either, and I haven't said anything to Michael. Besides, Grandpa Harry is the only grandpa Michael's interested in seeing. Aunt Mandy also called to tell Michael happy birthday and apologized for not being able to make the party, but she said his gift was being delivered. Apparently something came up…probably a new man." Kayleen rolled her eyes. "What is it with her and men, Mom?" she said, shaking her head sadly. "I just don't get it."

"Don't be so hard on your Aunt Mandy. She's been looking for a man who truly cares for her, her whole life. You know, it's really kind of sad to never find what you so desperately want."

"Well, maybe if she had a little class about her…"

"Kayleen Powell." Susie's voice was stern. "I know Aunt Mandy's a little rough around the edges, but she's never been anything but good to you. Good to the both of us, and she's your grandmother's best friend. Show a little respect!"

"Sorry, Mom, you're right. The class thing was a little harsh." She put the last birthday candle on the chocolate cake.

"We're here! Where's our great-grandson? Where's the birthday boy?" Liz and I called out in unison, stepping inside the foyer.

"Right here," Michael squealed, meeting us at the front door. "Is that for me, Grandpa Harry?" He eyed the wrapped present I held in my hand.

"It's for our favorite great-grandson, Michael. Oh where, oh where can our grandson be? Do you see him anywhere, Liz?" I searched the room.

"I'm right here, Grandpa Harry." Michael anxiously jumped up and down.

"So you are, Michael." I handed him the gift he so enthusiastically waited for. Falling to the floor he ripped away at the paper.

"Wow! Real boxing gloves!" His eyes were shining bright. "You going to teach me to be a southpaw like you, Grandpa Harry?" he asked, pulling the gloves from their box.

"Here, let me help you, Michael." I slid the gloves onto his small hands. "Now stand with your right foot out and knees bent… loose." I took my own stance in example. "Now put your gloves up." I raised my fists. "Always protect your jaw, Michael. Ready? Right jab, right jab, powerful hook." I threw a hard left. "The surprise punch," I said, smiling deviously.

"Yeah, the surprise punch." Michael's voice was sinister as he threw a hard left hook.

"Who's ready for cake?" Kayleen called out from the kitchen.

"Me, Momma," Michael called out, shaking the boxing gloves from his hands. "The birthday boy's ready." He ran into the kitchen. "I'll take a big piece." Climbing onto a kitchen chair, he eyed the chocolate cake.

"Okay, sweetheart, but first we have to sing 'Happy Birthday,'" said Kayleen, lighting the last candle.

"Okay, Momma." Michael's eyes were bright, looking at the small blaze atop his birthday cake.

"Happy birthday to you…happy birthday to you," we all sang in unison. Michael danced a little jig along with the song. "Happy birthday, dear Michael…happy birthday to you."

"Okay, son, make a wish and blow out all your candles." Michael squeezed his little eyes tight in deep concentration. His lips silently mumbled his birthday wish. We all watched in anticipation as seconds continued to tick by. "Son, open your eyes; it's time to blow out your candles." Michael, ignoring his mother's request, squeezed his eyes tighter and concentrated harder as the candles continued to burn down.

"Son?"

Michael's eyes suddenly sprang open, and he blew out all the candles in one fell swoop.

"Good job, Michael." Kayleen applauded. "You blew all your candles out in one breath. That means you'll get your wish. What did you wish for, Michael?" She pulled the candles from the cake.

"Give me a big piece, Mom, and I want lots of ice cream." Michael ignored his mother's question, looking hungrily at his cake.

"Sure, son, but what did you wish for?" she repeated, cutting him a large corner piece. Michael took a big bite of birthday cake and then another. "Son, is there a reason you won't tell me what you wished for?"

"I can't, Mom." Michael talked with a mouth full of cake. "If I do, it won't come true." He swallowed hard.

"I'm your mother, Michael; you can tell me."

"Can't, Mom. It's between me and the birthday wishers." Michael continued to enjoy his cake, determined in his silence. The doorbell chimed.

"Are you expecting someone else, Kayleen?" asked Josh, getting up from the table.

"Not really." Kayleen looked at her mother, wondering if her father had found his way to the party."

"It's a delivery for Michael…from Mandy." Josh set a large package that seemed to be whimpering on the kitchen table.

"It's Buster! It's my birthday wish." Michael ripped open the package. The ugliest wirehaired dog they'd ever seen popped out his head. “Isn’t he beautiful, Mom?” Buster licked Michael’s face in happiness.

“Mandy got him a dog?” Kayleen unpleasantly muttered.

“Isn’t he great, Mom?” Michael was overflowing with happiness. “I told you, Mom; you just have to believe.”

“You know?” Liz said, watching her great-grandson romp and play with his newfound friend. “Mandy has always known what a man desires, and apparently she knows regardless of age.” Everyone in the room burst out in laughter.

CHAPTER TWENTY-FOUR

Summer 1986

"You ready for lunch, Julie?" Susie asked, looking at the clock on the courthouse wall. "They just opened that outdoor café at the Whitley Hotel. I thought we could take a walk. It's such a beautiful day."

"I wish I could, Susie, but I'm leaving early today, so I'm skipping lunch. You go ahead and check it out." Julie was preoccupied with her work. "If it's good, we'll go another day."

"Sounds good." Susie hit the save icon on her computer and grabbed her purse from her bottom desk drawer.

At the café, the hostess led her to a nice corner table on the patio "Your waitress will be right with you. Enjoy your lunch." She handed her a menu.

"Thank you." Susie took a moment to bask in the sunshine before scanning the lunch menu.

"Good afternoon, my name is Denise. I'll be your server today. May I take your order?"

"Yes, an ice tea and the Cobb salad, please." Susie handed back the menu. "Denise, could you also point me in the direction of the ladies' room? I'd like to wash up before lunch."

"Of course, it's just inside the hotel to your left." Denise gestured with her pencil. Susie got up from her chair and entered the grand Whitley, reminiscent of something straight out of the forties.

"Good afternoon, Miss." The restroom attendant glanced at Susie as she entered the luxurious washroom.

"Good afternoon." Susie nodded, walking to the wash basin. The attendant returned to the straightening of her supplies. Hand cloths, perfumes, hairspray, and more—all free to Whitley patrons.

"Sabrina? I didn't expect to see you today." The attendant happily called out to a beautiful, young dark haired woman as she entered the ladies' room. She had an air of confidence and sophistication about her.

"I'm meeting Jack," Sabrina replied, taking a comb from her purse and running it through her perfectly coiffed hair.

"I thought Mr. Collins was your Thursday." She handed Sabrina a small bottle of perfume.

"Normally it is Thursday, but I don't mind the change." Sabrina lightly dabbed the perfume behind her ears. "I like Jack. He's respectful, friendly—yet strictly business. No attachments. Just the way I like it." She wiped away a small smudge of lipstick. "Besides, he's not hard on the eyes either." She winked. "Thanks, Shirley," she said, dropping a five-dollar bill into the jar on her way out of the restroom.

"Do you know that woman?" Susie watched the restroom door swing shut.

"Sabrina? As well as you can know a patron of the hotel."

"Is she a prostitute?"

"Solicitation is illegal, Miss. Let's just say Sabrina has a few friends…she meets from time to time."

"Do you know Mr. Collins?" Susie shook the water from her hands. Shirley handed her a dry cloth.

"Not personally, but I've seen him a few times—older gentleman, mid-fifties, but still a very attractive man."

"Try early sixties," Susie muttered.

"Excuse me, miss?"

"Nothing. Thank you, Shirley." Susie dropped a tip into the jar.

"You're welcome, Miss. Have a pleasant day," Shirley said, a confused expression on her face.

"It can't be. It has to be a coincidence." Susie stopped dead in her tracks, spotting her father on the other side of the hotel lobby. Sabrina was draped on his arm. "Harry Decker, a.k.a. Jack Collins," Susie muttered, watching her father and Sabrina step into the elevator. Tears of sadness and disappointment misted her eyes as she quickly left the Whitley.

"How was the Whitley?" Julie glanced up from her desk.

"Fine," Susie said shortly, picking up the phone. "Hello, Mom, is Daddy home?"

"No, I'm sorry, sweetheart; he's down at the Silver Center." Liz's voice sounded muffled.

"You sound a little funny, Mom; are you feeling okay?" Susie got an unsettling feeling in the pit of her stomach as she heard her mother softly moan in discomfort.

"I just have a terrible headache today, Susie."

"It's probably your blood pressure, Mom. Did you take your pill today?" Susie's voice was reprimanding.

"Yes, sweetheart. I took my pill, but it doesn't seem to be working today."

"Mom, are you alone?" asked Susie, feeling her anxiety rise.

"I am right now, but Mandy should be here shortly. We're supposed to take in the one o'clock matinee at the Regal, but I'm really not feeling up to it today."

"Then don't go, Mom; just rest. Aunt Mandy will understand."

"I think I will. Mandy's here now, sweetheart. I'll talk to you later."

"Okay, Mom. Talk to you later." Susie hung up the phone, her anxiety calming, knowing Aunt Mandy was with her mother. Yet her mind was still reeling from what she had seen at the Whitley.

Later That Day

"Have a good night, Ms. Jenkins," the parking-lot attendant said, lifting the gate.

"Thank you, Charlie." Susie took a left out of the lot instead of her usual right, heading in the direction of her mother's house. Her thoughts consumed by what she had seen at the Whitley earlier that day. She was unable to shake her womanly instincts telling her things weren't quite right with her family. As she took a right onto Leland Street, fear clenched her heart; there was an ambulance parked in the driveway of Twelve Forty. She accelerated her car and quickly brought it to a stop, running toward the house in a panic.

"What's going on here?" Susie demanded, entering the living room. "Daddy? Aunt Mandy?" She looked at her mother lying on the couch, flushed, surrounded by paramedics.

"Your mother's had another stroke." Mandy's eyes were filled with fear and sadness.

"That's impossible, Aunt Mandy. I know for a fact she took her medication today." She watched the paramedics put an oxygen mask over her mother's face.

"Daddy, tell them! Tell them Mom is fine. She just needs some rest."

"I'm sorry, sweetheart." I was unable to take my eyes from Liz.

"This is all your fault, Jack," Mandy said. "If you hadn't—"

"Shut up, Mandy!" I said, quickly silencing her, enforcing my words with a harsh stare.

"Don't tell me to shut up, Jack." Mandy glared.

"Please!" The paramedic silenced the room. "We need to get Mrs. Decker to the hospital, and we need to do it now. We'll be taking her to Saint Joe's Hospital. You can follow in your car." They lifted the gurney to a roll-out position.

This can't be happening, my mind shouted as I followed the paramedics in a state of shock. Standing outside the ambulance I looked at my beloved Liz lying on the gurney, her eyes seeming to plead to me as I stood there helpless as they loaded her inside.

"Sir? Please!" The paramedic attempting to close the ambulance door. "We need to go."

"Daddy, come on." Susie pulled my arm. The paramedics gently pushed me aside, shutting the ambulance door.

"Let's go, Daddy—now!" Susie's voice suddenly snapped me out of my state of shock. Both of us ran toward her car.

"I'll be right behind you," Mandy called out, jumping into her car.

"What happened, Daddy?" Susie hit the gas pedal hard.

"I don't know exactly, Susie; I wasn't home," I said, feeling surreal. "Mandy called me on my pager, and when I arrived home, your mother was lying catatonic on the couch."

"She's going to be all right, isn't she, Daddy?" Susie's voice was quivering.

"I don't know, sweetheart." I felt sick to my stomach.

"She has to be, Daddy...she just has to be." Turning into the emergency parking lot, she pulled up behind the ambulance, lights still flashing. Both of us jumped from the car.

"You can't park there," a security officer bellowed. "Hey! You can't leave your car here." Susie and I ignored his shouts, hot on the trail of the gurney carrying my wife, her mother, through the emergency entrance doors.

"Excuse me! Excuse me!" A nurse suddenly appeared between us and the gurney carrying my beloved Liz. "You can't go in there." The nurse stood firm in front of the doors marked NO ADMITTANCE.

"That's my mother." Susie looked though the small windows of the doors, seeing her mother being wheeled down the hall.

"Please, may we see her?" I pleaded. "Just for a moment."

"I'm sorry, sir. She's being assessed right now. Please take a seat in the waiting room. The doctor will be with you when he has some information."

"Come on, sweetheart." I gently took Susie from the small windows. My heart heavy, I led her to a room filled with nothing but uncomfortable chairs and a few outdated magazines.

"Have you heard anything?" Mandy anxiously came into the waiting room.

"Nothing yet. What happened to my mother, Aunt Mandy? Daddy said you were there when it all happened."

"I'm not really sure, Susie; everything happened so fast." Her eyes were searching. "Jack, can I talk to you for a minute out in the hall?" She walked out into the hallway, not waiting for an answer.

"Go ahead, Daddy. I'm okay. I'll come and get you if the doctor comes in."

"Okay, sweetheart. I'll just be right outside." I gave her hand a comforting squeeze. "What is it, Mandy? This isn't the time for one of your lectures on my code of conduct."

"Liz knows, Jack…about all the other women."

"That's impossible, Mandy. I've always been very careful. What makes you think she knows?"

"I'm sorry, Jack." Her eyes filled with regret. "I told her everything. She caught me off guard. I tried to tell her those other women meant nothing. That it was just sex—an uncontrollable urge. That you have always loved her, and only her."

"Mandy, what have you done?" My heart seemed to deflate. "Liz doesn't believe there can be sex without love."

"She hates me, Jack. I tried to explain to her that I kept your secrets out of love for her—to protect her."

"Did you really think she would see it that way, Mandy?" My voice filled with sarcasm. "That you were just trying to protect her? That you did it out of love?"

"She told me I wasn't her friend anymore, Jack," Mandy whimpered. "That she trusted me, and I betrayed her trust. We betrayed her trust."

"You need to leave, Mandy." My own guilt was consuming me.

"But, Jack?" Mandy's eyes filled with tears.

"Leave!" I ordered, furious with her. Mandy ran from the hospital, crying uncontrollably.

"Daddy?" Susie poked her head outside the waiting room. "The doctor is asking for you. Where is Aunt Mandy going?"

"She had to leave," I said, regaining my composure. "Take me to see the doctor, sweetheart."

"Mr. Decker. I'm Doctor Ryker."

"When can I see my wife, Doctor?"

"I'm sorry, Mr. Decker." His voice was filled with compassion. "We did an EEG; it showed no brain activity. Your wife is currently on life support. We need your signed permission to take her off the respirator and let her go in peace."

"Daddy?" Susie's eyes filled with tears.

"There must be some mistake, Doctor. My wife was fine this morning. We have reservations for dinner this evening."

"I'm sorry, Mr. Decker." He locked eyes with me. "Sometimes modern medicine just doesn't have the answers that will save our loved ones." I felt surreal as his word echoed in my ears. "Mr. Decker?"

"I'll need to see my wife before I sign any papers."

"Understandable, Mr. Decker. Go straight down this hall, and take your first left. She's in room 110."

“Thank you doctor.” I reached out searching for my daughter’s hand overwhelmed with sadness. I heard nothing but the echo of my footsteps as we walked hand and hand to the room that held the love of my life. Slowly, and with dread, I pushed open the door.

“She’s just sleeping, Daddy.” Susie sighed, going to her mother’s bedside taking her hand. “She’s cold, Daddy.” Her voice was soft and childlike. “She needs another blanket. You know Mommy always sleeps with two blankets. Could we get another blanket, please?” Susie looked to the attending nurse.

“Your mother doesn’t need a blanket.” The nurse was dismissive, preoccupied with her chart. “When you two are finished here, we’ll be taking her—”

“*Please*!” I raised my hand to silence the nurse. “My daughter asked you for another blanket…please?” My eyes pleading. “Just give her another blanket.”

“Of course.” The nurse seeming to find her compassion took a warm blanket from the cart and handed it to Susie before quietly leaving the room.

“There…that’s better.” Susie tucked the blankets tight. “Isn’t she beautiful, Daddy?” She adjusted a lock of hair that had fallen out of place.

“Yes, sweetheart.” My eyes filled with tears as I looked at the woman I’d loved for over forty years, wondering how I would live the rest of my life without her. I kissed her lips gently, lingering there in my good-bye. “We have to go now, sweetheart.” I extended my hand.

“Just another minute, Daddy.” A lonely, silent tear ran down her face. “Rest now, Mama.” She adjusted the blankets in one last final comfort kissing her mother ever so gently on the cheek. We walked out of the hospital in coma-like states. Hand in hand. Everyone and everything seemed distant and surreal. We drove home in silence until we rounded the corner and pulled alongside the curb of Twelve Forty Leland Street.

"This can't be happening, Daddy," said Susie, coming out of her coma. "You should have been home, Daddy. You could have saved her. Mandy's right. This is all your fault!"

"My fault? Susie, sweetheart. You heard the doctor. Your mother had a brain aneurysm due to a blood clot—a stroke. It's no one's fault. There was nothing I or anyone could have done to save her."

"You don't know that, Daddy, because you weren't home. You were at the Whitley Hotel with Sabrina. I saw you, Daddy." Her eyes filled with tears. "You were with a prostitute having sex while my mother was dying."

"What are you talking about, sweetheart? You're mistaken." "Stop it, Daddy," she cautioned. "Stop lying. I saw you. Your secret's out, and to think I defended you! How many were there, Daddy? Brandy…Sabrina…how many?" she screamed.

"Susie…those women." I was consumed with shame. "They meant nothing to me."

"Nothing! If they meant nothing to you, then why would you do it? Explain it to me!" Her eyes were merciless.

"Your mother is the only woman I ever loved or will ever love." My voice was sad and somber.

"That's it? That's your explanation, Daddy? I once told you if you ever hurt my mother…get out, Daddy. Get out of my car."

"Sweetheart, please, we need each other now, more than ever."

"Get out of my car, Daddy." Her bottom lip was quivering.

"Sweetheart, please?" My voice breaking, I opened the car door.

"Get out," she screamed. "It wasn't a stroke that killed my mother—it was you! You, Daddy! You broke her heart. You're responsible."

"Please, sweetheart," I pleaded to her through the car window. "We need to talk about this."

"Good-bye, Daddy." Susie stared straight ahead, driving away.

Tears filled my eyes as I watched my daughter's car round the corner. "Forgive me," I whispered, climbing the steps to Twelve

Forty Leland Street. Feeling like I'd just gone fifteen rounds, beaten, battered, and bruised, I entered the once-safe haven that had brought me so much joy and that now only echoed loneliness and heartache.

A Few Days Later

Kayleen and Susie were enjoying a hot cup of tea after their long day of shopping. Both had been in search of a black dress befitting the occasion for a funeral.

"Aren't you going to answer that, Mom?" Kayleen said, hearing the phone ring for the fourth time.

"The machine will get it. Besides, I don't feel like talking to anyone."

"Please leave a message after the beep." (*Beeeep.*)

"Hello, sweetheart, this is your dad. I was hoping we could go to your mother's funeral services together, but if you prefer to go alone, sweetheart, I understand. The memorial service is tomorrow, one o'clock, at Schwartz's Funeral Home. Please call me back, Susie. I love you…okay…I hope to hear from you. Good-bye, sweetheart." (Click.)

"Grandpa sounds so sad. You have to call him back, Mom." Kayleen picked up the phone.

"Put that phone down, Kayleen," Susie sternly ordered. "I have no intention of calling him back."

"But, Mom?" She set down the receiver. "What could Grandpa have possibly done that is so unforgiveable?"

"That's between me and my father, Kayleen. You and Josh can pick me up tomorrow, at noon. We can all go to the funeral together. Bring Michael, and I'll try to explain to him what has happened to his grandma Liz."

"Sure, Mom, if that's what you want." Feeling her mother's sadness, unsure how to console her.

"It's what I want, Kayleen. Now go home, sweetheart. I want to be alone."

"Whatever you want mom." She gave her mother a sympathetic hug. "I'll see you tomorrow." Sadly she closed the door.

Liz's Funeral

"Kayleen, Josh," I called out, giving a slight wave as I stood outside the entrance of Schwartz's Funeral Home. I smiled weakly, seeing Susie walking behind holding young Michael's hand. He was dressed handsomely in his blue suit.

"Hi, Grandpa Harry." Michael waved.

"Hi, Michael." Looking into his tiny face, I was consumed with love. "Hello, Susie." I opened my arms to her, only to have her walk on by as if I weren't even there.

"I'm sorry, Grandpa," Kayleen said. "I don't know why Mom is acting like this. For some odd reason, she blames you for Grandma's stroke. Josh and I both tried to tell her it wasn't anyone's fault. There was nothing anyone could have done to save her."

"It's okay, Kayleen. Your mother is in a lot of pain right now, and she needs someone to blame."

"That may be true, Grandpa, but she shouldn't be blaming you. Grandma had a stroke. It wasn't your fault. I love my mom, but—"

"But nothing, Kayleen. My little girl just needs some time. She'll come around. You just promise me you'll be there for her until she does."

"Of course I promise, anything for you grandpa" She nodded.

"Come on, you two. It's time to go inside." Josh took Kayleen's arm and escorted us to the seats designated for family. Susie was sitting two seats down next to Mandy, Michael on her lap.

"Grandpa?" Kayleen whispered, looking to a beautiful urn nestled next to a young picture of her grandmother in the famous emerald-green dress. "I didn't know grandma wanted to be cremated?"

"Your grandmother had a fear of being put into the ground, sweetheart. When this is all over, I'll be taking her home with me." My eyes were misting. "Where she belongs."

"Mr. Decker, we're ready to begin," the funeral director whispered.

"Thank you." Standing tall, I took the podium. I told stories of my beloved Liz and the never-ending love I would always have for her. I teared up only once when I spoke of our lovely daughter. "When Susie was born, she had the eyes of the black-eyed Susan flower—so dark and beautiful, and we loved her instantly." I looked at my daughter, only to have her turn away from my gaze. Sadly I continued, knowing how deeply I had hurt my daughter. Ending the eulogy, I gave an invitation to the memorial dinner.

"Would you like to ride with us over to the memorial dinner, Mandy?" asked Susie, adjusting Michael on her lap.

"I don't think so, Susie. I think I'm just going to sit here for a while and talk to my friend. I feel your mother here in the room today." Mandy hesitantly smiled, her eyes giving way to sadness and loss. "I loved your mother very much, Susie. She was my best friend…my only friend."

"She loved you too, Aunt Mandy." Susie gave her hand a gentle squeeze in comfort. "Mom often said you were more like sisters than friends."

"We were." Her eyes misted. "I'm going to miss her so."

"We all are," Susie murmured, pulling Michael close, nuzzling him.

"Are you ready, Mom? We need to get over to the memorial dinner." Kayleen took Michael from her lap.

"I'm ready." Susie sighed. "Mandy?" she said, opening her arms for a hug. "Thank you for always taking care of my mother."

"You're welcome, Susie." Mandy hugging her horary niece tight, looking to the portrait of Liz in her emerald dress. Nostalgia filled her in remembrance of the days they were just two young girls getting ready for a date.

"Come on, Grandma." Michael said, taking hold of Susie's hand seeming more like a little man than a child. He led her to the car taking care to put her safely in the back seat before retrieving his He-Man and Skeletor from the floorboard.

"Michael?" Susie pulled him onto her lap. "Do you understand why we're here today? That Grandma Liz is no longer with us?"

"Yeah, I know...take that, Skeletor!" He crashed He-Man into him. "Grandma Liz told me."

"What did Grandma Liz tell you, Michael?"

"She told me she had to go away, but not to worry. To always be a good boy and take good care of you, Grandma."

"When did she tell you that, Michael?" Kayleen interjected, looking to her mother in confusion.

"Yesterday, when I was playing in my room." He crashed He-Man into Skeletor once again.

"Did Grandma Liz say anything else?" Kayleen inquired searching his dark, innocent eyes.

"Just to look for her in the dimes—the dimes that don't belong," he said, crashing his action figures together in heated battle.

"The dimes that don't belong?" Kayleen sounded confused. "Mom, do you know what that means?" Susie unknowingly shook her head filing through the memories of her past. Her eyes lit up suddenly understanding.

"My penny loafers." Susie smiled.

"Penny loafers, Mom?"

"When I was sixteen, your grandmother bought me a pair of penny loafers. They were called penny loafers because we'd put a penny in the tongue of the shoe...for style. Your grandmother, however, insisted on putting a dime in my loafers. We argued for days that the dime didn't belong, but she insisted the dime stay. To be used for a phone call to keep me safe and close to her. I was embarrassed in the beginning wearing my dime loafers, but as time went on, the dimes brought me comfort. Whenever I was unsure, I would look down at the dimes securely placed inside my loafers and know everything was going to be all right, because the spirit of my mother was with me. Thank you, Michael." She gave him a big hug. "Thank you for reminding me of the dimes."

"You're welcome, Grandma." He-Man crushing Skeletor, who cried out in final defeat. Josh pulled into the parking lot where the memorial service was being held.

"I don't want to stay long, Kayleen," Susie said. "Just a respectful show, and then I want to leave."

"Whatever you want, Mom. Whenever you're ready to leave, just let us know."

"Come on, Grandma." Michael once again took his grandmother's hand in protection, leading her inside the reserved banquet hall.

"Mom, I'm going to get Michael something to eat. Would you like anything?"

"No, thank you, Kayleen," Susie said, taking a seat in the corner, wanting nothing more than the memorial dinner to be over.

I walked over to my daughter sitting quietly and alone. "Sweetheart? Can we talk?"

"We have nothing to talk about, Daddy," She said, her dark eyes looking straight through me.

"I want to try and explain, if I can."

"Explain? What's there to explain, Daddy? You cheated on my mother."

"It's not that simple, Susie."

"It is to me, Daddy," Susie said, getting up from the table walking past me. I never felt more alone in my life as I did at that moment.

"I'm ready to go Kayleen." Susie said taking Michael's hand.

"Mom? We just got here."

"I don't want to stay, Kayleen." Disregarding her daughter's objection, Susie exited the banquet hall with little Michael in tow.

"What am I going to do with her, Josh?" Kayleen was shaking her head, upset.

"You know your mother, Kayleen. Once she's made her mind up, that's it."

"Sometimes, Josh…my mother?" Kayleen sighed deeply. "Let's go and say our goodbyes. Her eyes searched the banquet hall for her grandfather. He was talking to an older gentleman she didn't recognize. "Excuse us, I'm sorry Grandpa, but mom's ready to leave." Her eyes were sympathetic. "Call me if you need anything." Giving a gentle hug.

"I will, sweetheart." Releasing her I looked around the memorial service wanting nothing more than for this day to be over.

"How can you just leave Grandpa here, Mom?" Kayleen said shutting the car door in upset. "Can't you see he needs you?"

"Just take me home, please." Susie gazed out the window. Josh and Kayleen respecting Susie's wishes, sat in discontented silence for the remainder of the car ride home. Only the sound of He-man and Skeletor waging battle to be heard.

"Do you want us to come in for a while, Mom?" Kayleen asked as Josh pulled alongside the curb.

"No, thank you, Kayleen." Susie getting out closing the car door.

"Good-bye, Grandma." Michael waved his He-Man through the open car window.

"Good-bye, sweetheart." Susie softly smiled.

"What a sad day," Kayleen said, her eyes misted as she watched her mother solemnly take the steps that lead to her home. Josh gave a few weak honks of the horn as he pulled from the curb.

Consumed by the events of the day Susie went to her bedroom closet and retrieved a dusty old shoebox from way in the back. Ever so gently she lifted the lid, safely tucked inside a pair of well-worn penny loafers. Dimes shining brightly from their tongues. Kicking off her heels, she slid on the loafers that had once caused so much disruption, and she instantly felt comfort. Bringing her knees to her chest, she began to hum "Sentimental Journey," mourning the loss of her mother and the life she once knew living in the safe haven known as Twelve Forty Leland Street.

Visiting Joe

As I pulled into the veterans' cemetery, the sun was slowly being taken over by dark clouds. The gloom of the day was befitting of the sadness consuming my heart. "Hey, buddy, surprised to see me?" I chuckled sadly. "My Liz is gone, Joe…a stroke" I fell to my knees…."She promised me, Joe. Promised me she would take care of herself. Promised me she would never leave me." I blinked back the tears.

"Mandy was with her when it happened, Joe. She told Liz everything—about all my infidelities. She said she had no choice. That Liz caught her off guard. I don't believe it, Joe." Hatred and loathing started to rise. "I think Mandy has always wanted to tell Liz. Whether it was to unburden herself of the betrayal or just hurt me, I'm not sure, but either way the secret's out—my beloved Liz died knowing of my betrayal.

"How am I going to make this right, Joe? Make Liz understand that I loved her, and only her? That the other women…were just bodies, fulfilling a need. My disgusting need." Exhaling sharply, I looked to the heavens in shame. The last of the sun was being consumed by dark, threatening clouds.

"Susie isn't talking to me, Joe. My daughter blames me for her mother's death. She claims her mother may have had a stroke, but it was a broken heart that killed her, and I was the deliverer of that broken heart. Maybe she's right, Joe. I just don't know anymore. I'm hoping in time Susie will forgive me; she's all I have left.

"My sister, Helen, claims that if the love Liz and I shared was a true love, our bond will carry over into the next life. That Liz and I will meet again in heaven. That we'll be rejoined in a better place. It's the gift given by God to see our loved ones once again. Is she right, Joe? Are you there, in this wonderful place my sister speaks of? Is Pappy with you? Have you seen my beloved Liz?

"This life, Joe? It's becoming so hard. Everyone and everything I care for seems to be taken from me. I don't understand the reason, Joe—the why of it all." The sky was turning black, giving a threatening rumble. Light rain began to fall.

"Tears from heaven, Joe?" I chuckled sadly, looking to the dark sky. Rain drops misted my face, joining my tears. "Help me, Joe." I muttered collapsing atop his grave in defeat. Thunder boomed as the skies opened, and heaven's tears fell. The small American flag became soaked. Droplets of rain slowly fell from its edges seeming to join me in my tears.

CHAPTER TWENTY-FIVE

Two Weeks Later

Turning off the vacuum Susie heard the beep of a recording voice mail.

"Hello Sweetheart it's me again, dear ole Dad. It's the anniversary of the day your mother and I first met. I'm going over to Brookston Park today to spread a few of her ashes around the bench and release an anniversary balloon in her remembrance. I would love it if you would join me, sweetheart. I'll be there around four this afternoon. Please come...I miss you...I love you...I'm sorry." The voice mail beeped, disconnecting the call.

"I'm sorry too, Daddy." Susie looked at the machine, eyes filling with tears of disenchanted love.

Sitting on the bench inside Brookston Park, ashes and balloon in hand, I patiently waited for a daughter who never showed. When it was clear she wasn't coming, I opened up the urn and gently poured a few of the ashes around the bench. Whispering my undying love I released the emerald green balloon. Park goers passing by, unaware and uncaring that the love of my life was no longer with me.

A Few Months Later

"Hello, sweetheart, it's your dear ole dad again. The Silver Center is giving a dinner this Saturday honoring the trainers for their dedication and hard work. I would love for you to come and join me, sweetheart. Please try and make it, Susie. Kayleen, Josh, and Michael are also welcome…I'll save you all a seat… I miss you, sweetheart…please come." The voice mail beeped; time was up.

Kayleen walked into the kitchen clutching a bag of groceries. "Your machine's flashing; you have a missed call, Mom." She set the bag atop the kitchen table and pushed the message button.

"Hello, sweetheart, it's your dear ole dad…"

"Give it up, Daddy." Susie pushed the delete button.

"Mom, why did you do that? You have to talk to Grandpa sometime. He sounds so sad. Just talk to him!"

"This is between me and my father, Kayleen," She uttered dismissively putting the groceries away.

The Honorary Dinner

"Harry Decker, a.k.a. Jack Collins. Please, Jack, come up and say a few words." Robert Spencer called me to the podium as applause and whistles erupted throughout the banquet hall.

"Thank you, Bob." Shaking his hand, I accepted the honorary plaque. I silently read the words inscribed below the intertwined boxing gloves: "In recognition of loyalty, devotion, and dedication in mentoring the youths of the Silver Gloves." I looked out to a sea of expectant faces and waved my hand to silence.

"I accept this plaque in honor of my mentor, Pappy O'Hare. The man that took the time so many years ago to teach me the great sport of boxing. Even if it was just to keep my nickel." I chuckled softly, in remembrance. "Thanks again," I loudly proclaimed, raising the plaque high, applause and whistles erupting once again. Bittersweet feelings consumed me as I made my way back to the table with its four empty chairs.

"Hello, Jack," a familiar voice said. I turned to find Mandy standing behind me.

"Mandy? What are you doing here?" I asked, feeling upset at the sight of the woman who had betrayed me.

"How are you, Jack?" She took a seat at my empty table.

"I'm good." Sitting down across from her I gave a nod of assurance.

"Are you, Jack?" She raised her brows in disbelief. "Rumor has it Susie isn't talking to you. Is that true, Jack?"

"My family is my business, Mandy. It's too bad you never understood that. I'll never understand why my wife befriended you. Liz was such a nice, innocent, sweet girl, and you, Mandy?" I shook my head contemptuously.

"We all start out as nice, innocent girls, Jack. Giving our hearts and love so freely. It's only after being betrayed and discarded that we change, giving the world the impression of being savvy and indifferent to protect our hearts. Think what you want about me, Jack. I really don't care. We both have our penance to pay in our betrayal to Liz, but this estrangement between you and Susie…fix it, Jack!"

"I tried, Mandy—she won't talk to me." I looked at the woman I had resented for years. "Tell me how." Sadness and defeat filled my eyes. "Tell me how to make amends with my daughter. Liz always said you were a wise woman, Mandy, so tell me."

Mandy sat silent, giving me the ole boxer's stare, before disappearing as quickly as she had appeared.

The Next Day

"Aunt Mandy? What a surprise. Come in; take a seat." Susie stepping aside for her to enter. "Can I get you something to drink? Ice tea? Soda?"

"This is not a social call, Susie. I'm here to talk about your father and your forgiveness of him."

"I can't forgive him, Aunt Mandy. I wish I could, but what he did to my mother? The betrayal?" Susie shook her head in sadness and disappointment.

"You have to forgive him, Susie. If not for yourself, for your mother. She would be very unhappy with the two of you being estranged from each other."

"Don't you think I want to forgive him, Aunt Mandy? I love and miss my father very much, but I just can't. The thought of him being with those other women just sickens me."

"Sit down Susie." Mandy gestured to the living room sofa. "I think it's time you understand a few things about your father."

"There is nothing you can tell me, Aunt Mandy, that will excuse my father's actions."

"Believe me; I'm not here to excuse him. I'm here to make you understand him."

"Understand him?" Susie scowled "I think I know my father very well."

"That's just it, Susie; you know him as a father—not as a man."

"Okay, then, enlighten me. Tell me. Why should I forgive my father?"

"Because men are weak, Susie. Especially when it comes to desires of the flesh. Sex for men is just a need. A desire to be taken care of, not much different than hunger. A craving, if you will. Some men, like your father, carry stronger cravings, deeper yearnings, uninhibited desires. They have what I refer to as sexual demons. These demons must be fulfilled in different ways, but not all women are capable of taking care of their desires, and unfortunately your mother was one of those women."

"Don't you dare blame my mother for my father's indiscretions!"

"I'm not blaming anyone, Susie. I'm just trying to make you understand. Your father's demons? They were so strong he couldn't ignore their calls. Your father may have had a lot of women, but he loved only one, your mother. Believe me, Susie—your father lives in his own turmoil because of his betrayal to your mother. Forgive him, Susie. He's a good man. He just has one big flaw."

Susie looked at Mandy, deciphering her words. Her eyes became misty. "I said such mean, harsh things to him, Aunt Mandy."

"Go see your father, Susie; make amends."

"I will, Aunt Mandy. Thank you." Susie gave her an appreciative hug as a horn blasted from the driveway.

"I'm coming," Mandy yelled from the front door to a disheveled man sitting behind the wheel of her car.

"Come on, baby. Let's go."

"Men." Mandy shook her head. "Who knows?" She smiled. "Maybe this one will be Mr. Right." The horn blasted longer, louder.

"Maybe?" Susie smiled.

Both knew he was just another loser in Mandy's long line of losers.

THE NEXT DAY

From the living room, I heard the front door slam "Daddy?" Susie happily called out. I got up from the couch to try and intercept her in the foyer, but I wasn't quick enough. She walked in, smiling broadly, and then stopped dead in her tracks.

"Susie?" I said. "I wasn't expecting you."

"Who is that woman, Daddy?" Susie's nodded to the woman seated on my sofa. Her dark eyes innocent and childlike.

"Her name doesn't matter." I bowed my head in shame. "She's no one, Susie."

"What do you mean, no one, Jack?" The woman said, sounding insulted. "You called me, remember, lover?"

"How could you, Daddy? How could you bring this woman into our home? Into my mother's home?"

"This woman means nothing to me, Susie. She was just leaving."

"I just got here, lover, but if that's what you want!" The woman stood to leave. "I'll need money for a cab."

"You don't have to leave." Susie looked at the woman, so different from her mother. "I'm leaving." She stepped toward the door.

"Susie, wait! Please don't go, sweetheart." My eyes filled with tears. "Please stay, and talk!"

"There's nothing to talk about, Daddy." Her voice was grave, and she kept her back to me. "Aunt Mandy explained to me about your demons, Daddy, but bringing these women into our home? My mother's home? It's just unforgivable. Good-bye, Daddy." Her voice quivered as she pushed open the door.

"Susie? Sweetheart?" I called out to her from the doorway. "Don't go. Please. Let me try and explain." Sadness gripped my heart as I watched my daughter pull from the drive of Twelve Forty Leland Street.

CHAPTER TWENTY-SIX

"Harry wake up. Come on, Harry. I need you to wake up." A soft yet firm voice pulls me from my slumber. As I blink my old, tired eyes, Sally, the chatty caregiver, slowly comes into view. "Well, good afternoon, Harry. Welcome back. I was having a really hard time waking you up. You didn't seem to want to come back from wherever you were. You were sleeping so soundly you slept right through breakfast. I've got chicken-noodle soup for lunch if you're hungry?"

"No." Sadly shaking my head, I look around the room that has become my living tomb.

"Well, if you're not hungry, Harry, how about a nice sponge bath and maybe a shave? You're getting a little scruffy." Sally squeezes the water from the washcloth. Closing my eyes, I desperately try to return to yesteryear as Sally goes about the cleaning of what used to be a strong, vibrant, virile man.

"There," she says, seeming to be satisfied, buttoning the last button on a fresh pair of pajamas. "Much better." She smoothed my pajama top, pleased with her finished work. "Would you like to watch some television, Harry? I'll turn on the History Channel. You like history, don't you, Harry?" She positions a chair next to my bed.

The TV announces, "The History Channel...World War II... the bombing of Pearl Harbor."

"You were in World War II, weren't you, Harry? Of course you were." She chuckles foolishly. "I've seen several pictures of you in uniform. You were quite the looker, back in the day. I bet the ladies really loved you, Harry." She returns her attention to the TV.

"Look at all the devastation, Harry," Sally mumbles. The historical documentary is scanning the widespread destruction, coming to rest on the USS *Arizona* battleship. "It must have been awful for those poor boys trapped inside, knowing it was their final moments." She shakes her head in despair. "They memorialized the *Arizona*, didn't they?" she says, turning her attention back to me. "Oh, Harry, I'm so sorry; what was I thinking?" She wipes the tears from my eyes. "Watching this must only bring back bad memories for you. I'm sorry." She shuts off the TV.

They're not all bad memories, I think. *I had my youth. I had Liz, Joe, Pappy, and a daughter who worshipped me. It's only now I feel sadness, realizing I've lost them all. Only to be left with a humbled existence...a mere shell of a man.*

"It's time for your medication, Harry, and then I want you to try and eat some soup." Sally prepares the injection.

"Not hungry," I grunt.

"You can pass on the food if you like, but your medication is a must." She injects it into the PICC line. "Rest now, Harry," she says, adjusting my blankets. "It should be taking effect soon."

Closing my eyes, nodding my head in understanding, I wait for the medication to take hold. Feeling it's effects I give way to slumber. Patiently I wait for The grandfather clock to begin its chimes. "Seven, eight, nine," I count along hearing its sound, "Ten." My lady appears right on schedule. Standing vigilant, silent, inside the shadows of her corner cove.

"Please?" I beg. "Please, talk to me?" Reaching out to her in desperation. "Please, step from the shadows, and show me your face." Collapsing back on the bed in defeated exhaustion.

"Harry?" a soft, warm voice calls out. The lady steps from the shadows, extending her hand. Tears fill my eyes in recognition as I reach out for her, inhaling sharply as our fingers touch.

"Harry?" Sally comes to my bedside, checking my pulse, feeling its final beats. "Rest now." She gently adjusts my blankets in a final comforting gesture. Turning off the lights, she quietly closes my bedroom door. She picks up the phone and dials the numbers she's come to know by heart.

"Hello, Regional Hospice Center, Marie speaking. How can I help you?"

"Hi, Marie, Sally Tillman. I'm calling to report the passing of Harry Decker. Can you check his file and make the proper arrangements for his removal from Twelve Forty Leland Street?"

"Yes, Sally, I'll take care of it right away. Is there anything else I can help you with?"

"No, thank you, Marie; that's all." Sally clicks the receiver, scanning her file for death-notification contacts. She finds only one name, Susie Jenkins, daughter. After dialing the numbers, she hears the phone line ring.

"Hello," a voice says through the receiver.

"Hello, may I speak to Susie Jenkins, please?"

"This is Susie Jenkins."

"Ms. Jenkins, this is Sally Tillman, one of your father's home-care hospice nurses. I'm sorry to inform you that your father passed away a few moments ago. He went peacefully; there was no..." Sally's voice becomes a distant mutter.

Susie's heart is pounding. She feels one emotion after another—grief, hatred, sorrow, disappointment, sadness, regret. Her dark brown eyes fill with tears as the last emotion consumes her...love.

ABOUT THE AUTHOR

Samanthy Jane is the granddaughter of Harry Decker, whose life was the basis for this story. She lives in Michigan, where she has resided for most of her life. She is a divorced mother of two sons, Chad and William Hinterman, and the grandmother of Henry.

Made in the USA
Lexington, KY
02 February 2017